# THE VAMPIRE'S TOMB MYSTERY

Written and illustrated by

## Dwight Christopher Kemper

ISBN 978-1-936168-73-6
Library of Congress Catalog Card Number 2017908352
Second Edition published by Midnight Marquee Press, Inc.
Manufactured in the United States of America
Published June, 2017

Dedicated to the memory of Uncle Forrest J Ackerman.
He now resides in that great Ackermansion in the sky.

# ACKNOWLEDGMENTS

This book was helped immensely with the generous feedback of Joe Moe, Forrest J Ackerman's friend and caretaker. Thanks to Joe, Forry's puns really came alive.

Special thanks to Conrad Brooks for talking with me and giving me some of his recollections about the funeral of Armand Tesla and his career with Ed Wood. And thank you to Gene Cothran for proofing and critiquing not one, but two revisions of this manuscript. Thank you to my editor at VideoScope, Joe Kane for providing me with back issues for this project.

A very big thank you to Gary and Susan Svehla at Midnight Marquee Press for picking up my third installment after my previous publisher decided to close down Helm Publishing to follow other pursuits. Now all three of my mysteries are under the same editorial roof.

# Cast of Characters

Armand Tesla—Hungarian character actor typecast as Count Dracula.

Hope Tesla—Tesla's fifth wife.

Lillian Arch—Tesla's fourth, and now ex-wife.

Armand Jr.—Tesla's son.

Charles Criswell King—Psychic to the Stars.

Edward D. Wood Jr.—ersatz writer, producer, director—and transvestite.

Forrest J (Forry) Ackerman—a literary agent.

Ray Bradbury—a science fiction writer.

Dolores Fuller—Ed Wood's former girlfriend, now a successful songwriter.

Kathy Wood—Ed Wood's common-law wife.

Conrad Brooks—One of Ed Wood's casual company of actors.

Paul Marco—Kelton the Cop in Ed Wood's horror films.

Loretta King—the actress who took Dolores's part in *Bride of the Atom*.

Tor "The Super Swedish Angel" Johnson—pro-wrestler turned actor.

Maila Nurmi—TV's Vampira and blacklisted former actress.

Andreas Orby—a teenage fan of Armand Tesla.

Reverend Manly P. Hall—hypnotist and philosopher, married Tesla and Hope.

Don Marlowe—Armand Tesla's former agent.

John "Bunny" Breckinridge—a millionaire and a headlining female impersonator.

Mae West—1930's sex symbol.

Chalky Wright—Mae West's chauffeur.

Lt. Karl Johnson—Tor Johnson's son and plainclothes detective.

Dr. Tom Mason—a chiropractor.

Lt. Jack Southern—an LAPD homicide detective.

Mr. Koenig—a distributor of food supplements.

Ralph Fleet—Vice President and chief mortician of Hollywood Mortuaries.

Hugo H. Bruckner—President of Hollywood Mortuaries.

# A Word from Criswell

Greetings, my friends, you are interested in the unknown, the mysterious, the unexplainable, that is why you are here, to learn the full story of what happened on that fateful day. We are giving you all the evidence based only upon the secret testimony of the miserable souls who survived this terrifying ordeal. Much of the dialogue has been transcribed verbatim from actual documentary sources, and then twisted wildly out of context for both your entertainment—and to protect the innocent from the horrible truth. The incidents, the places, the rumored happenings that are now part of Hollywood legend; they are all here, presented to you so that for the first time, you will find out how and why these events occurred. But be warned, my friends, do not accept what we say as truth, if only for the sake of your sanity. My friends, I must stress that this precious document is for entertainment purposes only.

So let us reward the innocent; let us punish the guilty. Now prepare your minds to accept the awful reality—presented as mostly harmless fantasy. My friends, we cannot keep this a secret any longer. Can your heart stand the shocking truth about *The Vampire's Tomb Mystery*?
—Criswell (from Beyond)

# A Word from the Author

Some of the names and places have been changed to protect the innocent, namely the publisher. Three names in particular, one of whom is central to the plot and a name that has been used in two previous novels, but because the story you are about to read is so controversial, even though the plot is so obviously fictional and the real background information is based on real events in the actor's life, the publisher of this book has asked the author, that's me, to not name certain names. So, you know who the Hungarian actor is, I know who the Hungarian actor is, but for legal reasons, it's not him. Instead I'm calling him Armand Tesla. Why? Because when he played his vampire for Columbia Pictures in *Return of the Vampire*, they changed Dracula's name to Armand Tesla. Also changed are the names of Tesla's son, a real life Hollywood lawyer, and a certain young fan of Tesla who shall now be called Andreas Orby, after the werewolf in *Return of the Vampire*. The name of the mortuary has also been changed because apparently mortuary owners have no sense of humor.
— Dwight Christopher Kemper

# Part One

Monsters to be pitied; Monsters to be despised

Eddie, what is this?

# Chapter 1

*"To die, to be really dead, that must be glorious."*
— **Armand Tesla**, Dracula (1931)

In the early evening hours of Thursday, August 16, 1956, the landlord of an apartment house at 5620 Harold Way was startled awake by impatient knocking on his upstairs apartment door. Shaking the cobwebs out of his head, the landlord wiped his face and squinted at the floor model Admiral TV squatting in front of him. With rabbit-ear antennas extended, it looked like a cyclopean chocolate-brown Bakelite bunny with a glowing 10-inch glass picture tube eye. What time was it? The last thing he remembered watching before falling asleep was *Criswell Predicts*, which was on every weekday at 5:30. The show was over and it was just getting dark out, so it must have been, what, maybe six or seven o'clock? Feeling disoriented, he tried to focus on the wall clock with the Tropic Isle topless hula girl on its face, but couldn't make out the time.

The loud knocking continued as he got up from his easy chair grumbling; "Aww, keep your goddamn shirt on!" He set the TV tray aside with what remained of a Swanson's Salisbury steak dinner, upsetting several empty beer cans in the process. The knocking continued as he reached over and twisted one of the Bakelite knobs on the television. "I'm coming, goddamn it! I'm coming!" The TV screen went dark, leaving only a slowly fading phosphorescent white dot on the bunny's big glass eye. The landlord shuffled to the door in beat up plaid house slippers, green work pants, and an undershirt with brown gravy stains down the front. He rubbed his eyes to get them into focus and had a look through the peephole.

Despite her image being distorted by the fisheye lens, the still groggy landlord recognized the cross-eyed blonde woman in the hall as his most fault-finding tenant. With a heavy sigh, he opened the door just enough to poke his face out and stare at her bleary-eyed. "What is it *this time*, Mrs. Tesla?" he asked. "Sink backed up? Toilet won't flush? What?"

"I need you to check on Armand," she said matter-of-factly. "I think he's dead."

That certainly woke him up. He opened the door wider and eyed her questioningly. "Come again?"

Hope gestured with annoyance toward the stairs. "I tried to get our neighbor to check him, but she's a Buddhist or something. She doesn't wanna see any dead people. I tried to wake him but he won't budge. Maybe he's dead or maybe he's just sleeping. I can't tell."

"What makes you think I can tell any better than you? Call an ambulance." He was going to shut the door on her, but Hope was too fast for him and used her foot like a pushy Fuller Brush man, barging her way in.

She glared at him and said, "I want you to make sure because I don't want to look like a fool, him waking up and being all half-crocked. That's all I need. You're in charge of the building, so you check to make sure."

Realizing there was no use arguing with her, the landlord said, "Okay, fine, whatever you want. Let me go put on a shirt and my shoes and I'll meet you downstairs."

He shoved her out into the hall and shut the door before Hope had a chance to use her foot again.

Twenty minutes later the landlord found Hope standing by the open door to the tiny downstairs apartment, glowering, and her arms akimbo.

"It's about time you got here." She curtly pointed. "Go in and see if he's dead already."

The landlord sighed and grumbled under his breath. He crossed the threshold and glanced around inside—and froze to the spot. He had almost forgotten the reason he hated coming into this apartment—besides having to face Hope and her constant nagging. Inside the gloomy abode with its Old World-style furniture and the gold drapes that guarded against even the harshest mid-day sun, was Dracula—the *real* Dracula.

There he was, staring with his mesmerizing eyes.

Count Dracula!

He wore the cape, the tuxedo, the medallion on a red ribbon around his neck—everything just like in the movies! He stood amid the backdrop of the Carpathian Mountains of Transylvania and the landlord was transfixed by those unflinching hypnotic eyes. It was as if the vampire were warning this mere mortal to approach at his peril—even if it was only to unclog the drain. *Enter if you dare,* the Count seemed to be saying from the full-length, life-size painting. *Enter, little man and face Dracula!* The landlord thought;

*God, how I hate that thing!* And he gasped when he felt a hand shoving him forward.

"What are you waiting for?" Hope asked gruffly. "See if he's dead."

She shoved him again. That was all it took to break the spell cast by the old oil painting. To his immediate left sat Armand Tesla, the actor who personified in the public's mind how Count Dracula looked and how he spoke. Tesla sat motionless in his favorite curved backed chair, the one he often received reporters in for those rare occasions when the press remembered that the Hungarian actor was still alive. The chair was facing away from the landlord, so he had to tiptoe around to get a better look. "Dracula" wore tortoise shell glasses, his head resting against the back of the chair. His eyes were closed and his mouth was hanging open. He had a script with a lengthwise crease open on his lap. The light of a small lamp sitting on a low table eerily lit the old man's face from below. The lamp was one of those gaudy sculpture things, the robed figure of a cross-legged Chinaman with a long white beard. The neck of the lamp came out of the top of the Chinaman's head, and ended in a light bulb covered by a cheery shade. Hope probably got it at a five and dime store to dispel the gloomy atmosphere, and somehow the tasteless lamp did help to shake off the creeps the landlord was getting staring at Tesla, who looked like anyone who had fallen asleep while reading. He was just an old man dressed in a short-sleeved striped shirt and dark pants, so divorced from the image of the screen vampire in a tuxedo and cape. The stench of garlic mingled with the aroma of fine tobacco. A thin stream of smoke issued from the end of a cigar resting in a square glass ashtray. The landlord noticed that the cigar was nothing like the crudely rolled stinkers Tesla usually smoked. It was a genuine Havana stogie, something beyond the Hungarian actor's meager earnings. Next to the ashtray was an empty glass. The landlord picked up the glass and took a sniff; it smelled of whiskey and a hint of bitter almonds. Maybe Tesla was celebrating getting a new part in a picture and he really *was* only half-crocked. The way he looked right now, the landlord half-expected Tesla to snore. As he bent down for a closer look, the landlord couldn't help glancing at another life-sized oil portrait. This one depicted the actor as a young man in a stylish gray suit, one hand on his hip, a coat draped over the other arm, the hand holding a Homburg-style hat. It was dominating a cluster of minor landscapes and seascapes that served as the backdrop for the actor's final death scene, and as the landlord studied the portrait, he couldn't help comparing it with its flesh and blood subject. The contrast was startling. Once devastatingly handsome, Tesla's body had been ravaged by time and drug addiction. Seeing the actor as he was now, reminded the landlord of his own mortality. How did that epitaph go? "As you are now, so once was I. As I am now, so soon you shall be."

He ignored the chill running down his spine, glanced back at Hope, and asked, "When did you find him like this?"

Hope gestured toward a small kitchenette where two brown paper bags of groceries sat on the table. "I came home from work and it looked like he was taking a nap. I wasn't sure whether to let him sleep or start dinner first, so I says to myself, 'I'd better wake him up.' He couldn't have been dead very long because he was nice and warm. So I patted him all over and nothin' moved. So I said to myself, 'Well, I guess he's dead.'"

The landlord got up the nerve to touch Tesla's face. The skin felt waxy, but still pliable, with just a hint of warmth. He wiped his hand on his shirt. "Maybe we should put a mirror up to his face."

"I got one here," Hope said, searching for her compact inside a gold-lamé clutch purse. "Here it is."

The landlord held the tiny mirror up to the dead man's nose.

"No breath," he said.

Yep, this was definitely a more permanent kind of nap. There was pasty white saliva congealed around the actor's mouth, his chest remained motionless, and there was a rapidly spreading urine stain that darkened the crotch of the old man's pants. But just to be sure, the landlord gave his shoulder a shake. "Mr. Tesla?" he called, "Mr. Tesla?" and got the expected reaction of no reaction at all. That's when the script fell from the old man's lap. The landlord picked it up and said to Hope, "You better call the police." He closed the script and involuntarily read the title page. A shiver ran through him as the landlord gasped, "Jesus!" The script bore the chillingly prophetic title of *The Final Curtain*.

Hope grabbed the script out of his hands and laid it face down on the small table. "Before we call the police I want you to give me a hand."

She collected the empty glass and the ashtray with the cigar burning in it. "We gotta clean Armand up and get this place presentable." Hope was about to head for the bathroom when she noticed the landlord staring apprehensively at the script. "Will you snap out of it!" she barked.

The landlord started, and then asked, "Why?"

"Because I need you in your right senses, that's why."

"No, I mean, why clean up? Isn't that tampering with evidence or something?"

"Look, he's old and he died, end of story. But the minute we call the police, reporters will be over here like a shot. I don't want Armand's last picture to be him sitting in wet pants."

She hurried to the bathroom where the landlord heard the toilet flush and water running in the sink. Hope came back with the glass and the ashtray sparkling clean and set the ashtray back on the small table, and then went to the kitchenette where she tripped over an empty water bottle on the floor by a water dispenser. Cursing, she kicked the bottle away, and then returned the clean glass to the proper cabinet, after which she drew closed the curtain that separated the kitchen area from the living room. Hurrying back to the chair, she knelt down and grabbed her husband's feet. "Get his shoulders. We'll carry Armand into the bedroom."

The landlord went ghostly pale. "You want I should help you wash up a dead guy?"

Hope rolled her eyes with annoyance. "Just help me carry him into the bedroom. You can collect liquor bottles while I clean him up. Armand has booze hidden all over this dump."

"Okay. I guess." The landlord reached under Tesla's arms and helped haul the late actor into the tiny bedroom.

While Hope stripped, washed and dressed Armand in fresh clothing, the landlord found an empty cardboard box under the kitchen sink and began reenacting a scene from *The Lost Weekend*. Bottles were hidden behind furniture, in light fixtures, inside the upright piano, behind kitchen appliances. There were even two brandy flasks stashed in the pop-up toaster. The man obviously loved his booze.

It was while rummaging in the kitchen cabinets that the landlord discovered four bottles of vitamin pills labeled *Criswell's Family Formula*. Being a regular viewer of *Criswell Predicts*, at least when he could stay awake, the landlord had heard of this much-hyped miracle food supplement. Occasionally a viewer would appear with Criswell, Psychic to the Stars, and declare just how *Criswell's Family Formula* had given them new found strength and vitality. Feeling a need for such new found strength and vitality himself, the landlord tried a nickel-sized tablet. It didn't taste too bad, kind of malty. Having felt no ill effects, the landlord placed all four bottles in the cardboard box along with the rest of "Dracula's" stash.

The bottles clinked together milkman-fashion as the landlord carried the box out behind the apartment house and to a row of sour smelling aluminum garbage cans. He was about to toss out the box when he hesitated. The late actor's booze looked mighty inviting. The landlord smacked his lips, and then took a quick furtive glance over his shoulder. The bottles made a hell of a noise and Hope was sure to catch him red-handed if he tried to sneak the whole box of booze up to his apartment. But maybe he could sneak one bottle, but which one? Looking through the box, he chose a bottle of whiskey that looked like some pretty expensive stuff. From the writing on the label, it might have been some Hungarian brand, and it was damn near full. There was a tag tied to the neck, "To Dracula – Cheers." The landlord kept the whiskey and a bottle of *Criswell's Family Formula*, the rest he tossed in the trash.

The landlord hid the bottles under his shirt like a kid trying to hide a stray puppy from his mom, and just as he expected, Hope caught him in the act the instant his foot touched the first step on the stairs leading up to his place.

"Did you throw away everything?" she asked.

The landlord froze. "Yeah. The booze is in the trash." He started up the stairs. "I'll be back in a minute."

"Where do you think you're going?"

The landlord hesitated; compelled to give an explanation. "Well, I gotta wash my hands."

"I just washed and dressed a corpse. You don't see me runnin' to wash my hands, do you?"

The landlord got defensive. "Jesus Christ! I'll only be a minute!" and hurried up the stairs. Once safely in his apartment, the landlord stashed the whiskey and the vitamins in his kitchen cupboard.

He heard Hope call from the stairs. "What the hell are you doing up there?"

"Nothing," he lied. "I'll be right there." He hid the whiskey behind a stack of canned goods.

"Well, hurry up!"

"Coming!"

Hope was waiting for him with the haunted script in her hand.

"What are you gonna do with that thing?" he asked as gooseflesh prickled his arms.

"You'll see," she said, and together they returned to the bedroom where Hope had staged the Count's deathbed scene. His newly washed body was clad in striped pajamas and a bathrobe; the covers were pulled up to his chin; fluffed up pillows supported the head, his glasses rested on the end of his nose. Hope took the script and laid it across the old man's chest, then placed his hand over it. The scene suggested he was just another aged celebrity who died peacefully in his sleep, dreaming of making a comeback that would never be. She studied her handiwork and nodded with approval. "Okay, now we can call the police." She looked over at the landlord, who was staring uneasily at the tableau. "What's with you?"

The landlord shivered, pointing at the script. "Where would he get a thing like that? *The Final Curtain*, it's almost like it predicted he was gonna die."

"Jesus H. Christ," Hope complained. "That's just some piece of shit written by that hack Eddie Wood."

"Who?"

She pointed at the byline on the title page. "Edward D. Wood Jr.," she said, "a real loser."

The day before he died, the man who would be forever called "Dracula" was sitting in a booth at the Brown Derby Restaurant wedged between Edward D. Wood Jr. and Tor "The Super Swedish Angel" Johnson. Too vane to be seen in public wearing his glasses, the Hungarian thumbed through the 20-page screenplay in question, scowling as he pretended to read it. Behind him was a gallery of celebrity caricatures. One caricature in particular was staring over his shoulder, a brush and ink rendering by Vitca with the inscription, "To the Brown Derby, Best wishes, Boris Karloff."

"Eddie, what is this?" Armand asked the handsome young man with a neatly trimmed mustache and features reminiscent of a young Errol Flynn.

Eddie Wood flashed the cunning smile of a used car salesman. "Why that's the script for *The Final Curtain*," he said. The brown business suit and tie Ed wore in no way belied the fact that beneath his conservative attire he wore a pair of women's panties and a stretched out angora sweater. Only the occasional bulge in his pants betrayed how those items of clothing kept Eddie in an almost constant state of arousal. "Oh, this is a great part for you," he chirped confidently.

"So you say," Armand grumbled, giving the ersatz writer/producer/director one of his patented skeptical leers.

Wood was working on his third martini. "You play a vaudevillian dying during the night of his last performance as Dracula." He grabbed the end of the toothpick which impaled a green olive, much the way the real Vlad Țepeș Dracula had impaled the Turks so many ages ago. He popped the olive between his teeth and pulled out the toothpick, discarding the mini wooden stake in a convenient ashtray. "It's perfect for you," he insisted.

The Hungarian knitted his brows. "Again Dracula?" He shook his head in dismay. "Dracula, it never ends."

Wood chewed the olive as he spoke, making what he said practically unintelligible. "*You're* not playing Dracula. You're playing *an actor* playing Dracula."

Tesla was about to make a caustic comment about Wood's mumbling when the sound of Tor Johnson's wolfish eating caught his attention. The big bald wrestler was devouring his lunch. That was the only accurate word to describe his table manners as Tor's big meaty hands shoved a whole roast chicken into his hungry maw. The wrestler gurgled contentedly as his jaws snapped and flashing white teeth rent flesh from bone while thick lips and slithering tongue slurped up the grease, juices and seasoning like an alligator at feeding time.

"Careful, big man," Tesla warned sarcastically. "Some of that chicken, it is getting in your mouth."

The wrestler smiled, his face glistening. "Is good," Tor said in a gravelly Swedish accent that bubbled up past chicken parts sliding down his gullet. Tesla was already feeling nauseous, but watching the 300-pound Tor feeding on his third whole chicken so savagely only added to the Hungarian's gastric distress. "You want some?" Tor offered, indicating the remaining two carcasses lying on the large serving platter before him like sacrificial victims to a cannibal god.

Armand could only frown with distaste as he turned back to Wood and demanded, "What happened to *The Ghoul Goes West*? I was looking forward to making a Western horror picture. To a reporter I boasted of it!"

In April of last year, the papers were filled with tabloid headlines like 'DRACULA' IS DOPE ADDICT. Photos taken in the recovery ward at Metropolitan State Hospital depicted the six-foot tall actor as a wizen gnome in a baggy hospital gown sitting on the edge of a white iron bed surrounded by reporters. The September 1955 issue of *Police Dragnet Cases*, described him as "like a zombie, an un-dead, a dead man walking." It was while suffering terrible withdrawal pains, "the worst pain one can ever feel," as Tesla later told a reporter, that Eddie Wood, accompanied by *Bride of the Atom* co-stars Loretta King and Tony McCoy, brought him the script to *The Ghoul Goes West* (and made sure the reporter from *Police Dragnet Cases* magazine knew about it. After all, what was wrong with a little free publicity?). When he was in a frame of mind to read the screenplay, he found to his surprise that he actually liked the thing. The opening scene took place in "a small Western cemetery… rough crosses, wooden headboards… a scattered granite headstone here and there." Tor would play one of two grave-robbing giants, "a man well over six-feet tall," the screenplay described, "and weighing close to 300 pounds. He holds a lantern." He would play the Boot Hill caretaker, "a man in his late 60s in faded shirt and pants" who ran a profitable Burke and Hare-style cadaver mill. The premise appealed to the Hungarian very much. There was something mythic about the story. Not just another monster movie, but something where the aging actor could *act!*

The day before the actual event, a newsreel reporter staged Armand's triumphant release from the state hospital. The grateful Hungarian shook hands with a receiving line of pretty nurses and Dr. Nicholas Lanser, the supervising physician. It was then that the optimistic Tesla announced to the world that he was cured and boasted of a new picture.

Glowering at Wood now, Armand said accusingly, "I even mentioned your name. What happened to that?"

Wood became pensive, as he often did when reality scuttled his grandiose ideas. "When Gene Autry dropped out, we, uh, lost the backing for *The Ghoul Goes West.*" He waved. "But that's okay. *The Final Curtain* is a winner! Like I was saying, your ghost is inexplicably drawn into an old theater, looking for some object. You don't know what it is, but you're compelled to seek it out. You meet Vampira—"

"Vampira?" exclaimed Tesla, dumbfounded.

"Yeah, you know, the late night horror show hostess on channel 5. She showed *White Zombie* last Halloween. High cheekbones, pale face, long black hair." He described a shapely feminine outline in the air. "Hourglass figure packed into a tight black dress."

"I know who she is," the actor said testily. "We ran into each other on Hollywood Boulevard."

This was literally true. The Charles Addams-inspired beauty was on roller skates and ran into Armand as he turned the corner. Not that he minded. Her huge breasts made a wonderful bumper.

The Hungarian eyed Wood narrowly. "Maila hates you. She told me so. She has big offers from big studios. Why would she even speak to you when a TV star, she has been?"

Wood cleared his throat and shifted uneasily before he spoke. "Uh, well, I guess 'has been' is the operative word. Vampira's been blacklisted and needs the money."

"Stop calling her Vampira!" Disgusted, Tesla reached for a shot glass of whiskey, his third. "Her name is Maila — Maila Nurmi! 'Vampira' is just her character." He raised the glass to his lips, and then glared angrily. "Do you, like everyone else, call me 'Dracula' to my back when it is turned?" He stared into his whiskey, sighed bitterly, and set the shot glass down. "Poor Maila," he muttered, gazing into his drink, "she used to be so proud. She said to me once, 'Why would you degrade yourself, Armand, by being in that horrible *Glen or Glenda*?' She said she would rather die than work for you in trash like that."

Wood was horrified. "But *Glen or Glenda* was a masterpiece!"

The masterpiece in question was originally meant to be a film called, *I Changed My Sex*, a fictionalized biography of she-male Christine Jorgensen. Wood rewrote the script into an autobiography about a man haunted by his compulsion to be a transvestite. Naturally, Wood cast himself as the lead. The man who had been and would always be Dracula portrayed Fate — or God — or a mad scientist. It was never clear to the actor just what he was supposed to be. All he knew was it involved convoluted dialogue and smoking test tubes.

"I agreed with Maila," he admitted glumly. "I felt degraded being in a sex-change picture. But we were broke. 'Make the film,' Lillian said to me." Lillian was the aged actor's fourth wife, although because of a clerical error on the original documents the July 27, 1953 issue of *Time Magazine* mistakenly said Lillian was his *third* wife when it published the announcement of their divorce. "'We need the money so make the film.' 'Some things,' I tell her, 'some things they are worse than being broke.' But I make the movie anyway." The Hungarian sighed bitterly.

"You gave one of your finest performances in *Glen or Glenda*!"

Armand watched horrified as Wood pantomimed pulling a bell cord while mimicking the actor's Hungarian accent, "Pull the string! Dance to that!" Wood sighed with wistful self-admiration. "It was perfect casting: Armand Tesla as the God who rules over our fate."

Darkly, the old man said, "If I had in front of me the God who rules over my fate, I would…." His hands clutched angrily, and then he demanded, exasperated, "What happened to *The Vampire's Tomb*? All day we shot in a cemetery, and later at Tor's house. For what?"

Tor Johnson stopped sucking what little flesh remained on a chicken bone. "I remember that," Tor said. "The cemetery, it was all dug up. Construction machines everywhere. My boy, 'Little' Karl, he moved all those tombstones so Eddie could shoot his movie and not take pictures of those machines."

"I remember, too," said Tesla. "I also remember Eddie got those machines in the shot anyway." He glared at Wood reproachfully. "Mr. Edward D. I-do-not-need-to-shoot-more-than-one-take Wood Jr."

Wood appeared genuinely concerned. "What's wrong? Money problems again?"

The Hungarian hunched forward glumly. "The money problems, yes. And Lillian will not speak to me."

"You're married to Hope now. She's a wonderful woman."

"Hope!" the Hungarian scoffed. "That cross-eyed bitch shows me no respect! She says that I am too gloomy!" He looked imploringly at Wood. "I am not gloomy, am I, Eddie?"

Wood gave the old man an appraising once over. His pinched face had a yellowish pallor. His gray hair was thinning. His breath smelled of garlic. His hunched posture and his suit of funerary black made the actor look like a grimacing vulture. Wood gave Tesla an encouraging smile. "Why, you look just…swell."

Sucking his fingers clean, Tor said, "You should eat more. You not be so thin."

Armand frowned and held his sour stomach. "Some of us, they do not have a constant appetite." He reached into his pocket for a bottle of Pepto-Bismol, took a large swig, and gestured at the bottle. "Lately, this is all I can do to keep what little I eat down." He grimaced and smacked his lips with distaste as he slipped the bottle back into his pocket.

"Food is good for you," Tor insisted, "makes you strong. My son, 'Little' Karl, the Police Lieutenant, is big and strong like his father because he eat like his father. That's why Eddie gave 'Little' Karl a part in the new movie." Looking to Wood, Tor asked, "Will the giant in the new movie be Lobo from the last movie, Eddie?"

Lobo was the monster Tor played in *Bride of the Atom*, a film that had since been re-titled *Bride of the Monster*.

Tor pointed at his head. "I been keeping my head shaved in case I play Lobo in the new movie."

Armand glared at the cue ball-headed Man Mountain. "There is no new movie! That is what I have been complaining about!"

He threw the script at Wood. "No more new projects, Eddie! When do we finish what we started?"

"But I already told you, Gene Autry backed out."

Tor waved. "That not important."

Tesla was beside himself. "It *is* important, Big Man, if it means we do not finish the picture!"

"Family is important," Tor insisted. "Picture or no picture, I am proud of my son and he is proud of his father."

This struck a chord with the old man. He fell silent, staring glumly into his whiskey. "Yes, a son *should* be proud of his father." With a heavy sigh, he said, "I fear that Lillian, she has turned my son against me."

"That's ridiculous," Eddie insisted. "Junior was best man at your wedding to Hope, remember?"

Armand glared angrily. "Do you know that Lillian, she calls him 'Bill' and not Armand Jr.?' She wants to make him ashamed to be my son!" He burned with renewed indignation. "I should never have left her!"

"I thought *she* left *you*," said Wood.

The old man scowled. "She left my home, but it was *I* who told her to go and not return!"

The ground for their divorce was "unfounded jealousy." Lillian complained in court, "He kept me under his thumb 24-hours a day. He would listen in on the extension phone when I talked to my mother; he checked up on me when I went to the dentist office; he charged me with infidelity."

Armand felt his jealousy was more than justified as he downed his whiskey in one gulp and slammed the glass down. "It is all that damn Brian Donlevy's fault!" he ranted. "He stole Lillian from me! I should have challenged that scoundrel to a duel as I would have done in the Old Country!" He looked down at his shaking, withered hands. It startled him how old he had become. "It is no wonder that my son is ashamed of his father." He sank back into his depression and sighed.

Tor squeezed Tesla's shoulder. "A son always loves his father, no matter what. You see. You worry for nothing."

Genuinely touched by the Swede's gesture, Tesla patted Tor's comforting hand. "You are a good man, Tor." then glowered in disgust as he realized the hand was covered with chicken grease. "You are good man, Tor," he repeated, reaching for his handkerchief, "But a sloppy eater." He sighed as he wiped the grease from his hand. "My son, he came to see me today."

"That's great!" Wood patted Tesla on the back. "So, it's just like Tor said, all this worry is for nothing."

Sticking his handkerchief back in his pocket, Armand fidgeted with his empty glass. "My son wants to be a lawyer and worries about my estate. He wants me to divorce Hope and write her out of my will." He looked up, tears welling in his eyes. "But I have nothing, only two lots of worthless land that I will bequeath to my nephew and a few pennies in the bank. My son, he is ashamed."

Wood picked up the discarded script and handed it back. "Okay, so you want your son to be proud of you. Great! Here's your chance. What I'm offering you now is a shot at television! Take the script home and read it. *The Final Curtain* will be the first episode of a new anthology series." Wood gestured grandly to suggest a title written in neon. "*Portraits in Terror*! It can't miss!"

Tesla shook his head. "You will be the death of me, Eddie."

The actor folded the script and pocketed it, little knowing how his widow would later use *The Final Curtain* to stage his death.

Photographers snapped pictures of Hope's handiwork as attendants from the Hollywood Mortuaries transferred "Dracula's" dead body from the bed to a stretcher. They strapped the body down and covered it with a gray blanket. More pictures as the mortuary attendants rolled the stretcher through the Harold Way apartment, past the painting of the actor as a young vital man in the gray suit and holding the homburg-style hat, past the table with the sparking clean ashtray and past the chair with the seat cushion turned over to hide the telltale urine stain. The police took statements and offered their condolences to the widow.

The next day, the obituary was not front-page news. Armand had been upstaged by both Adlai E. Stevenson's nomination as the Democratic presidential candidate, and by the Indians' Rocky Colavito hitting his first grand slam.

The following headline was buried as a minor item somewhere on the back page:


**Veteran Actor 'DRACULA' TESLA OF FILMS DIES**

But as a reporter was once told when Tesla was asked if there would ever be an end to Dracula, "No, Dracula never ends," he had observed with a wry smile. "I am not sure if it is a blessing or a curse, but it *never ends*."

# Chapter 2

Earlier that evening on August 16, as the thin black hands of the large school-style clock with the red-sweep second hand reached 5:30, the director, with a cigarette dangling from his mouth, sat in his tiny smoke-filled control booth and counted down on his fingers from five to one. The first of three cameras focused on Bob Shields standing at the ready before a floor mike with a page of studio copy in his hand. On zero, the chain-smoking director cued Shields, who then intoned in his announcer voice; "From the Lucky Channel 13 television studios in Los Angeles, we bring you live, *Criswell Predicts*."

Camera 2 dollied in on a riser stage upon which were arranged a mahogany desk and chair. *Pomp and Circumstance* heralded the arrival of Charles Criswell King. The handsome prognosticator with the blond pompadour placed his hands firmly upon his desk and stared intently into the camera. Under the studio lights the sequins on the lapels of his tuxedo twinkled like stars in the heavenly firmament as he proclaimed with practiced dramatic earnestness; "Good evening, dear friends. We are all interested in the future because that is where you and I will spend the rest of our lives, whether we want to or not. And future events such as these will affect *you* in the future." Gazing earnestly, as if reading from the book of time itself, Criswell intoned in his stentorian delivery, "I predict that very soon, perhaps within the next month, a celebrity will die and begin the first of a cycle of three famous deaths." Pause for effect. "I further predict that it will be discovered that these deaths are actually assassinations," another dramatic pause, followed by the shocking conclusion; "These assassinations, it will be disclosed, are being conducted by grave-robbing aliens from outer space." He gave the cameramen a challenging leer, as if daring them to laugh. They didn't. They were used to his predictions by now. One might say they even looked bored. "It will be determined that these creatures want our celebrity dead for their own hellish experiments." There was still no reaction from the camera crew, which Cris took as a personal challenge. "But fear not, for I predict that their evil plans will be foiled when our scientists discover a common, everyday seasoning found in every household is the one substance that will defeat them; That seasoning, mere table salt."

The crew wasn't so much as cracking a smile. Cris inwardly sighed, fearing he was losing his touch. For the next 15 minutes, he threw everything he could into the mix, including a prediction that he and his most famous client, Mae West, would be the first human beings to set foot on the moon. But the camera crew remained unmoved. With an inward shrug of resignation and his predictions now concluded, Criswell gestured over to a table set up on stage right. Camera 3 focused on a black felt tablecloth on which alabaster statues were arranged along with bottles of *Criswell's Family Formula*. Taking up one of the bottles Criswell prominently displayed the label. "Yes, my friends," he said. "I predict that if you take but one tablet a day of *Criswell's Family Formula* for only one month, you will notice a greater strength and vitality than you have ever known before. For only *Criswell's Family Formula* has the secret herbal ingredients passed down from my family for over six generations. But don't take my word for it, my friends. Here is a gentleman who will give his own remarkable testimonial of *Criswell's Family Formula's* unique properties." As camera 3 pulled back for a two-shot, Criswell introduced Edward D. Wood Jr. to the television audience. "This is Mr. Jones," he said.

"Hello, Mr. Criswell!" said Ed Wood with a phony smile and stiff department store mannequin pose.

"Mr. Jones here," said Criswell, unscrewing the cap on the vitamin bottle, "is a sterling example of what *Criswell's Family Formula* can do!" Criswell shook out two pills in Ed's waiting hand. Ed Wood smiled broadly as he enthusiastically popped the pills in his mouth and chewed vigorously. "Tell us, Mr. Jones," asked Criswell, "how do you feel?"

Swallowing, Wood declared through a manic smile, "Why, Mr. Criswell, I have never felt better in my life!" Overplaying his role, as Wood often did, he beat his chest like a glorified Tarzan. "WA-HOO! This stuff is amazing!"

Camera 3 zoomed in for a close-up on Criswell as he displayed the label and concluded, "And *Criswell's Family Formula* can do the same for you," declaring mystically, "so Criswell predicts!"

Bob Shields announced; "You have been watching *Criswell Predicts*, a production of the KLAC television studios in Los Angeles. Tune in tomorrow and every weekday at this same time for *Criswell Predicts*. And now, your local news."

From the cramped confines of the control booth, the director snuffed out the butt of his cigarette, one of many crowding the ashtray, and announced, "And we're clear." Slipping his headphones off, he exited the booth and approached the seer as he shook out a cigarette from a packet of Camels and clenched the end in his teeth, pulling it from the pack. "Mr. Criswell," said the director, the cigarette bobbing wildly as he spoke, "since this show is being kinescoped, do you want to do another take of the commercial?" He indicated Ed Wood with a nod. "I mean," he said, flipping open a lighter, "that guy looked pretty phony."

Criswell shook his head. "No, I think we'd better leave it as is. If things are too polished it won't look like a live broadcast."

"Does that really matter?" he asked, lighting the coffin nail and drawing smoke hungrily into his lungs. "The stations where this show is syndicated don't care if it's live or not." Smoke poured from his mouth like sea foam.

"My viewers care," Criswell insisted.

The director shrugged as he took another draw of smoke. "According to your numbers, your viewers are mostly elderly shut-ins."

"And because those elderly shut-ins are perceptive enough to watch my program, they are also perceptive enough to spot when a supposedly live show is rehearsed."

The director exhaled smoke through his nostrils and shrugged. "Whatever you say." He turned to the small studio crew and announced, "That's a wrap, everybody!" He gave Ed Wood a disapproving shake of the head before retreating back to the murky confines of his control booth.

"He's right, Eddie," Criswell said. "That was a bit much."

"So I got a little carried away." Wood shook out some vitamins, popped them in his mouth and chewed vigorously. "There's something about this stuff. I feel like I can stay up for hours!"

Criswell took the bottle and returned it to the display. "That's because they're loaded with caffeine."

"Wow! No wonder I feel antsy." Wood covetously eyed the stack of bottles as Criswell noticed Bob Shields talking to a black chauffeur carrying a covered pot. The announcer pointed Criswell out to the chauffeur, and then went to the snack cart to grab a donut before leaving the stage. Criswell gave the chauffeur a friendly wave as they approached each other and began talking. While Criswell's back was turned, Ed Wood took the opportunity to pocket one of the *Family Formula* bottles. Criswell happened to glance back at Wood in time to catch him in the midst of his wanton criminal act. "Eddie!" Criswell warned. Wood quickly put the bottle down while Criswell took the covered pot from the chauffeur and motioned Wood over. "Come on, Eddie," Criswell chided.

The chauffeur smiled and saluted. "So I can relay to Miss West that you'll extend the invitation, Mr. Criswell?"

"You bet, Chalky," Criswell said, hefting the pot. "And do thank Mae for this." He held the rim of the pot at nose level and sniffed. "Swedish meatballs?"

"Yes, sir," Chalky said. "Miss West is trying a new seasoning." Saluting again, he said, "Good day, Mr. Criswell." With a practiced click of his heels, Chalky smartly pivoted and marched from the studio.

"Who was that?" Wood asked.

"Oh, that was Chalky Wright, Mae West's driver. Used to be quite a boxer in his day."

"Say, I read something in *Confidential Magazine* about Mae having a love affair with a colored boxer. Is that him?"

Criswell grabbed Eddie by the arm, took him aside and hushed him. "Mae won't admit to it," he whispered. "She even made Chalky sign a statement steadfastly denying it." He checked to make sure no one was eavesdropping. "Let's just leave it at that."

Changing the subject, Ed asked, "So, what's in the pot?"

"Ah, this," Criswell said, hefting the pot, "is a little bit of Mae's home cooking."

"Smells terrific!" Wood said, reaching greedily for the lid.

"Ah-ah!" chided Criswell as he slapped Ed's hand away. "This is going to be someone else's dinner. Now behave yourself and follow me." Criswell headed for his closet-sized dressing room. He put the pot down in a chair and sat before his vanity, while Wood stood in the doorway.

"So," queried Wood, "who's gonna die?"

"Die?" asked Criswell absentmindedly as he checked his pancake makeup. It was perfect! Well, perhaps a touch up.

"Your prediction tonight," said Wood. "You said a celebrity was gonna die. Which one?"

Criswell shrugged. "Search me." Hmm, maybe more hairspray. Criswell picked up a can of White Rain and added to the many coats that already lacquered his spit curl firmly to his wide forehead. "There are lots of old celebrities out there, Eddie. One of them is bound to die sooner or later." He coughed and waved away the fumes.

"But you predicted grave-robbing aliens were responsible."

"I said that to add some spice." Criswell studied Ed's reflection. "Remember, Eddie?" he said. "I told you before. I'm not a psychic. I'm an entertainer. This is show business. I'm just Hollywood razzle-dazzle." He reached for a brochure from a stack of Civil Defense material on the vanity. "People believe in me because of stuff like this." The cover of the brochure he gave to Ed depicted a house in flames with the startling caption.

Wood stared at it and shuddered. "Gosh," he said.

"You see, Eddie," Criswell explained, "people listen to me because I represent a tomorrow where," in showman delivery, he pronounced, "you and I will spend the rest of our lives!" Taking the brochure back, Criswell returned it to the pile of CONELRAD propaganda with other titles like, *The **ATOMIC BOMB** and **YOU*** and *Facts about **FALLOUT** Protection*. He shook his head, flashing Eddie an ironic smile. "Our government offers fear; I bring hope." Grabbing a *Family Formula* bottle from a box by the vanity, he added, "Ironically, we both sell snake oil and wild predictions. The difference is, my brand of folderol is mostly harmless." He put the bottle down on the vanity.

Ed Wood was crushed. "But you have an 80% accuracy rate."

"I made that up." Remembering about the pot of Swedish meatballs, Criswell held up his finger. "Uh, pardon me, Eddie, I have to make a call." He picked up the handset on the dressing room telephone and dialed. There was a *click* followed by a sharp tone and a prerecorded voice announcing, "The number you have reached has been disconnected…" Criswell cradled the handset. Thinking aloud, Criswell muttered, "I guess I'll just have to make an extra stop." He noticed Wood's hangdog expression and smiled. "Say, I know what will cheer you up." He stood up and gestured grandly in the confines of the chicken coop-sized space. "Mae's throwing a big to-do at the Ravenswood this evening. Why not come with me as my guest?"

Wood's eyes beamed. "Me meet Mae West! Wow!"

"But just keep it social. No shop talk and, uh," he added, clearing his throat and talking out the side of his mouth like a felon in a prison picture, "no talky about Chalky. Get it?"

"Got it."

"Good."

"By the way, what's the occasion?"

"Two words, Eddie: Real estate. Mae made a killing."

"I thought real estate was one word."

"It's two words, Eddie. In fact, you're looking at the man who, as Mae West's personal psychic consultant, predicted the deal would make her a fortune."

"See there? That *proves* you're a psychic!"

Criswell placed his arm around Wood's shoulder. "I knew because Halo, my dear wealthy wife, wanted to unload some land. So I used my influence to steer Mae in the right direction and became a silent partner in the bargain." He patted Wood's chest. "I'm just lucky the deal actually reaped some benefits." He felt a bulge in Wood's breast pocket. "Say, what's this?" Leaning in he joked, "Is that half a brassiere you're wearing or are you just happy to see me?" With the skill of a pickpocket, Criswell deftly removed an envelope from the inner pocket of Eddie's jacket and turned it over in his hands.

"Oh, that," said Wood. "It's from Armand. Just got it in the mail today. Must be some kind of legal papers. He said Armand Jr. was pressuring him to get a divorce."

"So why would Armand send divorce papers to you?"

"I dunno," Wood said with a shrug as he took back the envelope. "Say, early on Armand had the crazy idea Hope and me were having an affair." He became apprehensive. "You don't think he's divorcing Hope on the grounds of infidelity, do you? Maybe these are legal papers saying I have to testify at the hearing."

Criswell shook his head. "Papers like that have to be hand-delivered."

"I guess you're right." Wood smiled, instantly reassured. "Maybe Armand addressed it to me by mistake. I was gonna stop over and ask him before I opened it." He pocketed the envelope. "But it can wait."

"No need to wait," insisted Criswell as he turned to get his topcoat. Wood took that opportunity to snatch the vitamin bottle off the vanity. Criswell placed the topcoat over his arm and turned back. "Mae wants me to extend Armand a special invitation." Not missing a beat, he reached into Wood's jacket pocket and pulled out the stolen vitamins. He displayed the bottle and clucked his tongue reproachfully. "Eddie."

Wood flashed Cris a sheepish grin. "See there! You must be psychic. How else could you know I took that?"

"I saw you in the mirror."

"Well, they just make me feel so darn alive." As an afterthought, Wood added, "And maybe Armand could use a bottle. He's been so tired and depressed lately."

With a sigh, Criswell handed the bottle back and gave Wood three more. "Just don't eat them all at once. Besides the caffeine and maybe a few vitamins, I'm not sure what's in those things. A fellow by the name of Koenig suggested I get into the food supplement business. Frankly, I'm surprised the FDA hasn't come after me." Criswell grabbed the pot of Swedish meatballs. "By the way, Eddie, how did you get to the studio today?"

"I took the bus. Kathy's got the car today." The Kathy to which Ed was referring was his new "bride" Kathy Wood, formerly Kathleen O'Hara Everett, Ed's common-law "newlywed."

"We'll take my car, then," said Criswell. "Do you think Kathy might like to tag along?"

"That would be swell, Cris! She's seeing her chiropractor right now. Dr. Tom's office is on Sunset."

"Good. We can drop by along the way to Armand's." Criswell stepped out of the dressing room and beckoned for Wood to follow.

"Uh, Cris, you're still in makeup."

"Haven't you noticed, Eddie? I never take it off. Shakespeare said all the world's a stage. And wherever I go, I am *Criswell!*"

# Chapter 3

The 1935 Chrysler Imperial 8 was the kind of relic one might see Norma Desmond tooling around in, which was rather appropriate since Criswell was driving up Sunset Boulevard. He and Eddie were sitting together in the chauffeur's compartment of the chocolate-colored limousine. Eddie was happily chewing vitamin pills, grinning maniacally and squirming in his seat with the pot of Swedish meatballs resting on his lap. "What a great car! Why don't you have a chauffeur, Cris?"

Behind the wheel, Criswell said, "I can't afford one."

"But this limo must have cost a fortune."

"It cost exactly two dollars. Every now and then, Mae sells me one of her used limousines for a couple of bucks."

"But why buy a used car?" asked Wood. "I thought Halo made a fortune during prohibition."

"She did," Criswell said, "but I don't like to take advantage."

Ed Wood shook out another vitamin pill and chewed it loudly. His eyes grew wide with caffeine-induced joy.

"Will you stop popping pills," Criswell scolded. "You're getting as jumpy as a dope fiend."

"I can't help it," Ed replied. "They're kind of habit forming."

Criswell shook his head and sighed wearily. He pulled up to a converted storefront with the legend "Dr. Tom Mason, Chiropractor" painted across the window. Inside, a receptionist with hard-angular features and dark hair, looked up from her copy of *Confidential Magazine* and smiled. "Hello, Eddie," she said in a voice breathy, low, and melodious, straight from the diaphragm, as if she were ready to burst into song at any moment. "Kathy's still in the exam room with Dr. Tom but I'll see if she's ready." She flicked a switch on her intercom. "Dr. Tom, Eddie Wood is here… with a friend."

There was a strange rhythmic ticking heard over the intercom as Dr. Tom said, "Kathy is still under, I'm afraid. Tell Mr. Wood to wait in the waiting room. That's why it's there."

Criswell leaned in and whispered; "Under?"

"Hypnosis," Wood whispered back. He made a trance-inducing gesture and emitted the spooky, "oooOOOOooo," of a Theremin.

"Hypnosis?" Criswell frowned questioningly. "What does *that* have to do with spinal adjustment?"

"Thank you, doctor," Nurse Leslie said. She flicked off the switch and smiled. "She won't be long, Eddie."

"Thanks, Leslie," Ed said.

A middle-aged man with gray hair at the temples pushed his way between Ed and Criswell and confronted Nurse Leslie. "I'm Richard Jeffrey," he said. "I have to see the doctor right away."

Nurse Leslie smiled nervously and checked her appointment book. "Oh, uh, yes, but you don't have an appointment until next week."

"I know, but I have to see him. It's an emergency."

"Your back?"

"No. I know this will sound crazy, but ever since I started coming here, the wife says I've been sleepwalking."

"I see."

"He's got to help me," the man anxiously pressed. "I don't remember doing it, but my wife says I act out like I'm, I don't know, doing strange things, all in my sleep and with my eyes wide open."

"Have a seat," she said, and indicated a young man with his arm in a sling and a large man dominating the couch in the reception area with a nod. "Mr. Irwin and Lt. Johnson are ahead of you. But I'll let the doctor know you're here."

"Thank you, Nurse," Mr. Jeffrey said.

The giant on the couch wore a brown fedora and gray suit that screamed "plainclothes police lieutenant." He smiled pleasantly and waved. "Over here, Eddie," he called. "How's it goin'?"

Wood smiled with recognition. "Karl! I didn't know you were one of Dr. Tom's patients!"

Criswell followed as the anxious man sat in the waiting room. It was a haphazard collection of folding chairs and the large couch, all situated around a coffee table. On the coffee table in an equally haphazard manner were old chiropractic magazines. As he surveyed the patients waiting their turn, the seer imagined the waiting room in purgatory probably looked a lot like this. Looking as bored as the rubber plant drooping in the corner was the teenager whose name Cris deduced was Irwin; his one good arm in a letterman's jacket; the other in a sling, either a torn rotator cuff or a sprain, Criswell thought. The boy's pretty blonde girlfriend sat beside him, resting her head on his good broad shoulder. In her lap was a gold-lamé clutch purse. Cris turned his attention to Lt. Johnson as he smiled and said, "So this is the 'Little' Karl that Tor's been boasting about."

Karl left a deep impression in the sofa cushion as he stood up and shook Cris's hand. "That's me!" Criswell's hand was lost in Karl's monster-sized grip. "So, Eddie, are you still coming up for some fishing this weekend?"

"Wouldn't miss it," Ed said. "But what are you doing here?"

Karl winced as he rubbed his lower back. "That time I was moving tombstones for you, I pulled something. I've been coming to Dr. Tom twice a week ever since."

"But that was last April. You've been in pain that long?"

"The pain has come down a lot. Just a couple more adjustments, he says, and I'll be as good as new."

Ed winced in sympathy. "Gee, I'm sorry about that. Why didn't you say something back at the cemetery?"

Karl shrugged. "It didn't hurt that bad at the time, but the next day… Jesus! That one marker must have weighed 500-pounds." With a half-smile, he added, "Dr. Tom's really good. And he's been helping me lose weight, too."

Criswell looked the giant up and down. In both breadth and height "Little" Karl exceeded his father's measurements. "I see," he said politely. "How's the diet coming?"

"No diet," Karl explained, tapping his temple. "It's all will power." He invited Wood and Criswell to feel his biceps. "Feel that! All muscle, no fat."

"Wow!" gasped Wood, squeezing the bulging bicep. "It's like a rock!"

Taking a tentative squeeze, Criswell said, "Very impressive."

Karl puffed out his huge chest. "All thanks to Dr. Tom! He's amazing!"

Criswell tried to hide his growing discomfort as he asked, "I take it Dr. Tom uses hypnosis on you, too?"

"He sure does. I feel amazing!"

"So you said."

The nurse receptionist approached with a clipboard. "Eddie," she said, "Kathy is coming right out." Cris found her even more striking standing up. She was statuesque, broad shoulders, firm breasts, slim waist and boyish hips. He noted that her hands had the tapered, yet strong fingers of a sculptress. He wondered if she might model on the side. "You're next, handsome," she said, smiling pleasantly at the detective, "Your session is in Exam Room 1."

"See you later, Eddie," Karl said, and followed the nurse down a short hallway, leaving Criswell to ask; "Eddie, just what does Dr. Tom do in his 'sessions'?"

Ed gave a sheepish shake of his head. "To tell you the truth, I don't remember." Adding with a broad smile, "But I feel *amazing*."

A man in a lab coat that Criswell surmised was Dr. Tom approached with his pretty patient. He was a tall, thin, cadaverous man with a set of huge ears. Kathy Wood wore a pleated gray skirt and a pink angora sweater; her blonde hair cascading about her shoulders and framing her perky, pretty face. She held a gold-lamé clutch purse similar to the one in the teenage girl's lap and gushed, "Oh, hi, Eddie! What are you and Mr. Criswell doing in here?"

"We're waiting for you, poodle," Eddie said. "Criswell and me are going to a party at Mae West's place."

"And," added Criswell, "we both thought you might like to come with us and make it a threesome." He smiled at the sexual connotation of that statement.

"I wish I could," said Kathy. "I have shopping to do."

"So," Criswell said, looking the doctor up and down, "I hear you use hypnosis in your sessions."

"And you are?" asked Dr. Tom.

Eddie made introductions. "This is the Great Criswell, Psychic to the Stars."

Dr. Tom smirked. "That explains your rather unorthodox attire."

Criswell step aside as Mr. Jeffrey approached. "I have to see you, doctor. Right now!"

"Is there a problem, Mr. Jeffrey?"

"Only if you consider somnambulism a problem," Criswell remarked.

"Somnambulism?" Dr. Tom quirked his eyebrow. "I don't understand."

"The wife says I walk in my sleep," Mr. Jeffrey explained. "You've got to help me."

Dr. Tom nodded down the hall. "Wait for me in Exam Room 2. I'll be there shortly."

"Thank you," Mr. Jeffrey said gratefully. "I really appreciate this."

Mr. Jeffrey hurried to the exam room as Dr. Tom smiled at Wood and Criswell. "An interesting case," he said. "He suffers terrible back spasms induced by stress; a perfect candidate for a combined spinal adjustment and hypnosis treatment."

"Perhaps," Cris suggested, "he's simply acting out his subconscious anxieties while he's sleepwalking. You ought to have his wife tell you what he's been up to in his somnambulistic state."

The doctor smirked at Criswell's sequined lapels. "You have some rather strong medical opinions for a cheap stage magician."

Criswell shrugged. "Who says I'm cheap?"

Dr. Tom dismissed Criswell by smiling pleasantly at Kathy. "Same time next week, Miss O'Hara."

"Thank you, Dr. Tom." She took Eddie's hand. "And it's 'Wood' now. Well, unofficially, anyway."

"Of course, I forgot." Dr. Tom excused himself with a nod and disappeared down the hall.

Eddie turned to his "wife" and asked, "So how about it, angel? How many chances will you get to meet Mae West?"

Kathy kissed Wood and played with his hair. "We haven't a thing in the refrigerator." Wood ran his hand up and down her back, relishing the feel of angora. "Besides," she added coyly, "I don't think you boys want a girl tagging along on a visit to Mae West's place."

Criswell considered the matter. "Well, you are rather pretty. Mae might get jealous." He wasn't joking, either.

"What a sweet thing to say." Kathy kissed Wood again, pressing close up against him. "You two have a good time. I'll see you when you get home."

"Well, poodle, if that's the way you feel about it." Wood kept feeling the softness of Kathy's angora sweater and getting very aroused. Kathy stepped back and giggled, "Eddie!"

"What?" he asked.

She gestured at the bulge in his pants and blushed. "You're getting too…excited."

"Oh." Wood tried to stand in a way to hide his erection and it wasn't working. He blushed. "Uh, sorry." He shrugged and said to Criswell, "What can I say? I really like Kathy in angora."

"Obviously," said Criswell.

# Chapter 4

Outside Dr. Tom Mason's Chiropractic Clinic, Criswell watched Kathy with apprehension as she traipsed gaily down the street to Wood's yellow convertible. Naturally, it was next to a red-flagged parking meter, and with a traffic ticket stuck under the windshield wiper.

"Uh, Eddie," Cris said. "Doesn't it kind of scare you, Dr. Tom hypnotizing Kathy like that?"

Wood shrugged. "Not really. Kathy's been Dr. Tom's patient for years. I go to him all the time."

"So you said. Are you sure you don't remember what Dr. Tom does in there?"

But Ed wasn't listening; he was too preoccupied admiring Kathy's bottom as she opened the door and slid behind the wheel. "Ain't she something?" he commented while flashing a broad smile.

Criswell remained uneasy as they walked back to the limousine. "I take it that Kathy isn't just suffering from backache."

"I can't tell you what Dr. Tom is treating her for, Cris. It's kind of personal, but I know for a fact that Kathy feels amazing! I do too."

"So everyone keeps saying."

Wood got back in the passenger seat and set the pot of Swedish meatballs on his lap. "Why, Dr. Tom even helped Armand with his addiction to pain killers. He even got rid of Hope's migraine headaches."

Criswell sighed as he slid into the driver's seat. "Well," he said with a shrug of resignation, "as long as *you're* okay with it." He turned the key, switched gears noisily and pulled back into traffic. Suddenly Wood's eyes bugged out. "Wait! Pull over!" he said.

"What's wrong?" Criswell asked as he stopped short. The drivers behind him leaned on their horns as Criswell looked around for anything amiss.

"See that guy over there?" Wood said, pointing to a well-dressed man with glasses and a mustache. He was sauntering along the street with a shorter, slight fellow in a bow tie with short dark hair and a dreamy cast to his eyes. They were window-shopping.

"Which guy?" Criswell asked, studying the pair.

"The taller one! That's Forry Ackerman!" Wood tugged on Criswell's sleeve like an excited two-year-old. "Pull up to him before he gets away!"

The name was vaguely familiar, but Cris couldn't place it. "Just who is Forry Ackerman and why don't we want him to get away?"

"Forry is my literary agent!" came Wood's startling answer.

Criswell was flabbergasted. "*You* have a literary agent?"

"I sent him the manuscript for a science fiction novel, and he hasn't gotten back to me yet, or returned my calls. Now I can finally talk to him."

With a shake of his head, Criswell sighed, "You have a literary agent." There was something about the "literary agent" in question that intrigued Criswell. Maybe it was the shape of his glasses, or the way he carried himself. Whatever it was, it suggested flamboyance. Criswell signaled and made a U-turn despite complaining traffic and pulled up along the curb beside the two men.

Eddie stuck his head out the window. "Forry!" he shouted as he waved Ackerman over. Ackerman wheeled around as if someone had just fired a gun over his head. "Over here! It's me! Eddie Wood!"

The minute he spotted Edward D. Wood Jr., Ackerman's body language expressed an undeniable exclamation of, "Shakatabulo!" which was Esperanto for Chess Table and an Ackerman substitute for "Oh, God!" or, as in this case, "Oh, shit!" With obvious reluctance, he forced a pleasant smile and approached the limousine. He draped his arm over the door ledge. "Oh, hello there, Eddie," Ackerman said, forcing enthusiasm. "Where have you been creeping yourself?"

Criswell noted one of two rather unusual rings on Ackerman's fingers, one was a scarab, the other, the one that drew Criswell's interest, displayed a silver crest with bats that Cris recognized as the Dracula crest.

"I stopped by your office five times last week," Wood said. "I called six times this week. No matter what time I stop by or call, your secretary says you're out."

Ackerman shrugged. "I was probably out at the House of Pies."

The shorter man with the bow tie approached and ducked his head down. "So this is Edward D. Wood Jr., huh?" he asked.

"Uh-huh," said Ackerman.

"Did you read my manuscript?" Wood asked eagerly.

"Oh, I read it," Forry said, "every last word." (Forry had flipped to the last page and had read the last word before circular filing the manuscript). In a hurry to change the subject, Ackerman focused on Criswell and extended his hand. "Aren't you the Great Criswell of *Criswell Predicts*?"

"I am indeed," Criswell said, taking Ackerman's hand and turning it over to get a better look at the ring. "Quite unusual rings you have there." Now the encyclopedia of celebrity gossip inside Criswell's brain kicked in and he immediately placed this man as the famous monster of filmland himself, Forrest J Ackerman, aka Dr. Acula, aka Uncle Forry, aka 4SJ. He was a rabid fan of science fiction (or Sci-fi, a phrase Ackerman himself invented) and horror. He was the first to dress up in costume at a science fiction convention, and a notorious womanizer, especially the younger ladies (a generation gap that grew as progressively wider with each passing birthday as his waistline). He was also a self-described atheist, a nudist, and allegedly had one of the largest collections of science fiction inspired pornography on the West Coast, of which Ackerman was rumored to be justly proud. Criswell took an instant liking to him. Having quite a few of his own skeletons rattling around inside his closet, Cris was drawn to kindred souls with an equally dark side.

"Ah, sir," Ackerman said with the flair of a carnival barker, "you have a good eye. The scarab ring was worn by Boris Karloff himself in his role as Im-ho-tep in *The Mummy*, this other one is the very ring worn by Armand Tesla in *Abbott and Costello Meet Frankenstein*. Upon this ring is the Dracula crest." He smiled wickedly, eyes a twinkle behind his glasses. "You can try it on, but if it sticks, I'll have added another finger to my collection. I'm a collector of sorts, after all."

His companion chuckled. "Of sorts, huh? Forry, you have more props than the Universal Studios warehouse, huh?"

"Wow," marveled Wood. His eyes grew large as he focused on the carved stone in its setting. "Dracula's ring."

Ackerman's friend nudged him and nodded at Eddie. "Hey, Forry, I'll bet if you made some magical passes, you could put this guy under, huh."

"Very funny, Ray."

"Ray?" Criswell said. "You mean, this is...."

Forry patted his companion on the back. "Mr. Criswell, meet my good friend, Ray Bradbury. Ray, this is *the* Charles Criswell King."

Bradbury smiled warmly. "No introductions are necessary, huh? I watch your show every night, Mr. Criswell." He took Cris's hand and shook it vigorously.

"Wow!" Wood gushed. "*The* Ray Bradbury!"

"Too late to deny it now," Ackerman joked. "*The* Ray Bradbury, a *real* science fiction writer." He gave Criswell a smile. "You should come by the

Ackermansion some time, Mr. Criswell. I'll take you on a tour so you can exercise your eyeballs."

Bradbury smiled. "Expect to spend the day there, huh?"

"Say," said Wood, "we were just on our way to meet *the* Armand Tesla. He's a good friend of mine."

"I know, Eddie," Ackerman said.

"Did you see his latest performance in *Bride of the Monster?*"

"Yes, I did."

"Well, what did you think of my movie?"

Ackerman smiled and remarked in his passive-aggressive way, "You're as fine a director as you are a science fiction novelist."

"Gee, thanks!" Wood said, completely oblivious.

Bradbury nudged Ackerman good-naturedly. "You gotta admire the guy's tenacity, huh?" The science fiction writer looked kindly upon Edward D. Wood Jr. "Mr. Wood, I will pass on to you what Mr. Electrico said to me."

"Who's Mr. Electrico?" Eddie asked.

"Mr. Electrico was a magician who used an electric chair in his act, huh. I was a boy at the time and it was a crowded tent show and I was flat up against the stage. Mr. Electrico sat strapped in an electric chair while his assistant announced, 'Here go 10 million volts of pure fire, 10 million volts of electricity into the body of Mr. Electrico!' The assistant pulled a huge knife switch, huh, and a voltaic charge ran through Mr. Electrico's body. His hair stood on end like a fright wig and sparks flew from his fingertips. He took up an Excalibur sword and brushed it over the heads of the kids in the crowd, putting their hair on end and making their skin tingle, huh. He used that very sword to tap me on the shoulder like a king bestowing knighthood to a commoner and he said to me, 'Live forever!' I was the only kid he spoke to that day, and it forever changed my life and instilled in me a sense of wonder."

"Wow!" Eddie gushed.

Bradbury extended his index finger and tapped Wood on the shoulder. "And now, I share that spark of wonder with you. Live forever and be wondrous, Edward D. Wood Jr."

Wood sat there transfixed as Bradbury joined Ackerman and waved farewell. "Nice to meet you, Mr. Criswell," Ray said.

"Same here," said Cris.

Ackerman called, "Okay, pal! See you on the merry-go-round."

Criswell pulled away from the curb and glanced over at a stunned Ed Wood. "Are you all right, Eddie?" he asked.

Edward D. Wood Jr. sat hugging the pot of Swedish meatballs, speechless. After a moment he whispered, "Be wondrous!" repeating the phrase softly to himself like a mystic chanting a mantra.

# Chapter 5

Criswell turned up North Wilton Place. "So, Eddie," he said, trying to break the spell cast on his moonstruck friend. "I hear you're making another movie, something about vampires?"

Distracted, Ed continued to chant softly, "Be wondrous!"

Criswell gave Wood a nudge. "Eddie? Hey, wake up."

Shaken from his revere, Wood said, "Oh, uh, sorry. The vampire movie, yeah. We shot some stuff in a cemetery but we ran out of money. But that's okay, I'll use the footage somehow." His eyes suddenly grew wide as an idea took hold. Whatever it was, it made Wood effervesce with sudden, frightening enthusiasm. "THAT'S IT!" he proclaimed.

"What's it?" Criswell asked startled.

"A *wondrous* idea! We already have scenes in a dug up graveyard! So we make a movie about grave robbers," and proclaimed in an eerie wail, "*Graaaave Robbers from Outerrrr Spaaaace!*"

Criswell sighed.

"It's perfect! Aliens come to earth to steal our dead! Just like you predicted!" The grip he put on Criswell's arm was wince-inducing to say the least. "It was your idea, Cris! Can I use it? Can I? Please!"

Criswell looked from the hand cutting off his circulation to Ed's earnest stare. "Would it stop you if I said no?"

"No."

"Then, sure. Go ahead." Adding as an afterthought, "As long as you get me a part in the picture."

Wood released his grip and smiled from ear to ear. "You want to be in my movie? Wow! You bet!" He pulled out a bottle of vitamins and was about to partake when Criswell grabbed it from him. "Oh no," he admonished. "You've had quite enough caffeine for one day!"

They arrived at the Harold Way apartment house in time to see Armand in the hall with a dark-haired teenage boy wearing thick tortoise shell glasses. "Thank you for coming to help me, Andreas," Armand said. "But a neighbor, he already helped me with the water bottle." Tesla appeared more tired and drawn than usual, if that were possible. He wore a bathrobe over an undershirt and dark pants.

Andreas Orby's eyes were bright with hero worship. "That's all right, Mr. Tesla," he said, clutching an 8x10 still of Armand as the Monster from *Frankenstein Meets the Wolf Man*. "And thanks for autographing this!"

"You are a good boy," Tesla smiled. "You and the other boys are my true friends." Eyeing Wood reproachfully, he added, "Not like some people who only want to use Armand for selfish aims."

Wood felt wounded. "That's not true, Armand. I really want to help you make a comeback."

Tesla remained dubious. "So you say." He acknowledged Cris with a nod. "Hello, Criswell. I will be with you both in a moment." He turned back to young Orby and smiled. "You go home now. I am tired and need to get some rest."

"Sure thing, Mr. Tesla."

"It is Armand, call me Armand."

"Okay…Armand, sir."

Tesla smiled again and patted the boy's cheek. "You are a good boy. Now run along. I have to talk business."

His nose obviously out of joint, Wood demanded, "Who is that?" as the boy headed out.

Tesla smiled wryly. "A fan, just a fan. He and his friends, they call Armand on the telephone one day and ask to meet with me. I say, 'Come over, boys.' They are good boys. They just want to see Armand for Armand. We have had many good times." Tesla scowled at Wood. "I have not read your script yet."

Criswell stepped between Wood and Tesla. "Forget about scripts," he said. "Eddie and I are going to a party."

"Yeah," Wood chimed in. "At Mae West's place. We came over to get you. A party might cheer you up, and she asked Cris to extend you a special invitation."

"Mae West?" Tesla bristled. "Never."

"But why?" Criswell asked. "She really wants to meet you."

"Mae West, she scares me," Tesla said. His shoulders sagged wearily. "And I am too old and too tired for parties." He shuffled back into his apartment, leaving the door open for Wood and Criswell to follow. They hesitated at the threshold as Tesla straightened up and forced a smile both charming and menacing. "Enter freely and of your own will," he intoned, adding flourishes with his beckoning hand and long tapered fingers. "Come freely. Go safely. And leave something of the happiness you bring."

"Wow!" Wood gushed. "That's from *Dracula*!"

Tesla resumed his former posture and waved. "Stoker's novel, yes. And speaking of great literary works—" He gestured curtly at the script on the small table beside his favorite chair. "You see? I have here your script. I pour some whiskey. I light a cigar. And I will read it."

He slipped off his bathrobe and shuffled into the bedroom. Wood and Criswell followed. Wood watched as Armand opened his dresser drawer and selected a striped short-sleeved shirt. As Tesla buttoned his shirt, he leaned forward and squinted, myopically studying his careworn face in the dresser mirror. Shaking his head, he sighed. "Now I know why Dracula hated mirrors." He opened a coffin shaped black enameled jewelry box that emitted a tinny rendition of "Swan Lake," a present from his young fans. Tesla pulled up one of the trays, exposing a stash of cigars, each preserved in its own glass tube. As the Hungarian selected one, he said, "Hope is trying to get me to quit smoking, so now Armand must resort to hiding his *el Ropos, el Stinkos*." He slipped the cigar out of its glass receptacle and returned the empty tube back to the makeshift humidor and replaced the tray. He reached for his eyeglasses case and stuck it in his pocket

Criswell gestured at the cigar. "There's certainly nothing *el stinko* about *that* cigar."

The corners of Armand's mouth formed a wry smile. "The cigars, they are a gift from a devoted fan."

"Uh, Armand," Wood pulled the envelope from his inner jacket pocket, "about this envelope you sent me—"

The wannabe director proffered it to Tesla, who turned on Wood angrily. "Why did you bring that *here?*" the Hungarian hissed. "Do not let Hope see that you have that!"

"What's in it?"

Tesla's eyes burned with rage as he grabbed the envelope from Wood and shook it in the startled director's face. "Idiot! In the first envelope there is a letter and a *second* envelope! The letter will give to you instructions about what to do with second envelope should I die suddenly!"

Wood took the envelope back, staring at it with awe. "You're entrusting me with—whatever this is?"

"No," Tesla snarled sarcastically, "I am going to give it to the young boy to hold for me! Who else can I give it to but you? Certainly not to Karloff! He is in London! My nephew Armand Loosz, he likes Hope too much to keep secrets from her. As for Basil Rathbone—" He frowned with distaste. "Forget about Basil Rathbone. So, Armand has no choice *but* to entrust it to you. So do not fuck it up!"

Wood held the envelope like a holy relic. "Gee, Armand, I don't know what to say."

"Of course you do not know what to say! You have not read the letter addressed to you yet!"

"I'll read it now." Wood was about to tear the envelope open when Tesla snatched it from him.

"Not now, idiot!" Tesla nearly tore Wood's jacket stuffing the envelope in his inner pocket. "Do not let anyone see you have it!"

"But why?" Wood asked, startled.

"*Agyilag zokni!*" Tesla swore in Hungarian. "Read the damn letter and your questions will be answered. Now go away and leave me with that damn script of yours in peace." He stormed into the living room and was about to sit in his favorite chair when he noticed the front door ajar. "Fools! Someone may have overheard!"

Tesla rushed to the door and checked the hallway. "Someone was here!" he insisted, shutting the door and pressing his eye to the peephole.

"Uh, Armand," said Criswell, "are you trying to tell us that someone is out to get you?"

Satisfied with his precautions, Tesla pushed Criswell aside. "Brilliant deduction, Mr. Holmes!" he scoffed. "You and Basil Rathbone should be consulting detectives together!" Tesla returned to his chair and grunted as he eased himself down. "It is horrible to be old," he muttered as he rubbed his aching knees.

Ed and Criswell exchanged worried looks, and then Ed asked, "Uh, Armand. Are you sure you're all right?"

The Hungarian glared indignantly. "I am not crazy! If that is what you are both thinking."

"Hope mentioned that a couple of nights ago you woke up insisting Boris Karloff was waiting to see you in the living room. What did you think Karloff wanted to see you about?"

Armand frowned glumly. "For a moment I thought it was like the old days — all for one and one for all." He sighed. "But those days are gone. The three of us, we are just tired old men."

Wood and Criswell exchanged worried looks again, and then Wood smiled at Armand. "Hope said it took a long time to convince you Karloff wasn't here."

Tesla grabbed the folded *The Final Curtain* script and angrily gestured with it. "That *kurva!* So she is poisoning your minds against me, too! Just because I was sleepwalking, that does not make me crazy!" He smacked the palm of his hand with the script. "But I show her! Tomorrow I see a lawyer! Nothing will prevent me short of my own death!"

Criswell gave Wood a nudge. "Come on, Eddie, we're just upsetting him. Maybe we should let Armand read in peace."

Wood hesitated. "I'm worried about you, Armand. I want to help if I can."

Tesla pointed to the kitchenette. "If you want to help Armand, pour me a drink. All this yelling, it has tired me."

Wood beamed. "Sure thing, Armand. What's your poison?"

"There is a bottle of whiskey hidden between the stove and the refrigerator, and there is a clean glass in the cabinet."

Wood found the bottle, got the glass, and poured Tesla a shot. "Here you go, Armand. To your health."

Armand downed the whiskey in one gulp and extended the glass for a refill. Wood complied, and then noticed the card attached to the neck of the bottle. "'To, Dracula – Cheers.' Say, who sent you this?"

Tesla downed the second glass. "I thought it was from you, a gift for all that you put me through in the cemetery." He shrugged. "It must be just another admirer." He reached for a book of matches by the square ash tray and lit his fine cigar.

"Are you sure you're going to be all right by yourself, Armand?" Wood asked as Tesla shook the match out and placed the burnt remnant in the ashtray.

Tesla puffed away, savoring the taste. Criswell's nostrils twitched. Did he detect the hint of garlic in the air? "You can run along, Eddie," Armand assured him. "Hope will be home soon from work."

Wood smiled at the old man, and then remembered the bottles of *Criswell's Family Formula* in his pockets. "I brought you something that might make you feel better. Criswell sells these on his program."

Tesla eyed the bottle suspiciously. "What is it?"

"Instant pep in a bottle," Wood said, shaking a pill in Tesla's palm. "I've had 50 of 'em and I feel great."

"Uh," Criswell interrupted, "I wouldn't eat that many. One or two are plenty."

"I do not need it," Tesla insisted. "Already I take a tonic." He studied the pill. "This stuff is good?"

"Try some," Wood encouraged. "It's chewable."

Tesla squinted at the pill with misgivings before finally popping it into his mouth. He bit down and chewed. Almost immediately, he grimaced in disgust and declared angrily, "It tastes like malt flavored billiard chalk!"

"See, Eddie?" Criswell joked. "*That's* how you make a product endorsement."

Tesla spat out what little of it remained. "Another whiskey, Eddie," Tesla insisted, holding out the glass. "I need it to take the taste away!"

"Take it easy, Armand," Wood cautioned as Tesla quickly downed his third drink. "It's still kind of early in the day for whiskey."

"As if that ever stopped you from drinking." The Hungarian glared accusingly at Criswell. "You should be ashamed for selling that atrocious concoction!"

Criswell shrugged good-naturedly. "What can I say, it pays the bills."

Wood ran to the kitchenette and opened a cabinet. "I'll just stick these up here in case you change your mind." He put away the vitamin bottles and the whiskey.

"Fine," said Tesla. "Later, I slip the pills into Hope's goulash. Maybe it will poison her."

Returning to the living room, Wood asked, "You don't mean that, do you, Armand?"

"No, of course not," Tesla said unconvincingly.

He slipped his eyeglasses from their case and hesitated putting them on, his vanity getting the better of him. Criswell waited by the door, his hand poised on the knob. He quickly read the meaning of Armand's gesture, sensed the Hungarian's embarrassment. After clearing his throat, he said, "Uh, Eddie, I think we should go."

"Yes, go, both of you," said Tesla, opening the script. "I read the script and tell you what I think in the morning."

As Wood and Criswell headed out, Wood said, "Sure thing, Armand. Believe me, you'll love it!"

"That I doubt very much," Tesla scoffed. "But I do it anyway. What choice do I have?"

Before leaving, Criswell bowed graciously to his host. "Good afternoon, Armand."

"Good-bye," Tesla said absently, his back to Criswell and waving the psychic away as a Count would dismiss a servant.

That was the last time anyone saw Armand Tesla alive.

A fully costumed Armand Tesla stood behind her.

# Chapter 6

It was a strange sight, an antique limousine pulling up to a curb in the Nickel; a quaint euphemism for LA's Skid Row, so named because it centered on 5$^{th}$ Street. The Nickel was notorious for its prostitutes, derelicts, and dope addicts. It was nightmare alley in a dream factory town.

Wood gestured at a shabby apartment house set starkly against the incongruous backdrop of blue skies and the Hollywood Hills. "Do you really think she'll come?"

"I hope so," Criswell said. "Maila could use a night out." He turned to Wood. "Aren't you going to open that?"

Wood looked down at the pot in his lap. "You said I couldn't have any."

"I meant the envelope in your pocket."

"Oh, that!" Wood smiled nervously. "I'm afraid to. Armand sounded so…crazy. There's no telling what's in it."

Criswell shrugged. "We'll never know until you open it."

Wood reached for the envelope, hesitated, then shook his head. "Maybe later. I'm not ready yet."

"If you wait too long, a mysterious stranger is liable to plug you and take it from you."

"Don't even joke about a thing like that!" Wood looked around anxiously. "You *were* joking, right?"

"Of course I was. I hate to say this, but I think Armand might be turning paranoid in his old age."

"Could we stop talking about this?" Wood pleaded.

"Okay," Criswell said, opening the door. "Let's see if Maila is in a party mood."

Maila Nurmi was definitely not in a party mood. She was sitting at her kitchen table; her angular features sans makeup, naked except for a mousy gray bathrobe cinched tightly around her waspish waist. She felt decidedly unglamorous, having taken a pair of scissors to her red hair during a fit of despair. As she smoked a cigarette and sipped her whiskey from a Vampira glass, she tried to figure just how she had gone from being the toast of late-night television, with featured articles in *Life Magazine* and *Newsweek*, to a down-and-out divorcee barely eking out an existence on $13 a week. With her TV career in the toilet, what was left? Moving back in with her mother?

"Modeling" for a sleazy camera club? Hustling for tips as a waitress? Of course, there was always the other alternative, becoming a hooker. When you got right down to it, was there really any difference between show business and prostitution? Then there was the *other* alternative, working for Edward D. Wood Jr. The thought of appearing in an Edward D. Wood Jr. production made Maila's skin crawl.

Her gaze drifted to a framed picture of her Vampira persona. A fully costumed Armand Tesla stood behind her, feasting hungrily upon her neck. Vampira was in ecstasy as the Count supped upon her throat, while her left boob got a reach-around squeeze from the naughty old letch. Vampira's hand rested over Tesla's bony clutching claw, pressing it closer to her breast, inviting him to squeeze it tighter. She raised her glass in a mocking toast as she remembered his hot breath on her neck. "To Vampira and Dracula," she said. "Here's hoping we both eventually rest in peace." As she drank to her toast, Maila saw distorted in the bottom of her glass the beckoning image of her kitchen stove. She wondered just how long it would take for gas to asphyxiate her. Then she remembered that she hadn't paid her utility bills and the gas had been turned off. "I can't even afford to kill myself," she sighed, smirking wistfully.

A knock at the door made Maila tense. Back in January, the actress had been the victim of an attempted rape. Provocative photos of Maila displaying bruises on her shoulder and upper thigh were circulated in the press. Sadly, the resulting publicity did nothing to resuscitate her career.

The knocks rapped out *shave-and-a-haircut*.

Snuffing out her cigarette, Maila eyed the door warily as she sprang to her feet and grabbed the baseball bat she kept by the door. "Who is it?" she challenged, Louisville Slugger at the ready.

"Cris-weeeell," sang the familiar friendly voice.

Maila relaxed and opened the door. Criswell stood hefting the pot of Swedish meatballs. "I hope you're hungry!"

Maila smiled. "Hungry? I'm starved."

As Criswell brought in the meatballs, Wood made his entrance. "Hi, Vampira!" He was about to step inside when Maila poked him in the chest with the business end of the baseball bat. "Edward D. mother-fucker-Wood Jr.," she growled. "As if I don't have enough vermin to deal with already!"

"Now, now, children," Criswell chided. "Play nice." He placed the pot on the kitchen table and then went for some plates. He recoiled as a cockroach wiggled its antenna at him from the depths of the kitchen cabinet.

"I see what you mean about vermin." He quickly closed the cabinet door and approached Maila, relieving her of the baseball bat. "Forget dining in," he said, returning the bat to its spot by the door. "We're going to a party at the Ravenswood. I was hoping you'd come along."

"Mr. Criswell," Maila said, using "Mister" with great affection, "you and I both know how Miss West hates competition, especially at one of her parties."

"I'll tell her you're my mistress."

"Oh, like she'd believe that," she teased, knowing Criswell's preferences for young men. "Besides, Mae doesn't want to have anything to do with me. She fired me from *Catherine the Great*, remember?"

"Water under the bridge. Come on, you'll have fun."

"I look like shit."

"At least Mae won't see you as competition."

Indicating her bathrobe, she said, "I don't have a thing to wear."

"Well, if you go dressed like that, then she *might* see you as competition."

Wood cleared his throat. "Uh, we can swing by my place. I probably have something you can borrow."

Maila rolled her eyes. God, how she hated him. "Thanks," she said, "but I don't think you're my size."

Wood put his arm around her shoulder. A chill ran through Maila as the producer said, "Have you considered taking that part I offered you in *The Final Curtain*? We're paying union minimum."

"Eddie," Criswell cautioned.

Wood ignored him with a dismissive wave. "Just today Armand was saying how excited he was about the script."

"You're very kind, *Mister* Wood," Maila said, this time giving "Mister" a decided chill as she pried his arm loose. "But I've been considering other things." *Like taking the gas pipe,* she thought.

Criswell went to the closet and pulled out Maila's Vampira costume and the Styrofoam head on which was pinned her long black wig. "You can dress up in these. You'd be a smash."

Maila took the costume and wig head back. "Vampira is dead." She hung up her costume and stuck the wig head on the top shelf.

"I thought that was the whole idea."

"I mean, really dead." She shut the closet door. The hinges creaked like a closing coffin lid. "TV producers drove a blacklist through Vampira's heart and then salted her grave. Trust me, Vampira's dead."

"Salted her grave?" Eddie suddenly smiled. "What a swell idea!"

Glowering, Maila said, "Yeah, I love you, too."

"Cris and I have been talking about a new project you'd just be perfect for."

Criswell tried to restrain him. "Eddie...," he said.

Wood made one of his grand flourishes. "*Grave Robbers from Outer Space!*" His eyes lighted on the framed picture of Maila and Tesla. He gestured excitedly as inspiration took hold. "VAMPIRA, the reanimated wife of Armand Tesla!"

"Not now, Eddie," Cris cautioned, but Wood wouldn't listen.

The would-be director waved his hands in Maila's face like a Svengali. "Aliens," Wood intoned weirdly, "use Vampira's gorgeous body as a vessel to harbor their evil minds!"

Maila was eyeing the baseball bat.

"And," he said, grabbing a shaker from the kitchen table and shaking some salt out into his palm, "just as Criswell predicted, salt sends Vampira back to her everlasting rest!" He blew the salt in Maila's face. She recoiled as Wood declared, "It's colossal! And you'll look terrific in the poster art! Come on, Vampira! What do you say?"

Wincing from the salt in her eyes, Maila shoved Wood out the door. "I say, get out and stay out!"

"But—" Wood was cut off by the door slamming in his face. Maila looked to Criswell and bit her trembling bottom lip. Criswell took her in his arms. "How, Mr. Criswell," she sobbed. "How did everything go so wrong?"

"I don't know, gorgeous," Criswell said soothingly. "I guess there are just some things even Criswell can't predict." Criswell surveyed the kitchen/living room/bedroom. "God, you deserve so much better than this." He smiled at Maila and used his handkerchief to wipe her tears. "I can put you up at my place. Halo won't mind the company."

Maila took Criswell's hanky. "Halo is a mad woman," Maila sniffled. "No offense."

"None taken," Criswell said. "But when you have Halo's kind of money you're not mad, you're eccentric." Criswell reached into his tuxedo jacket. "If you don't want to stay at my place," he said, "you're welcome to shack up at my office." He pulled $20 from his billfold and handed it to Maila. She eyed it with a saucy smile and said teasingly, "Why, Mr. Criswell, are you propositioning me?"

"Cab fare and an advance."

"An advance? For what?"

"You can be my secretary."

"I can't type."

"With your looks, you don't have to. Just charm my clients and answer the telephone. I keep a key to the office on the ledge of the transom. Just let yourself in. You'll find a cot in the supply closet."

"You're sweet," she said with a sniffle.

"No, just cheap. Where else can I get a secretary for $20 a week, and a pot of Swedish meatballs every now and then?"

"So," she said suggestively, "what kind of 'clients' am I expected to 'charm'?" She playfully opened the top of her bathrobe, exposing her breasts and striking a seductive femme fatale pose.

Criswell smiled coyly. "Well, not the kind where you have to flash your tits. Especially not for the little old ladies who want to contact their late husbands." Pausing to think, he added, "Then again, some of the cops that come looking for a fresh lead might want to dust you for fingerprints."

Closing her robe, Maila was agog. "You're kidding? Cops *actually* consult with you?"

Criswell shrugged. "Sometimes when a case grows cold they get desperate. I can't tell you how many times I've been asked to describe the Black Dahlia killer."

"But you're all the time denying you have any real psychic powers. Why would cops even bother?"

"I think they just send rookies to me as a hazing gag. But the LAPD pays well for my services, so I don't rock the boat. Do you want the job?"

"If you throw in a cup of coffee and a Danish each morning," Maila negotiated, "you got yourself a girl."

"Continental breakfast *and* Swedish meatballs? You drive a hard bargain for a nudist secretary who can't type."

In Vampira's sultry delivery, she said, "But I work nights. And people say I'm a scream." She let loose with her signature bloodcurdling shriek. Not so surprisingly, her neighbors didn't give it any notice. Somewhere, a dog barked.

"I love to scream," she moaned. "It relaxes me so."

I like a man who knows it's only polite to stand up for a lady.

# Chapter 7

At the Ravenswood, Criswell rang the doorbell. Through a tiny triangular "Joe sent me" peephole, an eye appeared.

"Yes?" the eye inquired in a deep Hungarian accent.

Criswell smiled and held up his invitation. "Charles Criswell King and Edward D. Wood Jr. Mae is expecting us."

The peephole shut and the front door opened. A muscleman greeter wearing only a black bow tie and tight swim trunks that left nothing to the imagination took their coats as he announced, "Edward D. Wood Jr. and Mr. Charles Criswell King."

As they passed through the entrance hall, Wood nudged Criswell and glanced back at the bodybuilder. "Say, that guy looks kind of familiar."

"He should. That's Mr. Universe, Mickey Hargitay."

Wood stopped short. "Mr. Universe is the coat check?"

"Punishment detail." Criswell leaned in to gossip. "Mickey's in Mae's touring muscleman stage review, and he's been a baaaaad boy."

Wood gleefully took Criswell aside. "What did he do?"

"Well, it seems Mickey made the mistake of getting his picture taken with Jayne Mansfield."

"And that's a bad thing?"

"It is when it gets circulated in all the papers. Mae had a royal fit."

"Why?"

"Look around, Eddie. Do you see Jayne Mansfield, or Marilyn Monroe, or any other sweet young thing around here that *might* steal Mae's thunder?"

Wood scanned the intimate crowd. Seated on the couch wearing one of her signature hats was gossip columnist Hedda Hopper, certainly no threat to Mae's sex symbol status. Beside her was Marlene Dietrich, a beauty perhaps, but well past her prime.

"Now that you mention it," Wood said, "no."

"And you won't. This is Mae West's exclusive domain. No competition allowed. That's why Mickey's in hot water. Mae has strict rules about the conduct of the musclemen in her show. Rule number one, thou shalt not make eyes at anyone but Mae, bad for her image."

"She's got a great image. Mae West is a goddess!"

Like Russian royalty, Mae held court from a lavish gold and white throne. It was also on this same throne that Mae greeted reporters and conducted interviews.

"Mae does like to make a good impression."

"I'll say!" Wood marveled. "What a living room!"

A writer once described the décor of Mae West's apartment as, "late wedding cake." This may have been too kind, and a trifle too conservative, a description. The tiny apartment was decked out like a whore's dream bordello. Mae's glamorous full-length portrait hung over the fireplace; three white polar bear rugs were stretched out spread-eagle on the floor.

Star struck, Wood said, "I'll bet Miss West lounges naked on those rugs!"

"She once described that big one there as the largest retail polar bear in Hollywood."

Every grandiose stick of Louis XIV furniture, every drape, right down to the fancy gold-plated telephones that bore her initials, acted as a constant reminder that you were in the presence of the one, the only, MAE WEST!

"This place is like a palace," Wood marveled. "How can such a tiny apartment look so big?" Squinting, he added, "And so *white*."

"Ah, Eddie," Criswell said as he made a sweeping gesture, "you've hit upon Mae's genius. The white washes out her crow's feet. In fact, everything serves to create the illusion that Mae is impervious to time or gravity. Specific curtains are open to catch just the right flattering light at a particular time of day. See there? Those mirrors hanging between the two large front windows, they're funhouse mirrors."

"Funhouse mirrors? How come?"

"They create a slim, tall reflection. In fact, it's the mirrors that make the place look so big. She's got them everywhere, on the walls, the tabletops, the baby grand piano, and, of course, over her bed. They're all backed with gold instead of silver."

"Wow. Now that's extravagant."

"It's not extravagance; it's illusion. The gold bathes Mae in an afterglow suggestive of youth, beauty, and…" Criswell whispered out of the corner of his mouth, "…consummated sex."

Ed whispered back, "Is it true that Mae owns this apartment house?"

"No. Actually, she bought the apartment house across the street *from* the Ravenswood."

"Why would she do a thing like that?"

Criswell glowed with admiration for the hostess. "She had it painted to give any reflected sunlight a more flattering hue."

"Wow! No wonder she looks so fantastic!"

"Make sure she knows you noticed."

"I'll say I noticed," Ed said ogling her. "Look at those bazooms!"

"She massages those girls with cold cream each morning and before she goes to bed each night. Mae says she does it to keep her breasts youthful. Personally, I think she just likes to touch herself."

"Who's the lug with her?" Wood asked, indicating a bodybuilder in a tailored suit.

"That's former Mr. California, Chuck Krauser. He's in the muscleman act, too. He lives in the spare bedroom."

"So they're an item?"

Cris shrugged. "In a Platonic sort of way."

In a corner of the living room, an overweight dowager Wood recognized as Liberace's mother shared the piano bench with her boy, while Lee played accompaniment for a husky-voiced drag queen. The drag was seductively draped on the mirrored baby grand, warbling a more than slightly suggestive comic French ballad about an underage prostitute named Yvette and her encounter with an overly endowed Toulouse Lautrec.

Pointing out the drag, Criswell said, "That's John 'Bunny' Breckinridge."

Breckinridge wore a sequin gown that reached clear to the floor; a wig and headdress that reached up to the ceiling, and waved around an ostrich feather fan that was damn near as big as he was.

Wood smirked. "I guess Mae doesn't see transvestites as a threat."

"He's filthy rich and headlines in all the best Paris nightclubs. Bunny is constantly threatening to get a sex change operation, but he never goes through with it." With an insinuating nod at some very familiar faces in the room, Criswell said, "Gays and drags gravitate around Mae like drones around a queen bee." He picked up a framed photograph resting on a mirrored table. "See that lady there?" he asked, pointing at the image of a stylish blonde dressed in a white mink coat and cap. "That lady *isn't* a lady."

"It isn't?" Wood took the photograph and studied it closely. He was genuinely shocked. "She" was leaning against a limousine similar to the one Criswell drove. Posed with the blonde were a young Chalky Wright and a tall man in a dark suit.

"That's really police detective Harry Dean disguised as Mae. Chalky you've met, and the other guy is police bodyguard Jack Southern." He took the picture and set it back on the table. "In 1935, Mae was getting extortion threats and Dean tried to catch the perpetrator by posing as Mae. Nothing ever came of it. Although, I understand he looks that good in a dress because he really *likes* to wear dresses." He pointed at two celebrities chatting by the wet bar. "Just like those two."

Wood was agog. "Danny Kaye and Tony Curtis…?"

Criswell nodded. "They're transvestites like you are. Lee and Bunny are gay, though."

"But I thought Liberace was straight."

Criswell blinked in astonishment. "You *must* be joking." Nodding toward the couch, he said, "And I know for a fact that *she* likes to yodel in the valley, if you know what I mean."

"Hedda Hopper!"

Criswell shushed him and shook his head. "No," he whispered, "Marlene Dietrich. And those older queens over by Mae's nude statue, they became part of Mae's entourage while Mae wrote and produced *The Drag*. By the way, make sure Mae knows you like girls. She doesn't see the difference between a queer and a drag."

"Got you," Wood said, making the OK sign. Three men came out of a tiny kitchen and passed by. Wood blinked in disbelief. "Oh, my God! Frank Sinatra and Dean Martin! You mean they're—!" He limply waved his wrist around.

Criswell rolled his eyes. "Don't be ridiculous. They're just investors. Those guys are as straight as they come."

"What about the guy with Sinatra and Martin? Is he—"

"No. That's Henry Doelger, Mae's cousin. He's a Big North California builder and developer and he's the one who OK'ed the real estate deal before Mae sunk in a penny. In fact, everyone in this room is part of the investment partnership."

"With Sinatra and Martin involved in the real estate deal, I guess Mae's opening a casino in Las Vegas."

Criswell smiled. "Nothing quite so flashy, it's just a high-class high-rise apartment in Sacramento."

Wood grinned. "Funny you should mention Sacramento. That's where we shot all that cemetery footage. In fact, some developer was moving all the bodies to make way for a new apartment complex. What a coincidence!"

"It's not a coincidence, Eddie. That *is* the real estate deal I was talking about."

"It is? I can't wait to tell Armand. Wouldn't it be something if he moved to an apartment built over a graveyard?"

"I doubt Armand could afford the rent."

Wood frowned questioningly. "Wait. Is my being a transvestite the reason you invited me here?"

"Don't let this go to your head, but I know for a fact that La West is one of the few people who actually liked *Glen or Glenda*. I think she even has her own print."

Wood gushed, "Wow! I've got a fan!" His eyes widened as he latched onto Criswell's arm and shook it with excitement. "If Mae liked *Glen or Glenda*, maybe we can get her to invest in *Grave Robbers from Outer Space!*"

"Eddie," Criswell cautioned as he disentangled himself, "I told you before, no shop talk."

"But when will we get a better chance? If Mae isn't interested, maybe we can convince Breckinridge to invest!"

"No, Eddie. And I mean it."

Wood pouted like a little boy who didn't get the toy he wanted. "Oh, okay. I won't say anything." He stuck his hands in his pockets and let his eyes drift around the room. He sighed.

"I mean business, Eddie. One word and I'll take you right home."

"Scout's honor," Eddie said, making the Boy Scout salute. "Not a word."

"You were never a Scout," Criswell scoffed.

"I sure was, when I was 13! And I was a G2 Marine Intelligence Officer in the War."

Criswell shook his head. "God, Eddie, you're so full of shit sometimes."

"Oh yeah?" Wood reached into his mouth and removed the dentures that took the place of his two front teeth. "How do you think I got these? A Japanese soldier got me with a rifle butt to the face, that's how!"

Criswell turned Wood around and took him out of sight of the other guests. "Put those teeth back in your mouth and behave yourself!"

Wood quickly complied. "I'm just saying, is all."

After a moment's hesitation, Criswell said, "*If* the subject of movies comes up, I'll casually mention you're working on *Grave Robbers from Outer Space*. But I'm not promising anything." Criswell patted Eddie's arm. "Now you be a good boy and I'll introduce you to Mae."

Criswell waited for Bunny's song to be over, and for the golf-clap applause to die down, and then escorted Wood to her Highness's throne. In an article about Hollywood's influence on American morals, *Police Dragnet*

*Cases* magazine credited Mae West for replacing Greta Garbo's flat-figured hungry look with flesh. The article went on to say that in her heyday, 'Come up and see my sometime' became the national invitation, as if her heyday had passed her by. What *Police Dragnet Cases* failed to realize was that in Mae's apartment, her heyday was now and forever.

Cris made introductions. "Mae, I'd like you to meet—"

"Edward D. Wood Jr.," Mae purred as she extended her hand. "Pleased to me'cha, Mr. Wood."

Wood was flabbergasted. "Wow, the pleasure is all mine, Miss West."

"Mmmm, I like the mustache. It gives you some character. And I hear you're quite a character."

"Cris tells me you've seen *Glen or Glenda*."

"I'll say this for you, honey, you really know how to fill out a dress." She indicated Criswell with a gesture. "So you and Mr. Criswell—"

Wood smiled broadly and blushed. "Oh no. We're just friends. I like girls."

"That's what they all say." Mae smirked knowingly at Criswell. "How's the wife, Cris?"

"Fine, Mae, just fine. Halo sends her best."

Mae said to Krauser, "Why don't we get these fine boys a drink. Criswell likes his Manhattan." She batted her long eyelashes at Wood. "And what's your poison, Woody?"

"Oh, well, uh, straight up whiskey."

"You heard the man."

After Krauser left them alone, Mae looked around and pouted at Criswell. "So where's Mr. Tesla?"

"Sorry, Mae. He wasn't feeling up to a party."

Sinatra and Martin stepped up. "Did I hear right?" Sinatra said. "Tesla ain't coming?"

"Looks that way, Frankie," Mae said with an alluring sigh.

"Gee, Mr. Sinatra," Wood said star struck, "I didn't know you were an Armand Tesla fan!"

"A fan?" Sinatra said with a smile. "Listen, friend, I love that guy. When I read he was in the hospital kicking his habit, I sent him some scratch to help him out."

"No kiddin'?" Wood asked.

Dean Martin put an arm around Ed's shoulder. "In fact," he said, "we wanted to make him a member of the rat pack and change the name to the *bat* pack in his honor."

"Wow!" Wood exclaimed.

Criswell whispered, "I think he's joking, Eddie."

"On the contrary, Cris," Mae purred. "We're all big fans of Mr. Tesla."

As Krauser handed Cris and Ed their drinks, Wood said, "Gee, it's too bad he couldn't be here. Armand would love to have met you."

Reaching into the air, Mae pantomimed yanking a rope. "Pull the string!" she said in a poor Tesla impression. "Pull the string!" She chuckled. As she chuckled, her breasts jiggled invitingly within the confines of her hourglass-defining dress. "I never get tired of seeing him do that." She stood up and played with Wood's tie. "Maybe you can ring Mr. Tesla up—you might change his mind."

"Uh, I, uh," Wood stammered. He felt a raging erection coming on.

"There's a phone in the bedroom. It'll give you some—privacy." It amazed Wood how anything Mae said sounded like a sexual proposition.

"Uh, sure, I'll be, uh, glad to."

Mae looked down at Wood's pants and smiled. "I guess you *do* like girls." She took his arm. "I think I'll escort you there myself."

Not so surprisingly, Mae's bedroom-dressing room suite was inspired by boudoirs of the great ladies of the 18th century. One could easily imagine Catherine the Great receiving gentlemen callers in the huge canopied bed with the mirrored ceiling and the quilted headboard. Mae sat Wood down on the plush mattress and handed him the gold inlaid handset. "What's his number?" she asked.

"H-Hol-Hollywood 9-5991," Wood stammered as he tried to ignore the bulge in his pants.

As Mae dialed the number she flashed him a saucy smile. "I like a man who knows it's only polite to stand up for a lady."

Embarrassed, Wood grabbed a throw pillow and put it in his lap to hide his erection.

"After you make the call," she continued, "maybe I can do a little somethin' about that."

After a pause, Wood said. "Uh, it's busy."

"Too bad," she said, taking the handset and cradling it. "Maybe we should try again in a few minutes."

"Maybe." Wood tried to ignore the lightheaded sensation of all the blood rushing out of his head and into his other head.

"I wonder," Mae said, pulling up a chair, "what we oughta do to kill some time." Mae took the throw pillow from Wood and set it aside. "Don't be shy, Woody." She reached for his belt and began unbuckling it. "I'd do this on my knees, but this dress ain't designed for kneelin'. Besides, I hurt my back during my review."

Wood became intensely aware of the sound of his zipper being unzipped and the trouser waistband slacking. "I, uh, kn-know a good chiropractor," he stammered.

"So do I," Mae smiled. "Dr. Tom is *amazing*." At a gesture from Mae, Wood raised his hips so she could pull his pants down around his knees, exposing a pair of red silk panties straining against the force of Eddie's erection.

Mae smirked up at Wood. "I can't say I fault you for your taste in ladies' undergarments. But I think 'Little Woody' could use somethin' with a fly. Take 'em off."

Wood quickly complied. Once free of any confining clothing it occurred to him that May could take his pulse just by looking at the darn thing jerk. He kept his eyes focused on those Cupid's bow lips and he speculated about what was going to happen next. Mae eyed him knowingly as if she had just read his mind. "I only do *that* for men I know don't have the clap." Mae pulled a wad of tissues from an ornate white Kleenex holder and set the tissues in her lap and then opened the bedside table drawer. She took out a jar of breast-preserving cold cream.

"Wha-what are you gonna do with that?" Wood asked.

She scooped out a dollop of cold cream and worked it between her hands, smirking at Eddie's manhood as only Mae West could. "As if you didn't know, big boy. Now lie back and shut up."

Wood felt butterflies in his stomach as he laid back. His heart began pounding in his ears as all sensation was focused on Little Woody between La West's hands. Ed couldn't believe that Mae West, *the* Mae West, was using her cold cream-lubricated hands to give Little Woody long, slow, rhythmic strokes — and, boy, howdy, she was damn good at it!

"Let me know when you're ready," Mae said, stroking in time to Eddie's palpating heart. "I don't wanna mess the bedspread."

A gasp escaped Eddie's lips and a rushing sensation down below took him by surprise. "R-," was all he could manage to say before what happened next happened.

Mae used the Kleenex to cap Old Faithful as Eddie gushed.

Wood's head was still spinning as Mae wadded up the Kleenex into a ball and sashayed to the bathroom. He heard the toilet flushing and water running in the sink. Moments later, Mae returned with a damp soaped up white washcloth and towel, both with MW embroidery. As Mae sat back in the chair, Wood reached for the cloth to minister to his needs, only to have Mae playfully slap his hand away and smile. "It's only good manners for the lady to take care of the gen'leman." Mae handed him the telephone. "You try getting Mr. Tesla on the phone, and I'll take care of Little Woody."

Ed did his best to keep his shaking finger in the holes long enough to spin the telephone dial around. While Mae attended down below to washing and patting dry, Eddie tried to concentrate on the sound of Armand's ringing phone. But it soon became obvious that Armand wasn't going to pick up. Checking his watch and comparing it to the alabaster clock on Mae's nightstand, Wood saw it was nearly six o'clock. He swallowed hard as Mae finished patting things dry. "Maybe Armand's taking a nap," he speculated with a gulp.

"Too bad," Mae said, admiring her handiwork and transferring a kiss from her fingertip to the tip of Little Woody's head. "I guess Mr. Tesla ain't home. Maybe we can try again a little later."

"Maybe," Wood said, reaching to pull up his panties.

"Wait a minute." Mae went to an antique white and gold dresser and pulled something out of the middle drawer. She came back and handed him something soft, pink and silky. "I think maybe you can use a change of underwear." With a wink, she added, "Only the best for 'Little Woody.'"

In a scene reminiscent of *Glen or Glenda*, Mae presented Wood with a pair of her silk panties. In the movie's climax, Dolores Fuller, Eddie's co-star and then-girlfriend, proffered her angora sweater in a gesture of understanding and commitment to Eddie's transvestite alter ego. What was happening now was 10,000 times better. He took the panties gratefully, feeling close to tears and could only managed to whisper, "Thank you."

"Don't mention it," Mae said with a wink. She turned back to her dresser and was about to close the drawer, when she frowned and began hunting around inside it. "Now, where'd it go?" she asked.

"Lose something?" Eddie asked, stepping into his new panties. He pulled them up slowly to appreciate their caress against his legs and buttocks, not to mention how the crotch comfortably cupped things up front.

Mae shut the drawer and shrugged. "Ah, it wasn't important; just a little trinket from the Hollywood C of C." She raised an eyebrow in admiration as she watched Eddie bend down to pull up his pants. "Darn thing was tarnished, anyway. Mmmmm. I like the view," she purred, no doubt noticing that the sensation of being in lady's underwear was inspiring a repeat performance. "I like a man with stayin' power." She offered Eddie her hand. "Come on, Woody; let's get back to the party. Play your cards right, and maybe you an' me can have a sleepover."

Eddie blushed. "I'm married, actually."

"Lucky girl," Mae purred.

"Actually," he added hastily, "w-we're just living together."

Mae smirked wickedly. "I also like a man who likes to keep his options open."

Twenty minutes later, Mae and Eddie returned to the party. Criswell was chatting up Bunny Breckinridge, who was still in a dress but had taken off the wig and headdress. Chuck Krauser stayed in the background, pretending to listen. Looking up, Criswell said, "So, Eddie, is Armand coming?"

Before Wood could answer, Mae playfully bumped her hip against Eddie's and said, "Armand ain't comin' but Woody sure did. You can come up and see me anytime." She took Krauser's huge arm and had him escort her back to her throne.

Breckinridge smiled. "I see La West has taken a shine to you, Mr. Wood," he said in an affected British accent. "You should be congratulated. Despite the act she puts on, Mae doesn't diddle around with just anybody."

Wood was still dazed. "She—gave me her panties. I'm *wearing* Mae West's panties."

Criswell patted Wood on the back. "I guess you really *did* make a good first impression. See what happens when you don't act like a nut?"

"You were right," Wood admitted. "And she goes to Dr. Tom."

Bunny gestured at a seat. "Please join us, Mr. Wood. Cris has been telling me about this new picture of yours. I'm intrigued."

Taking his seat Wood snapped out of his afterglow. "*Cris* told you?"

Criswell gave a casual shrug. "The subject came up in passing."

"*Grave Robbers from Outer Space,*" Bunny chuckled. "How delightfully droll. Might there be a part for me?"

The gears began turning in Ed's head as his Wood Productions persona came full to the fore. "Uh, why yes. I have the perfect part for you!"

"Do tell."

"How would you like to be," he stood up and gestured grandly, "Ruler of the Galaxy!"

Criswell held his breath. He relaxed when Bunny smiled and said, "*Queen* of the Galaxy at the very least. Tell me more."

The rest of the evening was like a dream to Edward D. Wood Jr. He was making friends in high places. People, important people, were actually listening to him. Tony Curtis complained to him about how Janet Leigh didn't understand his fetish for wearing dresses. Eddie listened sympathetically, sharing his own experiences with his ex-girlfriend Dolores. Ed bragged to Sinatra and Danny Kaye about being a Marine Corps Intelligence Officer, and that he could swim underwater for hours without a snorkel. When Bunny Breckinridge challenged Wood to prove it, Wood donned one of Chuck Krauser's trunks. With party guests crowding around Mae West's bathtub, Wood submerged himself. He could hold his breath for quite some time, then quietly, and without so much as a ripple, break the surface, catch a breath and then submerge again. Mae's reaction; "I love a man with breath control—Opens up all kinds of possibilities."

It was the greatest evening in Wood's entire life.

Around seven o'clock, Wood turned to Criswell. "I think I'll try calling Armand again." He asked Mae if he could use the phone in the bedroom and then retreated to make the call. After only three rings he got an answer. "Whoever this is," Hope's voice complained, "call back later. I'm using the phone."

"Hi, Hope," Wood effused. "It's Eddie! Is Armand there?"

In her usual matter-of-fact way of breaking bad news, Hope said, "Armand can't come to the phone, Ed. Armand's dead."

A dark abyss suddenly opened up before Edward D. Wood Jr. "He—he's what?"

"Dead. I came home and found him in bed with *your* script. He died reading it."

Wood felt the blood draining from his face again, but not from ecstasy. "Oh, my God—my God," he gasped.

"Now hang up, will ya. I gotta make some calls."

"Okay." Wood stared blankly off into space. "Good-bye." He slowly cradled the handset, and then groped around for a Kleenex.

Thirty minutes later, Criswell came looking for Eddie and found him balled up in a fetal position on Mae West's bed, sobbing uncontrollably. Criswell tried to console him, but Ed was beside himself with grief and parked himself at the wet bar where he was soon reduced to a blubbering mass of inebriated jelly. Criswell made excuses and helped the thoroughly smashed Edward D. Wood Jr. to the elevator. Criswell gave Wood a ride back to the small bungalow he and Kathy rented in a less than savory part of town. The whole drive home, Wood was sobbing about how he should have stayed with Tesla. "Armand died alone," Eddie wailed. "I let him die alone!"

Kathy was obviously used to her new husband coming home drunk. She didn't nag or scold. She just thanked Criswell for his kindness, then took Ed to the couch where he flopped in a pitiful heap. She sat down beside him and put his head in her lap, holding Ed tenderly as he cried.

"Maybe you'd better go," Kathy whispered to Criswell as Wood finally drifted off to sleep. "I'll take care of Eddie," she promised. Criswell hesitated, but Kathy assured him that she could handle things just fine.

# Chapter 8

Armand Tesla's time of death was estimated at around 6:45 p.m. The conclusion typed in under *Disease or Condition* on death certificate was "Coronary Occlusion with Myocardial Fibrosis." In other words, Armand Tesla had died of a heart attack, which only made sense since everyone knew Dracula's heart was his vulnerable spot. This conclusion was reached merely as a matter of course since no actual autopsy was performed. In forth-level autopsies on a man Tesla's age, "Coronary Occlusion with Myocardial Fibrosis" was the traditional cause of death. Coroner Harold Wise conducted no toxicology tests on the blood and urine samples he collected. What was the point? Tesla was an old man and a known former drug addict. Any number of things could have killed him, and Dr. Wise's workload was backed up anyway. So as was often done in such cases, Wise gave the body only a cursory examination, estimating the time of death based on liver temperature and taking a wild guess. Afterward he scribbled his signature on the paperwork that released the body to the funeral home, he moved on to the next metal slab, putting the Armand Tesla case behind him.

The mortuary attendants placed Mr. Tesla in a simple cardboard box and taped the death certificate to the lid. They slid the box into the rear of the coach. The box was taken from the County Coroner's office to the small garage at the rear of the Hollywood Mortuary located at 6240 Hollywood Boulevard. A student embalmer approached the coach with a wheeled bier. The attendants helped the student jockey the cardboard box into place.

From the garage, the young man conveyed Mr. Tesla to the undertaker's morgue or, "preparation room," as it was more politely described. It was here where Mr. Tesla's mortal remains were to be made ready for a simple cremation. No embalming (when Ralph Fleet, Vice President of Hollywood Mortuaries and funeral director for the Hollywood Blvd. branch, suggested embalming, the widow said, "Why embalm a body that's gonna be burned up anyway?") and no casket required. Tesla was just to be washed (embalmer Horace M. Steinmetz marveled at just how clean Tesla's body was, almost as if someone had washed it beforehand) and placed back in the cardboard box that would then be taken to the crematorium that serviced all 18 of the Hollywood Mortuaries. It would be by fire, and not the direct sunlight of vampire legend, that would reduce "Dracula's" mortal remains to nothing but gray powdery ashes. Those ashes would then be boxed in a smaller cardboard receptacle and returned to the mortuary wrapped up like a macabre birthday gift. This would then be presented to the widow in a burgundy-colored velvet drawstring bag rather than an urn. "What do I need an urn for?" Hope balked when Mortician Fleet suggested one. "I'm gonna spread the ashes anyway."

That was the plan — until the ringing of a telephone echoed off the tiled walls of the preparation room. Steinmetz reached for the handset, and then checked which of the line buttons was flashing to make sure the call was meant for the preparation room. Sometimes the circuits for the preparation room got mixed up with a call intended for the private office of Hugo H. Bruckner, owner of the Hollywood Mortuaries. It was definitely an in-house call meant for Steinmetz so he punched the button and picked up. What came next was a scene reminiscent of a stay of execution from the governor. "Steinmetz here," the embalmer said.

"Steinmetz," said the voice belonged to none other than Mr. Bruckner himself, and according to the lit up button, the old man was calling from the casket showroom. "I'm here with Tesla's family," Bruckner said. "The family wants a funeral, after all," Mr. Bruckner said. "The ex-wife does, anyway." He whispered, "She's going to break the news to the widow."

Upon the mention of Lillian, and if this had been a Universal horror picture, haunting organ music orchestrated by Hans J. Salter would have begun playing as a ghostly and transparent Armand Tesla floated up from his mortal remains to pass through the walls of the preparation room, and down to the casket showroom to eavesdrop on Mr. Bruckner. There, he would have seen Mr. Bruckner talking on the phone as Ralph Fleet escorted Lillian and Armand Jr. through the showroom, and Armand would have realized that it was Ralph Fleet who had alerted Lillian about Hope's plans for a cut-rate cremation. "Tesla's ex-wife has already picked out a casket," Armand would have heard Bruckner say. "Mr. Fleet will send someone to pick up Mr. Tesla's clothes as soon as possible." If phantoms had hearts, Tesla's would probably have leapt for joy upon hearing that Lillian still cared. He would have seen Lillian and their son standing by the coffin of their choice. Armand "Bill" Tesla Jr. was the very image of his father. Lillian was beautiful, as beautiful as her portrait that Armand had commissioned early in their marriage. Her dark hair, dark eyes and fair complexion betrayed her Old-World Hungarian origins. And if Armand had really been there as a ghostly presence, he might have thrown a poltergeist tantrum, because he would have also seen that scoundrel Brian Donlevy standing with his arm around Lillian's waist. In contrast to Lillian's delicate beauty, Donlevy was husky, with squared features and a thin mustache decorating his upper lip. He also sported a ruddy complexion of broken capillaries that betrayed a penchant for too much alcohol.

Mr. Bruckner hung up and called Lillian over. "You said you wanted to call the widow yourself?"

"Yes," Lillian said, and began dialing. She waited and said, "Hello, Hope. It's Lillian...."

Fade in to his former apartment where the spectral Tesla would have passed through the wall as easily as a Pepper's Ghost illusion projected onto glass. There, he would have seen his widow on the phone, growing angrier by the minute. Tesla's ghost would probably have chuckled at the sight, because Hope's eyes became more severely crossed when she got angry. At the moment, she resembled a furious Siamese cat as Lillian informed her of the change in plans.

"How dare you go against my wishes behind my back!" Hope shouted as she twisted and untwisted the cord in her clutching hand. "I can't afford a funeral! That's why I wanted a cremation!"

"I'll cover half the expenses," Lillian calmly but firmly said on the other end of the line. "It won't cost you anything extra. But Armand is going to have a decent burial. We're Catholic and that's just the way it's going to be. And don't worry. The coffin I picked out was the least expensive one in the showroom."

"Who the fuck do you think you are?" Hope fumed. "I'm Armand's wife! I make those decisions!"

"Bill and I felt you made the *wrong* decision."

"Funerals mean burials, and I haven't picked out a plot or a tombstone!"

"That's all taken care of. Armand will be buried in a lovely grotto at Holy Cross Cemetery."

"Armand told me he wanted to be buried at Hollywood Cemetery. But I guess that doesn't matter now. Bitch!" Hope slammed the handset back on its cradle and sat thinking.

Suddenly the phone rang.

Hope started. On the third ring, she picked up and growled, "Whoever this is, call back later. I'm using the phone."

"Hi, Hope!" effused the voice on the line. "It's Eddie! Is Armand there?"

Oh, Christ! It was that pest Edward D. Wood Jr. In her usual matter-of-fact way of breaking bad news, Hope said, "Armand can't come to the phone, Ed. Armand's dead."

Wood was obviously floored by the news. "He—he's what?"

"Dead. I came home and found him in bed with your script. He died reading it."

"Oh, my God—my God," he gasped.

"Now hang up, will ya. I gotta make some calls."

"Okay," Wood said, his voice hollow and in a near whisper. "Good-bye."

There was a fumble and *click* followed by a dial tone.

Hope hung up, picked up the handset and dialed Andreas Orby's number. Next to Edward D. Wood Jr., Andreas Orby was Armand's biggest fan. He was a dark-haired teenage boy who wore thick tortoise shell glasses. Hope heard the other party pick up the phone and Orby's pubescent voice crack, "*Or*-by- resid-*ence*." He cleared his throat. "Orby residence."

"Andreas, it's Hope. Armand died tonight. I need you to come over and help me find something for Armand to wear at the funeral." The boy dropped the phone. "Andreas? Andreas, pick up the phone!"

Moments later, the boy's shaking voice said, "Armand's dead?"

Hope didn't have time for this. "Yes," she huffed. "Armand's dead. I was going to have him cremated but I guess what I want doesn't matter. Get over here as fast as you can." She heard the boy sniffle and choke, and then clear his throat before saying, "I'm not allowed out this late on a school night. I gotta ask my mom first." Hope rolled her eyes. "Fine, ask your mom," she grumbled.

She heard Orby shout, "MOM! Mrs. Tesla is on the phone." He choked, then gathered the strength to say what had to be said next, "A-Armand died tonight and she wants me to come over and help her with stuff." There was the distant, somewhat unintelligible sound of parental authority. Orby listened, then relayed the verdict. "She said no. I'm real sorry, Mrs. Tesla."

Hope rolled her eyes again and sighed. "Fine. But I want you here first thing tomorrow morning. The funeral director will be over around nine o'clock so I need you here by eight." She hung up before Orby had a chance to answer, then started rubbing the bridge of her nose, trying to stave off an approaching headache.

And so it came to pass that the preparation and cosmetic rooms of the Hollywood Mortuary became Armand Tesla's dressing room for his last great performance as the deceased. Instead of sitting in a makeup chair at Universal Studios, Mr. Tesla was held in place with a Vari-Pose headrest for his head and a Repose Block to support his shoulders. An Edwards Arm and Hand Positioner for his upper extremities and a Throop Foot Positioner to hold his feet in place would have given the uninitiated the impression of some medieval torture device. Instead of makeup artist Jack Pierce giving Mr. Tesla the appearance of death, Tesla was naked and stretched out on the metal prep table as resident cosmetologist Horace Steinmetz worked to give him the appearance of life.

A white washcloth had been discretely placed over the late actor's genitals because, as embalmer Steinmetz explained to his apprentices as he worked, "even the dead deserve their dignity." Although there is very little dignity in having a long hollow needle called a "trocar" inserted into your abdomen, poked around much like ancient Egyptian embalmers of old had done, and have your entrails sucked out and replaced with "cavity fluid."

Looking very much like a surgeon as he worked, Steinmetz employed similar instruments in his restorative work, scalpels, scissors, forceps, clamps, needles, thread, as well as augers and basins, an embalming machine to drain the blood while simultaneously replacing that blood with embalming fluid, all served to present the dead with what the textbooks described as "a semblance of normality." For the removal of blood and injection of embalming fluid, Steinmetz chose the carotid artery and jugular vein as the means of fluid transfer. There was a certain irony not lost on the embalmer that the procedure would leave two tiny puncture marks on Mr. Tesla's neck. As gruesome as this all might have appeared to an outsider, these procedures brought to Mr. Tesla the simulacra of life and created a "beautiful memory picture" for the bereaved. In the morning, Mr. Fleet, or one of his staff, would deliver to the mortuary Mr. Tesla's clothes. Along with the clothes, Steinmetz would get any last minute instructions from the widow about how best to present the deceased for his final viewing.

"Don't take the shortcuts I'm taking now," Steinmetz explained to the student embalmer who passed him his instruments. "This is a bit of a rush job—It seems two families are fighting over the deceased, and this is a last-minute prep."

"You wouldn't know it to look at him," the student admired.

"That's what separates the artist from the journeyman," Steinmetz said.

# Part Two

I Woke Up Early the Day I Died.

# Chapter 9

*"People, all going somewhere; all with their own thoughts, their own ideas, all with their own personalities; one is wrong because he does right; one is right because he does wrong. Pull the string! Dance to that!"* – Glen or Glenda (1953)

It was Friday, August 17th at eight o'clock in the morning, and Andreas Orby was pumping furiously on his bicycle pedals, hurrying over to the Harold Way apartment where he found the door unlocked and Hope in the bedroom rummaging through Armand's closet. "How did Armand die?" asked Orby, his eyes still bloodshot from crying.

"He was old. He died." Hope was turning the pockets of a pair of Tesla's pants inside out, then balled them up in frustration and threw the pants on the bed. "Damn that Lillian! Damn her, and damn Armand Jr.! Where the hell is it?"

"Did you lose something?" Orby asked.

Hope tapped her foot impatiently as she tried to collect her thoughts. "A letter," she answered testily, and then started as if realizing she had said too much. "I mean, I can't decide what Armand should wear." She rubbed the back of her neck. The muscles were knotting up something fierce.

"Well," Orby said hesitantly, "Armand once told me he'd like to be buried in his Dracula cape."

"Oh yeah?" Hope said. She jerked her head in the direction of the closet. "The capes are in the closet there. Pick one."

It was funny seeing Dracula capes hanging on wire hangers like any regular articles of clothing. Then again, didn't Superman have a closet full of extra costumes? As he examined each cape, Orby saw something he never noticed before. All the capes had slits for Tesla's arms like any ordinary Ulster greatcoat. He took down the first cape. It was satin with a lining that blended from gold to salmon pink. The hem was scalloped to resemble bat wings. A label sewn into the lining read:

WESTERN COSTUME COMPANY
ARMAND TESLA
"BRAIN OF FRANKENSTEIN"

"Holy cow!" Orby could barely contain his excitement. *The Brain of Frankenstein* was the working title for *Abbott and Costello meet Frankenstein*, the very film that introduced Orby to his vampire hero. It would take a friend's uncle who worked for the *Hollywood Reporter* and some detective work on Orby's part to get Armand Tesla's phone number. After some prodding and double dog daring from his equally starstruck friends, Orby finally made the call that would lead to the greatest three years of his boyhood life. "What about this one?" he asked, holding the cape out reverently.

Hope shook her head. "Nah, he hated that one."

Orby was crushed. "Then why did he keep it?"

Hope shrugged. "He was a pack rat," she said. "He never wanted to get rid of nothin'. When times got tough, he had to sell some stuff, but that was before I met him. Anyway, pick another cape."

Orby returned the cape to the closet, treating it with all the dignity of an American flag at Boy Scout assembly. "Which movie is this from?" he asked, holding out a cape with gray lining.

Hope had to think a moment. "That's the one from the first Dracula movie," she said.

The next cape had braiding and a purple interior. "How about this one?" he asked.

"Oh, that one," she said. "That's the one he wore on the stage."

The next had an all salmon colored satin lining. "And this one?" he asked.

She sighed irritably as she thought hard. "Uh, let's see," she said. "Oh, yeah. That's from *Mark of the Vampire*."

"Wow," Orby marveled. *Mark of the Vampire* co-starred the exotic Carol Borland as Tesla's vampire daughter and she was Orby's first boyhood crush.

Hope grew impatient with the teenager's hero worship. "Look, kid," she said, "any cape will do. Just pick one."

"Definitely this one," Orby said, handing Hope the *Mark of the Vampire* cape. As she laid it out on the bed, the boy noticed a tuxedo hanging next to the remaining capes. Could this be *the* Dracula costume? He examined the holy horror relic. It was the complete costume including the white vest, hook on tie and, most amazing of all, the very Dracula medal Orby had seen hanging around the vampire's neck time and time again on Vampira's late night horror show. Orby got a crazy idea and was almost afraid to suggest it. He suggested it anyway.

**The Vampire's Tomb Mystery**

"Um, since we're going to bury Armand in his cape, why not bury him in the whole costume?"

He expected Hope to dismiss the idea as stupid. To his delight she said, "Sure, why not. Let's send Armand out in style." Her lips drew into a delighted smile that one might describe as fiendish. "It'll serve that bitch Lillian right. She wants a funeral; I'll give her a funeral."

There was a knock at the door. Hope went to answer it while Orby laid out Tesla's things. He found a pair of patent leather shoes with white spats folded inside them on the floor of the closet. He searched through the rack of hanging clothes for an appropriate shirt, but couldn't find any. Orby remembered that dry cleaners sometimes folded shirts and boxed them, so checked the closet shelf. No dress shirts, just hat boxes. Maybe Armand took his dress shirts out of the box and kept them in his dresser. Sure enough, in the middle drawer were two neatly folded stacks of dress shirts. As Orby selected a shirt appropriate for Count Dracula, he caught the sight of something glinting under the stack of shirts. Orby reached under and it felt like…but it couldn't be…but it was! A six-shooter! He pulled out a real, honest-to-goodness Western six-shooter from under the stack of shirts!

"Wow!" he gasped, marveling at the workmanship as he turned the gun over in his hand. It was silver-plated with fancy scrollwork and something engraved on the handgrip:

ARMAND TESLA

HONORARY SHERIFF OF HOLLYWOOD

There wasn't so much as a spot of tarnish on it. Armand must have been mighty proud of his honorary title. Orby was about to pose with the gun in front of the dresser mirror when Hope called to him from the living room. "The man from the funeral home is here to get the clothes," she said. Orby shoved the gun back under the shirts and shut the drawer. "Uh, I can't find the cufflinks," he shouted back.

"They're in that jewelry box on top of the dresser."

Orby opened the coffin shaped jewelry box he and his friends had given to Armand on his last birthday. "Swan Lake" played as Orby rummaged in red velvet lined trays where he found the cufflinks and matching pearl dress buttons. "Found 'em!" he shouted.

When he grabbed the cufflinks, the jewelry tray came up. Looking underneath, Orby found Tesla's stash of cigars. Orby picked one up and examined the glass tube that reminded him of the test tubes Tesla handled in many a horror movie. The cigars were nothing like Armand's *El Ropo, El Skinko* brand. These were obviously very expensive. As the boy turned the glass tube over in his hand, Orby thought it might be nice if Armand had some cigars handy for his trip to the afterlife. He slipped four cigars into the inner pocket of Armand's tuxedo jacket, and brought the complete Dracula costume out to the funeral director. Mr. Fleet gave the gothic *ensemble* a quizzical look. "Uh," he said, "are you sure you want Mr. Tesla buried in *this*?"

"It's what Armand would have wanted," Hope insisted. "So you just make Armand up to look like Dracula. You got me? Just like Count Dracula."

Mr. Fleet frowned. "I'll have to clear this with the ex-Mrs. Tesla first."

"Listen, asshole," Hope snarled, poking the mortician in the chest, "I'm the fucking widow, so what I say goes, got it? And don't think I don't know you had a hand in Lillian interfering with my wishes!" Her eyes narrowed. "I could get a good lawyer and soak your funeral business for plenty!"

The idea of getting lawyers involved made Mr. Fleet nervous. He was all too well aware that Mr. Bruckner hated scandal. "Okay, I understand completely," he said, giving Hope a capitulating smile. "After all, it's your funeral."

"You bet your ass it is," she said, "and remember, I want the funeral on Saturday, not Sunday. I want all my friends to be able to go."

"Right, Saturday. I understand completely."

Hope gave Orby a satisfied wink before sending the flustered Mr. Fleet on his way. Once they were alone, she turned to the teenager and pinched his cheek. "That was a great idea you had, kiddo. And you deserve a reward." Hope led Orby back into the bedroom and took the gray-lined Dracula cape from its hanger. "Armand would probably want you to have this."

Orby's eyes nearly bugged out of his head. As he took the cape in his arms he became flush with the same excitement Moses must have felt when he collected those clay tablets on Mount Errata. "I - I don't know what to say."

"Just be at the funeral tomorrow. You can be a pallbearer."

"I will," Orby said, shaking. "I sure will. You can count on me."
"I know I can, kid."

Fate would eventually intervene and rob Orby of this prized possession. Armand Jr. would later write a letter on legal stationary claiming that the costume piece was part of the Armand Tesla estate and demand its return forthwith.

But for now, young Andreas Orby was on top of the world.

# Chapter 10

That same day, at 9:30 in the morning, found Charles Criswell King in swimming trunks and a bathrobe. He was stretched out on a folding deck chair. Resting on his lap was a telephone with a long cord. As he dialed Ed Wood's number, Criswell glanced over at Halo who was lying on a nearly submerged inflatable raft in the middle of their swimming pool. She was wearing nothing but a pair of sunglasses. The sight of Halo's sagging breasts and rolling fatty folds bobbing buoyantly on the water reminded Criswell of a basking sea cow. Was it any wonder he preferred a casual homosexual watering hole on Las Palmas and Hollywood Boulevard called The Gold Cup?

Halo's huge standard poodle apparently found the sight of her blatant nudity equally distressing. Buttercup took to the diving board and began barking furiously as if to say, *God, woman! Put some clothes on!*

"Quiet, Thomas!" Halo barked back. Thomas was Halo's late cousin. She was unshakably convinced that he had been reincarnated as her poodle. Buttercup AKA "Thomas" shut up and ran to hide behind Criswell's deck chair.

Halo smiled. "That's better." She sighed contentedly, all the while drifting, drifting, drifting. Criswell sighed too, but not from contentment as Ed Wood's phone rang.

After a dozen or so rings, someone picked up, then dropped the receiver, then a lot of fumbling around, and then picked up the receiver again. Eventually Wood mumbled a groggy, "Hello."

"How are you doing, Eddie?"

Kathy asking, "Who is that, Eddie?" followed the sound of creaking bedsprings.

"I think it's Cris," said Wood. Criswell concluded that at some point, Eddie had gotten off the couch and crawled into bed. "It is you, isn't it, Cris?"

"Sure is, Eddie. I just thought I'd call to see how you're doing."

Wood's groaning sounded muffled by a pillow. "I don't remember a thing after Hope gave me the bad news," he said. There was a pause followed by an apprehensive, "Uh, I didn't make a fool of myself, did I? At the party?"

"No more so than usual," Criswell smiled.

"Oh, shit."

"Don't worry. Mae understood."

"Thank god for that."

"Listen, Ed, about the funeral tomorrow. Are you okay to drive? We can all go to the funeral in my limousine."

"I don't want to be a bother."

"It's no bother."

Wood hesitated, then said, "I was going to drive Paul and Conrad there in my convertible," referring to Paul Marco and Conrad Brooks, two of Eddie's bit players.

"There's plenty of room in the limo for everybody."

"Well, if you're sure."

"I'll pick you up tomorrow at one o'clock."

"We'll be ready," said Wood. "I promise."

"By the way, Eddie, I hesitate to mention this but you might want to open that envelope Armand gave you."

"Why?"

"You really ought to, Eddie. It was Armand's last request."

Another groan was followed by a capitulating, "Okay. I'll open it later."

"Why not right now?" Criswell coaxed, burning to know what Armand was so hard-pressed to keep from his wife.

Eddie emitted a long whine like a kid that didn't want to do his homework. "Not now, Cris," he said. "I haven't had my coffee. I can't even focus my eyes yet."

"Have it your way," Criswell relented. "But do open it before the funeral. Suppose they're instructions about something to do at the service."

"Okay, okay," Wood promised reluctantly. "You talked me into it. I'll open the envelope after breakfast. I'll tell you all about it when I talk to you later."

But Wood didn't call back.

One last picture with Armand.

# Chapter 11

Later that morning in the cosmetic and dressing room of the Hollywood Mortuary, Armand Tesla was getting his finishing touches. Gray hair had been blackened and slicked back. Emaciated features had been made plump and youthful again with the injection of massage cream into Tesla's cheeks. Lips had been skillfully sewn shut and presented with a slight hint of a smile at the corners. The eyes had been glued shut and the embalming fluid in Tesla's veins had been tinged with dyes, specifically B. and G. Products Company's Lyf-Lyk tint guaranteed to produce "nature's own skin texture" and a more lifelike color for that all-important "beautiful memory picture."

Tesla's extremities had been made supple enough to dress the actor in his tux without having to resort to slitting the costume up the back, thanks to Steinmetz working the joints back and forth to break rigor mortis. As Mr. Fleet handed Tesla's tailcoat to Steinmetz, he heard the four glass-encased cigars inside the inner pocket clinking together. Mr. Fleet noted the Havana label on the cigar band. Surely the deceased wouldn't mind if Fleet helped himself to an after-dinner stogie.

Mr. Fleet slipped the cigar into his breast pocket as Steinmetz clucked his tongue reproachfully. "You're asking for trouble, Mr. Fleet," the cosmetologist chided. "The dead take a dim view of grave robbing."

"Just attend to your business," scolded Mr. Fleet.

In a short while Mr. Tesla was fully costumed, except for his cape and the patent leather shoes and spats Orby had chosen. They would be returned to the widow after the service. Instead, Tesla's feet were clad in Ko-Zee-brand slippers that boasted of "soft, cushioned soles and warm, luxurious comfort."

Waiting on a collapsible transport truck was the casket Lillian and Armand Jr. had chosen for Armand's final repose. The casket was white with brass handles. It paled in comparison to Count Dracula's various movie and stage coffins, but, given the budget it was the best they could afford. Mr. Fleet grabbed the handles on the truck and rolled the casket up to the prep table.

"To casket" the deceased was an art all its own. Too low in the casket, warned textbooks, "and the body looks like it's lying in a box." Too high and the nose could get pushed in against the closed lid. Ideally, according to authorities on the subject, "the body should be tilted slightly to the right to soften the appearance of lying flat on the back." With this in mind, Steinmetz and Mr. Fleet lifted Tesla's body off the table and into the casket where the Dracula cape lay open and waiting. Mr. Fleet used a hand crank to adjust the height of the casket mattress to achieve the desired effect. Instead of crossing the deceased's hands over the chest, as was the tradition, Mr. Fleet positioned Tesla's arms straight at the sides. It would look better with the cape. The funeral director reached in and fastened the cape's high collar around Mr. Tesla's neck, then arranged the cape neatly around the body and straightened the Dracula medallion before taking a step back with Mr. Steinmetz to admire their workmanship.

"This may sound terribly unprofessional," Mr. Fleet confessed, "but seeing Tesla like this gives me the creeps."

Steinmetz nodded in agreement. "Makes me wish we had a wooden stake and some garlic handy." Steinmetz nudged the funeral director; "Although I could swear I smelled a bit of garlic on his breath." Leaning forward, he added an apologetic, "Uh, no offense meant, Mr. Tesla."

"I don't know which is scarier," said Mr. Fleet shaking his head, "Tesla made up like Dracula or you talking to the deceased."

"It pays to show the dead proper respect, Mr. Fleet," Steinmetz insisted. "Although I do wonder," he added as he contemplated the costumed corpse, "how the night staff will feel about Dracula lying in state until the service on Saturday."

"I'd rather not think about that," said Mr. Fleet, checking his watch. "Time to get the Count out to the slumber room."

As if on cue, Tesla's eyes snapped opened giving Fleet a scare. Steinmetz clucked his tongue as he reached for the adhesive. "This is what comes from buying cheap supplies, Mr. Fleet."

"Never mind, just make sure those eyelids stay closed, at least until the burial."

After Steinmetz had reapplied glue to Tesla's eyelids, Fleet closed the casket. The hinges were uncharacteristically silent.

Steinmetz lightly rapped on the lid and whispered, "Rest easy, Mr. Tesla."

Mr. Fleet grimaced. "Now you stop that!" He unlocked the wheels on the truck and did a K-turn, then pushed the casket out into the private hallway. "I swear," he said, "it's almost like you expect them to answer back." He shut the airtight door behind him.

Steinmetz made the sign of the cross and kissed his thumb for luck. "Sometimes they do," he said softly.

Mr. Fleet was about to push the casket down the hallway when Mr. Bruckner approached from the back stairs. "Is that Mr. Tesla?" he asked, gesturing with the black leather book he was holding.

"It is, sir. Is that the Tesla Register?"

"Yes," said Mr. Bruckner, handing Mr. Fleet the book, "fresh off the embossing machine."

Mr. Fleet gestured at the coffin. "Would you care to see—?"

Mr. Bruckner frowned. "Frankly no," he said. "The very idea. And holding a funeral on a Saturday. Absurd."

"Well, we do have two funerals today."

"Oh, yes. Another widow in a hurry." Mr. Bruckner shrugged. "No one cares about tradition anymore, Ralph. These modern times." He shook his head sadly, then decided to take a peek inside Tesla's casket, raising the lid slightly. The instant he caught sight of the glint coming from Tesla's medallion, he started and shut the lid. He straightened up and blustered, "Honestly, making him up to look that way, why, it's enough to make us the laughing stock of the industry."

"Or give us plenty of free publicity."

Mr. Bruckner paused to consider that. "Hmm. I hadn't looked at it that way." He raised the lid again for a better look. "The press is coming, right?"

"Try and keep them away."

Closing the lid Mr. Bruckner smiled. "Good. Make sure there are plenty of brochures in the foyer. I have a feeling this funeral is going to be a big draw. Get the 1950 Annuals."

"The A-Bomb brochures?"

"Exactly. Very timely, very effective."

"What about the prices?"

"I had the centerfold spread updated. You'll find them in the supply closet."

"Yes, sir."

"Carry on, Ralph," Mr. Bruckner said.

Mr. Fleet pushed the casket down the hallway, stopping by the supply closet where he grabbed a box marked *1950 ANNUAL*. He placed the box on the lid along with the funeral book and then wheeled the casket forward onto the ramp leading to the casket showroom, only to have the wheels hang up. He tried to pull back on the casket, but it wouldn't budge. Jostling it had no effect. Finally, he stood well back and lunged forward as hard as he could. The box of brochures and the memory book obeyed the laws of objects at rest staying at rest, and suddenly found themselves in midair without a casket beneath them. Mr. Fleet reflexively grabbed the book and box before they hit the floor, and then realized the casket was rolling out of control down the ramp and through the showroom, heading toward a display of high-end merchandise. Dashing after it, Mr. Fleet was able to get hold of the handle and steer the coffin out of harm's way. After checking for any signs of damage, and finding not so much as a scratch, he pushed the casket past the showroom and down the hallway to the slumber room reserved for Armand Tesla. "Slumber room" was the new euphemism replacing "viewing parlor" as the way to describe the place where Mr. Tesla would accept callers until the service in the mortuary chapel on Saturday afternoon. On the stand by the entrance, Mr. Fleet placed the funeral book. Freshly embossed in gold lettering on the cover was the inscription:

ARMAND TESLA
OCT. 20, 1882 – AUG. 16, 1956
MEMORIAM
HOLLYWOOD MORTUARIES
6240 HOLLYWOOD BLVD.
HOLLYWOOD, CALIFORNIA

He opened the book to the first page. The Friends' Register was for mourners' signatures. The opposite Floral Tributes page was for mourners who had sent flowers. Tomorrow, Ralph and his wife Marie would add their signatures to the funeral book that would eventually contain over 127 entries. Conspicuously absent would be the signatures of Lillian and Armand Jr.

An assistant slipped a card into the pedestal mount by the entrance announcing that ROOM A was reserved for "ARMAND TESLA – Visitation 3 p.m. – 9 p.m., Service 2:30 p.m. at Chapel."

Mr. Fleet went to the foyer and set out the A-Bomb brochures. The front page showed a large picture of a bursting A-Bomb and a panel of rules to be followed in case of an atomic attack. Inside, the double-page layout showed variously priced Hollywood Mortuary caskets. Thoughtfully included was a wallet-sized card to be carried by potential future customers. "To the County Coroner, Authorized Authorities or Whom it May Concern," it said. "In the event of my death, please notify Hollywood Mortuaries."

Satisfied that all was in readiness, Mr. Fleet returned to the hallway, opened the sliding doors and pushed Mr. Tesla's casket into the slumber room where two assistants were setting up folding chairs, while another fussed over flower arrangements. The funeral director positioned the hand truck at the front of the parlor beside the display bier. With an assistant's help, the casket was moved from the truck to the waiting bier and set up before a curtain backdrop. On either side of the casket were two floor lamps with rose-colored bulbs to further enhance the illusion of a healthy corpse. To the left of the display were a large arrangement of flowers and a framed photograph of the deceased on a gold easel.

The assistant gestured at the adjoining special room reserved for the immediate family. "Everything is ready for tomorrow's final viewing," he assured Mr. Fleet. "I have the kneeling pad ready, and the chairs. Only…"

"Only what?" asked Mr. Fleet.

"You only requisitioned *two* chairs. Shouldn't there be three? One for the widow, one for the ex-wife and one for the son?"

"Absolutely not!" Mr. Fleet insisted. "That room is there exclusively for the ex-wife and her son *only*."

"What? You mean, we're not supposed to allow the widow to be alone with her husband before the service? That's most irregular."

"Irregular or not," Mr. Fleet said sternly, "that's how Miss Arch wants it. There's to be as little contact as possible between Miss Arch, her son, and the current widow or any of her friends. And frankly, I don't blame Lillian one bit. Honestly, if you heard how callously the current Mrs. Tesla discussed the arrangements that she wanted…well, it would just make you sick. Which reminds me…." Clapping his hands, Mr. Fleet gestured for the rest of the staff to gather around. "All right, people, settle down. Which of you is acting as the usher during the Tesla service?"

One of the assistants raised his hand.

"Ah, Parker — good," Mr. Fleet said. "The ex-Mrs. Tesla left strict instructions that during the service in the chapel, she and the current Mrs. Tesla are to be seated as far apart from each other as possible. The ex-wife and her son sit up front. Seat the current widow in the back."

**The Vampire's Tomb Mystery**     89

"Sir?" Parker asked.

"You heard me," said Mr. Fleet as he scratched his eyebrow nervously. "I've been friends with Armand and Lillian for quite some time and I know Miss Arch very well, and whatever she wants, she gets. Had it not been for her, we wouldn't even be having a funeral, so we shall follow her instructions in this matter." Addressing everyone, Mr. Fleet said, "I know this next bit will sound very petty, but Miss Arch also made it quite clear about how she wants her son addressed by the staff. At no time is he to be called 'Armand Tesla Jr.' Understand?"

Everyone nodded. One staff member raised his hand.

"Yes, Anderson?"

"Uh, how should we address him?"

"He's to be addressed as Bill Tesla. Any other questions?"

No one could think of any.

"Good," Mr. Fleet said. "Now run along."

Mr. Fleet consulted his watch. It was 2:30; time to open the casket. As was traditional with Catholic funerals, a crucifix was hung from the open lid directly over the deceased; perhaps as a precaution should Count Dracula decide to wander about in search of virgin necks to bite. Mr. Fleet turned a knob hidden behind a drape. Pre-recorded music began playing softly in the background. On Saturday, a costumed violinist playing traditional Hungarian gypsy music would serenade passing mourners.

In a moment of supreme Hollywood irony, Tesla would achieve in death the very comeback he had longed for in the latter half of his life. Reporters and photographers from all the Los Angeles papers would record every last detail of the service for posterity. The "beautiful memory picture" of Tesla lying in state costumed as Dracula would become imprinted on the minds of young fans like Andreas Orby well into the 1960s. This would lead to the large-scale syndication of *Dracula* and its sequels in a TV package called *SHOCK!* Tesla's Dracula portrayal would be lampooned in TV shows like *The Munsters.* A popular magazine created and edited by Forrest J Ackerman called *Famous Monsters of Filmland* would further heighten Tesla's fame. This would translate into large-scale profits for Universal Studios thanks to merchandising Tesla's image in the form of games, Ben Cooper and Don Post Halloween masks, puzzles and Aurora model kits. By 1963, Armand Jr. would notice the money being generated by his father's image and put his law degree to use by suing Universal Studios for back royalties, which would lead to new laws giving family members control of the ownership and licensing of a late celebrity's likeness. But that wouldn't be for a few years yet. For now, Tesla was merely the lead in one of the most bizarre funerals in Hollywood history, and Count Dracula was now ready to take his last bow.

Friday afternoon after school, Andreas Orby and two friends visited the slumber room. Orby was dressed in a checkered shirt and his best jacket. He handed his camera to his friend Mike for one last picture with Armand. They each took turns, posing with Armand, finishing the roll of film by taking pictures of Armand as Count Dracula lying at rest in his coffin. Three years earlier, before Armand and Lillian's divorce, Armand had posed with the same three boys while Lillian held Orby's camera and snapped the picture. In that photo, Tesla flinched when the flash went off. The picture showed Armand with his arms around the three boys. He was smiling, but his eyes were closed.
Now Armand Tesla's eyes were closed forever.

# Chapter 12

Criswell tried to call Wood several times that day, but couldn't get an answer.

By 5:30, Criswell was back before the cameras at KLAC making his usual live prognostications that foretold of plane crashes, the launching of a space station, and the election of Mae West as the first lady president of the United States.

After pitching bottles of *Criswell's Family Formula*, Criswell retired to his dressing room and tried to call Eddie one last time.

He got Kathy instead. "I'm sorry, Cris," she said. "Eddie's out right now."

"Out? Out doing what?" asked Criswell, worried that Ed might have gone on another drinking binge. "It's after six."

"He wouldn't say," she answered casually. "But he was awfully excited about his new movie."

"*Grave Robbers from Outer Space?*"

"Something about getting money to make it."

"From Bunny Breckinridge?"

"I don't know about that. Our landlord was sure interested, though."

"Your landlord?"

"Ed Reynolds," she said. "He and Eddie were talking. I think Eddie convinced Mr. Reynolds to put up some money. That was this morning when Mr. Reynolds came by for the rent. Our check bounced."

"So Eddie and Mr. Reynolds are out together?"

"Oh, no. Mr. Reynolds had to talk to his reverend. Something about Eddie getting baptized."

"Baptized?" Criswell exclaimed.

"But that's not why Eddie left," she said. "He ran out after opening an envelope."

*That damn envelope again*, Criswell thought anxiously. "Did Eddie tell you what was in it?"

"No."

"When he left was he happy, sad, scared?"

"Just excited. He made some calls and ran out."

Criswell frowned. "Calls? Who did he call?"

"Some lab about developing film," she said.

"Film?" exclaimed Criswell, his interest piqued.

"He wanted to know if they could develop it today and how much it would cost to make two copies."

"What film?"

"I don't know," said Kathy. "He telephoned other people, too, but I don't know who. Do you want me to tell Eddie that you called?"

"He can reach me at home later this evening. It doesn't matter how late, just have him call me."

"I will," said Kathy.

She hung up.

That was Friday.

Eddie didn't call back.

# Chapter 13

On the morning of Saturday, August 18, 1956, papers carried the following item:

**ARMAND TESLA SHROUD TO BE DRACULA CAPE**

Armand Tesla will be buried today wrapped in the black cape of Dracula, the horror character that brought the greatest fame to his long acting career.

"It was his wish," explained his widow, Mrs. Hope Lininger Tesla.

Prior to this dramatic burial, funeral services for the 74-year-old actor will be conducted at 2:30 p.m. today at the Hollywood Mortuary Chapel, 6240 Hollywood Blvd. The interment will be at Holy Cross Cemetery. The body will lie in state until an hour before services.

# Chapter 14

Forrest J Ackerman arrived at 10:30 a.m. to drive Hope to the funeral. He remembered her reaction when he first suggested acting as her chauffeur. "What do I need you to drive me for?" she complained in her usual curmudgeonly way. "I did all the driving for Armand. I can get there myself." But Ackerman insisted and she begrudgingly gave in.

Hope came to the door with her hair in curlers and clad in a bathrobe. "Wait in the living room," she grumbled. "I'll be ready in 20 minutes."

The instant Ackerman set foot inside the Harold Way apartment he could feel it, that lingering sense of emptiness a place gets when someone who once lived there had passed on, as if the very air itself had an Armand Tesla-sized hole in it. The sofa still stank from those terrible smelling cigars Tesla enjoyed out of necessity. It was on this sofa where Tesla toasted Forry's health with whatever liquors the Hungarian had on hand (Forry himself never drank, but nursed whatever drink Tesla gave him and went through the motions of toasting). As Ackerman waited patiently on the sofa, he meditated on the times he and Tesla shared in this place while Hungarian records played solemn Gypsy refrains. He remembered the tall tales Tesla told of his homeland and its many legends and superstitions, his career in Hollywood and his eventual downfall, and his strange assertion that Boris Karloff owed his whole career to him, and as Forry often related it, speaking in an exaggeration of Armand's Hungarian accent, Armand would say to Ackerman and anyone else who cared to listen, "Dhey vanted me to play dhe part of Frank'stein's Monster, but I didt not vant to do it. I figured dhey could get any truck driver to put on all dhat stuff and grunt." According to Armand, the truck driver he recommended was Boris Karloff. "I suggested Karloff for dhe role. He didt the role, and of course, it vwas a hit. I created my own Frank'stein Monster by turning down dhe part." and, when the liquor flowed freely, there were even stranger stories of Karloff, stories tinged with murder and intrigue that involved not only Karloff, but Basil Rathbone and the comedy team of Bud Abbott and Lou Costello, exaggerated ghost stories of old Hollywood that included outlandish elements like gangsters and sultry lady spies, all ending with Tesla vehemently proclaiming to be a better detective than Karloff and Rathbone put together. "Karloff! Not only didt he owe to me his whole career, but I save his career vhen dhe mobsters, dhey try to frame him!" On such evenings, Ackerman would walk away thinking, "That Tesla, what a character."

Nearly 45 minutes passed before Hope stepped out of the bathroom. She was dressed in traditional black, fussing over a pair of non-traditional white gloves. "You're awfully quiet," she said.

"I was just remembering Armand," Ackerman said.

"Yeah," she said miffed. "I remember Armand, too."

Ackerman remembered Tesla getting drunk and bitching about how mean Hope was to him. The actor was a bit deaf and apparently didn't realize how loudly he was talking. Ackerman cringed for him as Tesla harped on and on about Hope, and all the while Hope was in the kitchenette with the curtain drawn and hearing every word. Ackerman felt for Hope. She had fallen in love with an ideal on the screen and apparently couldn't deal with the reality of having married a man so much older than she was. "It's going to be rough today," he said. "I'll help any way I can."

"Rough? You want to know what rough is?" She gestured around the room at all the antique furniture. "Look at this place! This dark, depressing, stinking place! Armand was like all Hungarians. I don't care too much for 'em. They have their high moments, all song and dance, and then they're all gloomy Gus again." She pointed at the portrait of Tesla as Dracula. "How many goddamn living rooms have a thing like *that* hanging on the wall?"

Ackerman shrugged slightly. "Actually, I have—"

"Okay, besides you." Hope shook her head bitterly. "I was a real sucker and he saw me coming." She glared at Ackerman. "But he was scared of me," she gloated. "He had all his other wives bullied but not me! I knew how to control him. He was superstitious and believed you had to sleep with a glass of water by your bed, something about keeping evil spirits away. Well, all I had to do was tell him if he didn't behave himself I'd remove the water."

Ackerman was feeling rather uncomfortable at this point. "Well," he said, "I'm sure the honeymoon—"

"Honeymoon?" she scoffed. "At a certain age you don't call it a honeymoon. That's really stupid. There's no such thing. We just took a wedding trip up to Big Bear Lake, Armand, Ed Wood and me. It didn't pan out. We turned around and came back."

"I see," said Ackerman, trying to be polite.

"Now I have to pay for a damn funeral!" Hope grabbed her gold-lamé clutch purse and rummaged through it. "Lillian!" she carped. "Oh, she says she'll pay half, but mark my words, I'll bet that bitch'll stick me with the bill." She snapped her purse shut and sighed heavily, rubbing the back of her neck. "Forget I said anything. I'm just tense, is all."

"That's all right," Ackerman said. "It's quite understandable."

"Before I forget, I've got something for you." She headed for the bedroom and came back with a large scrapbook. "Here," said Hope. "I think you'd appreciate this more than I would." She laid the scrapbook in Ackerman's lap.

Ackerman opened the book and flipped through pages filled with newspaper clippings dating all the way back to Tesla's 1930s Universal Studio days and ending with stories about his self-commitment to the State Hospital. Stuck in the middle of the scrapbook was a folded up poster. Carefully unfolding the poster, Ackerman saw depicted on it a King Kong-sized black haired giant with green skin, a greenish jacket and built up boots. Death-dealing rays fired from his eyes as he carried a woman screaming in his powerful grip. Ackerman immediately recognized the artifact as the advance publicity poster announcing to the world that ARMAND TESLA, "Dracula" himself, would be starring as the Monster in the upcoming Universal Super-Production, FRANKENSTEIN! There is was, the great turning point in Tesla's life, and his greatest regret, the point where he refused the role that went to his rival Boris Karloff, the role that catapulted Karloff to world fame and led to Tesla's typecasting and eventual downfall as a B-Grade movie villain. No wonder Tesla tried to soothe the pain by convincing himself that he had "given" the role to Karloff.

Ackerman looked up stunned. "You're giving me this?"

"I have no use for it," Hope shrugged. "To me they're just old newspaper articles. Sort of like Armand, they're old, brittle and smelly. There are three scrapbooks, but this one is about his movie career."

"Are you sure you want me to have this?"

Offhandedly she said, "If you don't take it, I'll just throw it in the trash."

Closing the book, Ackerman said, "I'll give this an honored place in my collection." Adding, "If you ever change your mind—"

There was a knock at the door.

"I won't," Hope said as she answered the door. It was Andreas Orby. He wore a different checkered shirt, but the same jacket he wore to his initial viewing of Tesla's body. "Sorry I'm late," he said.

"You're not late, kid," said Hope.

With the scrapbook tucked under his arm, Ackerman got up and shook hands with Orby. "Nice to see you again, Andreas." Orby was a Forry fan and the one who had introduced Forry to Armand Tesla in the first place.

"I can see why you two get along," Hope said. "You're both crazy collectors."

Orby smiled at Hope. "Mrs. Tesla gave me Armand's movie Dracula cape."

Ackerman patted the scrapbook under his arm. "She gave me something, too. Armand's movie scrapbook."

Orby reached out and touched the edge of the book, his young eyes filled with awe. "Armand showed it to me once." He looked at Ackerman. "Did you see the poster?"

"The *Frankenstein* poster? Sure did. It's right here."

Hope cleared her throat. "If you two are finished, could we get going?"

"Sorry," Ackerman smiled. "We collectors are an obsessive lot." He patted Orby on the back, then escorted Hope and the teenager into the hall. The landlord came downstairs, toting a toolbox. He pulled up short when he spotted Hope. "Good morning, Mrs. Tesla," he said.

"I doubt it will be," she sniped.

"I'd go to the funeral today," the landlord said, hefting the toolbox, "but I got repairs that need doin'."

"Don't lose any sleep over it," Hope said as she headed for the door with Orby on her arm.

"Say," said the landlord, pointing at Andreas's bike leaning against the stairway; "is that your bike, kid?"

"Yes, sir."

"You can't leave that there. It's a hazard."

The teenager was about to take his bicycle outside when Hope rolled her eyes. "Hold on, Andreas. You can leave it in my apartment." She rummaged in her purse for the key, muttering, "Son of a bitch landlord. Always making trouble. Piss ant little fuck."

She opened the door and left it ajar. "Hey, Forry," she said, pointing at the bike, "stow that inside and then lock the door." She motioned for Orby to follow her. He hesitated. She grabbed his arm. "Get a move on, kid." She dragged him after her as she headed out the door.

Shaking his head and smiling, Ackerman set the scrapbook on the stairs and rolled the bike into the apartment, then locked the door and tried the knob. The landlord watched him closely the whole time.

Ackerman picked up the scrapbook and nodded a good-bye as he headed for the door.

"PSST!" The landlord motioned for Forry to come back, then leaned in and whispered, "I had to come down and see if he was dead, you know." He gestured with his toolbox. "Armand Tesla, I mean."

"What?" Ackerman exclaimed with disbelief.

"Oh yeah," the landlord said with a nod. "Mrs. Tesla insisted I make sure. There he was, sitting in the chair, stone-cold dead."

"But Hope told me she found him in bed."

The landlord smirked knowingly. "Is that so?" he said. "My mistake. He was in bed, is what I meant." He nodded toward the door. "I'm warning you, she's as cold as a witch's tit, Mrs. Tesla is. Don't turn your back on her, whatever you do."

Right on cue, Hope flung opened the front door and glared at Ackerman. "Well, are you coming or not?"

"Be right there," Forry said. He gave the landlord a slight nod. "Nice chatting with you."

Ackerman and Hope departed together, leaving the landlord alone in the hall. He was about to return to his work when his gaze drifted up to his apartment.

"This is awfully thirsty work," he said aloud. He remembered the bottle of Armand's whiskey hidden in the kitchen cabinet.

Smacking his lips, he said, "Repairs can wait," and climbed the stairs.

# Chapter 15

It was around 11 a.m. At the home of Charles Criswell King, Criswell was just stepping out of the shower. Humming gaily, he slipped on a terrycloth dressing gown and slippers and padded into the large bedroom while wrapping his head in a towel turban. He went to the mirrored closet where he took out a garment bag and laid it over the back of a chair. Criswell rummaged through his many black sequin-studded tuxedoes, any one of which was more than appropriate for a funeral, a Hollywood funeral, anyway. Finding one to his liking (they were all identical), he laid his clothes out on the bed and then went to the vanity.

Criswell had learned from his mortician father about the best ways to apply makeup to a man's face and create a natural appearance. Although he looked okay for television, outside the studio the layers of pancake threatened to give him pallor to rival that of the deceased. Still, it did what he intended, gave him an eye-catching look.

After putting his hair up in rollers, he slipped a dryer cap over his head and set the dial on the dryer for 15 minutes. He took the telephone from the vanity and set it in his lap so he could feel the vibration coming from the ringer in case Ed Wood happened to call back; Ed Wood didn't call back. Criswell passed the time filing his nails and buffing them to a high polish.

Fifteen minutes later Cris's hair was dry and ready for a quick tease with a metal comb and a smoothing down with a hairbrush. This was followed by a liberal application of hair spray, followed by Kleenex (the all-purpose tissue) to blot the excess and shape the pompadour, then came the molding of the spit curl and a final application of hair spray. Perfection!

Criswell began dressing. His *ensemble* consisted of silk boxers, ruffled dress shirt with dress buttons and cufflinks with inlaid gold initials, and then the tuxedo and patent leather shoes, both sparkling. As he tied his bow tie, he kept eyeing the telephone that stubbornly refused to ring. He was admiring his reflection in the closet mirrors when Halo came waddling into the bedroom with Buttercup galloping behind her. The colorful moo-moo Halo wore billowed like a circus tent with each ponderous step. Criswell gave her a smile. "Are you sure you don't want to go to the funeral today?" he asked.

"No, pumpkin," she said, easing herself onto the bed over a chorus of complaining mattress springs. "You know how funerals upset me." She reached for a box of chocolate-covered cherries on the bedside table. "The spirits gravitate around me." Halo rutted through empty candy wrappers until she found an uneaten sweet. "I can't stand their chatter, chatter." She brought the cherry to her mouth. Buttercup begged for it. Halo ignored his whining and savored the chocolate the way most people savor sex.

"Of course, dear," Criswell said. He bent down and kissed her on the forehead. "I'm off, then."

Halo sat Buttercup up on his haunches and waved his foreleg. "Buttercup says good bye. Bye-bye, Daddy."

"Bye-bye," said Criswell as he gave Buttercup and Halo a cutesy wave good-bye, and then grabbed the garment bag.

Criswell's office was located in a Victorian house on Sunset Boulevard that looked like it might have hosted many a séance in its day. Only the miniature golf course next door served to detract from the stately wreck's unearthly aura. Maila Nurmi was sitting at her desk opening mail when Cris came tripping in as lightly as a Busby Berkeley dancer, keeping the garment bag behind his back. She looked up with a start and quickly stuck the letter she was reading in her desk drawer as Cris sang cheerily, "Guess what I haaaave!"

"Uh…," she faltered while forcing a look of innocence, and then joked, "…the clap?"

"That was last week," Criswell joked back.

"Then I don't know. What?" she asked.

"A present for my favorite secretary who can't type!" He produced the garment bag and unzipped it, displaying a black and stylishly tailored forties dress with a matching veil.

Maila was positively giddy as she jumped to her feet. "It's gorgeous!" she gasped.

She grabbed the dress and ran to the closet where a full-length mirror hung on the inside of the door. She held the veil on her head while holding the dress up to her chin, posing seductively. "And so tasteful! Where did you get it?" She raised her severely arched eyebrow. "Or shouldn't I ask?" She hung the dress up in the closet amid still more of Criswell's duplicate tuxedoes. "Armand told me how you helped Wood steal that rubber octopus."

"Oh, it's nothing like that," said Criswell. "I just happen to know a friend of a friend at Western Costume Company. I'm not sure, but I think Gloria Holden might have worn that in *Dracula's Daughter*."

Maila flashed an alluring smirk. "How appropriate." She reached behind for the zipper on the dress she was wearing, but couldn't quite reach. "Give me a hand?"

Criswell unzipped the dress and as Maila squirmed her way out of it, she nodded over at her desk. "That package was just hand-delivered by somebody named Koenig."

Cris gave the package a cursory glance before sticking it on the top shelf of the closet.

"Aren't you going to open it?" Maila asked, letting her dress fall to the floor, exposing black panties and a severely engineered Jane Russell-style bra.

"I already know what's in it. More of Mr. Koenig's food supplements."

There was a knock at the door.

"I wonder who that could be," Cris remarked.

"Some psychic you are," Maila teased.

Acting as sleuth, Criswell mused, "The silhouette on the frosted glass suggests a man in uniform. A policeman, maybe. Or a soldier, perhaps? I know, it's the Good Humor Man!"

The mystery man knocked again.

"I know one way you can find out," Maila said, reaching into the closet for the funeral gown. "Answer it."

"But you're almost naked."

Maila stepped inside the closet and closed the door. "And now I'm almost naked and invisible."

Satisfied, Criswell turned and gestured grandly. "*Enter*, whoever you are!" He asked Maila, "Too much?"

Peeking around the closet door, and with an equally grand gesture, she said, "You *are* Criswell after all!" and ducked inside.

A fully uniformed Chalky Wright entered and smartly saluted. "Good morning, Mr. Criswell," the chauffeur said. "Miss West thought you should have a driver for today's funeral, sir."

"Really?" said Criswell, all aglow. "Isn't that thoughtful of her!" He knocked on the closet door. "Hurry up with your mournin' duds, angel. Looks like we're going in style."

Maila poked out her shapely nude leg and wrapped it around the door. "Do you have any black stockings?" she asked from inside the closet.

As if it was perfectly normal for a naked girl to be in his closet, Criswell made introductions, "Oh, Chalky, that leg is attached to Maila Nurmi, otherwise known as TV's Vampira. Maila, this is Chalky Wright. He's Mae West's driver."

"We've met, Cris," Maila said, pointing her toe in Chalky's direction. "Nice to see you again, Chalky."

Even though Maila obviously couldn't see him, Chalky bowed politely. "Nice to, uh, see you again, Miss Maila."

She wiggled her foot. "Come on, Cris, my gams are freezing."

"Hold on a minute, I think I have a pair of stockings in my desk." Criswell went to search through the drawers. "Aha!"

"Sir," said Chalky, watching Criswell as he searched his desk, finding a hand mirror. Unable to resist, the psychic checked his reflection, "uh, while the lady is dressing, I'll see that your limousine is all spruced up for the service."

"Oh, uh, good idea, Chalky," Cris said absently, taken up admiring his reflection.

Chalky held his hand out expectantly. "Sir, I'll need the keys."

"CRIS!" Maila shouted impatiently. "Hurry up!"

Criswell snapped out of it and put the mirror back and remove a pair of black silk stockings from the bottom drawer. "Sorry, angel," said Cris as he hurried to the closet. "Say, did you hear what Chalky said? We're getting the red carpet treatment today." He reached down and tickled Maila's wiggling foot. Her leg quickly retreated as she giggled.

A waggling finger emerged. "Naughty boy," she scolded. Cris put the stockings in her hand. She took them, then stuck her head out and gave Chalky a wink. "Didn't you know," she said. "He keeps all his mistresses in the closet," and then closed the door.

Chalky remained taciturn and cleared his throat. "Uh, the keys, sir?"

"Of course." Criswell gave him the car keys and asked, "Anything else, Chalky?"

"No, sir," Chalky said, turning to leave. Under his breath, he muttered, "I guess Miss West was wrong about you, sir."

Cris chuckled and then snapped his fingers. "We're going to need some pocket money." He knelt down beside a small floor safe and began working the tumblers. "I'll get you the combination later. It's for petty cash and legal documents."

He pulled open the door. Maila let out an admiring wolf-whistle. "That may be cash, but it sure ain't petty."

Criswell grabbed a pack of 20s from one of the stacks and closed the safe. He split the money up 50-50. "Only the best for you, baby."

Maila riffled through the bills and smirked. "You sure know how to treat the help."

Cris had Maila on his arm looking like the cliché million dollars in her Vera West-designed mourning wear and a clutch purse filled with cash. The limousine was sparkling clean right down to the whitewalls. Chalky opened the passenger compartment for them, and then took his place behind the wheel. Using the car phone that communicated with the driver, Criswell asked Chalky to stop by the Wood residence.

"Right away, sir," said Chalky.

Criswell was about to give Chalky the address when the chauffeur turned quickly out of the driveway and negotiated the correct streets leading to Wood's house, all this before Criswell had a chance to open his mouth. Cris shrugged it off guessing that at some point during the Ravenswood party Eddie must have given Mae his home address. They pulled up in the driveway behind Ed's yellow convertible. "Coming in?" Cris asked Maila.

"Not on your life," she snarled. "It's bad enough I have to share the limo with him."

Cris smiled and gave her a good-natured shrug before getting out and stepping up to the front door. He pushed the buzzer. Wood came to the door looking quite presentable, if a bit hung over. Gypsy music played inside. "Hi, Cris," he said, wincing.

"What's going on?" Criswell asked, glancing behind Eddie. He saw Kathy play hostess to two of Ed's company players, Conrad Brooks and Paul Marco. They were sitting on the couch, each dressed in funerary black and nursing a drink. Cris noted that Conrad's shirt was buttoned wrong. "Toasting Armand's passing?" Cris asked Ed.

"I guess you could say that." Wood opened to door wider and gestured at the coffee table and a small record player. "Armand gave me that record. We'd tie one on and we'd sit together listening to that record and he'd get all weepy about the Old Country." Wood smiled wistfully. "It was like he was the character he played in *The Wolf Man*. Like the Armand in that movie, it was like he was cursed or something, and he would get drunk and moan about how Dracula never ends."

Marco came to the door and peered over Eddie's shoulder as he asked, "How's it going, Cris?"

"Fine, fine," Criswell said, nodding pleasantly.

"Hi, Cris," Connie Brooks said with a tipsy wave as he tried to stand on wobbly legs. He lost his balance and flopped back on the couch. By some miracle, he hadn't spilled a drop of Ed's whiskey. "We're gonna walk to the funeral, you know."

*More like stagger*, Cris thought. "Oh, no you're not," he insisted. "We're all going in my limo, chauffeured courtesy of Mae West."

"Wow, that's great!" Marco smiled like a kid about to spend a day at the beach.

Conrad made a second, more successful attempt to stand up. As he approached, he said, "Only, you know, I gotta be somewhere later, you know, so I'm not stayin' for the service, you know, just the viewing, you know, to pay my final respects and all. You know how it is, you know? I got things to do, you know." Whenever Brooks got drunk the "you know's" piled up in his sentences like rush hour traffic on the Hollywood Freeway.

"I know," Cris said, and took Eddie aside and whispered, "About last night; Kathy mentioned something about you getting some film developed?"

"Oh that." Wood reached into his pocket and pulled out a small film can. "This is the last footage of Armand ever shot. I thought I'd, uh, put it in Armand's coffin."

"The footage from *The Vampire's Tomb*? I thought you were going to use it in *Grave Robbers from Outer Space*."

"I am. I had two copies printed."

*Typical Eddie Wood*, Cris thought. "So what was in the envelope that Armand thought was so important?"

"Nothing," Wood assured him. "You were right. Armand was getting paranoid." He tapped his temple and whispered, "Early signs of dementia, I guess. He was convinced that Hope was trying to kill him."

"My God. Why?"

"Who knows? When you get old, you start thinking crazy things." Wood became shifty-eyed as he said, "Look, forget I said anything. Just check your mail."

"My mail? What for?"

"Never mind," said Wood, giving the psychic a wink.

Ignoring Wood's overly mysterious behavior, Criswell said, "We'd better be on our way." He escorted Eddie and Kathy to the limousine where Chalky held the door open and smiled. Marco eagerly piled into the passenger compartment, followed by the unsteady Brooks. That's when Maila got out with a huff. "Where are you going?" Criswell asked.

"I think I'll sit with Chalky," she said.

"But why, Angel?" Cris asked, concerned.

While giving Eddie a lethal glare, she said, "I don't like the company."

Chalky hurried to open the passenger door of the driver's compartment for her, and as Maila slid her shapely rear end onto the seat, Criswell sighed. "This is going to be a long day."

Ackerman pouted. "But *I'm* the one who found it."

# Chapter 16

The curtain rose at 1:30 p.m. A long line formed down the street as mourners arrived for the final viewing hours. A popular anecdote claimed that Boris Karloff had attended the viewing with fellow boogieman Peter Lorre. As they passed Tesla's body, Lorre was said to have joked, "Come on, now, Armand, you're putting us on." Actually, neither Mr. Karloff nor Mr. Lorre was in attendance—which is a pity because they missed a hell of a show. Photographers waited at the entrance to the Hollywood Mortuary hoping to capture celebrity mourners as they took their place on the viewing line, while other Speed Graflex cameras were trained on the funeral book to get shots of the bereaved adding their names to the register.

Standing by to greet mourners and give them words of consolation was Reverend Manly Palmer Hall. Mr. Hall was a self-described "writer, philosopher, ordained minister and long-time friend" of Armand Tesla and had married Armand to Hope Lininger. It was Hope's idea for Hall to preside over the chapel service, but Lillian got her way again, arguing that Hall really wasn't a minister ordained in a recognized church, pointing out that Mr. Hall's minister credentials were as the founder of the Philosophical Research Society in Los Angeles, a rather suspect Occult organization. His other claim to fame was as the hypnotist in the movie trailer for *Black Friday,* Armand's last Universal film teaming him with Boris Karloff. In the trailer the "Reverend" Hall, then a hollow-cheeked skeleton with an equally thin black mustache adorning his upper lip, implanted the suggestion to a mesmerized Armand Tesla that the actor suffered crippling claustrophobia. The publicity ballyhoo insisted this was necessary for an emotionally charged scene where Tesla's character was locked in a closet. Legend has it that when a reporter asked Karloff if he thought Tesla was really under, Karloff was said to have quipped, "He must be. I've never seen Armand keep his back to the camera for so long." No longer skeletal, the rotund Reverend Hall wore a pair of round horn-rimmed glasses that made him look less like a man of the cloth, and more like a black-haired barn owl. In an act of compromise, Mr. Fleet arranged for Reverend Joseph Vaughn to give the actual eulogy, while Hall was allowed to greet mourners and say a few words during the service, but was cautioned to make no mention of flying saucers, Freemasonry or Rosecrucianism, or conduct any Pagan occult ceremonies at the burial. Toward this end, Lillian had also insisted on a priest for the interment at Holy Cross Cemetery.

"So good to see you here, brother Tor," Reverend Hall said as Tor Johnson stepped up and signed for both himself and his wife, adding the name "Lobo" in quotes beside his signature. They made for quite a mismatched pair, Tor the man-mountain and his pretty wife Greta, barely five-feet tall. As Tor approached the casket, a close friend of Armand's, Gypsy violinist Duci de Kerekjarto, played a mournful lullaby in full costume. The big man broke down and cried like a baby. It made a most heart-wrenching photo.

"Ah, brother Weiss," Reverend Hall said as George Weiss stepped up next to add his name to the Friends' Register. "It's a blessing having you here. I know Armand was very fond of you."

George owned Screen Classics, a small-scale production house known for such quickie exploitation classics as *Test Tube Babies, Dance Hall Racket, Girl Gang, Hollywood After Midnight* and *Chained Girls*. A rather unassuming man, George Weiss had financed *Glen or Glenda*, the very film that made Tesla feel so degraded. A group publicity still taken on the set showed Weiss standing off to the right of the Ed Wood Company. In the photo, Weiss wore an electrician's jumpsuit, a costume he wore in a cameo in *Glen or Glenda*. Today, George wore a suit and tie and a black armband.

Outside, cameras were instantly raised as Criswell's limousine pulled up to the curb in front of the mortuary, and Chalky trotted to the passenger compartment to open the door. When Eddie, Kathy, Conrad and Paul emerged, cameras instantly lowered. They were nobodies. Cameras raised again as Criswell stepped forth and helped ex-Vampira Maila Nurmi down from the driver's compartment. Together they strutted proudly through the gauntlet of popping flashbulbs. The caption that would accompany the photo in tomorrow's paper would identify the couple as, "*Local Psychic to the Stars, Charles Criswell King and friend.*"

As Criswell and Maila, Kathy, Conrad and Paul took their place at the end of the line, Wood stopped short and excused himself. "I'll be right back," he said. "I, uh, left something in the limo." He hurried back to where Chalky stood waiting.

Criswell watched Wood and the chauffeur closely as they turned their backs. The way they were acting reminded Criswell of a couple of school kids passing notes in class. Ed reached into his pocket and slipped something to Chalky. Maybe it was a tip. But it sort of looked like Wood was passing Chalky the film can with *The Vampire's Tomb* footage in it. Then, Chalky slipped something back to Ed. The angle was bad, but as Ed slipped whatever it was Chalky had given him into his pocket, Criswell thought it looked like the same film can. After this brief exchange, Chalky excused himself and pulled the limo into the mortuary parking lot.

Ed turned around and bumped into a familiar bespectacled gentleman just coming out of the parking lot. The gentleman was escorting an equally familiar looking cross-eyed blonde and nearsighted teenaged boy.

"Forry!" Eddie gushed, grabbing the agent by the shoulders. "Forry Ackerman! Great to see you here! Armand would have appreciated it."

"Thanks, Ed," said Forry, disengaging himself from Wood's overly-exuberant grip.

"And Hope! Thanks again for asking me to be a pallbearer."

"Don't mention it," said Hope.

"And," Wood said, gesturing at Orby, "uh, it's, uh…Armand's number one fan."

"Andreas," said Orby.

"Come on, kid," Hope said, giving Wood the fish-eye as she took Orby's arm. "I'm gonna find a seat before Lillian hogs the best spot." She hurried the boy into the mortuary.

Ackerman felt abandoned. He tried to hurry after them, but Ed steadfastly blocked his way.

"Say, Forry," said Ed. "I was thinking about what you said."

"What I said about what?"

"About my science fiction writing. Frankly, I stink at it. Just forget about that manuscript I sent you."

Ackerman looked genuinely shocked, some might even say delighted. "Consider it done."

"I'm going to devote my time instead to writing a non-fiction piece."

Ackerman's face fell. "Really."

Gesturing broadly, Eddie pitched, "The life of Armand Tesla in his own words!"

Forry reached under his glasses and rubbed the bridge of his nose. "Here we go again."

"No, really, Forry," Ed interjected. "Armand and me had lots of conversations together where Armand shared his most personal anecdotes."

"No kidding," Ackerman said, suddenly intrigued.

"Everything," Wood said reassuringly. "All the gory details! For instance," he leaned in and whispered, "Did you know I drove Armand and Hope up to Big Bear Lake for their honeymoon?"

"I heard things got fairly grizzly up there," Forry punned.

"Well," said Wood, taking Ackerman aside, "here's the real story. We checked in at the motel, Armand and Hope sharing one room, and me in the room next door. Around two in the morning I wake up and there's Armand standing over my bed."

"What?"

"Standing over my bed. I swear. And he's making those hypnotic passes that he does as Dracula and he says to me, 'Eddie, what…do you want… with Hope?' Naturally, I tell him, 'I don't want anything with Hope.' Well, Armand just stares at me with those eyes of his, making Dracula gestures, and just says over and over again, 'Eddie…what do you want…with Hope!' The next morning, Armand had no recollection of the incident whatsoever, but Hope insisted I take them home."

"I see," said Ackerman thoughtfully.

"I have the notes to prove it. And I have a ton of other anecdotes. We can call the book, *Tesla: Post Mortem*!"

Ackerman stood there with arms crossed, deep in thought. "Okay," he said finally. "I *might* be interested, but I want to see those notes first."

Wood's eyes nearly bugged out of his head. "Really? You mean it?"

Ackerman raised his hands defensively. "Just don't hug me!" he said, stepping back quickly.

"EDDIE!" Criswell called from the end of the line. "Get over here!"

"Be right there, Cris," Wood called back. He flashed Forry a grateful smile. "I won't let you down. Or Armand either. I know he'd want his story to be told just right."

"Good," Forry said. "Now let's remember why we're here. Your friends are waiting for you."

"Talk to you later, Forry," Ed said.

As Ackerman entered the funeral home, Wood hurried down the line, stopping short as he recognized two ladies, one a pretty blonde, and the other a cherub-faced brunette. The blonde was Dolores Fuller. The brunette was Norma E. McCarty. The two ladies had something in common, namely Edward D. Wood Jr. "Dolores! Norma!" Ed gushed. "It's sweet of you both to be here! Say, Dolores I thought you were living in New York these days."

"I am," said Dolores, giving Ed a withering stare. "I flew here to pay my respects to Armand. Leave me alone."

"Brrr." Wood shivered and rubbed his hands together to stave off the chill of Dolores's cold shoulder. Eddie hurried down the line to join Criswell and the others and he just stood there, all the while keeping a wistful eye on what had once been.

Despite the frosty reception, Eddie could still feel the heat coming off Dolores during those glory days of their once passionate lovemaking. He had dabbled in 3D photography and in those days Dolores was his favorite subject. He still had the slides of Dolores socked away in a shoebox and kept from Kathy's prying eyes, especially the slide where Dolores was totally nude and draped seductively over a rock like Leda awaiting the rape of the swan. Dolores was there in her unabashed nakedness while surrounded by the splendor of Lake Arrowhead, just the kind of subject for which stereo optic photography was invented. He couldn't shake the memory of those perfect breasts and how milky white they were in the golden sun, or how those girls could fill out an angora sweater. He fondly recalled how he liked to kiss those half-dollar sized areolas of hers, and how they would crinkle up like swollen walnuts as he brushed his lips and the bristles of his mustache lightly over them. He also remembered how embarrassed she was the first time they had sex and Sam Arkoff came by Ed's tiny apartment for breakfast one morning. He knocked on the unlocked bedroom door and found Eddie in bed with a naked and humiliated Dolores Fuller.

Ed still wanted her, to watch her undress like she did back them, quickly and urgently, possessed with the desire for Eddie to screw her brains out. It was while he was enjoying these feelings that Maila eyed Wood's growing erection. Shaking her head, she sneered, "It looks like Armand isn't the only stiff at this funeral. You're disgusting."

Dolores felt Eddie's eyes on her and she didn't like it one bit. Or rather, she didn't like liking being undressed by those eyes of his. She tried to shrug it off, but she had fond memories of her own about Eddie. But those dreams of 69 embraces and other things were derailed when Norma decided to strike up a conversation. "I was married briefly to Ed," she confessed.

"Really?" Dolores said, trying to ignore her. Even though Dolores wanted nothing more to do with Ed Wood, it still didn't mean she wanted to hear about him from the lips of another woman. Unfortunately, Norma was totally oblivious to the cold shoulder Dolores was giving her. "I was on location out on one of the ranches the day we met," Norma effused. "Ed came out looking for locations and he said, 'Would you like to take a ride?' He had a nice convertible."

"I know," said Dolores icily. She recalled how *she* had met Ed Wood. He was looking for someone he could groom. Dolores had appeared on *Queen for a Day* and *The Adventures of Superman*. She had modeled for Diana Shore. Ed Wood had interviewed a lot of young actresses, but Dolores was the only one who came in wearing an angora sweater. And he loved angora. They fell in love and they became a team. Or so she thought.

"—and it boomeranged from then on," Norma said. "We decided to get married, and in two days he had the whole thing arranged, for heaven sakes."

"Wow," Dolores said indifferently. She helped Eddie with his movies; she got the entire wardrobe. She worked for some of the top manufacturers of clothing like Westward Knitting Mills and Chic Lingerie. So anything that she wanted she could say, "Yes, we could use that for this scene." and put their name on the screen. So Eddie never had to worry about wardrobe in his pictures for any of the women.

Norma went on chattering. "It was a very nice wedding, and Armand Tesla showed up for it," she said blithely. "It was so fast that I didn't ask a lot of people. But you should have seen all the people. Ed had a lot of friends."

Dolores sighed.

"Well," Norma continued, "we lived together—I guess about six or seven weeks. And Armand Tesla called and said Ed had been drinking too much."

Speaking slowly, Norma affected a deep Hungarian accent. "'Norma,' he said, 'would you come and pick up Eddie?'" Continuing in her own voice, she said, "I asked Ed why in the world he would go out and drink too much. He said, 'I'm a transvestite.' And I said, 'Well, what's that?' He said, 'I like to work in women's clothing.' I said, 'I can't live with you.'"

This was hitting a little too close to home. Dolores remembered *her* experiences acting in *Glen or Glenda* and about how very embarrassed and uncomfortable she was. Up until the moment she read the script she had no idea why all her angora sweaters were stretched out. Writing *Glen or Glenda* and putting Dolores in the lead was Eddie's way of breaking the news to her about his being a transvestite. She was the one who made Wood change his on-screen writing credit from "Edward D. Wood Jr." to "Daniel

Davis," hoping nobody would realize that *Glen or Glenda* was taken from their own lives.

Approaching the funeral book, Norma picked up the pen and began writing in her name. "So the next day I said I had to move. So I went to my mother's house and I came back a few days later and moved my things out. I had discovered that he had worn a dress of mine and I left it for him and said, 'You can have this dress of mine, you've ruined it.' So you can just imagine how he must have felt." Norma turned around and noticed that Dolores had given up her place on line. Mr. and Mrs. Ed Reynolds smiled politely, looking uncomfortable. "Oh," Norma said, getting red-faced. "Excuse me."

Standing eight mourners further down the line, Dolores sighed heavily. The memories Norma had dredged up depressed her. It was bad enough that Wood had broken the news to her about his being a transvestite by making *Glen or Glenda*. That was embarrassing enough! But the last straw came with the making of *Bride of the Atom*! She had put up with a lot from Ed Wood, but this was the final indignity! After all Dolores's hard work and sacrifice Ed gave Loretta King the starring role in *Bride of the Atom*, a role Ed had written especially for Dolores! But Wood was short on production funds and Loretta King had convinced him that she could cover the costs with her own money. Dolores was relegated to the thankless role of "File Clerk." She still remembered every line; there were only three of them! "Janet, I hear the boss wants those monster stories eighty-sixed. You've got the whole town in a panic." "I can't hear you," was Loretta's smarmy reply. "I said—" "Oh, I heard what you said," Loretta smirked, "I just can't hear you," leaving Dolores to smile dumbly and say, "I get it. See you later."

Exit through file room door.

"Cut! Perfect!" Wood in the director's chair had declared.

Ed tried to smooth things over by telling Dolores there would be other parts. But it's the betrayal that hurt! Dolores packed up her things and left Wood for a successful career as a songwriter.

Stepping up to the funeral book, Dolores wrote in her name as Reverend Hall smiled. "Sister Dolores," he said, "welcome." Dolores smiled politely, but that smile quickly faded when the Reverend looked past her and said, "And sister Loretta," he said to an all too familiar-looking brunette, "I know Armand will be pleased that you came to pay your respects."

Loretta King scribbled her name right below Dolores's. Apparently she had been standing behind Dolores the whole time. Dolores was outraged.

"That bitch!" their eyes seemed to communicate as Dolores and Loretta shared a mutual glare of hostility. Loretta King still stung with the memory of an incident connected with *Bride of the Atom*.

It was before the premiere, at four o'clock in the morning, that Loretta received a phone call that woke her and her mother out of a sound sleep. A woman's voice said, "How do you like doing what is mine?"

Half-asleep Loretta said, "Who is this?"

"How do you like having what I'm supposed to have?"

Loretta recognized the voice immediately. "Dolores?" she asked.

"Yes, this is me," Dolores admitted.

Loretta demanded, "What do you mean?"

"You're doing my role," was the scornful reply before Dolores hung up. Judging from Dolores's reaction now, it was obvious she still harbored a lot of hostility. "You have a nerve," Dolores said with venom.

Loretta stiffened. "Just to set the record straight," she said, "Ed Wood never asked me for money. He never referred in any way to it. As a matter of fact, when they stopped production I wasn't even told it was because they didn't have any money. I was just told they were going on hiatus. So I don't know where anyone could get the idea that I came up with the money because I didn't."

"Keep telling yourself that," sneered Dolores, "and maybe you'll start to believe it."

Reverend Hall stepped in. "Ladies, please," he said. "Be at peace."

"But it's the truth," Loretta insisted. "I was as astonished by those rumors as anybody."

"If you didn't give Ed the money," Dolores demanded, "why did he give you my part?"

Reverend Hall preached, "Let the past remain in the past."

"Well, Dolores, I had no idea I had your part! I received that role through my agent. That's when I met Ed Wood."

Dolores blinked in disbelief. "What do you take me for, some airheaded blonde? Ed and I both met you at the same time! It was at the Tail o' the Cock restaurant, that's when Ed brought up the $60,000 we needed to make *Bride of the Atom* and you said," Dolores effected a twittery girlish voice, "'Really, well that doesn't sound like very much!'"

Vexed, Loretta stamped her foot. "Stop that! My agent handled the whole thing with Ed Wood and the part I got in the picture. If Ed gave away your part, he did it because he didn't think you were right for it. So if you want to be mad at anybody, be mad at Ed Wood, not me."

Reverend Hall smiled earnestly. "And the truth shall set you free. Now let those feelings go, sister Dolores."

All sister Dolores could do was stand there speechless as George Becwar squeezed between them. "I'm terribly sorry, ladies," he said, "but I'm late for an appointment." That's when he looked up and recognized them. "Ah, Dolores! Loretta! So nice to see you both!" Becwar's claim to fame was playing the role of the foreign agent Strowski in *Bride of the Atom* and being "devoured" by the rubber octopus that Wood and company had stolen from the Republic Studios prop warehouse — without also obtaining the all-important motor to animate the tentacles.

"Hello, George," Loretta said politely. "Good-bye, Dolores. Reverend Hall." Loretta King entered the slumber room, leaving Dolores pale and overwhelmed.

"Are you all right, Dolores?" Becwar asked.

"Talk to you later, George," said Dolores, choking back tears. She glared resentfully at Ed Wood, who had just stepped into the foyer. Dolores ran to the ladies' room crying.

"Be at peace, sister Dolores," Reverend Hall said. "And a good day to you, brother Becwar."

"Good day, Reverend," Becwar said absently as he fretfully looked where Dolores had been looking. Ed Wood was standing there, talking to Criswell, Maila, Brooks and Marco. Ed could barely contain his excitement. "I can't believe it!" he said. "Forry Ackerman is actually interested in my idea!" He jumped up and down like a kid waiting to see Santa Claus.

"That's good, Eddie," said Criswell.

Maila leered at Wood in disgust. "Will you remember we're going to a funeral. Show some respect!"

"Right, right," Wood said, still hopping up and down excitedly. Becwar hurriedly grabbed the pen and scribbled in his name, praying Ed didn't see him. Wood blamed Becwar for insisting on being paid union minimum. Becwar complained to the Screen Actors Guild, causing additional production delays on *Bride of the Atom*. As a result, Wood openly hated Becwar's guts and even resorted to cutting Becwar's image out of all the production stills he was in. Becwar signed the book quickly, and then ducked into the slumber room.

After George's signature came well-wishes from the Rosu Family, then Frank M. O'Hara, followed by Mike Hewler, and David Oylen. Finally, there came the all-important signatures of Edward D. Wood Jr., Kathleen Wood, Conrad Brooks and Paul Marco.

"Edward, my son," Reverend Hall beamed. "I hear you've been asked by the widow to act as a pallbearer."

"That's right," Ed said as he wrote in his name, and gave the pen to Kathy.

"And dear sister Kathy," Reverend Hall said with a smile. "You look so lovely, so *wondrous* today."

Kathy gave the Reverend a sweet yet vacant smile as she and Ed said almost simultaneously, "Wondrous." As Kathy dreamily passed the pen to Connie Brooks, Ed Wood said to Reverend Hall, "It's funny you should say that word. Because Ray Bradbury—" Ed's namedropping was interrupted when he noticed George Becwar's signature in the Friends' Register and all hell broke loose. "That son of a bitch!" Wood bristled. "What's *he* doing here?" His reaction did not escape the notice of photographers who got a couple of shots of Wood's grimacing face.

"Keep your voice down, Eddie," chided Criswell as he scribbled his inscription. "What's all the fuss now?"

Wood stabbed his index finger at Becwar's name. "George Becwar! He has a goddamn nerve showing his face here!"

"Now, brother Ed," said Reverend Hall in a soothing tone. "Let us turn the other cheek."

"The hell with that!" Wood growled as he stormed into the slumber room. "If I see that bastard, I'll not only turn his cheek, I'll beat him to a pulp!" He pointed dramatically at Becwar, who spotted Ed at the same time. Becwar cringed as Wood growled, "There he is!" The other mourners and press people turned and stared, wondering what was going on.

Kathy took Ed into the hall and pleaded, "Eddie, please, don't make a scene. After making such a good impression, you'll ruin everything with Mr. Ackerman."

"Kathy's right, Eddie," Criswell said. "I don't know why George Becwar gets you so upset, but whatever the reason, you're just going to have to forget about it and act like a normal person."

Maila smirked. "At least normal for you."

Criswell shot Maila a stern look. "Not helping," he said. He looked up and noticed Becwar trying to slip out of the slumber room unnoticed.

"So, Eddie," said Criswell, positioning himself so Wood's back was to the frightened actor. He gestured for Becwar to beat it. "What's it going to be?"

Wood took a deep breath and nodded. "Okay," he said. "I guess it's the hangover talking. I'll just ignore him."

"Good," said Criswell as Becwar ducked down the hall toward the casket showroom, no doubt to find a back way out. Cris took Ed by the arm and led him back to the slumber room. "Now let's quietly pay our respects. And don't—" Criswell froze in mid-sentence as his eyes grew wide with inexplicable apprehension. "Oh, this is bad," he said.

"What's wrong, Cris?" Eddie asked innocently. Just then, a hand gripped his arm and wheeled him around. Ed suddenly found himself standing nose-to-nose with a furious Dolores Fuller, who glared at him with tear-reddened eyes. She snarled, "You and me need to talk, Ed!"

Wood's fear-strained voice cracked like a nervous adolescent on prom night. "Dolores!" he piped, then cleared his throat, pushing Kathy forward to block Dolores's advance. "Uh, have you met my wife? This is Kathy. Kathy, this is Dolores Fuller."

Dolores's eyes narrowed. "Wife, huh? You mean like I was your wife?" She looked Kathy up and down. "Did you know that he actually lied to his mother about *us* getting married? He used a still from *Glen or Glenda*'s wedding scene, only he cut out the devil acting as best man." She eyed Eddie. "At least he cut out the *other* devil!"

Ed nervously pulled on his collar. "B-but you said you weren't ready to get married again. I had to tell my mother something."

One reporter smiled and nudged his photographer. "This is gonna be good," he said.

From every corner of the room, cameras were raised in anticipation of a knock down drag out fight. Dolores did not disappoint them. "I said we need to talk," she growled. "*Now*, Ed!" Flashbulbs fired off a barrage as cameras captured Dolores grabbing Wood by the tie and dragging him by it to a far corner of the slumber room. Once there, Dolores acted the role of verbal pugilist. She jabbed Wood with a devastating; "You've got some nerve lying to me about Loretta King!" Ed was on the ropes, sweating and stammering unintelligibly as Dolores followed through with a resounding, "She told me the truth!"

"Uh, uh, uh, uh, uh," was Ed's only defense.

Dolores let fly with, "You're nothing but a lying, cheating...stinker!" She followed through with a swift kick to Ed's shin. The lying, cheating stinker could only scream and hop on one foot. Wood's howling got Lillian's attention, she charged from the private family room demanding, "What's going on here?" while her son, staying loyally beside her pointed accusingly and said, "It's that loser Ed Wood, mom! I told you something like this would happen!"

Squaring her shoulders, Lillian confronted Dolores and Ed. "This is Armand's funeral," she said. "How dare you!" Flashbulbs flickered like strobe lights as Wood smiled apologetically. "I'm sorry, Mrs. Tesla," he began.

"*Arch*!" Lillian fumed. "My name is Lillian *Arch*!"

"Ri - right, Arch," Wood stammered.

Dolores pushed Ed aside. "Look, lady," she said, "I have unfinished business with this…this *creep*!"

Armand Jr. stepped between Dolores and his mother.

"How dare you make a scene at my father's funeral," he said, firmly scolding Dolores. "And," he added, railing at Ed; "if I had my way *you* wouldn't even be here!" More flashbulbs burst. More film was exposed. More dirt collected for the late edition. "You're nothing but a loser and a user!"

"Here, here," chimed in Dolores.

Wood looked genuinely hurt as Armand Jr. continued his ranting. "I hated seeing my father in those awful movies of yours! Just look at him!" he said, pointing an accusing finger at the open casket. POP! POP! POP! Cameras captured the pose. "I'll bet dressing up my father like this was *your* idea! You've made his death a *joke*!"

"I can handle this, Bill," Lillian interrupted. "I want you both to leave," she demanded firmly, pointing toward the exit. "This instant!"

An anxious Kathy Wood ran over to Hope. The widow sat on the sidelines with Forry and Orby, wishing she had popcorn. "Please!" Kathy pleaded. "Do something!"

Happy for the excuse to interfere, Hope charged in with both barrels. "What the hell's going on here?" she demanded. One reporter nudged his photographer, "Get ready, Charlie. She looks like a biter."

Armand Jr. glared angrily. "We're handling this!"

Hope's eyes crossed with fury. "Listen, kid," she said, poking Armand Jr. in the chest, "like it or not, this is *my* husband's funeral. I'm the fucking widow! I call the goddamn shots around here! I'm the one who gave the funeral home Armand's costume. It was his last wish."

"That's a lot of bull!"

"Like you'd know what Armand wanted," she scoffed. "You hardly ever spoke to him the whole time we were married *except* when you tried to talk him into divorcing me! You got some nerve, kid!"

"Now look—" Armand Jr. began. His mother held him back as more flashbulbs popped. "Don't say another word, Bill," she said.

Ackerman approached Criswell. "Shouldn't we do something?"

Criswell sighed. "I've learned that it's best not to interfere." Turning to Ackerman, he asked, "How about you?"

"I've learned to stay out of Hope's way." Forry looked over at Brooks and Marco. "At least those two are paying Armand some attention."

Contemplating Armand, Marco said, "I always used to see Ed tickle Armand under the chin, and Armand would just shake and smile. It would just bring Armand to life again."

Brooks asked bleary-eyed, "Do you, you know, think that would work now, you know?"

Ackerman pointed at Tor. "Maybe we should get Mr. Johnson to break things up."

Tor was parked on two folding chairs, oblivious to everything, sobbing into a handkerchief as his tiny wife patted his huge arm affectionately.

Criswell shook his head and quipped, "It looks like Tor's too broken up to break up anything."

Just then, Mr. Bruckner hurried into the slumber room. Reporters blinded him with their flashbulbs. Mr. Bruckner squinted as blue blobs floated before his eyes. "Uh, is everything all right here?" he asked warily.

Hope glared at him. "Mind your own fucking business!"

"Why, I never—!" Mr. Bruckner exclaimed, not sure where to look.

"It shows, pal."

With an indignant, "Well!" Mr. Bruckner collided with Maila Nurmi and blindly groping her ample bosom. To say the least, the press photographers were thrilled. Bruckner started and hurried out of the room.

Ackerman gave Criswell a wan smile. "See what I mean about staying out of Hope's way?"

Hope redirected her withering stare back at Lillian and Armand Jr. "As for this funeral," she said with an admonishing finger wag; "I better not get charged even a penny extra! Not one penny!"

Lillian was outraged. "I've had just about all I'm going to take from you," she began.

Seeing his chance to make a break for it, Wood threw up his hands and shrugged. "Well, Dolores," he said, "I guess we'll talk another time." He hurried over and grabbed Kathy by the arm for a hasty exit. Dolores grabbed him by the tie and growled, "Not so fast, Wood!" She dragged Wood gagging for air and limping, while a curious mob of mourners, reporters, and photographers followed Dolores and a pleading Kathy Wood into the casket showroom.

Maila was giddy with excitement. "I gotta see this!" she said, intent on following after the mob.

Criswell held her back. "I really think," he said, "we should wait in the chapel."

"Definitely," Ackerman agreed. "Coming, Tor?"

Tor sniffled as he looked up. "I come," he said as Greta took his arm and helped him stand.

Criswell turned to Marco and Brooks. "Are you two coming?" he asked.

"Not me," Connie said. "I got someplace to be, you know. Like I said, you know."

As Brooks made his exit, Orby gestured at the casket. "I just want a few minutes alone with Armand. Please."

"Just stay out of trouble," Criswell cautioned.


Meanwhile, in his second floor office, Mr. Bruckner had regained his eyesight and was pacing the floor, rehearsing a face-saving speech for the press. His only chance to recover from such a disastrous public relations nightmare was to remain confident and to demonstrate Hollywood Mortuary's commitment to the bereaved.

He had it all planned out. Mr. Bruckner would act as though nothing whatsoever had happened. He would return to the slumber room and make a show of solemnly closing Tesla's casket, creating an excellent photo opportunity. This would be followed with his supervising the casket's gentle transfer to a rolling bier. Then the casket would be reverently taken to the chapel, again, providing another fine photo opportunity. This would lead directly to the service that would be conducted in a most respectful manner. After the service, the pallbearers would provide the press with a truly touching portrait of Tesla's last moments as they transported the actor's casket to the waiting hearse. Yes, that would solve everything!

Feeling prepared, Mr. Bruckner left his office and descended the foyer stairs. His confidence lasted exactly up to the point he entered the slumber room, finding only Andreas Orby contemplating the deceased. Bewildered, he looked around. "Where is everybody?"

Orby was about to answer when Bruckner became aware of the sound of angry voices. An assistant ran in, pointing excitedly down the hall. "Mr. Bruckner, sir! In the showroom! They're all in the showroom!"

Mr. Bruckner ran into the hall. "Oh, my God!" he exclaimed. There was a veritable mob crowding the entrance to the private half of the mortuary. "We could lose our license!" he fretted. "The Jeffery family will be here at three! Whatever will they think?"

Mr. Bruckner hurried back into the slumber room where he quickly, and with no solemnity whatsoever, shut Tesla's casket. "Get out!" he ordered Orby.

The teenager did as he was told. Orby sighed and sat on the foyer stairs, resting his chin in his fists.

Turning to the assistant, Mr. Bruckner ordered, "Stay with Mr. Tesla!" His jaw set heroically as he proclaimed, "I'll handle this!"

He marched into the hall and shut the slumber room doors. Then, feeling a bit like Custer on the morning of his Last Stand at Little Big Horn, Hugo H. Bruckner charged purposefully into the casket showroom to face God-knows-what.

God-knows-what manifested as a gathering throng of mourners that watched from the showroom as Dolores dragged Ed Wood down the private hallway with Kathy trying her best to intervene. Wood's gagging and protesting was drowned out by the sound of a revving engine. The sound came from the garage where Mr. Fleet was sending Horace M. Steinmetz to pick up two bodies from the County Morgue. Dolores used her free hand to shove the pleading Kathy Wood aside, then yank open the morgue's heavy door as Wood gasped, "Wait! That's the embalming room!"

Dolores shoved him in. "The perfect place for a dead duck!" she said. Dolores swung the door closed behind her. Kathy banged on it with her fists, her cries barely audible over the departing funeral coach's engine. *"Please!"* she sobbed. "Don't hurt my Eddie!"

In desperation Kathy grabbed the handle with both hands, pulled hard and found to her relief that the door was unlocked. She ran in, the door slowly swinging closed behind her.

In the garage, Mr. Fleet was so preoccupied with an apprentice embalmer that the funeral director failed to notice Kathy Wood dashing into the preparation room to help her husband. Mr. Fleet remained oblivious as he entered the hallway and focused his attention on a casketed client Steinmetz had left in the hallway, ready to be transported to the slumber room. As Mr. Fleet pushed the truck forward, he looked up and stopped abruptly. What were all the mourners and press people doing staring at him from the casket showroom?

The people thronging around her began pushing Lillian this way and that. She had seen enough. Shaking her head reproachfully, she turned to her son. "Come along, Bill," Lillian said, grabbing his wrist. "Mr. Bruckner should be told about this." With teenage son in tow, Lillian shoved her way through the crowd, emerging unscathed, but finding her way blocked by Hope Tesla.

"Hold it, sister," Hope said. "If anybody's gonna tell anybody about anything, it'll be me!" Hope marched up to a nonplused Mr. Bruckner and said in her usual tactful manner, "Hey, Bruckner, some broad is slapping Ed Wood around in your embalming room! Don't just stand there like a dummy, go help the poor bastard!"

"FLEET!" Mr. Bruckner shouted as camera shutters clicked, flashbulbs popped and Armand Jr. charged up demanding, "I want that loser thrown out of here!" followed by Lillian shouting, "Never you mind about Ed Wood! I want *this woman*," she said, glaring angrily at Hope, "out of here!"

"Up yours, Lillian!" Hope growled.

Back in the private hallway, the sound of the slamming morgue door made Mr. Fleet whirl around in time to see Ed Wood throwing his weight against the door. From inside the morgue, a woman's muffled voice shouted, "COME BACK HERE, YOU FUCKING CHEATING COWARD! I'LL KILL YOU!"

"You're crazy!" Wood fearfully exclaimed, fumbling for the locking pin as he struggled to keep the door closed. "What's gotten into you?"

Mr. Fleet exclaimed, "What! You can't be back here! What are you doing here?"

Having finally secured the latch with the locking pin, Wood smiled nervously at Mr. Fleet, then limped as fast as possible toward the garage, only to stop short when he saw the apprentice embalmer waiting by the door.

"Come here!" Mr. Fleet demanded as he lunged at the intruder. But even handicapped by a wounded shin, Ed proved too fast for him. Ed ducked quickly out of the way, then limped quickly up the back stairs.

Mr. Fleet was about to give chase when he heard Mr. Bruckner shout, "FLEET!" Mr. Fleet turned to the apprentice embalmer and pointed up the stairs, "Go after that man!" he ordered.

The apprentice didn't budge an inch. "Not me," he protested. "What if he's crazy? I'm not going to run after a crazy person."

In the casket showroom, Mr. Bruckner was understandably beside himself. He climbed up on a dual casket display rack and cupped his hands to his mouth. "FLEET!" he shouted again. "GET IN HERE! NOW!" Mr. Fleet hurried to help Mr. Bruckner while Mr. Bruckner addressed the agitated mourners. "PLEASE WILL YOU ALL CALM DOWN!" A hush fell over the crowd. "I assure you all," he said, mopping flop sweat from his brow, "I shall see to this matter personally. The service will begin just as soon as possible, and under the circumstances, I think we'll just dispense with the immediate family's final viewing."

"That's fine by me," Hope said, glaring smugly at Lillian. "That'll teach you to keep me out, bitch!"

Armand Jr. had to hold his mother back. Lillian lunged at Hope, claws bared for a cat fight. "Mom, no!" he pleaded. "Don't give her the satisfaction."

"PLEASE!" Mr. Bruckner shouted, and then implored, "Please, all of you wait in the chapel. We'll have things resolved just as soon as we can."

The mourners reluctantly did as they were told. The press lingered to see what was coming next. They didn't have to linger long. Climbing down from the display rack, Mr. Bruckner turned to Mr. Fleet and said, "We've got interlopers in the preparation room!"

Mr. Fleet exclaimed, "I know! I just saw one of them run up the back stairs!"

Mr. Bruckner groaned, "Can anything *else* go wrong today?"

Mr. Fleet led Mr. Bruckner down the private hallway with members of the press in hot pursuit.

In the chapel, Criswell sat with Maila in the pew closest to the hallway. Marco sat beside them and kept himself occupied by searching through the hymnals. "Do you think we'll have to sing gypsy hymns?" Marco wondered. "I think I remember the song they sang in *Frankenstein Meets the Wolf Man*." He softly sang, "*There is no music in the tomb, so drink to joy and down with gloom*, or something like that."

Maila rolled her eyes.

Tor and his wife sat in the pew behind them. Cris could hear the wrestler sniffling, and then he heard something else. It sounded like the distant sound of firecrackers exploding. But those sounds were soon muffled by the voices of approaching mourners.

Ackerman sat in the pew opposite Criswell and asked the usher to seat Hope next to him when she arrived. The usher explained that Hope's place was in the rear. "But Hope is the widow," said Forry as Lillian and Armand Jr. approached the pew and waited.

"Nevertheless," the usher said, "this pew is reserved for Miss Arch and young Mr. Tesla. I'm sorry."

Sighing, Ackerman said, "Okay, I'll sit in the back."

"No, Forry," Lillian said, "you're more than welcome to sit with us."

"Thank you, Lillian," Ackerman said rising. "But I can't abandon Hope. That just wouldn't be right."

Criswell smiled at the phrase. *No*, he thought, *none of us should abandon hope*.

Ackerman waited by the door as ushers showed everyone else to their seats. When Hope entered, Ackerman offered her his arm. As he escorted her down the aisle, he explained why she was sitting in the back.

"That fucking bitch," Cris and everyone else heard Hope exclaim as she directed dagger-stares at the occupants in the front pew.

Criswell saw three men sitting down in the chairs reserved for the pallbearers. Each chair had a name card in the seat. Don Marlowe was about to sit in a pew when he saw two empty pallbearer seats. Name cards reserved one chair for Ed Wood, the other for Andreas Orby. Acting like he owned the place, Marlowe removed Orby's card, stuck it in his pocket and sat with the pallbearers. Criswell looked around for Andreas Orby, but the young man was nowhere to be seen. Cris imagined that if Orby tried to protest, Marlowe would refuse to give up his seat like a player in a cutthroat game of musical chairs.

Then a commotion came from the hallway. Criswell got up to investigate and saw the press gaggle around Dolores, Kathy and George Becwar as a very angry Mr. Bruckner and Ralph Fleet herded the troublesome threesome from the premises. Bruckner had a tight hold on George Becwar's collar while Fleet stood between Kathy and Dolores and had both ladies by the arm.

"Take your hands off me!" Dolores snarled as Mr. Fleet hastened their departure.

"Honestly," Mr. Fleet scolded, "such behavior during a funeral service! Even by Hollywood standards, it's appalling!"

Cris wondered how Becwar had gotten mixed up in all this. Becwar answered this all-consuming question as he explained to Mr. Bruckner, "I wasn't trying to break into your embalming room! I wanted to get away from Ed Wood and I was looking for a back way out! He's crazy!"

But Mr. Bruckner would hear none of it, and made a grand show of authority for the press. "No more back-talk," he said firmly. "Hollywood Mortuaries won't tolerate this behavior."

"But," Kathy pleaded, "what about my Eddie?"

"Oh, rest assured," said Mr. Fleet, "Mr. Wood will be dealt with when we find him! Now get out!"

Having shown the interlopers the curb, Mr. Bruckner turned and addressed the crowding press people. "Please go into the chapel. There's nothing more to see!"

As the reporters passed by Criswell, one of them quipped; "And I was gonna cover an execution today. This show has that beat by a mile!"

The excitement over, Mr. Bruckner hurried in and signaled to the organist to start playing. He turned to leave, and then asked Criswell to return to his seat, which he did.

Time passed. The organist played one hymn after another. Everyone was getting restless, including the Reverend Vaughn. He looked at his watch and sighed. Cris checked his watch, too. Twenty minutes had passed and still no sign of Orby, or the funeral director—or the guest of honor, Armand Tesla, for that matter.

Sensing something was up; Criswell leaned forward, pretending to pray while really looking out into the hall. Mr. Fleet brought in a casket on a hand truck. He paused at the slumber room and knocked on the sliding doors. The assistant waiting inside opened the doors and helped wheel the casket inside just as Mr. Bruckner appeared.

"Leave the casket, Fleet," he said.

"What? But we have to get Mr. Tesla into the chapel." He gestured at the waiting coffin. "Mr. Jeffrey here has to be in the slumber room by three, and it's well past three now."

"Leave the casket," Mr. Bruckner insisted. "I called Mrs. Jeffrey and told her Mr. Jeffrey's viewing was pushed to four o'clock. We have to find that idiot Ed Wood. We simply can't risk another row."

Mr. Fleet sighed as the assistant parked Jeffrey's casket by Tesla's casket, and then returned to the hall. "He's upstairs."

"While you two check upstairs," Mr. Bruckner said, "I'll appease the mourners."

The assistant followed Mr. Fleet as Mr. Bruckner entered the chapel. He gestured for the organist to desist and took to the pulpit. "Ladies and gentlemen," he said, "I beg your indulgence. We're doing our best to insure this service will suffer no further interruptions…"

As the Vice President of Hollywood Mortuaries made his announcement, Cris continued to watch the hallway. To his amazement, he saw Andreas Orby slip into the slumber room and close the sliding doors. "What in the world?" Cris muttered aloud.

"…so please be patient," Mr. Bruckner said. "Just as soon as we're sure the mortuary is free of, shall we say, disruptive influences, we'll begin the service."

He gestured for the organist to begin playing again, and then left to join the search for Wood. Another 15 minutes passed, the congregation of mourners continued to grow restless. Very soon, an exasperated Mr. Fleet and his equally vexed assistant marched up to the slumber room. "What a waste of time that was," Fleet muttered. He and his assistant stopped short when they found doors closed. Mr. Fleet tried to open them, but they wouldn't budge. Fleet and the assistant each took a door and tried to pull them open. Finally, in frustration, Mr. Fleet grabbed the finger grips and shook the doors. Turning to the assistant he said, "Did you close these doors?"

"No, sir. Somebody must be in there."

Mr. Fleet banged on the doors. "Who's in there?" He put his ear to the doors. "I hear something going on in there." He pounded more forcefully. "WHO'S IN THERE, I SAY? OPEN THESE DOORS THIS MINUTE!"

Mr. Bruckner hurried over. "Stop that shouting, Ralph," he said. "Remember the press people."

"But somebody locked the slumber room doors."

"Well, don't call attention to it! Get the key."

A very chagrinned Andreas Orby opened the doors. Exasperated, Mr. Bruckner grabbed the teen by the jacket collar, demanding, "What were you playing at?"

"I just wanted to say a last good-bye to Armand," the lad explained.

"Fine," said Mr. Bruckner. "You've said your good-byes, now sit down!" He gestured to Mr. Fleet. "Take him to the chapel and see that he stays there."

Mr. Fleet took hold of Orby and roughly deposited him in the pew with Forry and Hope. Criswell could see Forry asking Orby what had happened. The boy was rather nervous as he said something that made Ackerman look around in alarm.

Soon after that the coffin was wheeled in with a large floral display decorating the lid. Mr. Bruckner parked the casket before the altar and sat on the sidelines.

Reverend Joseph Vaughn approached the lectern, briefly consulted his notes, and then began his sermon. "We gather here to bid farewell to Armand Tesla, a man much feared on the screen, and much beloved in real life, who as a baby was bounced upon his father's knee..."

Hope shook her head. "What a putz."


Criswell's curiosity got the better of him. With the service underway, he decided to slip out the side door to have a look around.

Mr. Fleet was just coming out of the slumber room while his assistant slipped a new card into the pedestal mount announcing Room A was now reserved for "RICHARD JEFFREY, Visitation 4 p.m. – 9 p.m., Service 9 a.m. Chapel." The "4" in 4 p.m. had been pasted over what had once been a "3." Mr. Fleet turned to the assistant. "I have to attend to the Tesla funeral," he said, consulting his watch. "Wait about 30 minutes, then open the casket." The assistant nodded. Before going to the chapel, Mr. Fleet saw Criswell and gave the psychic a dirty look. "If you cause us any trouble, out you go."

"I understand," Criswell assured him.

Criswell decided to check the showroom and the private hallway, in case Ed might have been hiding there for a chance to slip out unnoticed.

Criswell turned to leave when he saw Ackerman sneak out of the service and go to a potted plant standing by the door leading to the parking lot. Forry bent down and began feeling around the dirt.

Criswell approached. "What are you up to?" he asked.

"Andreas said he found something here," Ackerman said, pulling a silver-plated revolver from the dirt. "It looks like a Western six-shooter." He wiped the dirt away and blew on the barrel.

"And," Criswell said with a frown, "it looks like you've just destroyed the fingerprints."

Ackerman looked up. "Don't worry. Someday my prints will come."

Cris winced at the pun. "I know the proper way to handle evidence. I've worked with the police before as a psychic consultant."

Hefting the weapon, Ackerman asked, "Evidence? This?"

"Eddie is missing. You just found a gun hidden in a potted plant. Wouldn't you say that's rather suggestive of foul play?"

"Oh," Ackerman said shamefaced. "It looks like I jumped the gun."

Using his handkerchief, Criswell took the gun and sniffed the barrel. "It's been fired recently," he said. Examining the gun more closely, he spotted something on the handle. "There's an engraved message. Most of it's been scratched off but I can make out the words, 'Sheriff' and what looks like, 'Hollywood.'"

"Oh yes," Ackerman said. "Those used to be given out by the Hollywood Chamber of Commerce. 'Honorary Sheriff of Hollywood,' the title was. Boris Karloff gave me his as a birthday present a few years ago." He frowned. "How do you suppose it got here?"

"I don't know."

"There ought to be a name of the honoree on the grip."

Criswell brought the gun up close and squinted. "It's been scratched off. Must be old, though. The gun is pretty tarnished."

"Look!" Ackerman pointed at the carpet. Criswell saw five shoeprints made with blood or something that resembled blood. Cris knelt down and felt the carpet. It was still wet. Looking at his fingers, he saw they were definitely red with blood. "Now I'm really worried," Criswell said.

"You don't think that girl might have—"

"Dolores?" Criswell said, standing. "She's got a temper, but I don't think she'd do anything that stupid. Becwar, maybe. There was definitely no love lost between Becwar and Ed. As for Kathy, she's a saint. Besides,"

Criswell added, indicating the shoeprints, "those were made by a man's shoe."

"So it might have been Becwar."

"Looks like," Criswell said as he wrapped the revolver up in his handkerchief and slipped it into the inner pocket of his tuxedo jacket. "The gun shows premeditation. If Becwar shot Eddie, he came to the funeral prepared to do it. I'll keep hold of the gun, just in case."

Ackerman pouted. "But *I'm* the one who found it."

"And you're the one who messed up the fingerprints." Criswell nodded toward the chapel. "Why don't you get back to the service? I'm going to have a look there," he said, pointing beyond the fading trail of shoeprints toward the casket showroom. "It looks like whoever made those footprints was heading that way."

"Actually," said Ackerman, clapping the dirt off his hands, "I'd like to go with you. But I'm more inclined to check the parking lot first. That seems to be where the perpetrator came from."

"Good point," Criswell conceded.

Out in the mortuary parking lot, under the blue California sky, sat row after row of cars; some of them with press cards in their windows. Criswell fancied that the cars had faces, faces made up of headlight eyes and grillwork teeth. They were like rows of metal skulls, each flashing a mocking Cheshire cat grin. Standing out like a cliché sore thumb amidst contemporary Buicks and Chryslers and Fords was Criswell's anachronistic chocolate-colored Imperial 8. Chalky was leaning against the car. The chauffeur was talking to a distinguished-looking gent with a somewhat feminine demeanor. The gent was resting his foot on the running board and daintily wiping his shoe with a handkerchief. Criswell recognized the gent immediately as John "Bunny" Breckinridge out of drag.

Criswell took in the details of the possible crime scene. A wrought iron fence stood at both ends of the lot. The main entrance opened onto Hollywood Boulevard, the rear onto Selma Avenue. Cars parked along the mortuary and near the side door obstructed the view, making it plausible that a murder could take place in broad daylight and not attract attention. The tarmac in front of the side door had been freshly sprayed with water. There was a spigot close by and water was still trickling from it. Criswell turned the handle on the tap. Water sprayed out, splashing Criswell's shoe and flushing the area clean; the runoff went under the car to Criswell's left and down to the curb. "And away goes troubles, down the drain," he said, closing the tap and shaking his foot out.

"Where to now?" asked Ackerman.

"*If* Eddie's alive," Criswell said heading for his limo, "he might be hiding in my car until the heat's off."

Ackerman followed. "Now there's an idea!"

The chauffeur saw Criswell approach. He hurried to open the passenger door as Criswell asked, "Chalky, did Ed come this way?"

"Isn't Mr. Wood at the funeral, sir?" asked Chalky.

"Criswell," said Breckinridge with a pleasant smile. "Lovely day for a funeral, wot?"

"Hi, Bunny," said Criswell. "When did you get here?"

"I only just this instant arrived." Breckinridge looked around casually as he pocketed his handkerchief. "Lost Mr. Wood, have you?"

Looking inside, Criswell saw Kathy and Dolores sitting in opposite seats. "I just wondered if maybe Ed might have come out here." It wasn't likely with Dolores in the car.

Dolores said, "We haven't seen him."

Kathy stepped out of the limousine and asked anxiously, "Couldn't you find Eddie?"

Dolores leaned over and said, "Kathy, I know you have to be crazy to love Ed, but you're certifiable. Do you know that?"

"*You* loved Eddie once!" Kathy shot back, her voice choked with jealousy. "Does that make *you* certifiable, too?"

"Chalky," Criswell asked, "did you see or hear anything funny out here?"

Chalky nodded in the direction of the ladies. "You mean besides Mrs. Wood being thrown out of the funeral home with Miss Dolores and that Mr. Becwar?"

"Yes, besides that."

Chalky shook his head. "No, sir," he said. "Except for that, it's been pretty quiet." He paused a moment, then added, "Well, except for a car backfiring."

"I heard that, too," said Criswell, put his hand on the bulge in his tuxedo jacket. "Are you sure it was a car backfiring?"

"That's what it sounded like, sir," said Chalky. "*Bang! Bang!*"

Kathy put a hand to her mouth. *"Oh, Eddie!"* she gasped. "You don't think—"

Breckinridge patted her shoulder. "Calm yourself, my dear," he said. "No need to jump to hasty conclusions."

Ackerman asked, "Could you tell where the backfire came from?"

Chalky gestured toward Argyle Avenue. "Probably from that street over there, sir."

Kathy began to cry. "You don't think someone shot Eddie? Not my Eddie!"

"No, of course not," Criswell lied, trying to be reassuring. Turning to Chalky, he asked, "Could you see after Kathy until we get back?"

"Yes, sir," Chalky said, holding the door for Kathy, who anxiously lingered with Criswell.

"Don't worry, Kathy," Criswell said, chucking her under the chin. "I'm sure Ed is just laying low."

Kathy looked back at Dolores. "I hope you're right," she said. Dolores eyed Kathy narrowly.

Breckinridge shooed them along. "Do go back to the service. I'll stay and keep the ladies company."

Ackerman and Criswell returned to the mortuary. Forry jerked his thumb back at the parking lot. "That wet spot outside looks like a cover-up to me."

"Did you notice Bunny wiping his shoe?" Cris asked, pointing at his own wet foot. "Mighty suspicious."

Ackerman frowned. "Why would Breckinridge cover up someone else's crime? He couldn't be the shooter. The shooter ran from the parking lot, ditched the gun in the pot, then ran out the back way. At least, that's how it looks."

"Except that Chalky claims the gunshots came from the other side of the building."

"But can the chauffeur be trusted?"

"I used to think so."

"Shouldn't we call the police?"

Cris shook his head. "They'd classify Eddie as a missing person. Eddie has to be missing 48 hours before the police will do anything. Unless somebody finds—well, you know. Only *then* does it become a homicide."

"So what do we do now?"

Criswell sighed. "We're in a mortuary. We look for a body."

Criswell and Ackerman entered the casket showroom.

"Maybe," Ackerman suggested, "the killer dumped Wood's body in one of these coffins."

Criswell shook his head. "I don't see how. All these caskets are wide open." He pointed down the private hallway. "That's where Dolores took Eddie."

Searching the hallway, something on the floor near the supply closet caught Criswell's eye. "Hello, what have we here?"

"Find something incriminating?"

"I don't know how incriminating it is," said Criswell, picking up the object. "But it's a film can." He opened it. "An empty film can."

"Where do you suppose that came from?"

"Eddie had some footage of Armand in it. He must have dropped it in the struggle with Dolores."

"Why did he bring that to the funeral?"

Criswell pocket the film can. "He said he wanted to put it in Armand's coffin. You know, as a sort of tribute. Only—"

"Only what?"

"I don't know, just something funny that happened between Eddie and Chalky before." He shrugged. "It's probably nothing." He nodded toward the door leading to the garage. "That's probably where the suspect went."

"Lead the way, Sherlock."

Inside the garage, Criswell and Ackerman came upon a body bag strapped to a gurney. Steinmetz and a young assistant were wrestling to get a second body bag out of the back of a coach and onto a second gurney. As he was securing the body bag to the gurney, Steinmetz spotted Criswell and Ackerman.

"Hello," said Criswell, waving.

Steinmetz scowled disapprovingly as he pushed the gurney toward them. "Oh," he said flatly. "You're with the Tesla funeral." He jerked his head at his assistant. "I heard what went on. Are you going to cause trouble, too?" He parked the gurney beside its twin.

Ackerman asked, "Did you happen to see Ed Wood back here anywhere?"

"No, sir," said the embalmer. "I only just arrived with fresh deliveries. But Scott here had a look around earlier." He made a sweeping gesture. "Do you see your friend anywhere?"

Criswell asked, "Mind if we have look in that other coach over there?"

Steinmetz crossed his arms defiantly. "You're not allowed back here."

"Please," said Criswell, "I'm a mortician's son. And we're worried about Eddie."

Begrudgingly Steinmetz took them to the coach and opened the rear door displaying nothing in the back but an empty gurney and a couple of folded up body bags and some gray blankets. "Satisfied?" asked Steinmetz, shutting the door.

"Is this the only other coach?" asked Ackerman.

"We have a hearse waiting out front to take Mr. Tesla to Holy Cross Cemetery."

Criswell nodded back at the body bags on the waiting gurneys. "Mind if we have a look in those?"

"Oh, I see," Steinmetz scoffed as he approached the bags. "You think your friend might be in either of these? I would never show disrespect to the dead by hiding someone in an occupied body bag." He reached for the zipper on the first bag, then hesitated. "I should warn you," he said earnestly, "it's not pretty. Just picked the bodies up from the County Morgue." He nodded at the second body bag. "Double suicide."

Ackerman smiled. "I think we can take it."

Steinmetz shrugged. "Suit yourself." Before unzipping the bag, he said to the corpse within, "Forgive me, my dear. But these busybodies want a peak at you." The girl inside the body bag was naked; her skin displayed a pinkish blush. A sutured "Y" incision ran over both clavicles and down between her once pert breasts, all the way to the pubic bone. "Carbon monoxide poisoning," Steinmetz explained as he zipped up the bag. "She was barely 16 years old. The other one, the boyfriend, he was 17." Approaching the second bag, he said, "Both came from affluent families with everything to live for. Didn't you, young Mr. Irwin?" He unzipped the second body bag. The boy sported the same autopsy scars and had the same blushing pink skin. "Carbon monoxide gives the skin a nice healthy color so, in a strange way, they made my job a little easier." Zipping up the bag, the embalmer added, "She and the boyfriend chose to asphyxiate themselves in the garage belonging to the boy's parents. Imagine coming home and finding these two in the front seat of the boy's sports car, the garage choked with fumes—such a waste. No note, although I understand the boy aspired to be a professional baseball player—until he was benched after a sports-related injury. But surely *that* couldn't have been the reason for *both of them* to kill themselves."

"Did any of your recent deliveries leak?" Criswell asked. "It looks like somebody's been hosing things down in your parking lot."

"So?" asked Steinmetz.

"We found bloody footprints in your foyer."

Ackerman concurred. "They were on the rug by the side door."

Steinmetz sighed. "Mister, we try to keep things tidy at Hollywood Mortuary, but we're a high volume business. Every now and then some leakage is bound to happen."

"Did anything like that happen today?" asked Criswell.

Steinmetz jerked his head toward his young assistant. "We get student embalmers all the time. They're notoriously careless."

Ackerman asked, "Did either of you hose down the lot?"

"Not me," said the assistant.

"Like I told you already," Steinmetz insisted. "I only just now got here. It might have been the funeral director or any of the staff. Why do you ask?"

"We're just worried about Eddie," said Criswell.

Ackerman asked, "Why wasn't anyone from the funeral home in the embalming room?"

"Preparation room," Steinmetz corrected. "They don't call it an embalming room anymore. Again, why do you ask?"

"Because," said Criswell, "my friend here assumes rightly that if someone from the funeral home had been in the preparation room, they would have ejected Dolores, Eddie and Becwar immediately."

"Of course they would. There are health laws, you know. No one, not even family members are allowed back there; authorized licensed persons only." Steinmetz added with significance, "As I said already, you two shouldn't even be back *here*."

"Still," asked Criswell, "why was the preparation room left unattended?"

"I was out collecting these two," Steinmetz said, indicating the body bags. "My assistant here was waiting in the garage for my return."

"The whole time?" Criswell pounced.

"No," Scott admitted. "Mr. Fleet wanted me to go chasing after your friend and I wouldn't do it. Your friend ran up the back stairs. Then Mr. Fleet wanted me to wait by the stairs and ambush him. That's when I decided to go out for a smoke, instead. I'm not paid to chase after crazies."

"Did you smoke here in the garage?"

"No, just outside," he said, pointing towards Argyle Avenue. "They don't like us smoking in the garage."

"Fire hazard," Steinmetz explained. "We work with a lot of volatile chemicals."

"Where did Mr. Fleet go?

The assistant pointed. "He was attending to Mr. Jeffrey when Mr. Bruckner shouted for help. Mr. Jeffrey was left out in the hall."

"Whose Mr. Jeffrey?" asked Ackerman.

"Mr. Jeffrey," Steinmetz said, "is the new occupant of Slumber Room A. Just so you know, the Tesla Funeral isn't the only one we've got scheduled today. Although it does seem like it."

"And Mr. Fleet was doing what?" asked Ackerman.

"Like I said, we're a high volume business. I left Mr. Jeffrey already casketed and in the hallway for Mr. Fleet. So I presume he took care of things while I took care of things. At least until you folks made such a fuss."

Ackerman asked, "Are any of your funeral coaches prone to backfire?"

"Backfire? I should say not! We have a strict maintenance schedule for all our vehicles. Besides, apart from Jack Benny's Maxwell, cars don't backfire anymore."

"Thank you," said Criswell, pulling out his wallet and producing a business card. "If Eddie should come back, or if you should happen upon anything important, please give me a call at my office." He discretely slipped Steinmetz a folded $10 bill under the business card.

Steinmetz pocketed the money and examined the card. He looked up and gave Criswell an appraising look. "You're a psychic?"

"So they say," Criswell answered modestly.

Steinmetz stuck the card in his pocket and smiled. "If you're so psychic what do you need my help for?"

As the embalmer and his assistant pushed their cargo into the mortuary, a notion struck Criswell. "Hold it a second!"

"Now what?" Steinmetz asked.

"May I see that boy again?"

Steinmetz sighed and unzipped the body bag. Criswell said, "I've seen this boy someplace before. I just can't remember where."

"Can I go now?" asked Steinmetz. "It's a warm day and I want to get these two into the cooler."

"Yes, I'm sorry," said Criswell. "Only now it's going to bother me, because I know I've seen that boy before."

"I suggest you get back to the chapel before Mr. Bruckner finds you," said Steinmetz. "Go out that way," he said, pointing to the garage's outside door. "I don't want the boss catching you."

Criswell and Ackerman walked up Argyle Avenue. As they strolled along, Ackerman asked, "Where does this leave our investigation?"

Criswell shrugged. "I don't know. Nothing makes sense, starting with the killer's footprints. They're all wrong."

"Wrong in what way?"

Cris stopped. "If the killer dragged Eddie's body, he'd be walking backward like this," he said, acting out the action, "but the footprints show the killer was walking forward." Remembering how the footprints were placed he added, "Actually, he wasn't so much walking as limping."

Ackerman shrugged. "Maybe the killer carried Ed fireman style. That might also explain the limping gate."

"Across the shoulder?" Criswell shouldered an imaginary corpse. "Yes, the feet would have to be planted wider apart to compensate for the added weight." He straightened up. "But how did the killer move the body without being seen? People were pouring into the chapel and Dolores, Becwar, and Kathy were being escorted out of the building. The hallway was a heavy traffic area most of the time."

"Maybe we were wrong about the killer's escape route. He didn't go through the showroom at all." Ackerman acted out the action as he spoke. "Maybe he came in shouldering the body, ditched the gun, was about to run out the back when he saw people coming and ran up the front stairs, then through a second floor hallway, and down the back stairs."

Just then there was a *click!* that startled Criswell and Ackerman. Two tourists, a couple of fresh-faced newlyweds, had been watching their performance and the husband had just taken a picture.

"Thanks, guys," the husband smiled.

"I've heard all about street theater," the wife said. "You two are even better than those actors in the parking lot."

Cris and Forry exchanged excited looks. Criswell asked, "Oh, you liked that show in the parking lot, too, did you?"

"Oh, yes," said the husband. "Very convincing the way that guy shot that girl."

"What guy and what girl?" Ackerman asked.

"Well," said the wife, "we heard a shot, Harry and me. We ran into the parking lot and there was this man and a woman in black. The man looked a little like Errol Flynn. He was holding a gun."

"Just like the kind the Lone Ranger uses," said the Harry. "All silver."

"Then what happened?" asked Criswell.

The wife looked confused. "Don't you know? It's *your* play."

Ackerman smiled. "Well, this is audience participation. We're playing detectives and you're the witnesses."

"Oh, Harry!" the wife gushed. "I always wanted to do one of those murder mystery things!" She became very serious and said, "Well, detective, the woman in black was slumped in the man's arms. He looked scared, like maybe they were struggling with the gun and it went off by accident."

"I took a picture," said Harry. "The man saw me and hightailed it back inside the funeral home, leaving the woman dead on the ground."

"Pictures?" Ackerman smiled. "Did you say you *got* pictures? Of the crime?"

"Yep!" the husband said proudly.

"Then what happened?" Criswell anxiously asked.

"Then," said the wife, "this very well dressed man said in a British accent; 'Thank you for participating in our little play, old chaps.'"

"Breckinridge," Criswell whispered to Ackerman.

"Then Harry and me went to the drug store across the street."

"To buy some more film," said Harry, indicating his camera.

This gave Criswell an idea. He grabbed his lapels and said officiously, "Congratulations, both of you! On behalf of KLAC and Crime Stoppers, I say job well done!"

Harry smiled. "Gosh, did we win something?"

"I should say so! That is *if* you got clear incriminating photos showing the faces of both the perpetrator and his victim."

"Oh, we sure did!" said Harry.

"In that case, you win—"

"What?" asked Margaret. "What do we win?"

"Uh," said Criswell, stymied.

"You win," said Ackerman stepping in, "a television appearance!" He patted Criswell on the back, "With none other than Charles Criswell King, Psychic to the Stars!"

The young wife screamed for joy.

"And," added Criswell, "a lifetime supply of Criswell's Family Formula!"

"Wow!" said Harry. "Did you hear that, Margaret?"

"*But*," said Criswell, "in order to collect your fabulous prizes, we need the evidence. So if you'd just give us the roll of film—"

Harry said, "It's in the drugstore getting developed."

"Then if you'd just turn over your claim ticket—"

"But what about our vacation pictures?" asked Margaret.

"Oh, those," Ackerman said with a dismissive wave. "We'd return them to you, of course."

"Yes," Criswell assured them. "We just need the crime photos."

Margaret gave her husband an anxious look. "But, Harry, what about those other pictures? You know, the ones you talked me into posing for on the beach?"

Harry looked imploringly to Margaret. "Come on, honey! It was only a bathing suit."

"But the way you had me posing in the bathing suit, well, you know." She blushed.

"I'm afraid," said Criswell, "that if you want the reward, you have to give us the evidence."

"Yeah, honey," Harry pleaded. "They won't care about a couple of cheesecake shots."

"Well," said Margaret, furrowing her brow. Finally, she said, "I guess it's okay." She reaching into her bag and handed Criswell the claim ticket. "We're staying over at the Las Palmas Hotel, Room 310." She added shyly, "Please don't look at those beach pictures."

"You have our word," Ackerman promised.

"Thank you, Crime Stoppers," Criswell said in his over dramatic delivery. "And congratulations on keeping crime off of our streets!"

After the excited tourists had moved on, Ackerman asked, "So now it looks like Ed was the shooter—and he shot a mysterious woman in black."

"A mysterious woman in black who was trying to kill *him*," Criswell deduced, "but Ed used his hand-to-hand combat training to disarm her."

"But the gun went off during the struggle."

"She died."

"He panicked."

"The body was left in the parking lot."

"And *Breckinridge* is behind the cover-up."

"That means Chalky was in on it." Criswell started. "But are they covering things up to help Ed escape the assassins, or covering up a bungled assassination attempt *on* Ed?"

"Who knows? But one thing's for sure. Ed Wood is alive and laying low somewhere. But what happened to the body of the woman in black?"

"Good question," said Criswell. Consulting his watch, he added, "But looking for it will have to wait. Armand's funeral must be over by now." He frowned. "Oh, God, you don't think they stuck her body in the trunk of my car, do you?"

"If the chauffeur is in on it, that's a distinct possibility." Ackerman held his hand out expectantly. "Give me the claim ticket. You go back to the funeral and see that Hope and Andreas get to the cemetery. I'll go to the drug store and wait for the film to get developed."

"Good idea," Criswell said, handing the ticket over.

"Make an excuse to look in the trunk before you take off."

"Right," Cris nodded. "And if you miss the service at the cemetery, we'll meet back at my office." He handed Ackerman a business card. "This is the address."

"Okay." Forry pocketed the card and stopped on the curb to look both ways. "Now we'll see if this mystery has a photo finish," he said, and then hurried across the street to the drug store.

Criswell could only wince at the terrible pun.

"Where have you been?" Hope demanded. "The service is over!" She looked over Criswell's shoulder. "Where the hell is Forry? He's supposed to drive me!"

"He had to leave, but I'll see you and Andreas get to the cemetery."

"Fine, whatever," she said. "The bastard convinces me to let him drive me and then he sticks me and Andreas with you." Criswell was about to explain when she hushed him with a peevish wave. "Forget it! Look, Ed Wood left us high and dry and we need another pallbearer. So you're elected, hotshot."

She grabbed Criswell's arm and steered him into an empty chair next to the other pallbearers. That's when Hope noticed Marlowe sitting where Orby ought to have been. "You son of a bitch," she said. "What are you doing there?" She called Orby over and said, "Andreas, you're the pallbearer. You sit here!" When Marlowe refused to move, Hope snarled, "Get outta that fucking chair!"

That's when an exasperated Mr. Bruckner hurried over. "Never mind about that boy," he snapped irritably. "He has caused quite enough bother already."

Hope eyed him suspiciously. "What the hell is *that* supposed to mean?"

Mr. Bruckner said, "Never you mind. Now please sit down!" Mopping his forehead again, he told Criswell and the other pallbearers to wait for his signal.

When the moment arrived, the manager waved to the pallbearers with his by now sweat-saturated handkerchief. The five men stood up and each took a handle on the coffin and hoisted it off the bier. Slowly they marched in unison down the aisle and out the front door. The other members of the funeral party followed them. Once outside, Marlowe made sure his face was well in view of cameras when newspaper photographers' flashbulbs popped off.

Criswell helped slide the coffin into the back of the waiting hearse. The silver-plated gun in his pocket bumped up against him, reminding Criswell of the possibility that someone wanted to make Ed Wood a *dead* Wood.

Soon after, Criswell, Maila, and Marco, along with an embittered Hope Tesla and a glum Andreas Orby, piled into the limousine where Kathy and Dolores sat waiting and Breckinridge sat between them, regaling them with stories.

"So, Dolores," Criswell asked, "did you come in your own car or do you need a lift?"

"A friend dropped me off," she said. "So if you don't mind—"

"Not at all! Tag along with the rest of us." Criswell smiled at Breckinridge. "How about you, Bunny? There's still plenty of room," he said.

"No thanks, dear boy," Bunny replied, climbing over Kathy to get out. "I have my own car," he indicated a flashy Italian convertible. "Besides, I've decided to skip the burial. They're ever so depressing, don't you think?"

"Suit yourself." Criswell paused. "Uh, Chalky," he called.

The chauffeur saluted. "Yes, sir?"

"I need something from the trunk."

"Yes, sir."

Criswell watched Chalky closely for any signs of anxiety. The chauffeur flinching not so much as an eyelash, Chalky very calmly marched behind the limousine and unlocked the trunk. He opened it and stepped back so Criswell could inspect it. There was absolutely nothing incriminating inside. It was empty. No jack. No tire iron. No spare. No anything.

"What did you need, sir?" asked Chalky.

"Uh," Criswell ventured, "the jack and spare tire?"

"I don't know, sir. Do you really think we need them?"

"I guess we won't need one right now, no." Criswell gestured for Chalky to shut the trunk and then got in the passenger compartment. Chalky closed the door after him. Waiting for the chauffeur to get behind the wheel, Cris picked up the limousine telephone. "We're ready, Chalky."

"Yes, sir." Chalky turned on the headlights and waited. Lillian and Armand Jr.'s car took the lead behind the hearse, much to Hope's annoyance. "That bitch," she growled.

While Chalky waited to pull into the funeral procession, Criswell turned around and waved to Breckinridge. Bunny was leaning against the rear bumper of his sports car and waved back jauntily. As Breckinridge turned to go, he seemed to notice something about his trunk just as Chalky pulled out and made a right turn onto Hollywood Boulevard. The limousine was the last car in the procession.

Criswell kept watching from the rear window as Bunny poked what looked like a strap back inside the trunk of his sports car. It was then that Criswell caught a glimpse of something. "Son of a bitch," Criswell muttered. He sat back and frowned. "That looked like a body bag."

"What did you say?" asked Hope.

"Uh, nothing." *They came prepared to hide a body,* Criswell thought. He felt the empty film can in his pocket. Silently he wondered, *Was there something in this film can that was worth killing someone over? What does this have to do with Armand's mysterious envelope? Why did Eddie tell me to watch my mail? What did he send me?*

Criswell got the awful feeling that he was the next victim in an utterly insane and totally inexplicable murder plot.

As the procession drove slowly away, Mr. Fleet and Mr. Bruckner stood outside the mortuary and exhaled a collective sigh of relief.

"I'm glad that's over," Mr. Bruckner said.

"Amen," Mr. Fleet agreed.

Their relief was short-lived. Steinmetz stepped from the funeral home and cleared his throat. "Mr. Bruckner. Mr. Fleet," he announced calmly. "There's a problem."

"*Now* what?" groaned Mr. Bruckner.

"It's Mr. Fleet's fault. I told you, didn't I?" Steinmetz said, wagging an accusing finger in Mr. Fleet's face. "I warned you about stealing from the dead. They don't care for that sort of thing and now Mr. Tesla is showing his displeasure!"

"Stealing from the dead?" asked Mr. Bruckner, giving the funeral director a searching look.

"It's nothing," Mr. Fleet assured him. "Just a cigar." Before Mr. Fleet could say anything more, a commotion erupted from the slumber room. Sighing, Mr. Bruckner asked, "What's all the fuss now?"

Mrs. Gladys Parker Jeffrey was both crying and angry all at the same time. "Which of you is responsible for this outrage!" she demanded. "Where's my Dick?"

Mr. Bruckner reacted with a start. "I beg your pardon?"

"My husband Richard is gone!" she said, gesturing back at the slumber room. "Some practical joker has put a spook show dummy in his place! I'll sue!"

Mr. Fleet and Mr. Bruckner exchanged looks of horror, and then followed the fuming Mrs. Jeffrey to the slumber room. Family and friends were huddled around a high-end all-wooden casket with silver handles. Mr. Fleet' assistant stood by the open casket, pale with fright. Lying in peaceful repose within the casket was none other than "Dracula" Tesla.

Steinmetz looked over their shoulders and made the observation, "At least, Mr. Tesla traded-up his accommodations."

A very unhinged Mr. Bruckner ran outside. "Let's not panic," he said, trying not to pull his hair out. "We can fix this! If Mr. Tesla is here, then Mr. Jeffrey must be in Mr. Tesla's casket! Don't ask me how. All we have to do is intercept the funeral procession at the cemetery before they have a chance to bury the wrong person!"

"I don't know who or what they're burying," Steinmetz said smugly. "But it's definitely *not* Mr. Jeffrey in Mr. Tesla's casket."

"How can you be so sure?" Mr. Fleet demanded.

"Because that was the reason I came out to get you in the first place." Steinmetz gestured for them to follow. "This way, please." He led the funeral directors and Mrs. Jeffrey to the private hallway, and casually opened the supply closet. Standing stiffly with arms dangling at the sides, rather than folded across the chest as Steinmetz had arranged them, was the corpse of the late Mr. Richard Jeffrey, a middle-aged man with gray hair at the temples. The corpse teetered forward. Mr. Steinmetz caught the body before it fell.

Mrs. Jeffrey chose that moment to faint and nobody had the wits to catch her.


Meanwhile, somewhere on Hollywood Boulevard, Criswell rolled down his window and stuck his head out in bewilderment. "Where's the hearse going?" he asked.

For some inexplicable reason, the hearse had taken a detour down North Gower Street. Criswell pointed ahead. "We have to take the Hollywood Freeway to get to Holy Cross Cemetery." The buzzer sounded on the car telephone. Criswell picked up.

"Sir," the chauffeur said, "the hearse is—"

"I know," said Criswell stunned.

"Should I follow it, sir?" asked Chalky.

Watching the procession following the wayward hearse, Criswell said, "I guess so." Hanging up, he turned to Kathy. "Now what do you make of that?"

"I don't really care," she said. "I just want my Eddie back."

Dolores frowned at Kathy. "You need to see a shrink. Do you know that?"

Andreas Orby sat quietly, looking very guilty about something.

Paul Marco shrugged. "Maybe Armand's going for a joy ride."

The "joy ride" took them up North Gower Street and across Yuka to Vine Street. As the hearse turned South on Vine, Maila said, "We're heading for Hollywood and Vine."

Hope smirked. "You wanna know something funny? Armand used to walk to Hollywood and Vine for his newspapers and cigars."

"Spooky," Marco said with a shudder.

The hearse turned right onto Hollywood Boulevard—the opposite direction to where they needed to be.

"Now what's going on?" asked Criswell. The car phone buzzed again. "What is it, Chalky?"

"I don't see the hearse anymore, sir."

"What!"

"It turned down Highland Avenue—and then just disappeared."

Criswell looked out the window again. The rest of the funeral procession had pulled over in front of the Hollywood Historama, the very same wax museum where Dolores Fuller and Armand Tesla once posed for a number of publicity photos. Mourners and family members got out of their cars and gathered on the sidewalk, looking very lost. Needless to say, Lillian and Armand Jr. were fit to be tied. Hope was ecstatic. "So Lillian wanted a funeral! Serves that bitch right!" She threw her head back and laughed a croaking smoker's laugh.

Maila pointed behind them. "THERE IT IS!"

The hearse pulled onto Hollywood Boulevard from Las Palmas and waited at the light for the mourners to get back in their cars and follow.

"Okay," said Criswell. "That's just bizarre." The car phone buzzed again. "I see it, Chalky."

"Should I honk the horn and alert the rest of the funeral procession, sir?"

"Good idea." As Chalky honked the horn, Criswell hung out the window and shouted, "THE HEARSE IS WAITING AT THE LIGHT! FOLLOW US!"

The mourners hurried back to their cars with Criswell's limousine leading the way.

"I gotta say this for Armand," Hope smiled. "He's got one hell of a sense of humor!" She turned to look out the rear window. "Now Lillian and Armand Jr. are the caboose on this train to hell!" Sticking her head out the window, she shouted, "KISS MY ASS, LILLIAN!"

# Part Three


The Vampire's Tomb.

Slowly, they marched in unison.

# Chapter 17

*"They die dead. I die live."*
— **Armand Tesla**, *Son of Frankenstein* (1939)

If you were to consult the map of Holy Cross Cemetery provided by the Business Office (Open Monday to Friday 8 a.m. — 4:30 p.m., Saturday 8 a.m. — 4 p.m.), you will find Armand Tesla's burial plot; Plot L120, Space 1 in Section F, which the map key will identify as Holy Rosary. Here the gravesites are guarded by an artificial hillside. Dotted with beautiful lavender blossoms and green foliage and sheltered beneath lush shade trees, the cemetery map identifies the hill simply as the Grotto. Up a short flight of seven steps and set inside the largest of the Grotto's three caves is an altar where, as the map explains, daily Mass is performed "for all the faithful who rest in this Cemetery." Just inside the mouth of a smaller cave slightly higher in the Grotto stands a white marble statue of the Blessed Virgin. Day and night she watches over those aforementioned sleeping faithful, but only one of those faithful would be buried in a cape.

The Grotto and its grassy hillside looks out onto the M-G-M film studios, assuring that Count Dracula would soon be enjoying the finest in Northern exposures. It was at M-G-M that a young Armand Tesla was alleged to have played a bit part in Lon Chaney Sr.'s silent classic, *He Who Gets Slapped.*

The burial plot is about three rows from the Grotto and not far from the winding northward road that forks to the left of the main gate on Slauson Avenue. In later years, Armand would share the Grotto with close neighbors Bing Crosby in Plot L119, space 1 and "Tin Man" Jack Haley in L100, space 2. But that wouldn't be for some time. For the moment, Armand Tesla's neighbors were either forgotten Silent Era stars like Gypsy Abbott, or former wives of famous stars like Bing Crosby's first wife Lee Crosby. Ironically, Armand Tesla, who felt he had been denied top billing, especially when teamed with stars like Boris Karloff, would finally have the distinction of being the most famous "name" resident interred in Holy Rosary.

Everything was in readiness for his interment. Holy Cross Cemetery's resident padre, Father Harold Ross, stood graveside in priestly finery, holding his prayer book. A stainless steel and chrome casket-lowering device had been set up over a six-foot deep rectangular hole that had been excavated with a backhoe. An evergreen-colored chapel tent had been erected to shield both mourners and Vampire Count from the purifying rays of the California sun. A simple stone flush monument with the inscription, "Armand Tesla, Beloved Father, 1882—1956," was ready to be put into place once the hole had been filled and covered over by a "Lifetime Green" artificial grass mat.

In fact, there were only two things lacking in this peaceful scene, namely the guest of honor and the bereaved. Father Ross checked his watch. It was nearly four o'clock. Looking up, he saw a funeral coach pass through the main gates.

"Finally," he said. Clearing his throat, the priest opened his prayer book to the Last Rites. Looking over his reading glasses, Father Ross was startled to see the funeral coach parking by the graveside without a procession following it. He looked down the road. He waited. But there were no other cars.

What Father Ross didn't know was that this was the coach hastily dispatched from Hollywood Mortuary with Armand Tesla reposing quietly in a cardboard box. A frantic Ralph Fleet rolled down the window and gawked at the unoccupied folding chairs under the chapel tent and at the flustered priest staring back at him. "Where the hell is everybody?" he said.

"I better call Mr. Bruckner." The driver reached for the radiophone.

"NO!" Mr. Fleet said, grabbing the handset. "We'll just have to wait."

Mr. Fleet reached into his breast pocket for what had once been Armand's post mortem cigar. He slipped the stogie out of its tube and bit off the end. "Earl, have you got a light?"

The driver produced a lighter, flipped it open and struck the flint wheel. "So what happened to the hearse?" he asked.

Puffing on the cigar, the frustrated funeral director exhaled blue smoke through his nostrils. "Oh, who knows? Maybe Manny took a wrong turn." He frowned at the cigar. "God, for an expensive cigar, this thing tastes terrible!"

"Phew!" Earl pinched his nostrils closed and grimaced as he complained nasally, "What's that thing made with? Smells like garlic."

Mr. Fleet shrugged as he took another puff. "You know these Hungarians. They put garlic in everything." He glanced at the cardboard box resting in the rear. "Shame on you, Mr. Tesla, ruining a fine Cuban cigar like this." He caught himself talking to a dead man and sighed. "I've been hanging around Steinmetz too much."

Rolling down his window, Earl said, "Do you mind aiming the smoke out your window?"

"Fine." Mr. Fleet sighed and took another long drag.

Father Ross considered himself a patient man, but this was ridiculous. He marched purposefully up to the coach and bent down to ask where the rest of the funeral was, when Mr. Fleet turned his head and exhaled a plume of foul smelling smoke right in the priest's face. Father Ross grimaced and coughed and waved away smoke with his prayer book.

"Oh! I'm sorry, Father!" Mr. Fleet said with a start. "I didn't see you there."

Between hacking coughs, the priest sternly asked, "Is this… the Tesla… funeral?"

"Part of it," Mr. Fleet said.

Through fits of coughing, Father Ross said, "Well past four…cemetery closes…sundown…Most…irregular!"

"You don't know the half of it, Father," said Mr. Fleet. He took another long drag on his cigar. Smoke curled from his mouth in Earl's direction as he sighed heavily. "This whole day has been most irregular." Trying to be positive, he added, "I'm sure the rest of the procession will be here shortly."

Holding his nose, Father Ross said in a nasal twang, "I'll wait another 30 minutes, but no longer!" He marched back to the open grave and sat in one of the folding chairs.

Thirty minutes had passed and Father Ross was fed up. He was about to call it quits and return to the rectory when he saw the Tesla procession passing through the main gate. "It's about time!" he grumbled. He fumbled through his prayer book for the page containing the Last Rites. Standing at the open grave, he looked over his glasses at the approaching cars and realized, much to his confusion, that another Hollywood Mortuary funeral coach was leading the procession. "Two hearses?" he exclaimed.

Mr. Fleet looked up in the rearview mirror as Manny's coach pulled up behind them. He growled, "*Finally!*" as he snuffed the cigar butt out in the dashboard ashtray. He got out and slammed the door, and then stormed up to the hearse and motioned for Manny to get out.

Chalky opened the door of the Imperial 8 for Criswell, his friends, and the widow Tesla. The rest of the mourners emerged from their cars and were about to walk toward the gravesite when Mr. Fleet drew their attention by shouting, "What are you, Manny? Doped up or drunk or lord knows what?" The gathering bereaved watched with great interest as the driver made an inaudible excuse that caused the funeral director to exclaim loudly, "A *ghost!* You expect me to believe that a *ghost* told you to make a detour?"

Cris joined the five pallbearers, and as they approached the hearse, Kathy and Dolores tried to steer Hope graveside. But the widow was less interested in grieving and more interested in eavesdropping. Turning to Kathy, Hope said, "Let's go see what the hell the fuss is about."

They arrived in time to witness the driver pleading, "But it's the truth, boss! I heard the coffin open! I looked, but didn't see anybody in the back—but I *heard* Tesla!"

Mr. Fleet sniffed Manny's breath. "You don't smell like you've been drinking," he concluded while scratching his chin skeptically, "but I don't know."

"He told me to drive him to Hollywood and Vine! Then he told me to pull up in back of the Wax Museum! It's the God's honest truth, I swear!"

"That's the most ridiculous—" Mr. Fleet stopped abruptly when he noticed the mourners and press people advancing on them. "We'll talk about this later," he threatened, leaving Manny to stew for a bit.

Affecting a calm demeanor, the funeral director came forward to meet the pallbearers and bereaved. The press crowded around the hearse like vultures around a carcass. Mr. Fleet felt a little green around the gills as he smiled apologetically. "I'm sorry for the inconvenience," he began, "but there appears to have been some kind of mix-up."

The pallbearers and mourners exchanged confused looks while the press smirked with gleeful anticipation of another donnybrook.

"Mix-up?" Marlowe asked.

"What sort of mix-up?" Criswell asked.

Mr. Fleet was about to explain, when Lillian and Armand Jr. pushed through the crowd and confronted the funeral director. "I want that hearse driver fired!" an outraged Lillian demanded.

Hope put in her usual two-cents worth. "Nobody's firing that driver," she said. "He did good putting *me* where I ought to have been all along!" Glaring at Lillian, she added with emphasis, "*Up front* with *my* husband!"

Armand Jr. directed his anger squarely at the funeral director. "My mother and I have a good mind to sue!"

"Oh, listen to him!" Hope mocked. "Not even in law school and already talking like an ambulance chaser!" She jerked her thumb at the coach. "Or do I mean hearse chaser?"

Armand Jr. glowered. "I've had just about all I'm gonna take from you!"

Hope got in Armand Jr.'s face. "Or what? You gonna hit me? Go ahead! Hit me! Then I'll sue *you*, asshole!"

Mr. Fleet held up his hands in an effort to keep order. "PLEASE!" he said. "I'm sorry for the confusion. I don't know why Manny did what he did. I do apologize. But we've got a situation that needs fixing."

"You bet your life we do!" Armand Jr. said.

"What sort of a situation?" Criswell calmly asked.

Mr. Fleet scratched his eyebrow nervously as he tried to think of the most diplomatic way of saying what had to be said. "Well," he ventured, feeling a bit out of breath. "I don't know…quite how it happened, but Mr. Tesla isn't…in his casket. He's, uh, in the coach back there."

Lillian's eyes grew wide with shock. "WHAT!"

Andreas Orby approached with Tor Johnson and his wife. The teenager looked scared as Mr. Fleet explained, "Uh, I know you're not going to believe this, but somehow Mr. Tesla…wound up…," he nervously tugged on his collar and squeaked, "…in the wrong casket."

Lillian's eyes grew even wider with shock, if that were physically possible. "THE WRONG CASKET?" she exclaimed.

Mr. Fleet nodded sheepishly. "Don't ask me how, but that's what happened. He was in a casket reserved for a Mr. Jeffrey, and Mr. Jeffrey was—well, never mind about where Mr. Jeffrey was. Anyway, to make a long story short, you were about to bury…an empty casket."

Tor asked, "What is going on?"

"Didn't you hear?" asked Hope, gazing up at the wrestler. "Armand's been playing musical coffins and we were gonna bury an empty casket."

"At least," Mr. Fleet said, "we *think* it's an empty casket. We're not really sure at this point." He could feel a sudden wave of nausea.

Kathy Wood's face went pale with horror. "OH NO!" she screamed. She ran to the hearse and began pulling frantically on the handle. "EDDIE! MY EDDIE!"

Dolores pulled Kathy away and slapped her face. "SNAP OUT OF IT!" she shouted, and then shook her by the shoulders. "Really, Kathy, I think you need to see a doctor! WAKE UP!"

"Why?" Kathy broke free of Dolores's grip and cried, "You think I'm crazy just because I love my husband? You're the sick one, Dolores. You're still in love with him! I KNOW IT!" She returned Dolores's slap. Dolores held her smarting cheek as Kathy ran to Criswell and buried her face in his shoulder. "I just know Eddie's in that coffin!" she sobbed.

Criswell tried to soothe her as he addressed the funeral director. "Look, why don't we just take out the coffin and see if there's anyone in it?"

"By all means," said Mr. Fleet, rubbing his throbbing temples as he cleared his throat nervously. "Then we can put Mr. Tesla back where he belongs and lay him to rest."

He motioned for Manny to open the back door.

"Wow," Marco commented aloud, "Armand's had a pretty active day — for a dead guy." Adding regretfully, "I guess I shouldn't have tickled him under the chin."

The pallbearers were about to reach in the back of the hearse and rolled out the casket when Tor stepped up and said, "Let me." Tor handed the floral display to one of the pallbearers, then single-handedly removed the casket and hefted it in his arms. "It is too light," he said. "Don't worry, Kathy. There nobody in here." Kathy breathed a sigh of relief as Tor gently laid the casket on the ground.

The wrestler's observations were soon confirmed when Mr. Fleet opened the lid and displayed an empty casket. This struck Criswell as rather odd, because from the weight of the casket at the funeral home, it wasn't empty earlier. Leaning in for a closer inspection of the lining, he saw what looked like a heel mark made with dried blood. Andreas Orby joined him to sneak a peek. The teen went pale, and then looked up at Criswell. Their eyes met briefly, and then Orby blushed and looked away. Was that guilt Criswell saw written on the young man's face?

Mr. Fleet anxiously said, "If you don't mind, please, will the pallbearers bring the casket over to the coach so we can put Mr. Tesla where he belongs?" The other pallbearers joined Criswell and together they hoisted the empty casket and followed the funeral director. Tor brought the flowers.

As he led the way, Mr. Fleet loosened his collar and necktie. He felt like he was about to throw up. As they approached the coach, they found Earl on all fours, heaving up his lunch on the lawn. *What a picture that will make for the late edition,* Mr. Fleet thought glumly as the press photographers raised their Speed Graflex cameras.

Criswell grew concerned. "Is he going to be okay?"

"He'll be fine," Mr. Fleet said, anxious to get this over with. He opened the rear door and motioned for the pallbearers to remove the box containing Armand Tesla. Since a cardboard box wasn't as rigid as a casket, the five pallbearers and Mr. Fleet had to work in unison under the funeral director's instruction. "That's right," he said. "Don't let it buckle in the middle. Reach under to support the bottom. That's it. Now lay it on the ground." They placed the cardboard box beside Tesla's casket. Mr. Fleet opened the box, revealing Dracula in peaceful repose. Criswell thought wistfully that all they needed to have Tesla open his eyes was for a director to yell, "Cut!"

Mr. Fleet propped opened the casket lid, and then returned to the cardboard box. "Now, we'll just reach under Mr. Tesla and transfer him over." Grabbing one of the sides of the box, he looked at Marlowe. "Help me with this." Together they ripped down the sides, exposing the body. "You," he said to Marlowe, "support the head and shoulders. You two, get the feet. And you," he said to Criswell, "will work with me. We'll use the cape like a stretcher and support his body with it. Roll it up and take hold of it like this. That's right. Okay, everyone, we lift together on three—one, two, *three*."

A heave and a ho later, and Dracula was at rest again in his original burial box. It struck Criswell that the late actor was a lot lighter and a great deal stiffer than he expected him to be. Then again, Armand was getting awfully thin towards the end, and as for stiffness; they didn't call the dead "stiffs" for nothing.

Just as Mr. Fleet was about to close the lid, Hope approached. "Hold it a second," she said. She took off her glove, licked her hand and reached in to smooth down her husband's hair. Satisfied that he looked okay, she nodded. "Go ahead," and then stepped back so the funeral director could close the casket. Tor placed the floral display on the lid as tears began welling up in his eyes again.

The pallbearers bore the casket across the lawn to the Grotto and placed it on the straps of the lowering mechanism. Mr. Fleet stood graveside ready to trip the foot lever that would unwind the straps and lower the casket into the ground.

Father Ross cleared his throat, feeling a bit nauseous. "Into your hands, Father of mercies," he intoned, "we commend our brother, Armand Tesla, in the sure and certain hope that, together with all who have died in Christ, he will rise with him on the last day."

The nausea increased during the Rite of Committal with Final Commendation. Father Ross made it to the final prayer without disgracing himself, or the deceased, by vomiting on his prayer book. "In sure and certain hope of the resurrection to eternal life through our Lord Jesus Christ, we commend to Almighty God our brother Armand Tesla and we commit his body to its resting place. Earth to earth, ashes to ashes, dust to dust. The Lord bless him and keep him, the Lord make his face to shine upon him and be gracious to him, the Lord lift up his countenance upon him and give him peace."

Tor began weeping as Manly P. Hall took the floral display from the casket. He removed a lily and handed it to the widow, and then pulled out another for Lillian. Noting Tor's emotional distress, Hall handed the giant a flower, too. The wrestler took it gratefully.

Father Ross nodded to Mr. Fleet. The funeral director touched the foot pedal. Over the sound of Tor's heavy sobbing, and as the Gypsy violinist played a final farewell dirge, all in attendance watched respectfully as the casket containing the late Armand Tesla slowly descended into the ground. It was as the casket reached the bottom of the six-foot hole that Ralph Fleet grew deathly pale and feared he was going to vomit into the grave. He looked anxiously at the press. Photographers raised their cameras in anticipation of this most embarrassing of moments.

"Get ready, boys," one reporter said. "He looks greener around the gills than the Creature from the Black Lagoon."

Mr. Fleet did not disappoint. But it was not vomiting that was captured on film that afternoon. No, Mr. Fleet gave them a *real* story. The funeral director clutched at his throat, his mouth gasping like a fish out of water, as if he were suffocating in the open air. Before his anxious eyes, flashbulbs exploded as he turned, stumbled and fell backward into the hole, landing on the lid of the bargain-priced casket that crumpled on impact. Mr. Fleet lived just long enough to see the faces of the press peering down at him from the open grave. There was a flash from a Graflex camera, and then—presumably a brighter, beckoning light. We'll never know for sure. Mr. Fleet was dead, and silent.

"Oh, God!" Andreas Orby cried, hugging Kathy Wood for dear life. "It's all my fault! I killed him!"

Kathy tried to quiet him down. "It's not your fault," she said. "How can you say that?"

Orby looked at her with tear-stained eyes. "I helped Mr. Wood escape from the funeral home."

Kathy gasped. "You mean he's still alive?"

"When the funeral directors left the other coffin, and I was there alone to say good-bye to Armand, Mr. Wood's voice came from the other coffin and asked me if the coast was clear. He told me—," the boy hesitated, "—he told me *somebody* was trying to kill him and he had to sneak out. When nobody was looking, he stuck the real dead guy in a closet and got in his coffin. I helped him switch Armand into the other dead guy's coffin, and Mr. Wood got in Armand's coffin."

"But the coffin was empty when it got here," said Kathy. "Where's Eddie now?"

"I don't know." Orby sniffled and wiped his eyes.

"The ghost!" Criswell exclaimed.

Kathy blinked. "Ghost? What ghost?"

"Didn't you hear? The hearse driver claimed that Tesla's ghost spoke to him from the casket. There's a footprint in the lining of the casket, too—evidence that someone may have climbed out."

Kathy smiled. "So Eddie was pretending to be Armand's ghost and he escaped when the driver made a detour!"

"That was my suspicion," said Criswell.

A reporter exclaimed, "What a story! Quick, get a shot of the kid!"

The press fought each other to get close to the young man as Father Ross ran to call the police. He got as far as the last row of chairs before collapsing on the ground.

Criswell acted quickly, loosening the priest's collar and checking his pulse. Father Ross's heart was beating rapidly. "Can't…breathe!" he said, gasping for air.

Reverend Hall hurried to join Criswell. "I'll look after him. You run and call for an ambulance."

"And the police!" Criswell said.

# Chapter 18

Patrolmen Don Johnson and Daniel E. Corby were cruising along Slauson Avenue when the call came through from Dispatch. It was a Code 390 at 3855 West Slauson Avenue. Code 390 meant there was a man down. Officer Johnson responded. As he returned the microphone to the dash cradle he frowned at his partner. "Wait. That address. That's the cemetery." He pointed behind them. They had just passed the main gates. "There's a man down at the cemetery?"

His partner shrugged. "Sure makes things convenient."

With siren blaring and red globe flashing, Officer Corby made a U-turn and drove up to the main gates where Criswell was waiting for them. "It looks like one of the stiffs is trying to hitchhike," said Corby, commenting on Cris's pallor and the tuxedo.

"Only in Hollywood."

"Quickly!" Criswell pointed up the road. "The funeral director died mysteriously and fell into Armand Tesla's grave and Father Ross looks like he's going to die next!"

"Get in," said Johnson, pointing in the back seat.

Hope glared at the patrolmen as they pulled up behind a reporter's car. "It's about time you guys got here," she said.

"Who are you?" Corby asked.

"I'm Armand Tesla's widow."

"Well, please stay back while we work."

"So I can't be up there with my husband, but that clown Hall can play Svengali with the Priest?"

Criswell frowned as he got out of the patrol car. "Do what now?"

"Go have a look for yourselves," Hope grumbled.

A gaggle of reporters followed Criswell and the patrolmen as they hurried to the gravesite. Under the tent, Manly P. Hall was doing his best to keep a gasping Father Ross calm, swinging his gold watch back and forth before the Padre's panicked eyes.

Johnson glared at Hall. "What the hell are you doing?"

"I don't know first aid," Hall explained, "so I'm trying hypnosis instead."

"Is it working?" Criswell asked.

Father Ross turned blue and fainted.

"Not really, no," said Reverend Hall.

Corby turned to his partner. "Break out the oxygen tank."

"Right."

Johnson came back minutes later with the oxygen tank.

"Okay, step aside." Corby slipped the oxygen mask over Father Ross's face and turned the valve. Speed Graflex cameras clicked and flashbulbs popped as the priest clawed at the oxygen mask, his face registering panic. "I don't get it," Corby said, checking the valve and hose. "Oxygen is flowing, he's able to breathe, but he's still suffocating."

A reporter asked, "Could you spell your name, officer?"

Johnson turned on the press. "Hey, knock it off! Give the guy some air! Back off!"

Lillian stepped forward. "I want to know when we can put Armand to rest."

"And you are?" Johnson asked.

"I'm the widow."

"The funeral director's widow? And how did you hear about this?"

"Armand Tesla's widow," Lillian snarled.

Johnson turned to his partner. "How many widows does Tesla have?"

Corby shrugged as Paul Marco pushed his way through the crowd. "Can I help keep order, officers? I played a cop in one of Eddie's movies. Kelton the Cop. Maybe you saw me in *Bride of the Monster*?"

"Can't say I have," said Johnson. "Now stay back!"

Corby jerked his head down the road. "You want to help? Go wait for the ambulance."

Marco saluted. "Will do, officer."

The actor had no sooner taken off down the road when the siren of an ambulance could be heard and seconds later, the ambulance pulled up. Attendants got out as Marco said while pointing at the Grotto, "Up there! The priest is dying!"

While one of the attendants broke out the stretcher, the other hurried over with a first aid kit. He started as a discarded flashbulb burst under his foot, one of many spent flashbulbs littering the gravesite. A photographer getting a picture nearly blinded him. Johnson shoved the photographer away. "Do that one more time and I'll run you in!"

Checking the priest's failing vital signs, the first attendant said, "We've got to get this man to the hospital pronto!"

The second attendant hurried up with the stretcher. "What have we got?"

"Don't know. But the padre isn't getting any air."

Marco hurried over, with Earl at his heels. Marco saluted Johnson and Corby. "Officers, this man said he's feeling sick, too!"

Corby asked, "What do you mean sick?"

The driver pointed back to where he had vomited. "I heaved up my lunch over there. I don't know what Mr. Fleet was smoking, but whatever it was, I got pretty damn sick on the smoke."

"Who's Mr. Fleet?"

Criswell pointed down in the grave. "That, I believe, is Mr. Fleet...or was."

"And you are?" Johnson asked the driver.

"My name is Earl, Earl Warren. I'm the guy who drove Mr. Fleet up here." He nodded back at the coach. "I called dispatch," he said. "Mr. Bruckner is on his way. He's the director of the whole chain of funeral homes." He frowned, turning a slight shade greener. "I'm feeling pretty sick. I think it was the garlic cigar Mr. Fleet was smoking."

"Garlic cigar?"

"Yeah, it was a Cuban brand that Tesla must've soaked in garlic. Mr. Fleet said Tesla gave it to him. It stank something awful."

Johnson pointed back at the gravesite. "Tesla? The dead guy? How could a dead man give the funeral director a cigar?"

Earl shrugged. "I don't know." He gasped and sat down on a folding chair. "I'm just telling you...what he said." He tugged at his collar. "I can't...catch my breath!"

Criswell frowned with concern. "Just like the priest and the funeral director!"

"Oh, God!" Earl breathed harder, his eyes widening with panic. "I'm gonna die!"

The priest grabbed the ambulance attendant's white uniform top. "I...breathed...the smoke...too!"

"And it smelled like garlic?"

The priest anxiously nodded.

"Officers, it sounds to me like we've got three cases of *arsenic poisoning!*"

"I'm calling this in to headquarters." Officer Corby hurried to the patrol car.

"Call for a second ambulance, too!" shouted the second attendant as he worked on the priest.

Corby came back five minutes later. "Another ambulance is on its way."

Securing the straps on the stretcher, the first attendant said, "We're ready to take the priest to the hospital."

Johnson asked Corby, "What did the Watch Commander say?"

"He wants us to stand by for Detective Lieutenant Jack Southern. He'll know what to do about the body."

"OH, GOD!" Earl exclaimed.

"Not *your* body, the *other* body."

The priest gawked at Corby from the stretcher.

"I don't mean you either, Father, I meant…forget it."


They all stood around the open grave, Criswell, Reverend Hall, and Corby. They stared down at the funeral director's body. It was sprawled on the crumpled lid of Tesla's casket like a broken puppet.

Patrolman Johnson ran up to meet them. "The priest and hearse driver made it to the hospital," he said.

"Thank God," said Criswell.

"I wonder how we're going to get him out," Corby mused.

Johnson gestured at the casket-lowering device. "I guess we use this thing to bring the coffin up."

"That would qualify as an exhumation, wouldn't it?" asked Reverend Hall.

"Yeah, it does," said Corby. "We'll need a warrant, or at least get the immediate family's permission, since we'll have to bring Tesla's coffin up too."

"I doubt Hope would object," Criswell said.

"Which one is Hope again?"

"Armand's widow."

Johnson pointed at Lillian. "I thought *she* was Tesla's widow."

"That's Lillian Arch, the ex-wife, which I guess makes her a widow too."

Corby smirked. "Are you sure she knows she's an ex-wife?"

Marco ran up. "Officer, there's a car coming up the road!"

The Vampire's Tomb Mystery　　　161

A gray sedan pulled up behind the squad car. The press people pounced on it. Johnson eyed the crowding press photographers, scratching his chin thoughtfully, giving Marco the once over. "You want to do us a big favor?"

"Sure."

"I'm gonna deputize you."

"Gee!" Marco said, smiling broadly.

"Raise your right hand and put your left hand over your heart," Johnson ordered.

Marco eagerly complied.

"Do you, uh, what's your name?"

"Paul Marco," he said, standing erect.

"Okay, Paul Marco, do you swear to act appropriately as a duly deputized officer of the law? Say, 'I do.'"

"I do!" Marco replied.

"Okay, Deputy Marco," Johnson said, jerking his thumb at the press, "keep those guys away from the crime scene and the detective in that car."

Marco saluted, puffing out his chest and taking on a serious demeanor. He ran to the car and insinuated himself between the press people and the car, waving them back. "Okay, boys, there's nothing here to see! Get back there! Police line here! Back, all of you! Get back!" He herded complaining reporters and barked orders like a sheepdog with delusions of grandeur.

"Paul Marco with authority." Criswell shook his head. "Officer, you have no idea what you may have unleashed."

Johnson shrugged. "Hey, it got the press out of our hair, didn't it?"

A man Criswell recognized as Jack Southern got out of the sedan and put his brown fedora on at a jaunty angle. Jack didn't look much different from the photograph in Mae West's apartment, perhaps a little grayer and a bit of middle-age spread around his waist, but still recognizable. He approached the gravesite with "Deputy" Marco as an escort. The actor shoved a reporter back and said, "Now just go back there with the other civilians and leave the police work to the professionals!"

Lt. Southern eyed the actor. "Who did you say you were again?"

"Deputy Marco, sir. Officer Johnson appointed me as your bodyguard."

"What did I ever do to him?"

At the gravesite, Johnson saluted. "Lieutenant."

"Officer," Southern nodded. "Hello, Criswell," he said.

"When did you get kicked up to homicide?" asked Criswell.

Southern shrugged. "When I got tired of being a celebrity bodyguard." Southern pointed at the Grotto. "So we have a dead funeral director in an open grave, huh?"

"Actually, he's the vice president of the funeral home."

Officer Johnson pointed back at the road. "The hearse driver got pretty sick. So did the priest. The decedent's name is Ralph Fleet. The ambulance attendants thought arsenic might be responsible."

Southern eyed the patrolman. "Any idea how the arsenic was administered?"

"The hearse driver said something about a Cuban cigar smelling like garlic."

"And garlic odor is characteristic of arsenic. Where did the cigar come from?"

"Believe it or not, the driver said Armand Tesla gave it to him."

"A cigar from a dead man," Southern mused wistfully. "Sounds like the title to a Mickey Spillane novel." He pointed at Mr. Bruckner, who was standing by his car and looking frazzled. "Who's the old guy?"

"That's Hugo H. Bruckner. He owns Hollywood Mortuaries. The driver called him in before he collapsed."

Mr. Bruckner spotted the detective and anxiously hurried up. "Excuse me, detective," he said. "But may we finish the burial service? It'll be sundown before you know it."

"All in good time, Mr. Bruckner."

"And about my coaches, these policemen have two of my coaches tied up here."

"We don't want to overlook anything. The lab boys may need to examine them."

"But this is ridiculous! First the disruption at my mortuary, and now *this* happens!"

"You don't seem all that broken up about Mr. Fleet here."

"Of course, it's a tragedy," Mr. Bruckner said. "But we have a burial to perform!"

"Look on the bright side. Now you have two."

"Really, detective!"

"We'll do what we can to speed things along. The City of Los Angles appreciates your cooperation." Southern nodded over at Criswell's limousine. "What's going on there?" the detective asked.

Kathy Wood sat inside Criswell's Imperial 8 with Andreas Orby. A reporter with pad and pencil was trying to get the boy's story, but Orby was too busy crying. As the reporter's photographer snapped a picture, Johnson shrugged. "The kid confessed to helping a guy named Ed Wood switch places with Tesla."

"Come again?" Southern asked.

"That boy!" Mr. Bruckner huffed. "The chaos he caused at my mortuary was unforgivable! He was responsible for that the whole wrong body business! I want him arrested!"

"Cris, what are they talking about?"

"Young Orby helped Eddie escape an assassin by helping Ed sneak into Armand's coffin," said Criswell.

"An assassin?"

"It's a long story. But somewhere between the funeral home and the cemetery, Eddie got out of the hearse and disappeared."

"A regular Houdini, huh?" Southern said. "So let's say Ed Wood did like you said, why would he go through this elaborate switcher-roo instead of just running out the back door?"

Criswell shrugged. "That's sort of the way Eddie is."

"A real character, huh?"

"So, where do we go from here?"

"I don't know about you, but *I'm* going to get some statements." Southern started to approach the limo when he noticed Marco staying close at his heels. Turning to his "bodyguard," he jerked a thumb at the gravesite. "Deputy Marco, go guard the crime scene. Nobody goes near it. Got it?"

"Yes, sir!" Marco smiled broadly and saluted.

"So much for him." Lt. Southern led the way as he approached the Imperial 8.

Noting the detective, the reporter and his photographer met Southern halfway. "I'm Shelby from the *LA Times*," he said, smiling. "The photographer's name is Burns." Burns nodded as he snapped in a new flashbulb. "Care to give us a statement, Lieutenant?"

Southern pushed past the reporter and approached the limousine. "Hello," he said to Kathy. "I'm Detective Lieutenant Southern. I understand this young man has something he wants to tell me."

Shelby indicated Orby with his pencil. "The kid confessed to killing the undertaker."

The teenager continued crying on Kathy's shoulder while Kathy did her best to console him.

"Oh, yeah," Southern said. "The kid looks like a real desperado." He pointed at the Burns' camera. "I want copies." He indicated the other photographers. "From everybody."

"Okay," said Burns, raising his camera to get a shot of the detective with the young man. After taking the picture, he ejected the bulb and let it drop on the ground.

Southern eyed him sternly. "And stop messing up my crime scene with that shit."

"He's new," said Shelby.

Southern took off his hat and smiled pleasantly at Kathy and Orby. "Sorry about all the fuss. Look, kid, I don't think you're a killer. But maybe you can shed some light on what happened."

"It's all my fault," Orby tearfully confessed.

"What's all your fault? I heard about what you did with the bodies and that stuff, but what's all this about you killing a guy?"

"I killed the funeral director doing what I did! I guess he had a bad heart or something. What I did made him so upset that he dropped dead! I just know it!"

"You mean, because you helped switch the bodies around?"

"Yes," Bruckner said angrily, "Mr. Tesla was found in Mr. Jeffrey's casket, and Mr. Jeffrey was found in our supply closet, and now we know it was this boy who helped Wood do it!"

"Come on, kid," said Southern, "where's Ed Wood now?"

"I don't know," Orby insisted. "Even if I did, I couldn't say. He might get killed! I can't be responsible for killing *two* guys!"

Kathy said soothingly, "Andreas, if you know where Eddie is, tell the detective, please. And if you can't tell the detective, at least tell me. I have to know for sure Eddie is all right."

Orby frowned. "Don't be mad, Mrs. Wood. But he told me not to tell— you, especially."

"What?" Kathy was taken aback. "Why me especially?"

"I can't say. I'm sorry."

Kathy got out of the limousine and confronted Southern. "I know who Andreas is trying to save Eddie from."

"You do?"

Kathy pointed at Dolores. "That woman tried to kill him! That's why Eddie ran away!"

Southern looked the blonde up and down, rubbing his chin thoughtfully. "And the blonde would be…?"

"Dolores Fuller," Criswell explained. "Dolores was Eddie's ex." He leaned in and whispered in Southern's ear. "There's something I have to tell you." Cris looked at Kathy. "Alone."

"Well, aren't we being mysterious," said Southern. He pointed at the chapel tent. "Let's go and have a look-see and a chat."

Mr. Bruckner gestured angrily at Orby. "What about the boy?"

Southern turned to Johnson. "Why don't you take Mr. Bruckner's statement? When you're finished with him, round up all the mourners and start collecting names and addresses. This could take a while."

"Got you, boss." Officer Johnson took the funeral manager by the arm. "This way, sir."

"Now see here—" Bruckner began as Johnson took him up to the Grotto out of earshot of Criswell and the detective.

"Wait a second, Lieutenant," said Shelby, who was followed closely by his photographer as they reached the gravesite. "What about my readers? I need a statement."

"You couldn't print it," said Southern. He gestured at Marco, still standing watch. "Hey, Deputy Marco."

"Sir?"

"You're my bodyguard." He jerked his thumb at the reporter and photographer. "Guard me from them."

"Yes, sir!" Marco saluted and then herded the complaining press people back to the road. "Come on, there's nothing to see here! Move along! Move along!"

"Now," said Southern turning to Criswell, "what was so important you couldn't say it in front of the old guy or Mrs. Wood?"

"I found evidence that Eddie may have shot his attacker by accident. That may be the reason for the disappearing act. He was afraid to be seen outside the mortuary."

"What evidence?"

"This." Criswell reached into his tuxedo and handed the Lieutenant the silver revolver. "Forry found it, actually. But I collected it."

Lt. Southern took the weapon and unfolded the handkerchief. "Are you admitting to withholding evidence?"

"No, *preserving* evidence. It was found at the mortuary in a potted plant by the door leading to the parking lot. Unfortunately, Forry smudged the fingerprints removing it from the pot."

"Who's Forry?"

"Forrest J Ackerman, he's a literary agent." Smirking, Criswell said, "Eddie's alleged literary agent."

Lt. Southern looked around at the mourners. "Is he here?"

"No. He's at a drugstore across from the funeral home, investigating a lead."

Lt. Southern folded Criswell's handkerchief back around the gun. "Cris, you're not a cop. We don't appreciate amateur detectives screwing around with evidence. That's how evidence gets corrupted. We could lose this case because of you." Hefting the gun, he said, "This gun has been removed far from the crime scene. It's been in your pocket. It's been in your handkerchief. And God knows where the handkerchief has been. The chain of evidence has been fucked. If this case went to trial, a good defense attorney could rake me over the coals."

Criswell frowned. "Sorry, I thought I was helping."

Lt. Southern sighed. "Okay, so what was the 'lead' your friend was following up on at this drugstore?"

"Two tourists, a couple of newlyweds, they may have taken pictures of the crime in progress. They thought the attack on Eddie was street theater."

"So your friend is getting the pictures developed?"

"Waiting for them to get developed, yes."

"Okay, again," Lt. Southern scolded. "Chain of evidence has been fucked. Because of you Hardy Boys, I have no way of proving those photographs, however incriminating they may be, are *the* photographs taken by the eyewitnesses, or that they haven't been doctored."

"But I can tell you where the newlyweds are. They can verify the authenticity of the pictures."

"You mean the same two people who thought a murder attempt in broad daylight was street theater? Oh, yeah, they'd make swell witnesses. Do the LAPD a favor and stick to reading tea leaves or whatever the hell you do. Leave the investigation to the professionals."

"What about Eddie?"

The detective pocketed the revolver. "For now he's a problem for Missing Persons. And if you do happen to find his body, call the cops and don't touch anything. *If* he's been shot, we'll give the gun to ballistics to verify this is the murder weapon. As for this guy," said Southern, looking into the open grave, "we're going to have to treat this like a homicide." Lt. Southern took Criswell's arm. "That means, you stay behind the police line."

He escorted Criswell away from the scene.

# Chapter 19

The Blessed Virgin watched silently from her Grotto as Holy Rosary was transformed into a crime scene. A police line had been established with wooden sawhorses and blinking lights. Patrolmen segregated the bereaved to obtain their statements. Naturally, Lillian and Armand Jr. had plenty to say, mostly about Hope and how they felt about her and her friends like Edward D. Wood Jr.

Southern decided to question Dolores Fuller personally, partly because her name came up a number of times from other witnesses, and mostly because she was a stunning blonde. Even in her dress of funerary black, her outstanding figure was obvious. Taking her to the Grotto, he said, "Can you tell me what's been going on here, Miss? I understand you had an argument with an ex-boyfriend."

Standing there against the serene background of the Grotto, Dolores reminded Southern of a mournful, yet beautiful phantom. Her milky skin and hard expression suggested a stern Greek goddess. "What does that have to do with the undertaker dropping dead?" she asked coolly.

"Maybe nothing," Southern said, shrugging. "But things at the mortuary sounded like they got pretty wild, and you were a big part of it."

"Am I under suspicion of anything?"

It was all Southern could do to keep from smiling; the dialogue sounded like something straight out of *I, the Jury*, and right now Dolores looked as hot as any blonde who ever graced the cover of a Mickey Spillane potboiler. "Well, that girl there," he said, indicating Kathy Wood, who was giving her statement to Officer Johnson, "she made it sound like you might have killed her husband in a fit of jealousy."

Dolores's eyes flashed. "Oh, she did, did she?"

"There were a number of witnesses who said you were pretty violent. And after hearing what that girl there had to say about it, well...."

"That bitch!" Dolores's blue eyes narrowed, which made her pretty nose crinkle in a most alluring way. "She's making me out to be the crazy one, when all the while *she* was the one acting like a psychopath."

"That's not the way witnesses saw it."

"That's because they didn't see what *I* saw. Well, I've got a story to tell you."

Southern got out his notepad and pencil. He licked the graphite tip and smiled. "But first things first, I'll need your hotel room and a number where I can reach you later and whether or not you like Italian."

"What does that have to do with anything?"

"Well, I was thinking of asking you out to dinner later."

Dolores gave him a half smile. "I have two sons from a prior marriage," she said, obviously aware that such an admission was poison for the average guy on the make.

"Are they here in Los Angeles with you?"

"No. They're back in New York."

"So, like I said; if you're not doing anything later…"

"Can't I just give you my statement for now?"

Becoming all business, Southern cleared his throat and poised to write. "Sure thing, Miss Fuller, I'm all ears."

Dolores's testimony required a lot of exclamation points.


Standing by the open grave with Hope and Criswell were coroner Harold Wise and crime lab investigator Don Scott. Scott called Mr. Bruckner over.

"This winch," he said, indicating the lowering device, "does it work in reverse?"

"The mechanism might hold up under the strain of cranking it in reverse, but you'd have to be mighty strong to work it."

Scott glanced over at Tor Johnson. "*He* looks mighty strong."


Soon "Lobo" was lending a hand. As the giant turned the crank, Dr. Wise said to the wrestler, "Keep going. You're doing fine."

"I swear," Hope remarked to Criswell, "if I didn't know better, I'd say Don Marlowe arranged this whole thing as a publicity stunt. This is just the sort of thing Armand lived for."

"In a manner of speaking," Cris remarked.

It wasn't long before Dracula, along with an unexpected hitchhiker, had once again risen from the grave. As attendants wrapped Fleet in a gray blanket and strapped him to a stretcher, Lt. Southern walked over to the widow and flashed a genial smile. "Excuse me, Mrs. Tesla. I'm a fan of your late husband and I was wondering if I could have a look inside the coffin. I hear he's dressed as Dracula."

"You don't have to allow it, Mrs. Tesla," Mr. Bruckner advised. "Their warrant is for the removal of Ralph's body only. You have every right to refuse."

Southern glowered at the funeral manager. "Keep out of this."

"I'm merely looking after the best interest of the family, and your request seems frivolous to me."

"Well, let's see what Mrs. Tesla has to say about it."

Hope, being Hope, gestured begrudgingly at the crumpled casket. "Armand was a show off. You wanna have a look, be my guest." She left the detective with the coffin to join Kathy, and Marco down by Criswell's limousine, where policemen were getting their statements.

Mr. Bruckner stood by to oversee the opening of the casket, when Southern said, "Wait behind the police barrier."

"Indeed! I should be here to supervise."

"If I need you, you'll be the first to know."

Mr. Bruckner glared at Southern, refusing to budge as Lt. Southern opened Tesla's casket and smirked. "Well, well…cape and everything. I wouldn't have believed it if I hadn't seen it myself."

Bruckner fussily gestured. "Now that you've had your look, kindly close the lid."

Criswell frowned as he studied Armand's face. "Say, if I didn't know better, I'd say Armand's face was…sweating." He reached out to touch the corpse's face, only to have Bruckner slap his hand away. "That's the mortician's wax beginning to melt," the mortuary owner explained as he quickly closed the lid. "It's quite irregular for the body to be exposed this long to the hot California sun."

Lt. Southern jerked his thumb back at the road. "Okay, beat it or I'll sick that Marco guy on you,"

"Really!" Mr. Bruckner huffed and then stormed off, leaving Criswell to witness his retreat. "Why did you really want a look in the casket?" Criswell asked Southern.

"Do I need an ulterior motive?" The detective pointed at Dolores. "Miss Fuller told me about what happened at the funeral home. She made it out to be a pretty big row."

"Everyone was on edge more than usual."

"That's an understatement." Southern raised the lid again and studied Tesla's tranquil, perspiring face. Drops of flesh colored wax were staining Armand's satin pillow. "She also said the wife, or the lay, or whatever she is, Katherine Wood, tried to kill both Miss Fuller and Ed Wood."

"What!" Criswell exclaimed.

"It happened in the embalming room. Fuller said she was arguing with Ed Wood, when suddenly Kathy Wood went into a jealous rage." He eyed Criswell. "She came at both of them with an embalmer's scalpel."

"That's the first time I heard about this! That's not like Kathy at all!"

The Lieutenant gave a shrug. "Maybe you were all exposed to something that makes you sick or crazy if you inhale it. Maybe the whole place stinks with it. Maybe that's why everybody went nuts at the mortuary, and why the mortician dropped dead."

"You've had your look!" Mr. Bruckner protested as he skirted the police barrier. "Now get away from that casket."

"I thought I told you to stay back."

Bruckner slammed the coffin lid shut. "Please! You mustn't let the deceased be exposed to the direct rays of the sun."

"Afraid Tesla'll turn to dust?" Southern quipped.

Mr. Bruckner bristled. "That joke was in very poor taste."

The Lieutenant took out his notebook and licked the lip of his pencil. "Speaking of poor taste, tell me about the chemicals you use in your operation..."

"I overheard what you said just now. There's *nothing* exotic about the chemicals we use! They're all legitimate products available to every mortuary."

Don Scott approached. The Lieutenant turned to the lab investigator. "Have you got something?" he asked.

"Maybe," said Scott. He held a small evidence envelope. "While we were checking both the hearses —"

"Coaches," Mr. Bruckner corrected. "We don't call them hearses anymore."

Scott sighed. "Fine, while we were checking the *coaches*, we found a cigar butt in the ash tray of the one the mortician was driving in. Probably the cigar the funeral director smoked before he died." Using tweezers, Scott removed the butt from the evidence envelope and held it out to Southern. "Take a sniff."

The detective sniffed. "I don't smell anything except tobacco."

"And you won't smell anything queer until," Scott produced a lighter and struck the flint wheel, "you light the butt." He held it out. "Now sniff, but be careful. It's highly toxic."

Sniffing carefully, Southern smiled and said, "That's garlic, all right."

The lab investigator snuffed out the butt with his fingertips. "We'll know for sure it's arsenic after we run a few tests for heavy metals." He put the butt back in the evidence envelope and handed it to Lt. Southern.

"Say," Mr. Bruckner said, "our embalmer was rather upset because Ralph took a cigar from the deceased."

"Oh, yeah?" asked Southern.

"Mr. Tesla was to be buried with cigars in his pocket."

Southern smiled as he pocketed the envelope. "Is that so?" He reached down to search the body. "So that's how you get a cigar from a dead man."

Mr. Bruckner restrained him. "Wait, don't you need a warrant?"

"The widow said I could have a look. Now lay off."

"She said you could look, not touch."

Southern grumbled and gestured at the body. "Fine. You search the pockets. I want the rest of those cigars."

Mr. Bruckner searched every pocket and came up empty. "They aren't here."

The Lieutenant glared down at him and demanded, "Okay, what did you do with the evidence?"

Bruckner straightened up and fumed, "Me? What makes you think I took them?"

"Don't play dumb! The body was in your possession, wasn't it? Now what did you do with those cigars?"

"I tell you I didn't do anything with them." Bruckner snapped his fingers. "Say, I'll bet Fleet took them."

The lab investigator shook his head. "We found only one empty cigar tube on Fleet's body."

Lt. Southern set his jaw and glared at Bruckner. "Then in that case, as of right now your funeral is called off on account of murder."

"What!"

"Since the cigars have up and disappeared, Mr. Tesla himself has just become evidence."

"This is an outrage!" Bruckner slammed the casket lid shut again and angrily pointed back at the lead hearse. "I'm calling my lawyer right now! I'll have your badge for this!" He stabbed a finger at the casket. "And don't you dare open that until you get a proper warrant!"

As he stormed off, Criswell glimpsed the widow as she paced impatiently on the roadside. "You don't suppose Hope took those cigars when we weren't looking? To cover up a murder she committed?" He dismissed the idea with a gesture. "Oh, but what would Hope gain by killing Armand? He was practically penniless."

Southern shrugged. "Maybe he had more money than he was letting on, and she found out about it. The son said the widow knew she was getting cut out of the will." He called to a policeman standing nearby. "Hey, Pat!"

"Sir?" the policeman said as he hurried over.

"Keep your eye on this casket. Nobody goes near it."

"Yes, sir."

Southern headed for a nearby police car with Criswell padding after him. "So, what happens now?" Cris asked anxiously.

"I'm gonna get an arrest warrant sworn out on Mrs. Tesla, is what. Then I'm gonna look for the evidence. If she did take those cigars, chances are she's not dumb enough to keep them on her. We'll comb every grave and flower pot if necessary. But first we need to get an official exhumation order on Tesla; we'll want to do another autopsy. Arsenic has a way of sticking around in the body, even after embalming. Then I'll need a search warrant for Mrs. Tesla's apartment. We'll keep her busy here."

Cris grabbed Southern's arm as he reached for the police car microphone. "Now hold on, Jack. You may be jumping to conclusions. Armand said a *fan* gave him those cigars."

Southern pried his arm loose and glared at the psychic. "Did he happen to say *which* fan?"

Criswell shook his head. "No, he just said it was a fan."

Southern nodded in Hope's direction. "I'll bet my eye teeth *she* sent 'em, making it look like the cigars were from a fan."

Cris couldn't argue with the Lieutenant's logic. He sighed resignedly and said, "I'll let you get on with your investigation then. I still can't believe it."

Southern grabbed the microphone and smirked. "That's what makes me the cop and you just the amateur sleuth Hardy Boy. Now be a good boy and let me do my job."

As Criswell headed in the direction of the limousine he heard Southern calling after him, "And not a word to Mrs. Tesla about any of this. I mean it."

"My lips are sealed," Criswell glumly assured him.

Chalky opened the door for Criswell as he approached. "How long do you think we'll be here, sir?"

"Long enough for you and me to have a chat," Cris said, eyeing the chauffeur keenly.

"About what, sir?" Chalky calmly inquired.

"About Ed Wood."

"I really have nothing to say about Mr. Wood, sir."

"I know about you and Bunny hiding a body."

"Really, sir?" Chalky smiled. "A body, you say?"

"A woman. She's in the trunk of Bunny's car—in a body bag."

"A body bag, sir?"

"She was supposed to kill Eddie, but she didn't count on Eddie fighting back. He tried to disarm her and she got shot by accident."

"You don't say, sir."

"I saw you passing something to Eddie—and Eddie passing something to you."

"Really, sir?"

"You both swapped film cans. I don't see a bulge in the pocket of your uniform, so the only place the film can Eddie gave you might be is—" Criswell hurried over to the driver's compartment and opened the door, "—the glove compartment!"

"I wouldn't do that, sir," the chauffeur warned.

Cris reached for the glove box. Chalky pull him out bodily by his sequin lapels and pinned Cris against the car. Criswell was flabbergasted, but stubborn. "What's on that film you don't want me to see?" he pressed.

Chalky's grip on Criswell's lapels tightened. "That's none of your concern, sir."

"Is Mae mixed up in all this?"

Chalky's face remained inscrutable, but his hold on Criswell intensified.

"What? Is it some old stag film Mae made early in her career?" Criswell couldn't help smiling at the absurdity of his situation. "Come on, Chalky. I can't believe Mae would care if anyone saw her fucking in an old stag film. Knowing Mae, she'd probably sell tickets." An idea occurred to him. "Unless it's a movie of *you* and Mae fucking."

Chalky grimaced.

"Oh, my God. That's it, isn't it? Eddie was blackmailing Mae for movie funds! Kathy said Eddie was excited about getting enough money to make *Grave Robbers from Outer Space*. That's why you hired that woman in black to kill Eddie!" Criswell glanced over Chalky's shoulder at Lt. Southern. The detective was slamming his fist down on the hood of the police car. "Whatever's going on, Chalky, you don't want to get in trouble with the police." He saw the detective hang up the microphone and stride angrily in their direction. "Lt. Southern is heading this way."

Chalky released his hold on Criswell and smoothed out the wrinkles in the psychic's tuxedo jacket. "I know Lt. Southern very well, Mr. Criswell. And he knows me."

Southern didn't look happy. "Chalky, give us a minute alone, please."

Saluting, Chalky said, "Certainly, Lieutenant."

The chauffeur reached in the glove compartment and took out a film can identical to the one in Criswell's pocket and slipped it into the pocket of his uniform, then tipped his cap at a jaunty angle and took a leisurely stroll down the road while whistling a tune Criswell recognized as *I'll Be Glad When You're Dead, You Rascal, You.*

When Chalky was out of earshot, Criswell turned to Southern, about to tell him what was going on, when Southern grumbled, "The Chief just sank my ducks. Did I say sank? He shot them to hell."

Criswell blinked. "I beg your pardon?"

"He wants us to pack everything up and bury Mr. Tesla, no questions asked."

Criswell was stunned. "What? But why?"

"Something about National Security, which means it's the Feds, and the Feds means the FBI, and the FBI means J. Edgar Hoover."

"J. Edgar Hoover!" Criswell exclaimed. "What does J. Edgar Hoover care if Hope Tesla is arrested for killing her husband?"

"Don't ask me. But for whatever reason, this whole thing is getting swept under the rug."

Criswell was mystified. "What about Eddie?"

"The Feds want the case dropped like a hot potato, and Ed Wood is spud *numero uno.*"

Criswell would have run his fingers through his hair in confusion, if he hadn't lacquered his hair into an impenetrable helmet. "But Eddie is just a harmless transvestite who likes to wear angora sweaters and make bad movies." He held his aching head and asked, "What does that have to do with National Security interests?"

"You got me, Cris. But I will say this, I don't know what your friend's mixed up in, but whatever it is, as of now, it never happened."

"Tell that to Kathy. Tell that to Lillian and Armand Jr., too, while you're at it."

Southern grabbed Criswell's arm and looked around to make sure no one was looking. "Remember what I told you about not getting mixed up in official police matters?"

"Yes," said Criswell.

"Forget I said anything."

"You mean you want me to—"

"I'm not saying yes, and I'm not saying no. But if you do decide to snoop around on your own—" the detective took the Western six-shooter from his pocket and passed it to Criswell, along with the evidence envelope containing the cigar butt, "—watch your back," he whispered.

Criswell swallowed hard as Lt. Southern walk back to the gravesite and motioned for his investigative team to gather around.

A smiling Chalky Wright approached, looking where Criswell was looking. He pointed at the gravesite and asked, as if already knowing the answer, "Will I be speaking with Lt. Southern, Mr. Criswell?"

# Chapter 20

Night had fallen. It was only fitting that Armand Tesla was interred after sunset. At the request of Lt. Southern and Hugo H. Bruckner, the cemetery gates were kept open despite the lateness of the hour. After the burial was over, the bereaved and press people alike returned to their cars.

Criswell followed after Lillian and Armand Jr. "Excuse me," he said as Armand Jr. opened the door for his mother. Lillian got behind the wheel.

Armand Jr. glared at Criswell. "Leave us alone," he said. "Mom and I have had enough of Ed Wood and his cronies. That includes you."

"I'm sorry for the trouble Eddie caused. But I think you should know that there's something going on and it has to do with your father's death."

"Oh really?" the young man sneered. "What? Did Dad have a chat with you from Beyond the Grave?"

"No," said Criswell. "We spoke the day he died. He was convinced there was somebody out to kill him."

From behind the wheel, Lillian rolled her eyes. "Armand was having one of his episodes," she said. "He started sleepwalking and hallucinating. It was the drugs. When it wasn't the drugs it was alcohol." She started up the engine and turned on the headlights. "Get in, Bill. We're leaving."

"We're done here, Mr. Criswell." Armand Jr. crossed in front of the car when Cris grabbed him by the arm. They stood illuminated in the car's headlights as Cris said in his overly dramatic delivery, "Did you know there is evidence that your father was…," pause for emphasis, "…murdered?" There was no dramatic music sting to punctuate the moment, just chirping crickets, but it got Armand Jr.'s attention.

Leering skeptically, Armand Jr. asked, "Who would kill Dad?"

Cris glanced over at his limousine where Chalky held the door open for Hope. Criswell said in a whisper, "The police think your stepmother may have poisoned him."

Armand Jr. jerked his arm free of Criswell's grip. "Much as I would love to prove Hope guilty of such a thing, if the police believed Hope killed my dad, why did they let us bury Dad instead of perform an autopsy?" He marched around the car and put his hand on the door handle.

Criswell followed. "There's a cover-up going on," he insisted. "Don't ask me why. I don't know why. But for whatever reason, all the evidence of the crime is being suppressed."

"What does that have to do with you?"

Criswell shrugged. "I've been asked to investigate on my own... unofficially."

Armand Jr. got in the car. "You expect us to believe that the cops would ask a phony psychic to investigate a murder?"

Criswell sighed. It did sound rather ridiculous at that. He reached into his pocket and produced the evidence envelope containing the cigar butt. "The police believe this cigar butt is laced with arsenic."

"Oh, and they just gave that evidence to you?"

"Like I said, they're asking me to investigate on the sly." He proffered the envelope to Armand Jr. "Here, have it analyzed yourself if you don't believe me. It's allegedly from Tesla's own stash."

Armand Jr. took the envelope and turned it over in his hands. "A poisoned cigar killed my dad?"

"If you don't believe me, smoke it."

Lillian said, "My son doesn't smoke."

Armand Jr. pocketed the evidence. "I'll see about getting it analyzed."

"Do that. But before you go," Criswell flashed Armand Jr. his most earnest expression, "I have to ask you some questions. You have information vital to this case."

"Like what?"

"Armand said he was going to see a lawyer the day before he died. Was it about the divorce or something else?"

"That's privileged information."

Lillian changed gears. "We're finished talking to you, Mr. Criswell." The car pulled forward.

"WAIT!" Cris grabbed the car door. Lillian stepped on the brakes. "Your father gave Ed Wood an envelope," Cris said. "He said there were instructions in it about what to do in case he died suddenly. At the time it sounded like paranoid delusions, but then Armand really did die suddenly. Do you know what was in the envelope? Did it have anything to do with a roll of movie film?"

Armand Jr. frowned. "How do you know about that?"

"Because I saw Ed with my own eyes pass a can of movie film to my chauffeur. Chalky seemed to pass the can back to Ed. Then someone tried to kill Ed and now Ed is missing. Chalky threatened me when I tried to have a look at the film can. I think that film contains scenes of Chalky having sex with Mae West."

"You do, huh?"

"At least, I did until Hoover and the FBI started interfering with this investigation. What did Armand stumble on? How did he get that film?"

Armand Jr. looked to his mother, and then narrowly eyed Criswell. "I can't tell you, Mr. Criswell. You're named in the class-action suit as a partner in the real estate deal. It would seriously endanger our case."

"Real estate deal? What real estate deal?"

"The Sacramento High Rise Project," Armand Jr. said, "as if you didn't know."

"The cemetery property?"

"You and your partners will get served with papers soon enough. They'll explain everything. But," Armand Jr. added, indicating the envelope in his pocket, "if this cigar butt *does* turn out to contain poison, you're going to need a good lawyer."

"What for?"

"For criminal conspiracy." With a nod from her son, Lillian drove off.

Criswell called after the retreating car. "Wait! What conspiracy?"

Criswell was left standing in the road as the rest of the procession of cars drove slowly past, briefly illuminating him in their headlight beams. Once the last car had driven out of sight, Criswell was plunged into darkness. The Grotto became a haven for eternal peace once again. Darting fireflies twinkled over cemetery plots like lost souls in search of their graves. Cricket chirping mixed with the noise of distant traffic.

Criswell gazed over at the Grotto. Its hillside was an indistinct mound in the blackness. The sheltering trees were like claws blocking out the starlight. He felt no protection from the cold marble Virgin hidden out of sight in the dark Grotto cave. Then, as if in response to his thoughts, colored lights directed at the Blessed Virgin's grotto suddenly broke the darkness.

For a moment, Criswell felt safe. This sense of peace was swiftly shattered by the sound of the Imperial 8's engine turning over. Criswell started, shielding his eyes as the car's headlight beams flashed on.

Pulling the limousine up beside him, Chalky asked genially, "Shall we go, sir?"

Chalky put on the safety brake and left the engine idling as he got out and opened the passenger door for Criswell. "This way, sir," he said.

Criswell sighed resignedly and got in the limousine.

# Chapter 21

For Criswell the ride back was a bit awkward to say the least. First stop, the Biltmore Hotel where Dolores Fuller was staying. The limousine pulled up along the Olive Street entrance. As Chalky opened the door, Dolores gave Kathy a scornful look. "I can't say it's been fun," she sneered. "I *can* say that I've had all I ever want from you or Ed. Ever!"

Criswell studied the two women closely as Kathy returned Dolores's look of malice. "I can certainly say the same thing about you," she said.

Hope sat next to Andreas Orby. She rolled her eyes and sighed heavily. "You can both kiss my ass," she said. "This has been the longest goddamn day of my life."

As Dolores stepped out, Maila leaned forward and asked the chauffeur, "Chalky, could we stop by the Union Bus Station next?" She pointed over at South Broadway. "It's just a little down that way."

"Why, of course, Miss Maila."

"Union Bus Station?" exclaimed Criswell. "Where are you going?"

"Nowhere," said Maila with a shrug. "There's just something waiting for me there, that's all."

"Like what?"

Maila shrugged again. "Just some stuff I was keeping in a locker there." She paused, and then added, "Now that I'm living at your office I need a few things."

Chalky offered Dolores his arm. "Right this way, Miss Dolores."

A colored doorman in a navy blue dress uniform and cap held the door open as Dolores stepped inside.

Criswell turned to his guests. "Excuse me, everyone. I'll be right back."

He was about to follow Dolores, but Chalky blocked his way. "Something you need, sir?" the chauffeur asked.

Criswell stiffened. "You're not going to try and stop me, are you?" He gestured at the waiting doorman. "In front of witnesses?"

Chalky smiled and stepped aside. "I wouldn't dream of it, sir."

Criswell kept a wary eye on the chauffeur and hurried into the Biltmore. Dolores was getting her room key from the clerk at the front desk.

"Dolores!" called Criswell. His voice echoed off the marble walls of the palatial lobby and added to the cacophony of other voices and footsteps.

Dolores gave him a disdainful look and tried to lose herself in the crowd milling about the huge Main Galeria. Criswell followed. She tried to slip in amongst hotel guests waiting for available elevators, but Criswell caught up just as the doors to three elevators parted simultaneously and exiting passengers poured out.

An elevator operator announced, "Going up."

Dolores allowed herself to be swept in with the embarking guests.

"Dolores, wait," Criswell called, trying to squeeze in.

The doors began closing. Cris stuck his arm out just as the doors came together. The startled elevator operator stammered, "Uh, I - I'm sorry, sir. W - we're full up." He pointed across the way. "There are two available cars there."

"But that's my wife," Criswell said, pointing at Dolores Fuller, whose eyebrows raised in surprise. "We're, uh, on our honeymoon. We don't want to get separated. It's bad luck."

The elevator operator waved Criswell in, then closed the doors and depressed the control switch, sending the car up. Criswell squeezed in next to Dolores.

"Your wife, huh?" she asked.

"I needed to talk to you for a minute," Criswell said. "I think someone is trying to kill Ed Wood."

"I know someone is trying to kill Ed Wood. Kathy Wood."

The elevator operator exchanged worried looks with the other passengers.

"Someone besides Kathy, I mean," Cris insisted.

Dolores watched the position indicator as the elevator drew closer to her floor. "Could we talk about this some other time?"

The elevator stopped. The doors parted.

"Uh, third floor," said the now nervous elevator operator. Anxiety-stricken passengers hurried off, while those still onboard flattened against the walls of the tiny compartment.

"But you're flying back to New York."

"That's right. My plane leaves in the morning."

"Back at the cemetery, Lt. Southern told me about what went on in the embalming room. But I wanted to hear it straight from you. What really happened?"

"Kathy went crazy and came at Ed and me with a scalpel. End of story."

"How did Kathy look just before she attacked you?" Cris asked.

Dolores rolled her eyes impatiently. "How do you think? Like a crazy woman."

"I mean how did she look *before* she picked up the embalmer's scalpel?"

The doors parted again. "Fifth floor," said the elevator operator.

More passengers stepped off. Two couples were about to get on when the elevator operator held up his hand. "If you know what's good for you, get the next car."

The doors closed. Now only one nervous couple and the elevator operator occupied the car with Criswell and Dolores.

Dolores sighed impatiently. "What are you driving at?"

"Did Kathy act weird in any way?"

"She came at me with a scalpel. That's acting pretty darn weird."

"Yes, but before that, how did she behave?"

"Before that she just acted like a nervous wreck, pleading with me not to hurt Ed. Then all of a sudden she turned into this wild-eyed shrew and called me a slut and accused Ed of cheating on her. Then Becwar came out of nowhere, I guess he was hiding in a locker or something, all I know is, he said something to Kathy, and she calmed right down."

"She did? What did Becwar say?"

"I don't know, but since then, she's been pretending not to remember anything." She tapped her temple. "I think she's nuts." The elevator doors opened onto her floor.

"Eighth floor," announced the elevator operator, who swallowed nervously. "All out."

Dolores was about to step off when Criswell held her back. "Did this change in behavior, both before and after the attack, did it happen instantly?" Criswell snapped his fingers. "Like that."

"Yes," Dolores said, snapping her fingers. "Just like that." She held up her key. "Can I go now?"

She stepped off the elevator. Criswell followed. Then the nervous couple exited, staring after Dolores and Criswell. The couple hurried down the hall in the opposite direction. The elevator operator stepped off and peaked around the corner, watching as Criswell caught up to Dolores. She was fumbling her key into the lock and was about to turn the knob when Criswell put his hand on hers.

"Dolores, please. There's something very strange going on. I was hoping I might persuade you to stay in Los Angeles a few more days."

Dolores gave a scoffing laugh. "Not on your life!"

"I'll pay for the room. I'll even buy you a return ticket. But I really need you to stick around for a few more days."

"Why?" she asked, looking past Criswell.

"Because—!" Criswell stopped abruptly when he felt a gloved hand on his shoulder. Criswell tensed, and then turned to see Chalky smiling broadly at him.

"Miss Nurmi and Mrs. Wood were getting worried, sir," Chalky said.

Criswell smiled back. "I'll be right along, Chalky."

"I'll be waiting by the elevator, sir."

Sighing, Criswell turned back to Dolores. "Well," he said, "have a good flight home."

"I plan to." Dolores shook her head disdainfully and sighed, "It was a mistake coming back here." She stepped inside and shut the door after her. Criswell heard the key turn in the lock and Dolores trying the knob.

"Sir," Chalky called. "The elevator operator is getting impatient." He gave Criswell a beckoning wave.

"Coming," Criswell said mournfully.

As Criswell got in the elevator with Chalky, he noticed the bulge in Chalky's pocket. The chauffeur still had the film can on him. Cris patted the duplicate film can in his own pocket and as they stopped on the next floor to take on additional passengers, Criswell got an idea.

The first principle of picking pockets as described in the *Professional Pickpocket's Guide for Stage Magicians*, no one can concentrate on more than one thing at a time. The best time to pick someone's pocket is when he or she is preoccupied with something that misdirects their attention, like when a commuter is hurrying for a train. Their mind isn't on their wallet; it's on catching their train. This is when most instances of theft occur. In the case of the stage magician, some other means of misdirection is necessary. For Criswell, the sudden jostling around as people got on the elevator afforded the perfect opportunity to switch film cans. Reaching into his own pocket, Criswell palmed the small film can. The embarking passengers pushed and shoved, giving Criswell the opportunity to bump up against Chalky. Without Chalky realizing it, Cris got his hand in the chauffeur's pocket. Out went Chalky's film can; in went Criswell's. The switch was made quickly and effortlessly.

"Are you all right, sir?" Chalky asked, helping Criswell regain his balance.

"Fine, Chalky, thanks."

Chalky escorted Criswell to the Olive Avenue exit and to the waiting limousine. Chalky held the door open for Criswell, who flashed a smug cat-that-ate-the-canary smile as he sat in the passenger compartment.

Glowering from the opposite seat, Hope asked, "What's up with you?"

Cryptically, Criswell said, "The hand is quicker than the eye." He reached forward and pulled a quarter from Andreas Orby's ear.

"Gee," said Orby, smiling for the first time since the funeral. Cris gave him the quarter.

Hope grumbled, "You should work for fucking kids' parties," as the limousine pulled away from the curb.

They drove down West 6th Street to South Broadway. Five minutes later, they were pulling up to their next stop: Union Bus Station.

# Chapter 22

The limousine didn't have to wait outside the Union Bus Terminal for very long. In less than 20 minutes Maila came back with a black zippered satchel. As she climbed in, Criswell asked, "What do you keep in that?"

"Just…things," she said.

"What kind of things?" He reached for the satchel only to have Maila slap his hand.

"None of your business, Mr. Nosey," she said.

Thirty minutes later they were pulling up to 5620 Harold Way. As Chalky drove the limousine up the street, Hope looked ahead and said, "What the fuck is going on up there?"

There were police cars and an ambulance clustered around the apartment house. Passersby watched from the sidelines as two attendants from the Hollywood Mortuaries wheeled out a stretcher bearing a gray-blanketed figure.

Chalky parked the limousine and escorted Hope to her door. Criswell followed. A policeman stopped them at the steps.

"No one is allowed inside," he said.

"I live here, asshole." Hope brandished her apartment key.

"Are you Hope Tesla?"

"Who wants to know?"

Lt. Southern stepped out wearing rubber gloves and holding two brown paper evidence bags. "I do," he said, then nodded a hello to Criswell. "Hey, Cris. We keep running into each other, don't we?"

"It would seem so," said Criswell. He indicated the stretcher being loaded into the mortuary coach. "Who's the new passenger?"

Smiling grimly, Lt. Southern said, "It's the landlord. The downstairs tenant found him." He gestured toward the apartment house. "The tenant was supposed to get a leaky faucet taken care of, and the landlord never showed up. She went to his apartment to complain, the door was unlocked, and there he was, slumped over the kitchen table, stone-cold dead."

"Any calls from the Feds?"

"Not a peep. I guess the landlord of a crummy apartment house isn't in the same league as a dead Dracula." Smiling at Hope, he added while hefting the paper bags, "I've got you dead to rights, lady."

"What's in the bags?" asked Criswell.

"I'm glad you asked." Lt. Southern pulled out a whiskey bottle. "He died with this in his hand." He held it out for Hope to see. "Look familiar, Mrs. Tesla?"

Hope appeared not the least bit fazed. "Listen, flatfoot, a *fan* sent Armand that whiskey."

"I know. The card attached to the neck of the bottle says, 'To Dracula, Cheers.' I'm gonna need a sample of your handwriting."

Hope glared at the label. Criswell recognized the handwriting and his eyes widened with shock. It was Maila Nurmi's handwriting!

"Something wrong, Cris?" asked Southern.

"Uh, no. I mean, yes. Uh, Eddie found that bottle up in Armand's cabinet. Armand had a couple of slugs out of it earlier but he didn't suffer any ill effects. At least, not right away."

Hope smirked. "The handwriting doesn't look nothing like mine *and* the landlord stole that bottle out of the garbage."

"Even so, I want you to write out, 'To, Dracula, Cheers' on a piece of paper. I'll give it to our handwriting experts for a match." Motioning for a policeman, Southern tucked the bags under his arm and scribbled on his notepad. "Take Mrs. Tesla to her apartment and have her write out this phrase about 20 times." He tore out two sheets of paper and handed them to the policeman.

"Yes, sir," he said.

Hope offered no resistance as a patrolman escorted her inside. When she was out of earshot, Lt. Southern took Criswell aside. "I did some snooping in Armand's apartment." He reached into the second evidence bag and held up a bottle. "We found this in the medicine cabinet, something called Bayer's Tonic."

"Armand said something about a tonic he was taking."

"Bayer's Tonic is made in West Germany and distributed to places like Hungary. It's illegal in this country because the active ingredients are arsenic and strychnine nitrate."

"He took *poison* as a nerve tonic?"

"In small doses they act as a stimulant." He held the bottle up to the porch light. "See those white crystals? The arsenic and strychnine are heavier than the solution so they settle to the bottom. To take it safely you have to shake the bottle first. If you don't, you can get a lethal dose by accident. See?" He shook the bottle vigorously. The crystals quickly disappeared. He gestured back at the apartment. "Obviously having this stuff around makes it easy for the Black Widow to collect arsenic for things like making poison cigars."

"You really think Hope…?"

"It figures, doesn't it? She buys expensive cigars, cigars she knows Tesla could never resist. She makes it out that they're from a fan. He smokes them, no questions asked. It's a perfect set up for murder."

Returning the medicine bottle to its evidence bag he said, "We found other remedies in the cabinet too, including Pepto-Bismol. It works by coating the stomach lining. *If* Tesla took it before drinking the whiskey, it might account for his not kicking off right away."

"Are you going to arrest Hope?"

"I'm sure gonna try. She works for a film studio, right? Reading scripts and such?"

"I think so. Why?"

Lt. Southern shrugged. "So maybe we're gonna see if any of those scripts has to do with a mad poisoner who knows how to distill arsenic and strychnine from Bayer's Tonic." Smiling, he added, "Then of course, there's the fact that Armand was in the touring company version of *Arsenic and Old Lace*. Maybe she got some pointers from that."

A plainclothes detective hurried up. "Lieutenant, there's a call for you on the radio. It's headquarters."

Lt. Southern's face fell. "Don't tell me. Let me guess. A federal agent wants a word with me, right?"

"How did you know?"

"Wild guess." He turned to Criswell. "Cris, about these bottles…"

"I know. Hand 'em over."

Shaking his head as he headed for the squad car, Southern grumbled, "Maybe I should take early retirement."

Cris returned to the limousine and found Orby standing with Chalky.

"Is Mrs. Tesla in trouble?" the boy asked anxiously.

Chalky smiled and patted Orby's shoulder. "Don't trouble yourself about it, sir. Mrs. Tesla will be just fine, I'm sure."

"Oh definitely," Criswell said. "She has a guardian angel." He took Orby's arm. "Come on, Andreas. We better get you home. It's getting pretty late."

# Chapter 23

As they drove to Orby's house, Maila noted the bags that Cris had stuck under the seat.

"What have you got there?"

"Wouldn't you like to know, Miss Nosey?" Criswell smirked. He reached down and pulled out the whiskey bottle. "Care for a shot?"

He held it so the card tied to the neck was visible. Maila was about to grab the bottle when she hesitated. She smiled and sat back.

"Thanks, but I'm not in the mood right now."

"I didn't think you would be." Criswell put the bottle back in the evidence bag and stuffed it under the seat. He smiled sweetly at Maila. She avoided his gaze and kept a tight hold of the satchel in her lap.

At 1544 North Formosa, Andreas Orby's parents were waiting on the porch. Chalky escorted the boy to the door and gave Orby a snappy salute and a warm smile.

"Have a good evening, Mr. Orby," he said. "It's been a pleasure, sir." Adding, "And don't worry. I'm sure Mrs. Tesla will be just fine."

It wasn't long before Criswell found himself back in his driveway. Chalky opened the door and gave him a warm smile that sent a decided chill down Criswell's spine.

"Last stop, sir," the chauffeur said.

As they got out, Maila pointed at a silver 1954 300 SL Coupe parked by the curb. "Is that your car, Chalky?" she asked.

"Yes, it is, Miss Maila."

Maila approached the car and caressed the Mercedes-Benz. "Mmm, sexy," she purred.

"Miss West is very generous." Chalky checked his watch. "I dare say she must be wondering what happened to me. It's quite late."

Maila leaned seductively against the car. "Do you have time to take me for a drive?"

"Why, I'd be delighted, Miss Maila."

"Just call me Maila."

"I'd be delighted…Maila."

Criswell stepped between them. "Uh, no, Maila. I really don't think that's a good idea."

"Why? Just because Chalky is colored? I didn't think you were prejudiced, Mr. Criswell."

"Well, no. It's not that."

"Then what?"

Criswell glanced at Chalky who seemed to be greatly amused by his predicament. "It's like Chalky said, Mae will be worried about him. The funeral was supposed to be over this afternoon and it's past 10 o'clock."

Maila caressed her breast and gave the chauffeur a smile. "You want to give me a ride, don't you, Chalky?"

Chalky smiled. "I certainly would, Maila."

He approached the car and raised the passenger-side Gullwing door. She slid in with feline grace and let her shapely legs peak out beneath her black *Dracula's Daughter* gown. She set the satchel in her lap.

The chauffeur gave Criswell a salute. "Don't worry, sir. I'll have the young lady back before dawn."

Criswell could only smile nervously and wave as Chalky got in the driver's seat. Maila turned and waved to Criswell from the rear window.

The Coupe took off down the street—along with any answers Maila Nurmi might have supplied.

# Chapter 24

On a bench in the hallway outside his office, Criswell found a snoring pile of newspapers.

"Forry?" Criswell asked.

Ackerman stirred; he peered out bleary-eyed from under the papers, adjusted his glasses and yawned. "Hello, Criswell," he said. "What time is it?" He squinted at his watch and started. "Wow, you're late."

"Sorry, Forry, I forgot to tell you." Criswell put down the evidence bags and reached up and felt around the transom. "I keep a spare key up here." He opened the door. "It's been a very eventful day."

"I guess it must have been. Sorry about messing up your evening paper."

"Don't worry about it," Criswell said as he returned the key to the transom.

"Oh." Forry reached for a package he had been using for a pillow. "Somebody left this for you."

Criswell took the package and frowned at the label. "More food supplements? Koenig must be overstocked." He tucked the box under his arm and grabbed the evidence bags. "Come on in."

Tidying up the newspaper as best he could, Forry folded it to a particular article and followed Criswell into his office. "I was reading this item about the Hollywood Historama. Somebody broke in and vandalized the *Double Indemnity* and *Dracula* displays."

"The Hollywood Historama?" Criswell asked, putting his bundles down and taking the paper.

"Yep," Forry said, pointing at the news item. "Barbara Stanwyck's waxwork figure was found stripped completed naked, and I mean naked, they took her wig and clothes, and I mean all of her clothes, the dress and the underwear, and then, like that wasn't bad enough, they took the whole darn Dracula figure with them." Ackerman smirked. "Me personally, I would have much rather taken Barbara."

"I'll bet you would," Criswell remarked, taking the paper.

Forry gestured in the direction of the hallway. "Oh, a process server came by earlier with a summons for you."

Criswell sighed as he scanned the newspaper article. "I'll bet I know what *that* was all about." It was just as Ackerman related. The article went on to say that the likeness of the Tesla waxwork figure was taken directly from the actor's own face. He had submitted to a life cast done by Don Post himself, who had hopes of using the life cast for a mass produced rubber Halloween mask. It was then that Criswell remembered about the body lying in Tesla's grave, and the "mortician's wax" that sweated under the hot California sun.

Ackerman's voice intruded on Criswell's thoughts. "I told him you were out."

"Told *who* I was out?" Criswell asked absently, unable to take his eyes from the paper.

"The process server. So who's suing you, anyway?"

"Armand Jr. is—for some undisclosed reason." He pointed at the article. "Did you read this bit about Tesla's waxworks dummy?"

"You mean about how Don Post cast the life mask? Yeah. As a matter of fact, I have a life mask of Tesla myself."

"You do?"

With obvious pride, Ackerman boasted, "I got it from Jack P. Pierce himself. It's the hallmark of my collection." Forry gestured behind him. "Say, where's Maila?"

"With Chalky. I hope she'll be okay. Chalky's mixed up in something nasty. I don't know what, but it has something to do with what happened to Eddie." He pointed at the newspaper. "Forry, I have a very bad feeling about this article. Look at when the break-in was discovered. It was around the same time that we found out the funeral home had given us the wrong body to bury."

"So?"

"How much do you want to bet that the body that's buried in Armand's grave is actually the stolen waxworks dummy?"

"So what's that got to do with the naked and bald Barbara Stanwyck?"

Cris shrugged. "I dunno. Maybe they did it to throw us off the scent."

Forry gave Criswell the fisheye. "Yeah, that's gotta be it." He spotted something on the desk and picked up one of the evidence bags. He pulled out the bottle of whiskey and gave Cris a smirk. "I see you've been to the liquor store. Are you sure you're not a little tight?" Eyeing the label and then Criswell, he commented. "Because that's the kind of thing I'd hear from a guy who's had a snoot full."

Criswell smacked the paper down and grabbed the bottle back. "I'm perfectly sober. And I wouldn't drink this if I were you."

"I don't drink. Sci-Fi is my high."

"Good, because this stuff has a hell of a kick. It just might be poisoned."

Ackerman quirked an inquisitive eyebrow, reached for the bottle, opened it and took a sniff. "Poisoned? Who poisoned it?"

"I have my suspicions, but I can't figure out her motive."

"*Her* motive? Do you think Hope—?"

"No, not Hope. I don't see how *she* could have substituted Armand's body for a dummy. That's something the funeral home did, I'll bet my life on it."

Ackerman gave Criswell a searching look as he handed the bottle back. "Okay, suppose the body in the ground is the stolen dummy. Why would they go to all that trouble?"

Criswell bagged up the bottle and set it down. "I think they were afraid of leaving the evidence of a poisoning behind. They're going to cremate the real body and do it right under everybody's noses."

"You bet your ash."

"Enough of your puns, Forry, this is serious."

"There can never be enough puns," Forry insisted. "But I can see what you're driving at."

"I swear, if you make a reckless driving pun…"

Forry smirked. "Shouldn't all good driving be wreck-less?" He held up his hands and said, "But I digress. Everybody at the funeral could swear on a stack of Bibles that they saw Armand buried." He chortled. "That is, if swearing on a stack of Bibles really meant anything."

Cris eyed Forry. "Speaking of evidence, what happened at the drug store? Did you get the pictures?"

Forry held up a photo envelope. "Right here."

"And?"

Taking out one of the photos, Forry ogled the picture. "That girl was right. These snapshots of her are really something. Bettie Page, eat your heart out!"

Criswell glared impatiently as he reached for the pull cord on his desk lamp. "Come on, Forry, don't keep me in suspense. I'm not in the mood." Criswell went to his closet.

"Sorry." Ackerman pulled out the other pictures and began shuffling through them. "You're awfully tense. Present tense, past tense, and future tense, even."

"I have good reason to be." Criswell pulled out a gray case containing a Bell & Howell movie projector. He put the movie projector on his desk and unlatched the case.

Selecting a photo, Ackerman said, "Well, I'll let you have a look for yourself. Here."

Criswell took the picture and examined it under his desk lamp. It was a very clear shot of Edward D. Wood Jr. holding the slumped form of a blonde woman in a black dress.

Forry pointed at Eddie's hand. "His hand is either covered with chocolate syrup or blood. I'm betting that's blood."

Cris fumbled around on his desk and found a magnifying glass. He focused on the face of the woman in black and then exclaimed, "Oh, my God."

Ackerman leaned in. "Do you recognize her?"

"No, I recognize *him*."

"Of course you do. That's Ed Wood."

"That's not who I was referring to." Criswell pointed at the woman in black. "I meant her. She's not a she; she's a *he*. More specifically, he's an old friend of mine…Mae's and mine…That's Harry Dean, a Los Angeles police detective and a known transvestite."

Forry blinked in disbelief. "A killer in drag? You're kidding." He took the photo and studied it more closely.

"Sounds like something Eddie might write about, doesn't it?" Criswell flipped up the projector reel arms and snapped in the take up reel. "Still, that's who it is. I'd know Harry anywhere." He unwrapped the cord and plugged in the projector, and then pulled the film can from his pocket.

"What are you doing?"

Holding up the film can, Cris said, "Do you like home movies?"

"Only the kind that Lionel Atwill used to show at his tennis parties back in the day. They were stag films he used to make himself, and with him as the star."

"Then you'll love this one."

Criswell pried open the film can and slipped the reel on the spooling arm and inserted the leader into the slot. Turning the knob to "Autoload," the film threaded through the projector and wrapped itself around the take-up reel.

"What's on it?"

Criswell aimed the projector at a blank wall. "If I'm right, it's footage of Mae and Chalky going at it hot and heavy."

"How did Armand get hold of a thing like that?"

"Search me," Criswell said with a shrug. "Lights;" He turned off the desk lamp and took his seat. He motioned for Forry to sit down in a chair next to his, and then reached behind him and fumbled for the projector control knob; "Camera and *action*."

The film ran through the gate. After the usual countdown there was a steady, *click, click, click* on the soundtrack timed to coincide with a pulsing white dot. The white dot began pulsating faster and faster as the rhythmic clicking increased.

After a minute of this, Forry frowned in disappointment. "This is the worst stag film I've ever seen." He pushed up his glasses and rubbed his eyes. "And it's giving me is a hell of a headache."

"Wait a minute," Criswell said leaning forward. "This isn't a stag film. But I've heard that clicking before."

"You have; where?"

"Back at Dr. Tom's office, he was hypnotizing Kathy Wood and I heard that same sound coming from the exam room." He blinked. "Wait, what was that?"

Forry asked hopefully, "What was what? Did you see breasts?"

"There was a brief frame of something that flashed on for just a moment."

"Was it breasts?"

"Anyone ever tell you that you have a one track mind?"

"Yeah, and I really like where it takes me."

Criswell ran the film in reverse, and then forward in slow motion, five frames at a time. Eventually a frame came up that displayed one word, "WONDROUS." This was followed by single frames of other words like, "GUILT," "DESIRE," and "HATE," except they were all projected as mirror images.

"Why are the words backwards like that?" Forry asked.

"I wonder." Cris searched his desk. "Assuming Kathy was lying down, the easiest way for her to see the projected image…" He took his hand mirror and used it to watch the movie over his shoulder. "Uh huh, just like this. You use an angled mirror much the way a patient in an iron lung uses a mirror to see more than just the ceiling."

"What? Do you think maybe he's brainwashing his patients?"

"It looks like Dr. Tom is doing more than curing migraines and backaches."

Ackerman took off his glasses and rubbing the bridge of his nose. "I'll say this for the movie, it sure hurts my eyes." He put his glasses back on and stared earnestly at Criswell. "How do you suppose Ed Wood got hold of it?"

Cris shrugged. "He could have sneaked it out after one of his sessions. But more to the point, what was Chalky doing with it?" Criswell rewound the film.

"What if Chalky deliberately switched the real stag film for this thing. I'll bet Mae's got the stag film safe at her apartment right now."

"You may be right." The film now rewound, Cris turned off the projector and slipped the reel off its spindle. "Still, I better get this back to Chalky before he misses it, just in case you're wrong."

Ackerman stood up and put his glasses back on. "Well, I think I'll get back to the Ackermansion. Wendy hates me staying out too late. Besides, my head is killing me."

Criswell rubbed his aching temple. "Yeah, mine, too. Funny, but Kathy didn't complain of a headache after Dr. Tom snapped her out of her trance."

"She probably got used to it." Forry smirked. "The last time I had a headache this big was at a 3D movie premiere; *House of Wax*. Armand made a live guest appearance at that premiere, too. One of the few times he allowed himself to be photographed with his glasses on."

"I didn't know he was in that picture."

"He wasn't. Don Marlowe arranged a weird publicity stunt that had nothing to do with the picture. Armand walked down the red carpet in his Dracula costume, and with a gorilla on a leash."

"A real gorilla?"

"Nah. It was a guy in a costume. Bob Burns, I think."

Criswell sighed as he put the reel back in its film can. "The things Armand did to make ends meet." He pressed the two lids of the film can together and stared wistfully at it. "Maybe Chalky didn't switch films at all. Maybe Armand stole the movie from Dr. Tom just to feel important. He told Eddie he was sitting on some big secret and Eddie tried to blackmail Mae based on whatever Armand told him."

"So Mae never actually saw the picture?"

"And maybe she really did make a stag film of sorts with Chalky. That would explain everything."

Forry shrugged. "I guess. But, what kind of hocus-pocus is Dr. Tom up to with that thing?"

"I'm not sure. All I know is that everyone who claims to be a patient of Dr. Tom is acting mighty strange."

Stretching, Forry said, "Well, whatever's going on, I'm going home."

"Good night, Forry."

Forry waved as he headed out the door, intoning one of his signature exit lines; "Up, up and away, with 4SJ!"

With a weary shake of his head, Criswell finished packing up the projector and returned it to the closet. As he closed the door, he caught his reflection in the mirror and was horrified at the condition of his makeup. Going to his desk, he rummaged around for his supplies, but came up empty. Searching around his office, he remembered that he had a stash of pancake and rouge in Maila's desk. Cris tried to open a bottom drawer — it was locked.

He wondered aloud, "Why would Maila lock her desk?"

Criswell jimmied the lock with a letter opener and pulled open the middle drawer. He found his pancake makeup, and something else — an envelope addressed to him and postmarked yesterday — with Ed Wood's return address.

He remembered what Ed had told him about watching his mail. Cris also remembered bringing Maila the black dress and Maila looking a bit flustered and maybe a tad guilty as she stuffed something in her drawer.

He opened the envelope and found it was empty. Cris rummaged through the middle drawer and found a note stuffed toward the back. The outline of a small key was impressed in the notepaper — the kind of key one might use to open a bus station locker.

Reading the note, Criswell discovered it was the kind of annoyingly cryptic letter that only Ed Wood could have written.

CRIS,

NO TIME TO EXPLAIN. GO TO UNION BUS STATION. USE THIS KEY. GUARD WHAT YOU FIND IN THE LOCKER WITH YOUR LIFE.

EDDIE

Criswell rolled his eyes and sighed heavily. Why didn't Ed just *say* what was at the bus station?

The phone rang and gave Criswell a start. Answering, he said, "Hello?"

A voice whispered, "Come to the Gold Cup. Come alone."

Cris couldn't tell if it was a man's or a woman's voice. "Who is this?"

"Who do you think, Pudgyface?" the voice whispered.

Criswell was taken aback. "Pudgyface? Look, I think you have the wrong number."

"Oh, I have the right number, Pudgyface. I bet you thought calling me from payphones kept your identity a secret. But I got wise quick enough."

"What's this all about?" Cris demanded.

"Come to the Gold Cup. Come alone." *Click!* The stranger hung up.

Criswell stared at the handset before hanging up the phone. He stuffed the letter back in its envelope and stuck it in his pocket. He was about to leave his office when he checked to make sure the six-shooter in his pocket was loaded. There were still four unfired bullets in the cylinder. He pocketed the piece and headed out, locking the door after him.

# Part Four

The Sinister Urge.

# Chapter 25

*Down at the Golden Cup*
*They set the young ones up*
*Under the neon light*
*Selling day for night*
**— Jackson Browne**, *On the Boulevard*

The weight of the six-shooter in his pocket was reassuring as Criswell entered the smoky dankness of the Gold Cup. He sauntered up to the bar, feeling a bit like the new fast draw that had just come in on the noon stagecoach and asked, not for a straight whiskey like he might have done in a Western, but for his usual, an Irish coffee with very little coffee.

"Someone's been looking for you, Cris," said the leather-clad bartender.

"Oh?"

"He's pretty, a bit older than you like, but he's pretty enough if you're not in the mood for chicken."

Criswell looked around the coffeehouse. Boy prostitutes called "chickens" were hustling for drinks and dates from "chicken hawks," self-described family men leading double lives. There were drag queens, too. Many of them were very poorly made up big ugly men with six o'clock shadows under pancake makeup and unkempt wigs.

The bartender nodded at a figure standing at far end of the bar. "That's him. Like I said, he's pretty. Or at least he would be if he'd shave off that mustache."

"Oh?" Criswell glanced at the attractive-looking fellow in full drag holding a gold-lamé clutch purse. He wore a blonde wig and filled-out pink angora sweater. It struck Criswell that the visage was vaguely familiar — the blonde wig especially. It was an exaggerated 1940s-style coif. The bangs sat like an egg roll across the drag's pale forehead. Soft waves cascaded and rolled under at the shoulders, like the wig Barbara Stanwyck wore in *Double Indemnity*. The drag's true identity finally dawned on Criswell as the vision of Barbara Stanwyck approached with a seductive wiggle. Like the bartender said, in the dingy lighting, he could have easily pass for a real girl, that is if not for the Errol Flynn mustache gracing his top lip.

It was Ed Wood!

Ed took the empty stool beside Criswell. "Buy me a drink, Pudgyface," he said speaking out of the corner of his mouth. "Make it look like you're hitting on me."

"Eddie," Cris whispered. "That was *you* on the phone earlier, wasn't it?"

"Yeah. Put your arm around me. And it's 'Glenda,' not Eddie."

Criswell did as he was told. "Whatever you say, *Glenda*. And what's with this Pudgyface business?"

Wood ignored the question. "Take me to a booth," he insisted. "Buy me a drink first."

Criswell ordered Eddie a whiskey and they went to a dark corner booth. "So you're the one who vandalized the Hollywood Historama," Criswell said, sliding in next to Eddie.

"You heard about that?"

"It was in the evening paper. I should have realized you were behind it when I read that somebody had stripped the dummy in the *Double Indemnity* display. Barbara Stanwyck's outfit looks just the way you dressed in *Glen or Glenda*. But where did you go after that?"

"I've been lying low, keeping out of sight," Ed opened his purse, "waiting for my chance."

Criswell studied Wood carefully. "Waiting for your chance to do what?"

Eddie pulled out a compact Beretta M 1934; once described by an expert as a lady's gun for a lady who wasn't a very nice one. He poked the snub muzzle of the Italian 9mm automatic in Criswell's ribs. "I was waiting for my chance to kill you, Pudgyface."

"Oh, shit," Criswell exclaimed as he reached for the six-shooter in his pocket.

Eddie poked him harder. "Keep those hands where I can see them, Pudgyface."

Criswell did as he was told. "Okay, Eddie. Here are my hands. See?"

"I told you, it's Glenda! Call me Glenda, Pudgyface."

"All right, *Glenda*, why do you keep calling me Pudgyface?"

Eddie rolled his eyes. "Didn't you read the script?"

"Script? What script?" He was about to lower his hands when Wood stuck the muzzle in deeper. Up went the hands again.

"Pudgy is the guy that turned Glenda, a harmless transvestite, into a vicious killer for hire. Pudgyface wears a bowler hat and a greatcoat."

There was a mad glint in Wood's eyes as he spoke. "He gives Glenda her instructions, tells her who she's going to kill for the Mob." He prodded Criswell's ribs with the gun barrel again. Under other circumstances, it might have tickled. "Now say the line so I can shoot Pudgyface." Eddie acted as if this was a perfectly sane thing to do. When Criswell remained mum, Wood rolled his eyes and sighed irritably. "You're spoiling the take. You said you wanted a part in my next picture, and this is it! Now say, 'Glenda, be reasonable. We can work this out.'" The muzzle poked deeper. "Say it," he whispered. "We're running out of film. Say the line."

"Oh, my god, you're sleepwalking!" Criswell exclaimed. "Just like that man complained about at Dr. Tom's." He stared earnestly. "Listen, Eddie, you're having a bad dream. You're really sleepwalking and acting out what you're dreaming. Only," he glanced at the gun and the gold purse, "only where'd you get the gun and, that purse, I've seen it before."

"Quit wasting film and say – the – line," Wood pressed.

"Kathy and another patient of Dr. Tom's, that pretty teenage girl, they had the same gold purse! Eddie, you've got to listen to me before you do something we'll both regret." But it was no use reasoning with him. Eddie continued to act like they were making a picture together. "Say the line," Eddie repeated.

Okay, so if he thought they were making a picture, maybe there was a way to reach Wood after all. Acting quickly, Criswell said, "Uh, Eddie, we have to cut."

"Hey, I'm the director! Only I get to say cut!"

"But Armand is furious with you."

Eddie's glassy, staring eyes grew wide with concern. "What? Armand's furious? Why?"

It was working. "He's upset because his part is too small. He says my part is upstaging him."

"But—but I gave Armand the role of Delton Van Carter, a millionaire and Glen's closest friend."

"Don't you hear him?" Criswell pointed at thin air. "He, uh, he wants Delton Van Carter to be an emotional part, a part where he can *act*! Armand wants you to stop shooting and write some new pages this instant!"

Eddie sighed. "Well, if that's what Armand wants—"

Wood put the gun down on the table and pantomimed rolling a fresh page into a typewriter. His fingers flew furiously across an imaginary keyboard as Criswell grabbed the gun and pocketed it. Clutching his throat, he swallowed hard and sighed, "That was too close."

"Hey," Eddie said with a smile. "I like that line. I'll have to use it somewhere."

Cris chuckled. No matter what, Eddie Wood could be counted on to act like Eddie Wood. Criswell got up and said, "Wait here, Eddie. I need to make a couple of phone calls."

Cris left Ed happily typing away on thin air.

The phone booth was located in the corner by the men's room. A beautiful boy was making a call, no doubt to his lover or maybe his pimp. But something about the young man's body language made Criswell hesitate. Usually the caller had his back turned to create a needed sense of intimacy inside the confines of a glass box, especially when calling a lover. But the boy was watching Criswell as if he was the subject of the conversation. Maybe it was his nearly getting shot by his best friend that made Cris more than a touch paranoid, but it was the way the boy kept staring at Criswell, his gaze intense, his dark eyes fixed on Criswell's eyes. It was not the come hither intensity of a chicken looking for a chicken hawk, but more the reverse: Cris felt like the intended prey, and not for a quick fucking.

As he approached, and for the second time today, Cris had the strange feeling he was looking at a familiar face. He couldn't place the young man, much as he couldn't recall where he had seen the dead boy back at the funeral home, but he was sure he had seen the occupant of the phone booth before. The boy was tall, slender, broad shoulders, short dark hair with bangs. He looked 17, but was probably older, 20, maybe, no older than 22. The boy's features were angular, severe; his lips full and dark, like a drag who had forgotten to take off his makeup. His eyebrows were ached and shapely to give his features a more feminine look, which meant he was more than likely a drag queen, someone who wore women's clothing, but was not attracted to girls. He wondered if the boy had a knife, or maybe a gold-lamé clutch purse with a lady's gun inside. He hung up the phone and exited the booth, as he did, Criswell noted the hands: long slender fingers, yet strong; an artist's hands, a sculptor's hands. The hair on the back of Criswell's neck prickled as the young man's dark eyes sizing him up. The boy smirked and said in a low, melodious voice; "You're next, handsome." And for the first time in his life, Criswell felt the kind of revulsion a straight might experience if he were to be hit on by a gay in a men's room.

It was then that Criswell put two-and-two together. That melodious voice was the clincher. Cris watched the boy's hips sway in a girlish fashion as he left the bar and imagined the boy in a dark wig and a nurse's uniform, a clipboard clutched in those tapered hands: he had first encountered the boy at Dr. Tom's clinic; the young man wasn't a man when Criswell first met him: back then he was in the guise of Nurse Leslie!

Criswell tried to tell himself that he was just imagining things, that he was just shaken up. It's only natural to see conspiracies around every corner after what he just went through. Still, he found it awfully hard to keep his hands from shaking as he yanked the phone booth door closed and as he tried to insert a coin in the slot and dial.

It was awfully hard.

The literary agent ushered in his lovelies.

# Chapter 26

It was around 11 o'clock when Ed and Criswell left the Gold Cup. Eddie was acting like they were out for a leisurely stroll and Cris had to urge him along. The psychic couldn't get out of his head the image of Nurse Leslie making a call in the phone booth. Paranoid delusion or not, he felt sure he/she was ordering someone to finish the job that Eddie had failed to complete. There were questions to be asked and it was now or never. As he glanced around nervously, Cris asked, "Uh, is it true that Kathy tried to kill you?"

Oblivious to any danger, Eddie spoke with a dreamy smile plastered all over his powdered puss. "Oh, she went a little nuts, I guess. She gets that way sometimes." He giggled girlishly. "But today, wow, I never saw such murderous rage in her eyes. At least, not while she was sober." He said this with all the blissful joy of Jack Haley's Tin Man.

"What's that supposed to mean?" he asked, pulling on Ed's arm. "Uh, come on, Eddie. Step up the pace."

Eddie pulled back. "Why? What's your hurry?"

"Oh, uh, Armand's waiting for his new script pages back at my office."

Eddie frowned. "But he was with us at the bar."

"Well *now* he's waiting at my office."

"Why didn't you say so?" Eddie stepped lively.

Criswell had to hurry to keep up with him. "Anyway, you were saying about Kathy?"

"Oh, Kathy's a mean drunk. When she gets tight, she's like a different woman." He stopped short and gazed earnestly. "When we're both tight, watch out. We fight like hellcats. And you should see Kathy when she's got the shakes. Kathy practically tears the bag out of my hands when I come back from the liquor store."

"I never realized." He pulled Eddie by the arm, mindful of every shadow, every passing car. "Hurry up."

Wood gladly let Criswell lead him and said with a smirk, "But the make-up sex is *great!*"

"I can imagine." Criswell stopped abruptly. Was he seeing things or was that barefoot raven-haired young damsel wearing nothing but a pair of white panties and a pink angora sweater? The streetlights lit her dramatically as she came drifting toward them like one of Ed Wood's adolescent wet dreams.

Ed remained oblivious. "Dr. Tom, he's been trying to help Kathy get off the booze."

"Has he?"

It was cold and girl's nipples stood erect like twin bullets of jutting desire against the pink fuzz of angora. The young woman was joined by two other girls, one golden haired; the other ginger. They all wore the same white panties and matching angora sweaters. Cris noted a shadowy triangular patch behind the opaque silkiness of the blonde's panties, suggesting her golden locks came from a peroxide bottle. Gulping nervously, Cris slowly backed away and pulled Eddie with him.

"Did Dr. Tom happen to use hypnosis on her?" the psychic asked anxiously.

"He sure did. He tried to help me get off the stuff, too. The sessions work, but it doesn't last. We have to go back for follow-up treatments. His office is always crowded with satisfied patients."

Criswell pointed at the surreal scene. "Satisfied patients like *them?*"

They wafted forward like Dracula's undead brides; each wore a necklace with a dangling sorority medal. But Criswell's anxious attention was drawn to their identical and fatally familiar looking gold-lamé clutch purses; suggesting that these saucy somnambulists were Eddie's replacement killers.

The golden one spoke in a Southern drawl as thick as Tennessee mud; "All right, honey lambs, it's time we Angora Debs soaked us some little ol' freshmen!" Brandishing her Beretta, she said, "Get out your water pistols!"

As Raven and Ginger complied, Criswell muttered, "Oh, shit," grabbing Eddie and ducking behind a mailbox just as the sorority sisters opened fire with their 9mm "water pistols." Bullets ricocheted off the red and blue metal box as Criswell struggled to think. He appealed to Ed by bringing up Armand Tesla. What could he say to distract three angora clad sorority sisters hypnotized into thinking they were hazing freshmen with water pistols?

Of course!

He grabbed his handkerchief and waved it in the air, shouting: "Ladies! Hold your fire! It's the Dean! Stop this nonsense immediately!" The handkerchief was shot out of his hands. "LADIES!" he shouted. "THIS IS THE DEAN! HOLD YOUR FIRE!"

"The Dean!" the girls all gasped at once.

The sorority sisters held their fire and their breaths as Criswell emerged and grabbed his glittering lapels in a gesture of Deanly authority. "What is the meaning of this?" he demanded.

"Gosh, we're awful sorry," said Raven.

"We thought you were a couple of freshmen," Ginger explained.

"Why, Ma'am, it's only hazin' week," elaborated Blondie, displaying her Beretta. "There ain't no harm in givin' a freshman a little ol' bath, is there?"

Criswell harrumphed. "Do you girls realize that you nearly soaked your House Mother's brand new angora sweater?" He gestured for Eddie to step out. Ed emerged while adjusting his wig, obediently taking on the role assigned to him. "Why, you're bringing shame to the very angora sweaters of your sorority," Eddie scolded while caressing his sweater and adopting a feminine pose of exasperation. "Now give the Dean those water pistols this instant!"

"We're sorry," the shamefaced girls chorused as they quickly complied.

Eddie passed the weapons to Criswell. "Now you girls scoot. It's cold and you'll all catch your deaths."

"Yes, Ma'am." The sisters clutched their angora sweaters to their throats and ran shivering into the night.

Criswell pocketed the guns. "Okay, Eddie, let's—"

Eddie was checking his makeup in a storefront window.

"Eddie?" Cris was about to pull Eddie away from his reflection when he noticed a familiar figure in the window glass. Turning around, he saw Nurse Leslie watching them from the phone booth across the street.

"Come on, Eddie," Cris said, urging his friend along, "I think we'd better get back to my office—fast."

Once they were safely inside Criswell's office, Cris led Eddie to a chair and commanded him to sit down. Wood complied. He sat demurely and crossed his legs. Then Cris hurried to the window and peaked out from behind the shades to make sure the coast was clear. "I don't think we were followed. At least, I hope not."

"I hope Armand likes these new pages," Wood said with a feminine lilt. He was holding an imaginary sheaf of revised script pages in an imaginary folder.

"I'm sure he will, Eddie." Cris pulled out the folded envelope.

"So you did get my letter," Eddie said with a smile.

"No, Maila got to it first. Tell me what was in the satchel you left at the Union Bus Station."

Eddie said offhandedly; "A human skull."

"What!"

"It was evidence Armand collected for the class-action suit."

"Class-action suit? Eddie, what are you talking about? Start from the beginning."

Wood said in a low whisper, "It all started that day at the cemetery, back before Armand committed himself for treatment. Armand was still on dope and pretty shaky. What he found that day could have been the last straw convincing him to get clean."

"What does that have to do with a skull in a satchel?"

"Rain must have eroded the cemetery grounds or maybe it was all the digging. But the coffins were close to the surface and while Armand was playing vampire in the graveyard, his foot sank into one of the graves and went right through a skeleton's chest."

"Coffins? Wait, I though the developers had moved the coffins."

"That's what they wanted people to think. The developers were gonna save a few dollars by building their apartment houses over the graves without moving the bodies, just the headstones."

"You saw all this happen?"

"No, it happened while I was helping Karl move headstones around. Armand explained all this in his letter."

"What was he hoping to do with the skull?"

"Armand was going to get a dentist to identify who it belonged to. That along with the names Armand Jr. collected from the discarded tombstones. That would prove the bodies hadn't been moved."

"This was for a class-action suit against the real estate partnership?"

"Yep. I guess that's why Armand refused to go to the party. Everyone there was going to be named in the class-action suit."

"Including me." Criswell frowned. "But if Armand had this evidence as far back as last April, why didn't he bring it to the families' attention sooner or get a restraining order?"

"He committed himself to the State Hospital, remember? Kicking his drug habit made him forget. Withdrawal will do that to you. But the minute he got clean he contacted a lawyer. Armand told him about the skull. The lawyer didn't believe him at first, of course. Then Armand told him he had other evidence. He was going to bring it to him the day after he died."

"What other evidence?"

"The footage I took at the cemetery for *The Vampire's Tomb*."

Criswell reached into his pocket and produced the film can. "You think that's the film you slipped to Chalky?"

Eddie nodded and pointed at the can. "I captured the evidence without realizing it. If you take one of the frames and blow it up, you can see the bones sticking out of the dirt."

"I hate to disappoint you, but the only things on this film are a bunch of flashing dots, some words and a clicking soundtrack."

"That's ridiculous."

"I'll show you." Criswell went to the closet and got out the projector. "Why was Armand trying to keep this a secret from Hope?"

"Armand was convinced she was selling him out to the Mob. See, Armand thought the Mob was behind the land deal. I guess because of Dean Martin and Frank Sinatra."

"And you tried to blackmail Mae to finance *Grave Robbers from Outer Space*?"

"I was going to show her the film first, and then threaten her with the skull if she didn't cave."

Criswell threaded the film through the projector. "It's hard to believe she took you seriously."

"She took me seriously enough to set me up for a Mob hit."

"See for yourself." Criswell turned on the projector. "This is the movie I took from Chalky. You tell me if this is worth blackmail."

The film ran the same as before. Blips of light timed to clicks, words appearing and disappearing too quickly to register consciously. Wood's eyes were transfixed on the wall. He jumped up and pointed excitedly. "See! You didn't believe me, but there it is! That's the graveyard! See the bones?"

Criswell was stunned. "Do you see anything else?"

"Wow!" Eddie ran up to the wall and pointed at the projected image of flashing dots. "I actually caught the moment Armand put his foot through the shallow grave! See that?"

"No," said Criswell as realization dawned. "But you obviously do."

Things were finally beginning to make some weird kind of sense. Cris smiled as he shut off the projector and rewound the film. Instantly, Wood calmed down and returned to his seat.

"Okay, Eddie, now I want you to tell me where you've really been all this time."

Eddie flashed his usual conniving grin. "Why, I was just at my good pal Dr. Tom's."

"And I'll bet Dr. Tom helped you to relax with one of his treatments, right?"

"Of course."

There was a knock at the door. "Don't move, Eddie. Stay right there."

Criswell found Forry Ackerman, his face covered with red lipstick cupid's bows. He was standing in the hallway in a raincoat over striped pajamas, and wearing three very familiar angora clad girls like trophies of feminine pulchritude; two on each arm; one hugging his neck. "Can you believe it? I offered to give them a lift and they said yes!"

"Oh, dear god," Cris exclaimed. "Forry, those girls…."

"…are adorable!" Forry gushed. "This is Clara," nodding at Raven, "Matilda," squeezing Ginger, "and Mary Sue," winking at Blondie. "I especially like, Mary Sue. She's from Georgia. A real peach." He hugged his harem. "So what's so important?"

Criswell beckoned. "Bring them inside. There's something I want you to see."

The literary agent ushered in his lovelies, and then stopped short and blinked at Ed. He smiled nervously at Criswell. "Cris, why didn't you tell me you had company?" He clutched his raincoat closed and tried to step away from the girls, who refused to disentangle themselves from Forry's clutches. "Oh, sorry, miss!"

Closing the door, Criswell said, "That's not company; that's—"

"Our House Mother," said Clara.

Cris leaned over and whispered; "Actually, that's Eddie Wood. They only think he's their House Mother, and don't tell them otherwise."

Confused, Forry gawked and said, "House Mother? You mean— My God, he's alive!" He looked Wood up and down. "Funny I didn't notice the mustache. But why's he dressed like Barbara Stanwyck?" He blinked with realization. "You mean he's the guy that vandalized the Wax Museum?"

"That's Eddie's way of blending in." Cris added with a whisper, "I think he's in a hypnotic trance." He jerked a thumb at the tasty trio. "They're in a trance too. That's why they'll do anything you ask them." He whispered in an aside, "They tried to kill us earlier."

"What? You're crazy."

Criswell pulled one of the Berettas from his pocket. "See? They were armed with these. Eddie had one too, in that purse there." He nodded at the ladies. "They all had similar purses, and guns, no doubt supplied by Dr. Tom."

Forry nodded nervously. "I see. I see."

"Talk to him if you don't believe me. Go see for yourself."

As Criswell locked the Berettas and his six-shooter in the safe, Ackerman cautiously approached the hypnotized Ed Wood. Eddie reached into his purse, and then took out a file and started filing his nails, humming contentedly. Forry waved his hand in front of Wood's face. "Uh, hello, Eddie."

Wood ignored him completely. He sat there happily filing his nails, smiling demurely.

Ackerman was astonished. "Hey, Wood isn't pitching a story or asking about a manuscript." He looked over at Criswell. "My God, Wood really *is* hypnotized!"

"What did I tell you," Cris said. "He'll just sit there completely oblivious until—" He frowned and pointed. "Say, what's he looking at?"

"What do you mean?" Forry glanced at Wood and saw his eyes were transfixed on something. Forry stuck both his hands in his bathrobe pockets and shrugged. "Huh, that's odd."

Wood stopped looking at whatever it was that fascinated him a moment ago and continued filing his nails, humming happily.

Criswell nudged Forry. "Take your hands out of your pockets."

"Why?"

"Just do it. And show him your hands."

"My hands?" Forry shrugged and pulled out his hands and displayed them, palms up. Eddie took no notice. Forry waved them under Eddie's nose, and still no reaction. Ackerman shrugged and said, "Whatever he found so fascinating, he's ignoring now."

"Yeah, I guess you're right. But *this* I know Eddie will find interesting. And maybe your fan club, too." Cris returned to the projector and gestured at the chair next to Wood. "Have a seat, Forry." Assuming his Dean character, he addressed the sorority sisters. "Ladies, it's time for an instructional film. Gather around."

Forry frowned. "Hey, you're not going to show that movie of Dr. Tom's, are you?"

"Yes, I am."

"But I just got over my headache."

Just then, Lt. Jack Southern barged in. "This better be damn good, Criswell," he snarled. Southern was also garbed in hastily put on attire; a trench coat over pants and a pajama top. His feet were shod in a pair of bedroom slippers. "It's been a long day." Southern stopped short when he spotted the girls. "What the hell?" He spotted Ed Wood and repeated, "What the hell?"

Criswell closed the door. "That's Eddie Wood in drag. And as for those girls, well, I'll explain as we go." Cris gestured for the detective to sit down beside Ackerman and made introductions. "Oh, uh, Lt. Jack Southern; Forry Ackerman. Forry, this is Jack Southern."

Southern sighed and shook his head. "Oh yeah; Ackerman, the other Hardy Boy."

Forry frowned at Criswell as the psychic began rummaging through his desk. "Hardy Boy?"

Criswell smiled. "That's what the Lieutenant calls amateur sleuths like us."

Lt. Southern gestured at the girls. "So who are they, the Andrews sisters?"

"No, they're three very unlikely assassins."

Southern leaned forward and studied Wood more closely. "Say, he looks like Barbara Stanwyck in that movie, what's it called?"

"*Double Indemnity*?" Ackerman suggested.

"Yeah! *Double Indemnity*!" He did a double take. "Did you say 'assassins'?"

"That's what I said." Changing the subject, Criswell asked; "Jack, do you happen to know if Harry Dean ever visited a chiropractor?"

"A chiropractor!"

Criswell pulled out the envelope of photos. "Well, we have evidence that Harry Dean was the woman in black that tried to assassinate Eddie."

Lt. Southern jumped up. "*What!*"

"We've got the picture to prove it." Cris passed a magnifying glass to Southern and pointed at the photo. "I think you'll agree that that's Harry Dean under the veil."

The Lieutenant squinted through the lens and shrugged. "Okay, it's Dean, but so what? Dean may have been a little eccentric, but he was no killer."

"Those three girls there aren't killers either, at least not under ordinary circumstances. But I'm telling you, they shot at Eddie and me."

Southern looked askance at the sorority sisters as they flirted with him. "They don't look very dangerous to me."

"That's the trick. They didn't think they were doing anything dangerous. They thought they were playing a college hazing prank on Eddie and me. They were convinced their guns were water pistols."

Southern shoved the photos back at Criswell. "What's that got to do with Harry? As for your photo evidence; you say Dean is attacking your pal, but this could be a picture of your pal shooting an undercover cop in cold blood."

Criswell turned off the desk lamp. "Well, this might change your mind. Sit down and watch this. Eddie is going to have a very interesting reaction to this little film, maybe the girls, too." He turned on the projector.

The film ran the same as before. Southern noted the look of awe on Wood's face. "He looks like he's on dope."

"He's not drugged. He's in a trance." Cris nodded at the girls. "Look. They're fascinated, too."

The sorority sisters sat cross-legged on the floor and stared up wide-eyed at the screen. A dribble of drool formed at the apex of Mary Sue's chin.

"Now observe." Criswell leaned forward and whispered in Wood's ear. "What do you see, Eddie?"

Wood instantly jumped up and pointed at the wall. "This is the film I was telling you about! That's the graveyard! See the bones?"

Southern frowned. "He's faking."

Eddie pointed. "There's the graveyard, and there's Armand putting his foot through the coffin!"

"Where did you get this?" exclaimed Matilda. "I swear; I only stole that scarf because I had to. It was part of my initiation."

"Scarf?" said Mary Sue. "Why, sugar, I don't know want you're talking about. Why, that's me in the back seat with the captain of the football team. If my Daddy sees it, there'd be a shotgun wedding for sure."

"You're both loopy," Clara insisted. "That's me and my psychology professor." She blushed. "I wasn't getting very good grades, and…well, all the girls do it."

"You mean," Forry asked, "They see all those blips and dots and words as something different?"

"Not just something different, but something that means a lot to them." The Lieutenant waved his hand in front of Wood's face. "This is just plain screwy."

Criswell leaned forward. "Eddie, when you showed this film to Mae, was she alone or was Chalky with her?"

"Chalky was with her."

Criswell stopped the projector and rewound the film. "Mae is another one of Dr. Tom Mason's patients. Chalky used to be a prizefighter. I'll bet his back needs adjusting every now and then, and knowing Mae, wherever she goes for treatment, he goes, too. Chances are, when Mae and Chalky saw this film, they saw each other caught in the act of screwing."

Lt. Southern shrugged. "Okay, so whatever a person is guilty about, this movie somehow makes them see it. So what?"

"Don't you get it? Somehow this movie gives Dr. Tom a window into the subject's unconscious, making the subject reveal their deepest hopes and desires and secrets. It probably has something to do with the words hidden between the flashing dots."

"Words?" asked Lt. Southern. "I don't see any words."

Criswell pointed at the projector. "There are words that flash on the screen too fast to be consciously aware of, but fast enough to give you a headache. I think they're trigger words. Words like 'hate,' 'desire,' and 'wondrous.'"

"And he uses this for what, blackmail?"

Criswell turned on the projector and pointed at the flashing dots. "No, not blackmail. Something far more sinister. Dr. Tom conditions his subjects to kill on command."

"That's impossible," Forry insisted. "You can't get a person to do anything under hypnosis that they wouldn't do while awake. Or so I've always heard."

"It looks like Dr. Tom found a way around that."

Wood held his head and groaned, teetering back and forth on his heels. The girls did likewise, rocking back and forth from their lotus postures like Hindu monks.

"What's with them?" Southern asked.

"I think they're coming out of it!"

Southern jumped up and he and Criswell each grabbed an arm and steered Eddie into a chair just as the three sorority sisters looked down and realized they were practically bottomless in front of a group of strange older men. They screamed harmoniously and tried to cover themselves.

"WHITE SLAVERS!" Mary Sue shrieked.

Southern flashed his badge. "It's okay, Miss. I'm a cop."

His trench coat opened, revealing a well-endowed part of him was falling out of his pajama bottoms fly. The girls screamed again. Southern hastily covered up.

"What's going on?" Eddie said, confused.

"Are you okay?" Criswell asked.

"Yeah, I think I am." He looked around like a man roused from sleep. "Uh, where am I? This doesn't look like the funeral home." He blinked and rubbed his eyes. "Isn't this your office? How did I get here?" He pointed at the girls who were huddled in the corner. "Who are they?"

"Don't you remember anything?" Southern asked.

"I remember signing the guest book. After that, it's a blank." He grabbed Cris's arm desperately. "I didn't go on another bender, did I?"

"You'll be just fine, Eddie. Don't worry."

Without warning, an axe blade crashed through the beaded glass in Criswell's office door. There was another chop, and then another, and another.

"I changed my mind. Worry."

Lt. Southern waved them back. "Behind the desk, everybody MOVE!"

The girls all screamed and ran behind Southern as a heavy foot kicked the door down. "Little" Karl Johnson stormed in, his face a mask of rage.

Lt. Southern instinctively reached for his holster, and then remembered he wasn't wearing it. "Damn it, I didn't bring my gun!"

Criswell reached for his Western six-shooter. "The guns! I locked them in the safe!"

"Well open the fucking safe!" Southern grabbed the desk lamp and leveled it at the intruder. "Stay right where you are, or I'll shoot!"

"With a lamp?" Forry asked.

"He's in a trance, maybe he'll buy it."

Karl emitted a guttural hiss of rage and brought the axe down on the desk.

"Or not."

The sorority girls began to cry and scream, huddling around Ackerman for protection as Criswell's shaking hand fiddled with the dial on the safe.

Whack! Whack! Whack! The blade flashed in the light of the desk lamp. Southern placed himself between Karl and his potential victims. "Hurry up with that gun!" he said.

"I'm hurrying! I'm hurrying!" Cris yanked on the safe handle. "Got it!" He grabbed the six-shooter and passed it to the Lieutenant.

"What are you waiting for?" Ackerman fretted. "Shoot!"

Southern took aim and then hesitated. "I can't. He's a cop, and he might be in a trance!"

Karl continued chopping his way through the desk.

"*Might be* in a trance?" Forry exclaimed.

Southern suggested, "Maybe he'll respond to one of the control words."

Karl was like a lumberjack possessed. Chop! Chop! Chop!

"KARL!" Criswell shouted. "Listen carefully: *Hate!*"

Karl continued his onslaught, snarling, "Kill…the…bastards! Kill…the…bastards!"

"Hate?" Southern exclaimed. "You're trying to calm the guy down with a word like hate? TRY ANOTHER WORD!"

"*Desire!*"

Karl eyed the girls hungrily, his expression a mask of growing lust. "Old enough to bleed, old enough to butcher!" He chopped furiously, laughing maniacally, repeating with each chop, "Old…enough…to bleed…Old…enough…to butcher!"

"Try another word!" they screamed, covering themselves like triplet Venuses, backing into a corner.

"Right. Another word… another word." Criswell wracked his brains. "Okay, uh, *Envy!*"

Karl hesitated and then snarled, "I hate assholes that have things better than me!" He resumed his attack. The desk was very nearly split in two as he repeated the mantra, "I…hate…assholes! I…hate…assholes!" The contents on the desk were scattered to the floor. Karl trampled the newspaper, leaving a black shoeprint over the article about the missing dummy. Criswell barely had time to save the movie projector. He hugged it protectively as the giant advanced.

"What about 'stop'?" Ackerman suggested. "What's wrong with 'stop'? It worked in *Revenge of the Creature!*"

Cris shook his head. "That wasn't one of the words in the film."

"Sure it was," Forry insisted. "The Creature was carrying off Lori Nelson and John Agar yelled, 'STOP!'"

"Not *that* film, *this* film," Cris indicated the projector, "the *hypnotic* film!"

Southern trained his weapon right between Karl's eyes. "Oh, the hell with this."

"Wait!" Criswell turned on the projector and aimed it in Karl's face. The effect was very surreal. A pulsing white dot illuminated Karl's furious features. The hypnotized hulk guarded his eyes from the blinding light, growling and turning to face the wall. He staggered back and watched the unfolding movie.

Criswell turned to his companions. "*Now* would probably be a good time to run."

Cris, Southern and Ackerman dashed for the exit. Wood and the girls stood spellbound, as did Karl; they all stared at the wall, quirking their heads like a pack of curious canines, their movements a synchronized choreography of somnambulistic fascination.

"Get out!" exclaimed Criswell. The psychic shoved Southern and Ackerman out the door. "Get out! I'll get Eddie and the girls."

"Fuck that," Lt. Southern growled. "I'm the cop here. You get out and *I'll* get them."

"Little" Karl kept staring at a rectangle of light on the wall as Southern edged his way toward Eddie and the three girls. It was while Southern tried to herd them to safety like a sheepdog protecting his flock that the detective wasn't looking where he was going and kicked the wastebasket, alerting Karl. The giant snarled and blocked their escape, axe at the ready. Southern brandished his gun and warned, "Listen, officer, I don't want to have to shoot you, but get out of the way if you know what's good for you!"

Eddie watched all this with the same dopey look of naïve wonder he displayed earlier. "Wow!" he marveled. "Karl, you look just swell! I'm glad I listened to your dad and gave you the part. That is so darn convincing!"

Karl hesitated a moment, smiled—and slowly lowered the axe. "Gee, thanks, Eddie! So I look monstrous enough?"

"You sure do! Hell, I was ready to wet my pants!"

Criswell edged into the room and peered from around Karl. He motioned Lt. Southern over. Southern worked his way around Karl, his piece at the ready.

"What the fuck is going on?" Southern asked.

"Karl thinks he's in one of Eddie's movies. Probably that Western Ed was going to make, what was it called?"

Wood peered around Karl. "*The Ghoul Goes West*," he said. "And it's gonna be a *smash!*" He stepped forward and patted Karl on his huge arm. "You and your dad will be a *sensation*! So, let's set up for the next shot." Ed took him aside.

"Okay," said Karl, dragging the axe along the floor after him.

Lt. Southern grabbed the handle. "I'll take that."

Karl tightened his grip on the weapon. "Who the hell are you?" he asked menacingly.

"The prop man."

The giant's grip instantly released. "Oh, that's okay, then."

Taking the axe, Southern steered Karl to a couch. "Coffee break. You better have a seat in this nice chair with your name on it."

"Thanks." Karl smiled and turned to his director. "What's the next scene, Eddie?"

"We can't shoot the big scene until Armand gets here," Eddie said. "But we can get some nice pick up shots while we wait." Wood made a rectangular aperture with his hands and framed Karl's face. "You'll scare the pants off the drive-in crowd!"

Lt. Southern shook his head. "This is just sad. So what now?"

Criswell shrugged. "Figure out how to snap them out of it, I guess. But first, Forry...."

Forry seated on the sofa with the sorority sisters. "You girls remind me of Mary Shelley, the teenage girl who wrote *Frankenstein*. I don't know if Frankenstein ever wrote back."

Southern shook his head. "Forget him," he said "We should put the 'cuffs on these two." Out of habit, he reached for his handcuffs and then froze. "Only I didn't bring my damn handcuffs."

Criswell smiled as he crossed over to what was left of his desk drawer. "That's okay. We'll use mine."

Southern took the handcuffs and eyed Cris questioningly. "Why do you keep a pair of handcuffs in your office?"

"Ask me no questions and I'll tell you no lies."

Criswell sat Ed down next to Karl as Southern handcuffed them together. Wood's slender wrist was easy, but getting the other bracelet around Karl's huge wrist was anything but.

The telephone rang.

As Southern struggled with the handcuffs, Cris said, "Get that, Forry, will you?"

"Don't go anywhere," Forry said to the girls. He picked up the phone and said, "Criswell's office…" He paused and frowned. "You're who? Hold on." He held out the handset to Criswell. "It's Vampira."

"You mean *Maila*."

Forry shrugged. "She said she was Vampira."

Criswell grabbed the phone. "Who is this?"

"This is Vampira," said the low seductive voice with a hint of a Hungarian accent.

"Come to me, Mr. Criswell. I am lurking for you."

"Maila? What's wrong? Why are you talking like that?"

"I love to scream. It relaxes me so." Maila let out her patented Vampira scream that ripped right through Criswell's eardrum.

"What's wrong?" Lt. Southern asked.

"Maila thinks she's doing her television show."

"You mean she's in a trance too?"

Criswell nodded. "Maila, where are you?"

Maila's voice sounded distant. "Where do you think, darling?" There was a *click* followed by a dial tone.

He desperately clicked the plungers. "Maila? Hello? Hello?" Looking worried, Criswell hung up.

"Did she tell you where she was?" Forry asked.

"No, but I have a pretty good idea. Five will get you 10 she's at Dr. Tom's Chiropractic Clinic."

"Say, why don't you go and check the clinic out and I'll stay here and, uh, keep an eye on… things?"

"Nothing doing, Casanova," the Lieutenant said. "The girls come with me. You want to keep an eye on somebody; keep an eye on the Bobbsey Twins here." indicating Eddie and Karl.

Forry shook his head and chortled. "Hardy Boys. Bobbsey Twins. For a cop, you sure have some interesting tastes in literature."

Southern eyed Forry narrowly. "Okay, wisenheimer, what fine literary works do you read?"

"Actually, I've always had a fondness for *Amazing Stories*. An issue of *Amazing Stories* JUMPED off the shelf, grab hold of me and said, 'Take me home, little boy, you will love me.'"

Southern turned to Criswell, "We can drop the girls back at their sorority house on the way."

Matilda jumped up and squealed. "We get to ride in a police car? That's so boss!"

"With the little ol' siren on?" asked Mary Sue.

"And the lights flashing?" Clara chimed in.

"Yeah, yeah, yeah." Southern gestured. "Come on, ladies, up and at 'em."

Cris gallantly held the door open. "Right this way, girls…."

Southern was on his way out when he hesitated and glared despairingly at his makeshift attire. "Damn it, I can't go charging around in a trench coat and pajamas!"

Criswell sized up the detective and headed for his closet. "What's your size? You look like a 42 long."

Apprehensively, Lt. Southern asked, "Why do you ask?"

# Chapter 27

Criswell pulled up in front of Dr. Tom Mason's office and got two flashlights from the glove compartment. He handed one to Southern and then got out and headed for the alley. When he realized Lt. Southern hadn't join him, Cris did an about face and returned to the limousine. "Aren't you coming?" he asked. "There should be a back way in. Let's go."

Arms crossed defiantly, the detective stubbornly remained in his seat. "If the boys back at the station saw me dressed like this, I'd never hear the end of it!"

Criswell gestured around the street. "There's no one out here. Come on, you look fine."

Reluctantly, Lt. Southern emerged wearing a tuxedo identical to Criswell's. Tugging on his glittery lapel, he groused, "I look like the best man at Liberace's wedding!"

"You look adorable."

Southern glowered. "You just better be right about this, Criswell."

"I really do think you look adorable."

"I meant being right about the *chiropractor!*"

They went around to the rear entrance. The door was locked. Criswell reached into his pocket and produced a lock-picking kit. Selecting a pick and a tension wrench, he began working on the Yale lock.

"What are you doing with a burglar kit?" Southern asked.

"I once toyed with the idea of being a stage magician." He turned the tension wrench in the direction of the lock and then inserted the pick and began working the pins.

"Oh, escape artist stuff. So that's why you got handcuffs."

Criswell looked up from what he was doing and smiled. "Sure, why not?" He began to feel the pins fall into place. In a few minutes he had the door open. With a sweeping gesture Criswell said, "After you, Lieutenant."

Shining his flashlight, Southern led the way. They tiptoed down the connecting hallway.

"Say," whispered Criswell, "this is the exam room where Kathy Wood got her treatment." Criswell reached for the knob. Southern slapped his hand away.

"Let a real cop go first, will ya?" Southern carefully opened the door and shined his light around the exam room. "Okay. Wait here," he whispered.

Reaching for his weapon, he held it at the ready and entered the room. After checking behind the door and around every dark corner and cranny he announced, "Clear."

Criswell joined him.

The darkened exam room and its elaborate medical paraphernalia reminded Criswell of something Armand Tesla's Dr. Eric Vornoff might have used in *Bride of the Atom*. The walls were decorated with charts of the human spine. Sitting on metal shelves were elaborate control boxes with toggle switches, copper coils and backlit electrical meters. One black metal box identified as an "Electronic Muscle Stimulator" had a number of dials, gauges and two long coiled wires that terminated in square electrode paddles. Hanging on a hook by an adjustable examination table reminiscent of a setpiece from *Frankenstein*, was the largest vibrator Criswell had ever seen. Cris grabbed the end of it and let go, causing the vibrator to swing pendulously from its hook. "I suppose he uses this to relax his lady patients by inducing prescribed paroxysms," he said, smiling ruefully.

"Inducing what now?" Southern asked.

"In the 19th Century, doctors used to induce orgasms in ladies with 'nervous maladies.' It also insured that their practices would be kept going." Cris noticed a swing arm next to the vibrator with a mirror mounted on it. "Uh huh. Just as I thought." He noted a rolled up movie screen on the wall behind the head of the exam table. "Hmm," he mused aloud. "So if this mirror allows the patient to see what's projected on the screen..." He approached the screen grabbed the ring and pulled the screen down and locked it in place. He glanced back at the table and mirror. "Then where is the projector?" He noted a panel amongst the soundproof ceiling tiles that suggested a possible trap door. He reached up and found a hidden pull. "Aha!" The movie projector was hidden in a compartment in the drop ceiling. "And this way, Dr. Tom shows his susceptible patients his unique home movies."

Southern wasn't paying attention. The detective was too busy inspecting a full-length mirror attached to the wall. He shined his light around the frame and felt along the edges.

"What are you doing?" Criswell asked.

"This mirror, it's hinged like a door." He manipulated a catch. The mirror swung open. Southern smirked at Criswell as he said, "Yeah, just as I thought; a room hidden behind a two-way mirror." He turned back and screamed as the stiffened body of Armand Tesla in full Dracula attire fell on top of him.

Criswell hurried to rescue the Lieutenant as he struggled to get out from under Tesla's corpse. "Get him off of me! Get him off of me!" As Criswell did just that, the psychic shined his flashlight into Armand's peaceful face. "Why did they bring his body here?" Cris wondered aloud.

"To make me crap myself," Southern complained as he got to his feet. "Let me see that a minute." Southern searched the tuxedo and produced three Cuban cigars. "Uh huh, here are the missing cigars."

Criswell glanced inside the tiny room. He pulled out a movie camera on a tripod. "Oh, my God," Criswell said. "Dr. Tom films all his sessions!"

"Nice little films they must be, too." Southern examined the camera. "Looks like it's loaded and ready."

Criswell aimed his light on the wall opposite the mirror. "See there? A clock and a calendar."

"So what?"

"Well, you'd want to include things like the day and time if you're keeping film records of hypnosis experiments."

"Experiments nothing," Southern scoffed. "This guy's running a dirty movie racket."

"What?"

"Sure. He dopes up a bunch of pretty unsuspecting dames, then plays doctor for the camera. There's a lot of scratch to be made in smut peddling."

"But the movie back at my office, the one Eddie and Karl responded to…"

"A put-on. I'll bet they're both in on it. Wood makes movies, doesn't he? Who's to say he isn't in on the whole dirty movie racket? As for Karl, I'll bet my badge he's a dirty cop out to get his cut. That how it is in the LAPD sometimes."

"But Karl works out of Sacramento."

"Okay, so he's a dirty *Sacramento* cop."

"But what about the phone call from Maila? I was so sure she was in a trance."

"She was faking." Southern stuck Armand back in the hidden closet and closed the secret door. "It's the old story. She's all washed up as a TV star, so she gets by making smut. I can just see her now, wearing a skimpy nurse's uniform and Dr. Tom in nothing but a lab coat."

"What about Chalky? He was so anxious to get that film."

"Wood switched movies on him. Mae is one of Dr. Tom's patients, right? A smut film with a drugged Mae West in it would make a fucking fortune."

Criswell nodded at the body inside the secret closet. "Okay, so what about Armand? Why did they steal his body?"

"Okay, so they're making a smut film that caters to necrophilia."

"What about the FBI?"

"I'll bet they're working a sting operation and didn't want the local PD to screw it up. It happens all the time."

"Do you really think so?"

"That makes a hell of a lot more sense than 'everybody's in a trance.'" Southern headed for the door. "Come on."

"Where are we going?"

"We gotta find Dr. Tom's secret stash. You take the exam rooms; I'll search the waiting room and his office."

Somewhere in the clinic, a door opened and slammed.

Southern froze. "Somebody's coming!" He pushed Criswell back into the exam room and inside the hidden closet and then shut the door after them. Criswell suddenly found himself squeezed inside the cramped space with Lt. Southern and Armand's cold corpse wedged between them.

Through the two-way mirror they saw Dr. Tom enter with John "Bunny" Breckinridge. Following them was someone carrying a body bag fireman's carry style over his shoulders.

Dr. Tom said, "I was sure I heard voices in here."

Bunny coolly assured him, "It's just your nerves."

With a gesture from Bunny, the man heaved the body bag onto the Frankenstein table, where it landed with a dull thud. Turning robotically, the man turned out to be Conrad Brooks. By the now familiar glassy-eyed stare, Criswell deduced he was one of Dr. Tom's "patients."

"So this is the appointment Conrad had to keep," Cris remarked.

Southern shushed him as Dr. Tom turned on the light. They watched as Breckinridge removed his top hat and mopped the sweat from his brow. "You'll feel better once *this* has been properly disposed of." He set his top hat on the stomach of the body bag's occupant, and then began to pull at the fingers of his kid gloves, removing them with a practiced nonchalance. He tossed the gloves into his top hat and approached the two-way mirror. "And we dispose of poor Armand, too."

Dr. Tom noticed the top hat and snatched it off the dead body and set it aside on an instrument table, glaring at Breckinridge with distaste. Gesturing at the body bag, he grumbled, "I don't see why we didn't just take it to the crematorium directly," and then pointing at the hidden closet, "And why did you insist they bring Tesla *here*?"

"In case the police or that interfering Criswell decided to go sniffing about the funeral parlor, of course." Bunny took out a comb and began preening before the mirror. "I don't know what you're complaining about. I'm the one who had to drive around all day with a dead body in the boot of my car."

"Well, never mind about that," Dr. Tom said. "Do we get the contract or not?"

Bunny admired himself as he talked to Dr. Tom's reflection. "You were supposed to convince us that your technique is foolproof." He gestured over his shoulder at the body bag. "I'd hardly call Lt. Dean proof-positive that your technique is a success."

"Is it my fault that Wood had combat training?"

Criswell whispered to Southern. "Still think this is a smut ring?"

Southern hushed him.

Breckinridge turned to face Dr. Tom. "My superiors are rather fussy about accuracy. You said that Harry Dean would successfully assassinate Mr. Wood and yet Mr. Wood was victorious."

"You're missing the point! We triggered Wood's programming and he demonstrated ingenious survival skills. Frankly, I thought he was a complete buffoon. Who knew?"

Inside the secret room, Criswell reached up and turned on the movie camera. Southern was about to protest when Cris put a finger to his hushing lips.

"*You* were supposed to know, that's who." Breckinridge approached the operating table. "All of your talk about mapping a man's psyche, what rubbish."

"We told you from the start that there was a plus or minus 20% margin for error. Your superiors accepted that." Dr. Tom unzipped the body bag and indicated the corpse with a sharp gesture. "Here we had two equally matched opponents with nearly identical psyches, both transvestites, both with combat training. We assumed a police officer would have the edge over Mr. Wood's tour of duty training. I believe Dean died because he hesitated."

"Aha! So you *admit* that he hesitated."

"Our brainwashing methods are good, Breckinridge. But there are some innate reactions we can't fully override."

"The whole point of Plan 9 was the promise that you *could* override them."

"I'm sure with further treatments we can—"

"Promises, promises," Bunny sniped as he zipped up the body bag. "I seriously doubt that there will be time for further treatments."

"And just what is that supposed to mean?"

"There are too many people asking too many questions."

"What people?"

"Lt. Jack Southern for one; Criswell for another."

"The Tesla experiment? But it was a complete success!"

"A complete success; with all the folderol that went on at the mortuary and later at the cemetery? I hardly think so. And there's the nasty mess involving Ralph Fleet and Tesla's landlord. Their deaths attracted way too much attention."

Dr. Tom's elephantine ears turned bright red with rage. "You can't blame us for *that!*"

"I most certainly can. Mrs. Tesla was supposed to dispose of *all* the evidence."

"Closing those cases for National Security reasons was *your* idea! Maybe you can get away with that kind of thing once, but *twice*? No wonder Southern and Criswell became suspicious!"

"Perhaps that was a tad overzealous on my part." Bunny shrugged. "Oh well. Live and learn. That doesn't change my decision. It's time to close up shop."

"You'd be a fool to give up now," Dr. Tom insisted. "We're so close! Observe." He picked up a metal probe and stabbed Brooks in the arm. "See? This subject is totally impervious to pain."

Brooks muttered in a stentorian voice: "Ow, you know."

Bunny cast Dr. Tom a jaundiced eye. "I see."

"But those three suicides were especially promising!"

"*Two* suicides, you mean. The teenagers, we authorized. Mr. Jeffrey was supposed to kill his wife, not himself."

"Teenagers are so moody they could have easily harbored suicidal tendencies. But a successful business man like Mr. Jeffrey doing himself in—"

"Bosh!" Bunny said as he approached Dr. Tom's desk and reached for the telephone. "You did it to cover your ass. Mr. Jeffrey demonstrated awareness of his predicament and you tried to hide that from us. Fortunately, your nurse kept us well informed." Bunny began dialing.

"She was *spying* on me?"

"I prefer to think of it as keeping you honest."

Dr. Tom opened a drawer and pulled out a gun. "Put the phone down, Breckinridge."

Bunny smiled. "Oh, honestly, put that away." He indicated the body bag with a nod. "I'm merely calling to have *that* disposed of."

"I don't care. Hang up the phone."

Sighing wearily, Bunny complied and raised his hands. "I know you haven't the nerve to pull the trigger."

"Oh, don't I? Nothing is going to interfere with Plan 9, do you understand? Nothing!"

There was a gunshot. Lt. Southern was about to spring into action when Criswell held him back.

Screaming in pain, Dr. Tom held his bleeding hand.

Chalky Wright entered holding a .38. "Are you all right, Mr. Breckinridge?"

"Of course," Bunny said with a smile. He picked up the phone and began dialing. "Dr. Tom merely got a tad overzealous, that's all."

Chalky confiscated Dr. Tom's gun and pocketed it, then pulled out his handkerchief. "That's a nasty wound, sir. You might want to attend to it."

"Did you take care of the girl?" Bunny asked as he waited for the party to pick up.

"She's in the car, sir, quite pacified." Much to Criswell's shock, Chalky produced a bottle of *Criswell's Family Formula*. "Formula 8 proved most effective."

Breckinridge glared at Chalky. "You were supposed to eliminate her."

Chalky flashed Bunny a disarming smile. "I really saw no need for that, sir. She believes the cover story completely. The skull was most convincing."

Bunny smirked. "Oh, you heterosexuals—always letting your cocks do your thinking. Although I suppose I'm sometimes guilty of—" Bunny stopped abruptly when his party picked up. "Yes, this is Breckinridge. We have another loose end ready for pick up." He gave Dr. Tom the once over. "Make that *two* loose ends—perhaps three." He listened, then said, "Dr. Tom Mason's Chiropractic Clinic. That's right, on Sunset. Yes, we'll wait." Hanging up, Bunny addressed Chalky. "After we take care of the good doctor, *I'll* decide about Miss Nurmi." From a secret pocket behind his jacket lapel Bunny produced a tiny syringe and eyed Dr. Tom. "It's time to tidy up."

The chiropractor's eyes grew wide with horror. "You can't kill me! You need me!"

"*Au contraire*, I've decided your role in Plan 9 is superfluous." He removed the cap from the needle. "Your partners are more than capable of continuing on their own." He raised the syringe and applied a gentle pressure to the plunger sending a spurt of liquid into the air. "Your notes are quite thorough."

"They'll never agree to it!"

"The example of your execution will insure their full cooperation, I'm sure." He advanced menacingly. "Now, Dr. Tom, to quote an oft used bromide in your profession," he brandished the syringe, "this won't hurt a bit."

Dr. Tom tried to run. Chalky blocked his escape. "It really is useless to resist, sir." He grabbed the chiropractor and forcefully extended his arm.

"We'll just see about that." Dr. Tom addressed Brooks. "Protect me!"

Brooks reached into his pocket and produced a hipflask. He brandished it like a gun. "You know, let my Master go, you know, or I'll shoot, you know."

Dr. Tom sighed. "I'm a dead man."

Lt. Southern had seen enough. He burst from his hiding place, drawing his six-shooter, which was getting tangled in Tesla's Dracula cape. "All right, everybody," he wrenched his gun hand free while Criswell tried to keep Armand upright, "drop your weapons!"

Chalky and Breckinridge complied and raised their hands. Dr. Tom fell to his knees. "I surrender!" he said. "Gladly!"

Not the least bit fazed, Bunny smiled and said, "Well, what have we here...A not so *plain*clothes detective. Love the sequins."

"Can it, queer," Southern growled. "You're all under arrest." He indicated the Frankenstein table with the muzzle of his gun. "Line up over there!"

"So that's where La West's gun got off to. I was wondering."

Cris frowned, pointing at the weapon. "That's Mae's gun?"

Breckinridge nodded. "I purloined it during that little soiree Mae was throwing."

"Why did Mae insist on Armand being there?"

"Isn't it obvious? Mr. Tesla's time was very short. All that poison circulating 'round his system. It would have been ever so much easier disposing of the evidence had he expired at the party." Bunny smirked at Dr. Tom. "I didn't trust in Dr. Tom's assurances that Mrs. Tesla would follow her preprogrammed instructions to have the body cremated."

Dr. Tom glared angrily. "How was I to know Tesla's ex-wife would interfere?"

"I'm obviously better at predicting these things than you are." Bunny smiled at Criswell. "And I don't need to wear a tacky tuxedo to do it, either."

Southern glared at Breckinridge. "Never mind the funny stuff. Keep those hands up!" Calling behind him he asked, "Got the camera, Criswell?"

"Right here."

"I don't know what kind of shady racket you guys are running, but whatever it is, we got the goods right here."

"If you'll allow me to explain," Bunny said as he reached into the inner pocket of his jacket.

Aiming his piece, Southern warned, "Keep those hands up, fancy pants. You can do your explaining downtown."

Smiling pleasantly, Bunny said, "I merely wish to show you my identification, officer." He twiddled his fingers. "May I?"

"Okay, but no sudden moves."

Slowly Breckinridge produced a black leather ID wallet. Southern grabbed it and flipped it open.

"Holy crap," the detective exclaimed.

"What?" Criswell asked.

"If this badge is on the level, he's..."

"...CIA," Bunny said with a smirk. "Might I put my hands down now?"

# Chapter 28

Back at Criswell's office, Forry Ackerman sat with his arms folded, watching Ed and Karl as they chattered away happily.

"Do you really think I can make it as an actor?" asked Karl.

"Oh, sure, Karl," Wood chirped pleasantly. "Why, I can think of a dozen movies you're just perfect for."

"Gee."

Someone knocked on the doorjamb. Ray Bradbury was beaming with excitement. "I came right over," he said, and then noticed the chopped down door and Ackerman's sequin lapels. "Say, what gives?"

"Long story, Ray." Forry pointed at Eddie and Karl. "The big guy's name is Lt. Karl Johnson, he's Tor's son." He waved his hand before their faces. "They're both under a hypnotic spell."

"Wow. No fooling?" Bradbury waved his hand in front of Wood's face.

Eddie remained totally oblivious and continued talking to Karl. "Now in this next scene, you're going to get shot."

"That's good," Karl said. "I've been shot. I can play it real good."

Noting Eddie's attire, Ray said, "Say, he looks like—"

Forry rolled his eyes. "Yeah, yeah, I know, like Barbara Stanwyck in *Double Indemnity*." He sighed. "It's a long story."

With boyish glee, Bradbury asked, "Can you make 'em cluck like a chicken and stuff like that?"

"I really haven't tried that, Ray." Forry nervously tugged on the collar of his dress shirt. "I'm just happy not to have Karl trying to chop my head off."

The phone rang. Forry went to answer it, leaving Ray to playfully suggest to Wood, "Say, Eddie, there's a fly on your nose."

Wood wiggled his nose and batted away at an imaginary fly.

"Criswell's office," Forry said.

"Who is this?" asked the party on the phone in a nervous whisper.

"Forry Ackerman. Who is *this*?"

"Horace Steinmetz, the cosmetologist from Hollywood Mortuaries."

"Oh, yes. Mr. Steinmetz. We met in the garage. Remember? I was with Criswell. What can I do for you?"

"It's more what I can do for you," Steinmetz whispered. "It's vital that I speak to Mr. Criswell right away."

"Cool!" Bradbury effused. He pointed at Wood as he swatted the imaginary fly buzzing around his head. "Hey, Forry, you gotta see this."

Ackerman covered the mouthpiece. "Not now, Ray!"

Sensing this was serious, Bradbury said to Wood, "Okay, the fly's gone now. Just keep still, huh."

Eddie relaxed and continued his conversation with Karl. "Now, about that scene—"

"I'm sorry," Ackerman said to Steinmetz, "Criswell went to help a friend trapped at a chiropractor's office."

Steinmetz gasped with alarm, and then said in a tense whisper, "You've got to warn him. He's in danger. Mr. Bruckner, he's involved in something shady. Remember those two young people, the suicides, and that other fellow, the one whose coffin Mr. Tesla wound up in?"

"I remember the suicides. How could I forget? But what's this about Armand's coffin?"

"That's not important right now," Steinmetz insisted. "The point is Mr. Bruckner is sending the out the bodies this very minute to be cremated!"

"I don't see what—"

"It's being done without the family's knowledge. Mr. Bruckner is planning to bury empty coffins! And I know why they're going to be cremated. I accidentally picked up for a call meant for him, thinking it was for me. The lines get mixed up sometimes. The call came from somebody named Breckinridge."

"Bunny Breckinridge," Forry exclaimed.

Ray frowned. "What does *he* want?"

Forry gestured curtly for silence as Steinmetz said, "He was the one who *told* Mr. Bruckner to cremate those bodies…because they're contaminated with some sort of experimental drug, and there was something about a dummy…"

Forry glanced down at the trampled newspaper. "I know all about the dummy."

"But here's the worst of it; Breckinridge just called again a few moments ago and told Mr. Bruckner to pick up Tesla's body and some other 'loose ends' at the office of the chiropractor whose name is Dr. Tom."

"Shakatabulo! And Criswell's on his way over there right now!"

"You'd better do something," Steinmetz said. "As for me, I'm going to—" There was a *thud*, followed by a clatter and then dead air.

Forry anxiously pumped the plungers as Bradbury asked, "Who is that, huh?"

"Hello? Hello?" Forry said frantically, and listened. There was only dead air; no dial tone.

"Why do people do that, huh?" Ray wondered. "It's not like Sarah's at the switchboard to help reconnect your call."

"I'm doing it to break the connection. I can't get a dial tone." Forry sighed and hung up. "Somebody deliberately left the phone off the hook."

"Who was it?"

"The embalmer from Hollywood Mortuary, and if we don't do something and fast, Criswell and Lt. Southern could be in real trouble, assuming they aren't dead already."

Bradbury reached for the telephone. "So let's call the police."

Ackerman took the handset from him. "Didn't you hear what I said? I can't get a dial tone. The police won't do anything anyway." Hanging up, and with a determined look, he said, "It's up to us."

Bradbury smiled. "So we're gonna charge to the rescue, huh?"

"It looks like." Forry searched the drawers for a weapon, and found what he thought was a gun, but turned out to be a metal dildo that began to vibrate in his hand. He set it down, where it hummed and rolled around under its own power. Forry continued his search. He found a leather paddle and a whip. "I knew there was something about Criswell I liked." He put the items back in the drawer. "But none of these playtime toys are going to help us now."

Ray hefted Karl's axe. "We've got this!"

"You don't know the kind of trouble we're heading into. I doubt that will be enough."

"Okay," said Bradbury with a shrug. "What about them?"

"Them?" Ackerman pointed at Wood and Karl. "What good would they be?"

"Eddie is highly suggestible. I'm sure the big guy is too."

"Ray, we're going to be dealing with the people that hypnotized them in the first place. How do you know they won't turn Ed and Karl against us?"

Bradbury noted how Eddie and Karl suddenly stopped speaking to give Forry's hand their full attention. "Say, what's up with them?" Ray asked.

Forry shrugged. "I don't know. Earlier this evening, Eddie couldn't take his eyes off my hands."

Ray looked from Eddie and Karl to Forry's hand. "Not your hands," he said, pointing at the Dracula ring and smiling. "It's your ring!"

Forry stared at the ring and frowned. "You're kidding?"

Bradbury grabbed Forry's wrist and moved Forry's hand around. "It is the ring, all right! See?" Ed and Karl's eyes obediently followed the ring. "They can't take their eyes off of it!" Ray let go of Forry's wrist. "Say, what about using *that* to keep them in our control!"

Ackerman sighed. "Ray, this is just a movie prop."

"Maybe to *us* it's just a movie prop, but to *their* unconscious, the Dracula ring is something they're supposed to obey." He made magical passes. "To them, it's a symbol of ultimate power. oooOOOooo." Ray smiled and nudged his friend. "The movies conditioned them before the hypnotists did, huh?"

Ackerman looked from his ring to Eddie and Karl. "Say, maybe you've got something there." He drew himself up and affected Armand Tesla's accent and demeanor as he displayed the Dracula ring and made magical passes. "Edvard, Karl, listen to meeeeee."

Ed and Karl focused on the ring with wide-eyed fascination. "Yes, Master," they intoned together.

Bradbury gave Ackerman a nudge of encouragement. "Keep it up, Forry. It's working!"

"You vill listen to me—and to no one else."

Ray frowned. "Hey, what about me?"

"You vill listen to Ray Bradbury and me—and no one else."

"What about Criswell and Lt. Southern?"

Ackerman gave Ray an irritated look. "Hey, who's doing the hypnotizing around here?"

"I'm just saying."

Clearing his throat, Ackerman said, "Okay, you vill listen to Bradbury, Criswell, Lt. Southern and me," glaring at Ray, he added, "*and no one else!*"

"Yes, Master," Ed and Karl said.

"Now," Ackerman said, gesturing Dracula fashion, "you vill rise."

Karl and Eddie stood up slowly.

With an aside to Bradbury, Ackerman instructed, "Okay, Ray, take off the handcuffs."

Ray held out his hand expectantly. "Give me the key."

"What key?"

"The key to open the handcuffs."

"I don't have the key."

"Well, how am I gonna open the handcuffs, huh?"

Ackerman groaned. "Great. We have shackled-together zombies. That'll be useful."

"Maybe they can break the handcuffs, huh."

"Ray, they're hypnotized, not supermen."

Bradbury stared intently at Ed and Karl, intoning in a poor Tesla impression, "You vill break the handcuffs that bind you!"

Forry sighed. "Ray, that's the most ridiculous—"

Wood and Karl said, "Yes, Master."

With a quick hard yank, they broke the chain that linked their wrists together.

"Wow," Forry marveled.

"Say," Ray said eagerly, "do you think they can crash through a wall, too, huh?"

With forced patience, Forry said, "Lead the way, Ray."

# Chapter 29

"You do realize," Breckinridge said, "that if you don't surrender your weapons and that camera to me this instant, you'll be interfering with National Security interests."

Lt. Southern tossed back the badge. "Keep your blouse on, Shirley. For all I know, you got that out of a box of Cracker Jacks."

"Since when," Criswell demanded as hefted the camera, "does the U.S. Government experiment on American citizens?"

Smiling coyly, Breckinridge said, "I'm surprised, Charles. You are so delightfully naïve in spite of your talk about how the Government manipulates its citizens. We do this sort of thing all the time. Whether it be feeding retarded children radium pills, or putting fluoride in the drinking water, the ends justify the means, and all that."

Criswell's face flushed with anger. "How dare you use my television audience as Guinea pigs! You fiend! My viewers—"

"—made excellent test subjects for Plan 8." Bunny giggled and elaborated, "Dr. Tom's rather silly and unimaginative designation for the eighth attempt at this experiment."

Southern asked, "An experiment to prove what exactly?"

Breckinridge smiled sweetly. "To prove whether or not the public can be brainwashed into becoming unwitting assassins. Plan 8 was a pharmaceutical approach devised by Dr. Tom and his associate, Dr. Koenig, who has been trying to perfect the drug, but hasn't quite got the recipe right yet."

Criswell gasped. "So that's why Koenig has been sending me all those extra bottles!"

"Exactly. Those vitamin pills you peddle on your TV program, Charles, contain a trance-inducing stimulant. We chose your audience because they were primarily retired shut-ins." He shrugged. "But the Formula 8 is proving to be too unpredictable, no matter what combination of chemicals Koenig fiddles with. Some subjects became over-stimulated nervous wrecks."

Criswell thought back to how Eddie was so jumpy after taking the supplements. "And I thought Eddie was acting like that because of the caffeine."

Dr. Tom started. "Do you mean Wood actually ate some of those tablets?"

"Quite a few, actually."

Dr. Tom nudged Breckinridge. "See? *That's* what gave Wood the edge over Harry Dean, the combination of Plan 8 and its stimulants, and the mental conditioning of Plan 9! That's the answer! We have to combine techniques."

Bunny scoffed, "Except that in some cases the subjects that were given the Plan 8 formula became lethargic zombies," he gave Chalky a knowing smile, "just the way Miss Nurmi is right now."

Lt. Southern glared at Breckinridge. "Okay, so exactly what *is* Plan 9, Tinker Bell?"

"Plan 9 was the non-pharmaceutical approach devised by Dr. Tom Mason and his colleagues."

Dr. Tom gestured at Brooks. "For years we've believed that a subject could not be hypnotized into doing anything that they wouldn't ordinarily do while they're awake."

"Like committing cold-blooded murder?" Lt. Southern snarled.

"Exactly!" Dr. Tom stepped forward. "But we learned to tap into an impulse we call The Sinister Urge."

"The what?" Criswell asked.

"The Sinister Urge, those base primitive resentments responsible for things like nervous disorders and ulcers. We discovered that by creating the illusion of a non-threatening scenario, we could bypass the conscience and redirect those resentments toward a specific target of our choosing. Thus we can turn anyone into an unstoppable assassin, housewives, teenagers, businessmen, anyone. Once indoctrinated—"

"You mean, 'brainwashed,'" Southern growled.

"If you like—once *brainwashed* our subjects would lead perfectly ordinary lives." He looked Conrad Brooks up and down. "Well, mostly ordinary."

"Until you give them a trigger word," said Criswell, "a trigger word like...'wondrous?'" He waited for Brooks to respond, he remained silent.

Dr. Tom smirked. "Yes, a simple post-hypnotic suggestion, but a word that means something special to each subject."

"That's the reason for the films and the conditioning. You try to find that special word that has meaning to them."

"Exactly. After receiving their instructions, along with any necessary weaponry—" He snarled at Brooks, "Which was in your *other* pocket!" He pulled out Brooks gun and slapped it in the actor's hand.

"Or in something like a gold clutch purse?" Cris suggested.

Dr. Tom shrugged. "I had a supplier that could get them for me at cost. Anyway, the assassin would eliminate the target, clean up the mess, destroy any evidence and resume their ordinary lives with no knowledge of what they had done."

"Or so you claimed," interjected Bunny.

"You can't deny our initial trials were successful! Harry Dean, Ed and Kathy Wood, Armand and Hope Tesla, they were all oblivious to having committed any wrongdoing."

Southern asked, "What about the suicides?"

"One of the requirements we had to fulfill was a pre-programmed self-destruct order to be triggered should the assassin be captured." Dr. Tom scratched behind his ear as he proudly proclaimed, "Overriding the self-preservation instinct was a real breakthrough. The difficulties we encountered were almost insurmountable."

"Who exactly is 'we,' Dr. Death?" Southern asked.

The detective felt something poking in his back.

"Drop your gun, please," said the man standing behind him.

Southern dropped his weapon and both he and Criswell raised their hands.

"Keep your hands up, gentlemen." Reverend Hall grabbed the movie camera away from Criswell. He was about to hand his gun over the Bunny when Dr. Tom stepped forward.

"No, Manly, Breckinridge tried to kill me! He said you and Koenig could continue on without me! He said I wasn't necessary to complete the project."

Hall looked to Bunny. "Is this true?"

Breckinridge smiled. "Well, yes. Dr. Tom is proving difficult. And should he be eliminated it would mean more money for the remaining specialists working on Plan 9."

Hall returned Bunny's smile. "Very true," he said and leveled his gun at Dr. Tom. "Would you please join Lt. Southern and Mr. Criswell over there?"

"Manly! You can't mean that!"

"Oh, I'm afraid I do."

In utter shock, Dr. Tom joined the ranks of the captured.

"Well, well," Southern said, "it looks like there's no honor among thieves *or* hypnotists."

Hall shrugged. "What can I say? I'm a practical man with expensive tastes."

Picking up his syringe, Breckinridge said, "Oh dear, it looks like the Hollywood Mortuary crematorium is going to be *very* busy tonight."

"So," said Criswell, "Hollywood Mortuaries is in on all this, too?"

"They're a high volume business," said Breckinridge. "Mr. Bruckner was overjoyed to help in the Cold War effort, especially at a profit."

"I'll bet," said Southern.

Bunny pointed at Criswell. "Chalky, if you please?"

The chauffeur grabbed Criswell. Cris put up a fight, but found that Chalky was too strong. Chalky bared the psychic's forearm as Breckinridge approached with the needle.

"This will be over in just a moment, Charles," Bunny assured him.

Hall kept Dr. Tom and Lt. Southern covered as Breckinridge prepared to jab Criswell with the needle. Cris waited until the last second, and then jerked his arm so Chalky received the fatal dose. The chauffeur's face registered shock before his eyes rolled up in his head and he dropped to the floor, dead.

Bunny glared at Criswell and chided, "Well, *that* was uncalled for!"

Bradbury looked Maila up and down.

# Chapter 30

Forry pulled up outside the chiropractic clinic. Ray sat beside him; Karl and Ed sat quietly in back.

Ackerman indicated the Imperial 8. "That's Criswell's car, all right."

"Great." Ray reached for the door handle. "Let's go save them, huh?" Bradbury got out and ran down the street.

Jumping out of the car, Forry raced after Bradbury and grabbed his arm. "Hold on. We're not just going to charge in there."

"I guess you're right," Ray said. He noticed Chalky's car. "WOW! What a swell car!"

"Yes, it's very nice." Forry gave the Coupe a cursory glance, then gawked in astonishment. "Hey, it's Maila!"

She sat staring straight ahead. Forry knocked on the window.

"Maila," he said. "Hey, Maila, it's me, Forry Ackerman. Maila!"

She sat transfixed, unblinking.

"She's a zombie, too, huh?" asked Ray.

"Looks like."

Ray nudged Forry. "Hey, try the ring."

Leaning over the windshield Forry made magical passes in Maila's eye line and intoned, "Maila, you vill obey me vithout question."

"I don't think she can hear you."

Forry shouted, "OBEY ME, MY MISTRESS OF THE NIGHT! OBEY ME!"

Maila's gaze slowly met Ackerman's.

"Step out of the car," Forry commanded dramatically.

Slowly Maila reached for the handle and lifted up the gullwing door. She stood erect, a vision of hypnotized Vera West-gowned sensuality; shoulders well back, ample bosom jutting proudly, eyes as lifeless as a doll's. Ackerman ogled her, working his hands together eagerly. "What I wouldn't give to have her to myself for a couple of hours." He reached out to touch those perfect breasts.

Bradbury slapped his friend's hands away. "Forry!" he admonished.

"Come on, you were thinking the same thing."

Bradbury looked Maila up and down, stopping to stare at her incredible cleavage. "Yeah, okay. I have to admit you're right."

Forry jerked his thumb back at the car. "Go get Ed and Karl."

"Will do, huh," Ray said. "Whoever we're facing doesn't know it yet, but tonight is the Night of the Ghouls."

Forry sighed. "Sure it is, Ray."

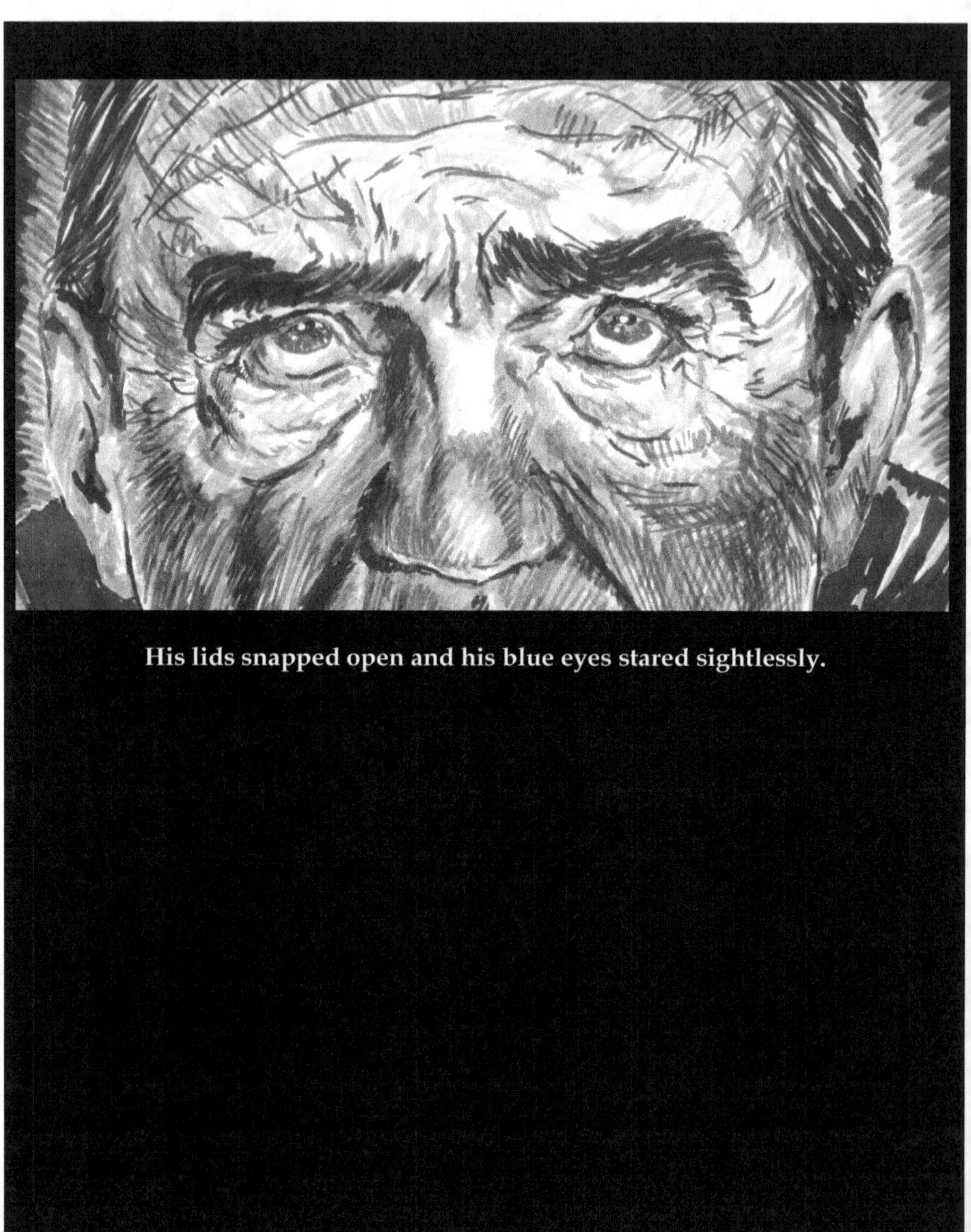

His lids snapped open and his blue eyes stared sightlessly.

# Chapter 31

Lt. Southern struggled against the rubber surgical tubing Reverend Hall was using to tie him back to back with another chair in which Dr. Tom was bound and gagged. The movie camera with the incriminating footage rested on Dr. Tom's desk along with Southern's gun.

"Honestly, Charles! How you've inconvenienced me," Breckinridge complained as he tightened the straps binding Criswell to the Frankenstein table. "Now we'll have to arrange the disposal of poor Chalky's body too."

"Another pickup for the funeral home?" asked Hall as he finished binding his captives.

"No, no. We'll take him back to the Ravenswood. If we create a slight contusion to the back of the head, it will appear he slipped in the bathtub. Once we manipulate Miss West's recollections, she'll be able to file a very convincing police report."

"So what's in store for us, twinkle toes?" asked Southern. "A jab with your hypo?"

"Afraid not," Breckinridge said. "That little stunt depleted my supply of poison. A pity, because it's both undetectable and painless." Satisfied Criswell was quite securely bound, Bunny ripped open Criswell's dress shirt and reached for the Electronic Muscle Stimulator paddles. "You and Charles and the good Dr. Tom are about to suffer massive heart attacks." He dialed up the current. "A bit unlikely the three of you would all suffer heart attacks at the same time, but we really don't have time to be subtle."

Criswell braced himself as he felt cold metal on his bare chest. "Just tell me one thing," he said.

"Yes?" Bunny said wearily.

"Did you have anything to do with moving the headstones, but not the bodies at the cemetery in Sacramento?"

"You can thank your fellow investors for that. Honestly, what some people will do to cut corners." He reached for a toggle switch. "Good bye, Criswell. Give my regards to those on the other side."

At that moment, Reverend Hall's pudgy bulk came flying over Breckinridge's head and came smashing against the metal shelves, effectively ruining the Muscle Stimulator.

"What in the world!" Bunny whirled around in time to see "Little" Karl bearing down on him, his huge hands effortlessly slapping Breckinridge to the floor.

"That is good, my mindless zombies!" said Forry as he gestured at Southern and Dr. Tom. "Free them, Edvard and Maila. Karl, keep those two at bay!"

Ray rushed in and surveyed the carnage. "Aww, I missed it!"

As Maila freed Lt. Southern's hands, the detective rubbed his wrists to get the circulation back. "I don't know what's going on, but I'm glad you guys are here."

Southern grabbed his gun and marched over to Bunny.

Breckinridge sat up and commanded, "WONDROUS! Do you hear me? WONDROUS! Obey me, all of you! Subdue these intruders!"

Southern wielded his weapon as the zombified trio looked to Ackerman. Forry raised his Dracula ring and intoned in Armand Tesla's voice, "You vill obey only me," adding hastily, "and Criswell, Bradbury, and Lt. Southern."

"Mason!" Breckinridge demanded. "Get control of these people *now!*"

"You were going to kill me!"

"Get control of this situation and I'll spare you!"

Dr. Tom turned to Conrad Brooks. "Stop them!"

Brooks raised his weapon and fired. There was click after click as he fired one empty chamber after another.

"Your gun isn't loaded?!" Dr. Tom exclaimed. "I loaded it myself!"

"You know, people could get hurt, you know," explained the hypnotized Brooks. "So I took the bullets out, you know."

Dr. Tom snarled in frustration. With a gesture from Forry, Maila kneed Dr. Tom in the groin. The chiropractor dropped to the floor into a fetal position, writhing in intense pain.

Struggling to his feet, Reverend Hall said, "Enough of this! All of you listen to me! You are my brothers and sisters. They are the sinners. You will strike down their evil for they are false prophets."

The three zombies looked at Forry Ackerman. Ackerman smiled nervously. "Uh, that guy," he said pointing at Hall, "just put the kibosh on your big chance to all be famous movie stars."

The zombies bared their teeth and advanced on Hall. "THAT DRACULA RING IS PLASTIC!" Hall pointed out. "IT IS FALSE! THEY ARE NOT YOUR MASTERS!"

The zombies snarled at Ackerman and Bradbury. "They are not our Master!"

"Uh oh," said Ray. "If anybody has an idea, now would be the time to use it."

Criswell was backed up against the two-way mirror. He swallowed hard and then remembered what was waiting behind the hidden door. "Wait!" he said to the zombies. "You want to see your real Master. Here he is!" He opened the hidden door to reveal Armand Tesla's corpse. In a moment that could only have been written by Ed Wood himself, the glue keeping Tesla's eyes shut chose that moment to melt away. His lids snapped open and his blue eyes stared sightlessly at the hypnotized trio.

"Master," they said, and then turned on Breckinridge and company.

"I don't understand," Bunny said. "Why aren't they obeying their programming?"

Ackerman nodded at the tuxedoed corpse as he polished the Dracula ring and placed it on Armand's stiff finger. "Armand Tesla brainwashed them first."

Lt. Southern grabbed Breckinridge by the arm. "Show's over, Buster Brown."

Bunny looked contemptuously at the detective. "You can't arrest us. The CIA will simply step in and make this all go away."

Southern hefted the movie camera. "When I take this home movie to the press, the CIA might just make *you* go away."

"You wouldn't dare!"

"Try me."

Breckinridge adjusted his shirt cuffs and smoothed back his hair. "I suppose we could make some sort of arrangement, something mutually beneficial."

"If I hear you guys are so much as hypnotizing a gerbil, I'll develop this film and take it to all three networks. By the time I'm finished, your name will be Mudd. Got it?"

"It really doesn't matter." Breckinridge surveyed the damage and sighed wearily. "Plan 9 is a wash, anyway."

"What!" Dr. Tom gasped. "But why?"

"Your assassins were turned against us by something as trifling as a movie prop and a poor Hungarian accent!" He adjusted his lapels with a quick tug. "Face it, doctor, Plan 9 is kaput, finished, ended." Reaching into his pocket, Breckinridge took out a pad and a pen and began scribbling a list.

"What are you doing?" Criswell asked.

"Giving you the names and phone numbers of all the Plan 9 test subjects."

"Why?"

Tearing out the page, Bunny gave it to Criswell. "We don't want any trace left of the experiment and I doubt you'd trust me to bring them out of it."

"You got that right," Southern said.

"Call them up; say this phrase and all their programming will be erased. The same goes for your friends here—Miss Nurmi being the exception, of course. Her Formula 8-induced trace will eventually wear off after a few hours."

Two attendants from Hollywood Mortuary entered with a stretcher. "You called for a pick up?"

"Yes," said Bunny, indicating the body bag, "that one there."

"What about him?" the attendant asked, pointing at Chalky's body.

With a dismissive gesture, Bunny sighed and said, "I'll take care of him myself," and handed the attendant his car keys. "Just pop him in the boot of my car, will you?"

The attendant took the keys and nodded. "Sure thing," he said.

"So that's it?" Lt. Southern asked, gesturing at the body bag being strapped onto the stretcher. "We all just walk away like nothing happened?"

Ackerman grabbed the detective's arm and glared at Breckinridge. "You can't let him get away with this," he insisted. "The embalmer back at the mortuary might have been killed."

One of the attendants looked up. "You mean Mr. Steinmetz?" He exchanged looks with his partner who shook his head and said, "Poor guy."

Ray swallowed hard. "What happened to him?"

The first attendant appeared genuinely saddened to say, "Heart attack."

Bunny shrugged. "What can I say? Politics makes strange bedfellows."

Southern sneered, "And they don't come stranger than you, twinkle toes."

Breckinridge smirked knowingly as the stretcher was wheeled silently and reverently out.   "You don't know the half of it, darling," he said, winking.

# Chapter 32

Outside the clinic, Lt. Southern watched as the Hollywood Mortuaries attendants rolled out blanket covered stretchers and heaved them into the funeral coach. Maila Nurmi, Ed Wood, and "Little" Karl Johnson stood by as stiff as waxworks figures, their eyes glassy and staring. Criswell hugged the all-important movie camera and sighed. "Well, *this* is certainly anticlimactic."

Southern remarked grimly, "I don't feel any better about this than you do. Harry Dean was a good cop, a little weird maybe—but a good cop."

Breckinridge chose that moment to emerge from the clinic. He paused to slip on his kid gloves, again as nonchalantly as a gentleman just leaving a dinner party. He glared at the police detective and the amateur sleuth. "All right," he pressed irritably, "what did you do with him?"

"Do with who?" asked Criswell.

"Don't play the innocent. What did you do with Tesla?"

Criswell and Southern were nonplussed. "You have Tesla's body," Southern insisted. Criswell pointed at funeral coach as it pull away with the evidence. "Didn't they just take his body away?"

"You know perfectly well…," Breckinridge began peevishly. He sighed and explained with forced patience, "He wasn't in the closet and we're missing a body bag. So obviously you had something to do with Tesla's disappearance."

Southern chuckled and smirked. "Maybe he turned into a bat and flew out the window." The Lieutenant playfully nudged Cris. "Right, Criswell?"

Criswell was about to say something when he noticed lurking in the shadows of the alley behind the clinic two skulking figures who looked a lot like Forry Ackerman and Ray Bradbury. They were struggling to get something into the trunk of Forry's car. "Uh, right," Criswell said, trying not to register the astonishment he was experiencing. "Just like you say, Tesla turned into a bat." He shook his head and tried to change the subject. "Forry Ackerman told me something about a mortician?"

Breckinridge sneered. "Horace M. Steinmetz, I suppose you mean. What about him?"

"What happened to him?"

The dandy removed his top hat and placed it over his heart in a mocking gesture of reverence. "He made the ultimate sacrifice for his country."

Popping the hat back on his head, he smirked and said, "Pity, dying from a heart attack like that."

Lt. Southern raised an eyebrow questioningly. "Heart attack, huh?"

"That's what it will say on the death certificate. Of course, there won't be any evidence to the contrary. Ashes to ashes, as it were. With one glaring exception, I'm afraid."

Southern nudged Criswell. "Get him. *He's* afraid."

Forry pulled away from the curb and pulled up beside them. "Well, there's no sense sticking around here anymore," he said affecting innocence.

A nervous looking Bradbury waved. "Good night, huh."

Criswell glanced anxiously at Breckinridge, who regarded Forry and Bradbury with only passing interest. "Uh, good night, Forry," Cris ventured, swallowing hard, "be good. And if you can't be good," he added with an uneasy smile and a voice tense with hidden meaning, "be *careful*."

Ackerman grinned like Cheshire cat, a Cheshire cat with canary feathers in his teeth. "I'm always careful. Good night, Pal. See you on the merry-go-round." Ackerman sped away into the night. As his car passed under a street light, Criswell experienced a weird sense of *déjà-vu* and something Ackerman casually remarked upon their first meeting echoed in Criswell's head, "*I'm a collector of sorts, after all.*" because the Hollywood psychic could *swear* he caught a glimpse of a body bag strap poking out from under the hood of Forry's trunk.

This detail either escaped Breckinridge's notice or Criswell had imagined the whole thing. Bunny gestured at the still zombified trio. "Wait until I'm out of sight before you revive them, would you?" He climbed into his sports car. "No sense creating yet more loose ends to cope with."

Criswell nodded. "We sure don't want to do that."

"Very wise." Breckinridge said, and then waved and chirped, "Cheery-oh," then drove off into the night, a silver ghost.

Criswell shuddered. "I really hated to do what I had to do to Chalky."

Southern put an arm around his shoulder. "It was you or him, Cris. Forget about it." He glared at the dust settling in the road under the street lights. "At least we've seen the last of Yankee Doodle Dandy. Now let's—" He was interrupted by Dr. Tom as he shoved Reverend Hall out of his clinic.

Hall was hobbling and holding his aching back. "Come on, Tom, have a heart! That big ape nearly broke my spine."

Dr. Tom glowered at Hall. "Find another chiropractor, you dirty double-crosser! And just wait until I tell Koenig about what you did." He slammed the door in Hall's face.

"I should sue," Hall grumbled as he limped to his car.

"Speaking of law suits," Criswell said, "I wonder if this will affect the case Armand Jr. was working up against the Sacramento high-rise project — and me."

"If Junior gives you any problems," Southern said, "just give me a call. I'll pull a few strings."

Criswell indicated the silent sentinel forms of Ed, Karl and Maila. "I guess we'd better snap them out of it." He unfolded the paper Bunny had scribbled on.

"So," asked Southern, "what's the phrase that brings them to?"

"Actually, it's very apropos." Criswell cleared his throat and intoned, "Cut. Print. That's a wrap."

Ed Wood and Karl rubbed their eyes as if they had just awakened from a long nap. Ed suddenly smiled like a boy on Christmas morning.

"I just thought of a great movie title," he said. With a sweeping gestured he proclaimed, "*Plan 9 from Outer Space!*"

"Wow, Eddie," Karl said. "Where do you come up with these things?"

"It just came to me!"

Criswell shook his head. "No matter what, Edward D. Wood Jr. can always be counted on to be Edward D. Wood Jr." He looked at the camera in his hands. "I guess we'll have to find a safe place for this."

"Hey, nice camera!" Wood said.

Lt. Southern scratched his head. "Got any ideas about where you can hide a thing like that?"

Criswell smiled wryly as he petted the camera housing. "I think I do."

# Chapter 33

It was several hours later before Maila Nurmi finally came 'round. Criswell had driven her back to his office and sat patiently waiting for the light to return to her eyes. Her first words were not the typical "where am I?" But rather, "I think I'm going to throw up!" whereupon she ran for the toilet and let loose loudly and wetly.

When she finally emerged from the bathroom, her face dripping from having splashed it with water, Criswell pulled the bottle of poisoned whiskey from the paper evidence bag and displayed it like a product endorsement.

"Do you want to explain this?" he asked. "You couldn't have been one of Breckinridge's test subjects. Chalky wouldn't have had to resort to using my Family Formula on you if you were. So why did you send Armand Tesla a bottle of poisoned whiskey?"

As Maila sat on the couch, she gave Criswell a saucy half smile. "Do you really want to know?"

"Yes, I do." He leaned in. "I thought you liked Armand."

"I *loved* Armand," she said earnestly.

"So why did you try to poison him?"

Maila seemed to sink inwardly as she confessed, "I sent that bottle to him after that business in the cemetery. He came to my apartment and we got drunk and cried on each other's shoulder, me, about my failed career and Armand about how degraded he felt having to be in Ed Wood's movies. He cried about Lillian leaving him for another man. He cried about being in a sex-change film. He just poured out his heart to me, and that's when we—"

Criswell started. "You and Armand—?"

"We were both so lost and we both needed somebody, so we made love." She shrugged. "Or tried to, anyway. Armand was having trouble getting hard." Maila smiled. "But we managed somehow and we felt better afterward, especially Armand. He said I had nice jugs."

Cris held up the bottle. "Then why did you send this?"

Tears ran down Maila's angular cheeks. "It was a mercy killing. I really wanted Armand to be at peace. I was going to kill myself and I knew Armand wanted out, too."

Criswell sighed, staring at the bottle in his hands. "We'll never know for sure what finally killed him. Ed poured Armand his first drink from this bottle on the day Armand died. Before that, Hope was feeding him poison-laced cigars."

"Are you going to give that to the police?"

Criswell stood up and went to the bathroom. Uncorking the bottle, he upturned it and poured out the contents in the sink. "The police aren't interested. No one will exhume Armand's body for an autopsy. Even if they did, all they'll find is a wax dummy."

"A wax dummy?!" Maila exclaimed.

"All part of the cover-up. It's a long story."

"What happened to Armand's body, the real one, I mean?"

Criswell chuckled. "Oh, I have my suspicions." He imagined somewhere in the Ackermansion, a hidden room, perhaps, Armand Tesla would be preserved under glass, lying in a prop coffin from one of his films, protected from the elements and decay in a perfect vacuum, surrounded by memorabilia from his many roles, the ultimate and much prized collector's item of 4SJ.

"But never mind about that, gorgeous." Criswell slipped the empty bottle back in the bag and dropped it in the wastebasket. "So I guess all things considered you won't have to go to jail."

Maila sighed. "Who says I'm not in jail already."

"Well," said Criswell, "I know Ed needs a vampire for his next picture. If you want to pay your debt to society you can do community service by being in *Plan 9 from Outer Space*."

Maila stared glumly at the wastebasket, wishing there might be a few drops of poison left. "This is the end," she sighed.

"I predict that this is...THE END."

# Epilogue: Post Mortem — Presenting the Awful Truth

Edward D. Wood Jr. never achieved the fame he craved, at least while he lived. Much like Armand Tesla, Eddie died of a heart attack, and in poverty. He died in 1978 at the age of 54. Amongst his possessions tossed in the trash at 5635 Laurel Canyon Boulevard, the only copy of his manuscript, *Armand Tesla: Post Mortem*. Eddie was cremated at Hollywood Mortuaries. Kathy Wood, who stayed with Eddie until the bitter end, scattered Eddie's ashes at sea. Wood's fame would be posthumously recognized when the Medved Brothers labeled him as The Worst Director of All Time in their book, *The Golden Turkey Awards*.

Maila Nurmi played Tesla's dead wife in *Plan 9 from Outer Space*, and insisted on playing the role mute, hoping no one would recognize her. In the early 1960s, after making a living installing linoleum flooring, Maila opened a boutique in her Melrose Avenue home called Vampira's Attic and started a craft jewelry business. In later years, she worked the horror convention circuit with fellow Ed Wood alums Conrad Brooks and Paul Marco. She died in her sleep of a massive heart attack at the age of 85 on January 10, 2008 in her North Hollywood home.

Hope Lininger Tesla left Los Angeles for the tropics of Hawaii, where she contracted stomach cancer and eventually died at home on April Fool's Day, 1997. Her marker bears the epitaph, "Beloved Curmudgeon."

Lillian Arch Tesla married Brian Donlevy in February of 1966. Donlevy was a notorious alcoholic and was often assigned minders during film and television productions to watch that he didn't drink. In 1969, Donlevy contracted throat cancer. Lillian, who described Donlevy as "the love of my life," remained at his side until her death on October 18, 1970 at the age of 70. Donlevy died two years later on April 5, 1972.

Armand Tesla Jr. went on to become a prominent attorney. Forever afterward, when asked about Edward D. Wood Jr., he would describe the director as, "a user and a loser." In the years since the funeral, Armand

Jr. has stated that it was his mother's idea about Armand being buried in his Dracula cape, despite contemporary newspaper articles reporting that Hope insisted on it because it was Armand's final wish.

When interviewed, Andreas Orby maintains that it was his idea that Armand ought to be buried in full costume.

Dr. Tom Mason would be asked to stand in for Armand Tesla in the now infamous *Plan 9 from Outer Space*, keeping his face hidden behind a Dracula cape.

A rather bored John "Bunny" Breckinridge did his stint as "Ruler of the Galaxy" for *Plan 9*, finding the whole thing rather insipid. Shortly after *Plan 9*'s release, Bunny would be convicted on 10 counts of "sex perversion" for taking two underage boys on a trip to Las Vegas. He lived to see Bill Murray play him in Tim Burton's 1994 biopic *Ed Wood*. Bunny died in 1996 at age 93, in a Monterey hospital. He was quoted in his obituary as saying, "I was a little bit wild when I was young, darling, but I lived my life grandly."

The Sacramento high-rise apartment complex was eventually erected on the spot of the former cemetery. To this day, it is rumored that there are bodies still left buried beneath the foundation.

Patrolmen Don Johnson and Daniel E. Corby were the first officers on the scene in the apparent suicide of actor George "Superman" Reeves on June 16, 1959, another actor type-cast by his most famous role.

Forrest J Ackerman was better known as Uncle Forry to millions of Monster Kids who grew up with his *Famous Monsters of Filmland Magazine*. Amongst his other notable achievements, he was named an honorary lesbian, a title bestowed upon him by the Daughters of Bilitis, a gay women's group, when they found out that he wrote fiction under the pen name of Laura Jean Ermayne for the lesbian publication *The Ladder*. In *Odd Girls and Twilight Lovers: A History of Lesbian Life in Twentieth-century America*, Laura Jean Ermayne is quoted as a formative figure in the development of lesbian fiction. Indeed, Forry was a pioneer in every sense of the word. Uncle Forry left this world on December 4, 2008. Inscribed on his crypt marker is the appropriate epitaph: "Sci-Fi was my high."

Charles Criswell King played in several of Ed Wood's movies, including providing the introduction, narration, and epilogue to *Plan 9 from Outer Space*, as well as appearing as the un-dead host in *Night of the Ghouls* and as the "King of the Night" in a monster-movie, girlie-romp called *Orgy of the Dead*. He moved into a modest Hollywood apartment in his later years and after writing a book of predictions, and appearing as a regular guest on *The Tonight Show*, Criswell passed away quietly at St. Joseph's Medical Center in Burbank at the age of 75. The official cause of death: "cardiac arrest." He was cremated on October 7, 1982. Criswell's ashes are interred at Pierce Brothers Valhalla Memorial Park in the Niches of Remembrance, F—10, space 2, behind a plaque that reads, *"Criswell Predicts" Charles Criswell King, 1907—1982.*

Although this cannot be confirmed, it has been rumored that amongst Criswell's personal effects was a locker key that he had apparently been wearing around his neck since 1956. An alleged secret sealed codicil of his will told executor Robert Harrison to use the key to open a locker at the Union Bus Terminal. Inside the locker was allegedly found a small can of 16mm film. It was Criswell's final wish that the can of film be placed inside the columbarium along with his cremains, and there be sealed forever.

It is also alleged that on the film can is a label with an inscription written in Criswell's own hand;

<blockquote>
"I predict that this is...THE END<br>
Filmed in HOLLYWOOD, USA"
</blockquote>

# THE FACTS BEHIND THE FICTION

(Warning: Contains Spoilers)

While its complete fiction that Ed Wood had anything approaching sex with Mae West, as well as the slapstick farce concerning a fictional switching of bodies and ruckus at the funeral of a certain Hungarian celebrity, and the business about Ed Wood's chiropractor working with Manly P. Hall to perfect a means to subvert the human will under the supervision of John "Bunny" Breckinridge is complete hokum straight from the author's twisted imagination, other things, like Hall being a hypnotist and certain character's dialogue and recalled past incidents of scandal are true and taken from biographies and documentary sources like Spinning Our Wheels Production *Lugosi: Hollywood's Dracula*, written and directed by Gary Don Rhodes, and in particular the supplementary interview with Hope Lininger as told to Richard Sheffield, is the basis for the portrayal of incidents leading to the discovery of a certain late actor's body and things said by that actor's wife. Watch the interview. The dialogue is taken practically verbatim from Hope's own account of the incident.

Image Video's *The Haunted World of Edward D. Wood Jr.*, directed by Brett Thompson, provided much of the dialogue presented by the real people while waiting on line at the funeral, particularly the relating of past incidents involving Delores Fuller and Loretta King, and their animosity toward each other on the set of *Bride of the Atom (Monster)* and King's assertion that she was hired through an agent. This includes stories related to Delores waking King up in the middle of the night with harassing phone calls, and what Fuller said to King, and the description of Delores's hurt feelings after King got her lead role in that movie. They are all taken from their interviews, practically verbatim. This source also quotes a certain son of a certain Hungarian actor saying that Ed Wood was "a user and a loser."

*The Ed Wood Story* in Passport Video's release of *Plan 9 From Outer Space*, *Flying Saucers Over Hollywood: The Plan 9 Companion* in Image and Corinth Film's release of *Plan 9 From Outer Space* (that's right, God help me, I have two copies of *Plan 9*), and the Wade Williams Collection version of *Glen or*

*Glenda* provided this author with other strange but true Ed Wood related trivia.

Book and other printed reference sources include: *Nightmare of Ecstasy* by Rudolph Grey, provided other recollections of past strangeness including the incident at Big Bear Lake involving a certain Hungarian actor waking Ed Wood out of a sound sleep and trying to hypnotize a confession out of him, it was taken practically word for word from another source and put into Ed Wood's mouth. This is also the book that alleges the transvestite practices of both Danny Kaye and Tony Curtis (and even alleges that they tried on dresses with Ed Wood in the costume department of a motion picture studio!), *Lugosi, His Life in Films, on Stage, and in the Hearts of Horror Lovers* by Gary Don Rhodes, *The Immortal Count, the Life and Films of Bela Lugosi* by Arthur Lennig, *Bela Lugosi – Dreams and Nightmares* by Gary Don Rhodes and Richard Sheffield, provided all the information about a certain Hungarian actor and his drug addiction, his recovery, and his relationships with the people depicted in this book. *A Fuller Life: Hollywood, Ed Wood and Me* by Dolores Fuller, provided information about Delores and her affair with Edward D. Wood Jr., including their lovemaking and the taking of a nude photo, which Ms. Fuller even provided a print of in her own autobiography. The only thing I made up was Delores beating the snot out of Ed Wood at the funeral and any involvement with deaths at the burial, all of that was fiction, *The American Way of Death* by Jessica Mitford, published by Simon & Schuster, provided information about the preparation of a dead body for burial, and *Killer in Drag* by Ed Wood Jr., published by Four Walls Eight Windows, gave me the references to "Pudgyface," the article *I Was A Woman For Ed Wood Jr.: The Delores Fuller Story* as told to Tom Weaver, published in Winter 1996, No. 17 issue of *Phantom of the Movies VideoScope*, the article *Bring Me The Soul of Ed Wood Jr.: Rev. Lynn Lemon* as told to Robert Rees, Fall 1996, No. 20 issue of *Phantom of the Movies VideoScope*, all gave me additional information on Ed Wood and the making of his movies and his relationships with certain celebrities, the articles *Hollywood and American Morality* and *New Thrills for Jaded Passions* appearing in the Sept., 1955, Vol. 1, No. 5 issue of *Police Dragnet Cases* gave me descriptions of what happened at the hospital where a certain vampire celebrity was recovering from drug addiction, and *Criswell Predicts: The Life & Prophecies of the Amazing Criswell* by Edwin L. Canfield, appearing in the April/June 2006 No. 110 issue of *Filmfax Plus* provided details of what it was like on the set of *Criswell Predicts* and about Criswell's Family Formula (which had no hypnotic powers whatsoever). Criswell's homosexuality and visits to the Gold Cup and stories related to his marriage are taken from a Wikipedia article concerning his life and other sources.

Other sources: information about Forrest J Ackerman, how he spoke, what he was into and so forth, were related to me through correspondence with Ackerman's caretaker Joe Moe. Certain recollections of a certain late Hungarian actor's funeral and facts about Conrad Brooks are taken from my phone conversation with Conrad Brooks, who really does say "you know" as often as I portrayed.

The things that are completely made up: All the incidents at the chiropractic clinic; the incident involving Maila Nurmi's brief affair with a certain Hungarian; the plot concerning her attempts to poison a certain Hungarian actor; a certain Hungarian actor finding bodies on the property of a future high rise, all fiction, but the stories about bodies under a certain high rise were taken from related rumors presented in *Nightmares of Ecstasy*.

So as you see, sometimes truth *is* stranger than fiction.

# ABOUT THE AUTHOR/ILLUSTRATOR

DWIGHT CHRISTOPHER KEMPER is the writer, producer, director, and performer of Murder Mystery Theater for special events like the Arts Festival in North Charleston, South Carolina, where he has appeared for an unprecedented three seasons in a row as a returning performer. He has conducted mystery weekends for bed and breakfasts like The Inn at East Hill Farms in Troy, New Hampshire, The Benjamin Prescott Inn in Jaffrey, New Hampshire, and The Edge of Thyme Bed and Breakfast in Candor, New York. He has also appeared in mystery dinner shows for hotels like the Chestnut Inn at Oquaga Lake, Deposit, New York and at the Holiday Inn Arena in Binghamton, New York.

Mr. Kemper makes regular guest appearances on actor/director/horror host Michael Legge's *Dungeon of Dr. Dreck* Halloween specials as Uncle Mess, a madcap zombie scientist Kemper based on Boris Karloff in the *Thriller* episode, *The Incredible Doktor Markesan.*

Mr. Kemper is also a champion power lifter with six awards under his weight-lifting belt.

Mr. Kemper's writing ability runs in the family according to the Judah L. Magnes Museum in Berkley, California, which informed him that his great, great aunt on his father's side was author Gertrude Stein.

His first novel, *Who Framed Boris Karloff?* was nominated in the Best Book of 2007 category by the Rondo Hatton Classic Horror Awards. His second novel, *Bela Lugosi and the House of Doom* was nominated for a Best Book of 2009 by the Rondo Hatton Classic Horror Awards. Visit Mr. Kemper online at www. murdermysterytheater.com.

www.ingramcontent.com/pod-product-compliance
Lightning Source LLC
Chambersburg PA
CBHW071753190726
48292CB00003B/961